VENGEFUL SPIRIT

'WE FOUR AND the Emperor travelled to Molech. It complied, of course. What planet would offer resistance to Legion forces led by the Emperor?'

'An overwhelming force,' said Mortarion. 'Was heavy resistance expected?'

'Far from it,' said Horus. 'Molech's rulers were inveterate record keepers, and they remembered Terra. Its people had weathered Old Night, and when the Emperor descended to the surface it was inevitable they would accept compliance.'

'We remained there for some months, did we not?' asked Fulgrim.

Aximand glanced at Abaddon and saw the same look on the First Captain's face he felt he wore. He too remembered Molech, but like the primarchs was having difficulty in recalling specific details. Aximand had almost certainly visited the planet's surface, but found it hard to form a coherent picture of its environs.

'According to the *Vengeful Spirit's* horologs, we were there for a hundred and eleven standard Terran days, one hundred and nine local. After we left nearly a hundred regiments of Army, three Titanicus cohorts and garrison detachments from two Legions were left in place.'

'For a planet that embraced compliance?' said Mortarion. 'A waste of resources if ever I heard it. What need did the Emperor have to fortify Molech with such strength?'

Horus snapped his fingers and said, 'Exactly.'

THE HORUS HERESY®

Book 19 – KNOW NO FEAR
Dan Abnett

Book 20 – THE PRIMARCHS
edited by Christian Dunn

Book 21 – FEAR TO TREAD
James Swallow

Book 22 – SHADOWS OF TREACHERY
edited by Christian Dunn and Nick Kyme

Book 23 – ANGEL EXTERMINATUS
Graham McNeill

Book 24 – BETRAYER
Aaron Dembski-Bowden

Book 25 – MARK OF CALTH
edited by Laurie Goulding

Book 26 – VULKAN LIVES
Nick Kyme

Book 27 – THE UNREMEMBERED EMPIRE
Dan Abnett

Book 28 – SCARS
Chris Wraight

Book 29 – VENGEFUL SPIRIT
Graham McNeill

Book 30 – THE DAMNATION OF PYTHOS
David Annandale

Novellas
PROMETHEAN SUN
Nick Kyme

AURELIAN
Aaron Dembski-Bowden

BROTHERHOOD OF THE STORM
Chris Wraight

THE CRIMSON FIST
John French

Many of these titles are also available as abridged and unabridged audiobooks.
Order the full range of Horus Heresy novels and audiobooks from
blacklibrary.com

THE HORUS HERESY®

Graham McNeill

VENGEFUL SPIRIT

The Battle of Molech

BLACK LIBRARY

To my Mum and Dad, the best I could have wished for.

A BLACK LIBRARY PUBLICATION

Hardback edition first published in 2014.
This edition published in 2014 by
Black Library,
Games Workshop Ltd.,
Willow Road,
Nottingham, NG7 2WS, UK.

10 9 8 7 6 5 4 3 2 1

Cover illustration by Neil Roberts.

A CIP record for this book is available from the British Library.

UK ISBN: 978 1 84970 594 3
US ISBN: 978 1 84970 738 1

See Black Library on the internet at

blacklibrary.com

Find out more about Games Workshop
and the world of Warhammer 40,000 at

games-workshop.com

Printed and bound by CPI Group (UK) Ltd, Croydon, CR0 4YY

THE HORUS HERESY®
It is a time of legend.

The galaxy is in flames. The Emperor's glorious vision for humanity is in ruins. His favoured son, Horus, has turned from his father's light and embraced Chaos.

His armies, the mighty and redoubtable Space Marines, are locked in a brutal civil war. Once, these ultimate warriors fought side by side as brothers, protecting the galaxy and bringing mankind back into the Emperor's light.
Now they are divided.

Some remain loyal to the Emperor, whilst others have sided with the Warmaster. Pre-eminent amongst them, the leaders of their thousands-strong Legions are the primarchs. Magnificent, superhuman beings, they are the crowning achievement of the Emperor's genetic science. Thrust into battle against one another, victory is uncertain for either side.

Worlds are burning. At Isstvan V, Horus dealt a vicious blow and three loyal Legions were all but destroyed. War was begun, a conflict that will engulf all mankind in fire. Treachery and betrayal have usurped honour and nobility. Assassins lurk in every shadow. Armies are gathering.
All must choose a side or die.

Horus musters his armada, Terra itself the object of his wrath. Seated upon the Golden Throne, the Emperor waits for His wayward son to return. But His true enemy is Chaos, a primordial force that seeks to enslave mankind to its capricious whims.

The screams of the innocent, the pleas of the righteous resound to the cruel laughter of Dark Gods. Suffering and damnation await all should the Emperor fail and the war be lost.

The age of knowledge and enlightenment has ended.
The Age of Darkness has begun.

~ DRAMATIS PERSONAE ~

The Primarchs

HORUS LUPERCAL	The Warmaster, Primarch of the XVI Legion
MORTARION	The Death Lord, Primarch of the XIV Legion
FULGRIM	The Phoenician, Primarch of the III Legion
LEMAN RUSS	The Wolf King, Primarch of the VI Legion
ROGAL DORN	The Emperor's Praetorian, Primarch of the VII Legion

The XVI Legion 'Sons of Horus'

EZEKYLE ABADDON	First Captain
FALKUS KIBRE	'Widowmaker', captain, Justaerin Terminator Squad
KALUS EKADDON	Captain, Catulan Reaver Squad
'LITTLE' HORUS AXIMAND	Captain, Fifth Company
YADE DURSO	Line captain, Fifth Company
SERGHAR TARGOST	Captain, Seventh Company, lodge master
LEV GOSHEN	Captain, 25th Company
GRAEL NOCTUA	'The Warlocked', sergeant, 25th Company
MALOGHURST	'The Twisted', equerry to the primarch
GER GERRADON	Luperci

The XIV Legion 'Death Guard'

CAIPHA MORARG	24th Breacher Squad, Second Company
IGNATIUS GRULGOR	The Eater of Lives

The XIII Legion 'Ultramarines', Battle Group II (25th Chapter)

CASTOR ALCADE	Legate
DIDACUS THERON	Centurion, Fourth Division
PROXIMO TARCHON	Centurion, Ninth Division
ARCADON KYRO	Techmarine

The IX Legion 'Blood Angels'

VITUS SALICAR	Captain, 16th Company
ALIX VASTERN	Apothecary
DRAZEN ACORAH	Appointed lieutenant, formerly of the Librarius
AGANA SERKAN	Warden

Legio Crucius

ETANA KALONICE	Princeps, *Paragon of Terra*
CARTHAL ASHUR	Calator Martialis

Legio Fortidus

UTA-DAGON	Princeps, *Red Vengeance*
UTU-LERNA	Princeps, *Bloodgeld*
UR-NAMMU	Warmonger

Legio Gryphonicus
OPINICUS   Invocatio

The Mechanicum
BELLONA MODWEN   High Magos, Ordo Reductor

House Devine
CYPRIAN DEVINE   'The Hellblade', Knight Seneschal
CEBELLA DEVINE   Adoratrice Drakaina
RAEVEN DEVINE   First Knight
ALBARD DEVINE   Firstborn scion
LYX DEVINE   Adoratrice Sybaris

House of Donar
BALMORN DONAR   Lord-Knight
ROBARD DONAR   Scion

Imperial Personae
MALCADOR THE SIGILLITE   Imperial Regent, First Lord of Terra

BRYTHON SEMPER   Lord Admiral of Battlefleet Molech
TYANA KOURION   Lord General of the Grand Army of
                         Molech
EDORAKI HAKON   Marshal of the Northern Oceanic
ABDI KHEDA   Commander of the Kushite Eastings
OSKUR VAN VALKENBERG   Colonel of the Western Marches
CORWEN MALBEK   Khan of the Southern Steppe

NOAMA CALVER   Medicae corps

ALIVIA SUREKA   Larsa harbour pilot
JEPH PARSONS   Dock worker
MISKA
VIVYEN

The Chosen of Malcador
GARVIEL LOKEN   Knight Errant
IACTON QRUZE   'The Half-heard', Knight Errant
SEVERIAN   Knight Errant
TYLOS RUBIO   Knight Errant
MACER VARREN   Knight Errant
BROR TYRFINGR   Knight Errant
RAMA KARAYAN   Knight Errant
ARES VOITEK   Knight Errant
ALTAN NOHAI   Knight Errant
CALLION ZAVEN   Knight Errant
TUBAL CAYNE   Knight Errant

BANU RASSUAH   Pilot of the *Tarnhelm*

Non-Imperial Personae
THE RED ANGEL

'And therefore is the glorious planet Sol
In noble eminence enthroned and sphered
Amidst the other; whose medicinable Eye
Corrects the ill-aspects of planets evil,
And posts, like the commandment of a king,
Sans check to good and bad: but when the planets
In evil mixture to disorder wander,
What plagues and what portents! what mutiny!
What raging of the sea! shaking of earth!
Commotion in the winds! frights, changes, horrors,
Divert and crack, rend and deracinate
The unity and married calm of states
Quite from their fixtures!'

– attributed to the dramaturge Shakespire (fl. M2), cited in *The Prophecy of Amon of the Thousand Sons* (Chapter III, Verse XIII)

'Horus had called the dark and savage furies latent in the most ruthless, contradictory and ill-starred power of the Immaterium. He had conjured up the fearful idol of an all-devouring Molech of which he was the priest and incarnation. All his powers, hitherto dissipated and scattered, were now concentrated and directed with terrible energy to one terrible aim.'

– from *The Age of Revolution: Suppressed Monographs of Choirmaster Nemo Zhi Meng*

'The line separating good from evil runs not between species, not between ranks and not between competing faiths. It runs through the heart of each and every mortal soul. This line is not stationary, but shifts and moves with the passage of time. Even souls ensnared by evil maintain a small bridgehead of good.'

– *The Keeler Amanuensis* (Volume II, Chapter XXXIV, Verse VII)

PART ONE
FATHERS

Where are the tombs of dead gods? What wailing mourner pours wine over their grave-mounds? There was a time when a being known as Zeus was the king of all the gods, and any man who doubted his might and majesty was a heathen and an enemy. But where in all the Imperium is there the man who worships Zeus?

And what of Huitzilopochtli? Forty thousand maidens were slain in sacrifice to him, their dripping hearts burned in vast pyramid temples. When he frowned, the sun stood still, when he raged earthquakes destroyed entire cities, when he thirsted he was watered with oceans of blood.

But today Huitzilopochtli is magnificently forgotten.

And what of his brother, Tezcatilpoca?

The ancients believed that Tezcatilpoca was almost as powerful as his brother. He consumed the hearts of almost thirty thousand virgins a year, but does anyone guard his tomb or know where it is to be found? Does anyone weep or hang mourning wreaths upon his graven image?

And what of Balor of the Eye, or the Lady of Cythera? Or of Dis, whom the Romanii Qaysar found to be the chief god of the Keltos? Or the dreaming serpent, Kajura? Of Taranis, only dimly recalled by a dead order of Knights and early historians of Unity? Or the flesh-hungry King Nzambi? Or the serpentine hosts of Cromm Crúaich, driven from their island lair by the Priest of Ravenglass?

Where are their bones? Where is the tree of woe upon which to hang memorial garlands? In what forgotten abode of oblivion do they await their hour of resurrection?

They are not alone in eternity, for the tombs of dead gods are crowded. Urusix is there, and Esus, and Baldur, and Silvana, and Mithras, and Phoenicia, and Deva, and Kratus, and Uxellimus, and Borvo, and Grannos, and Mogons. All mighty gods in their day, worshipped by billions, replete with demands and commandments, ascribed the power to bind the elements and shake the foundations of the world.

Civilisations laboured for generations to build vast temples to them; towering structures of stone and steel, fashioned by technologies now lost in the unknowing of Old Night. Interpreting their divine desires fell to thousands of holy men; lunatic priests, dung-smeared shamans and opium-ravaged oracles. To doubt their pronouncements was to die in agony. Great armies took to the field to defend the gods against infidels and carry their will to heathen peoples in far off lands. Continents were burned, innocents butchered and worlds laid waste in their name. Yet in the end they all withered and died, cast down and justly unremembered. Today there are few so deranged as to do them reverence.

All were gods of the highest eminence, many of them mentioned with fear and trembling awe in the ancient texts of the White God. They ranked with the Highest Power; yet time has trampled them all underfoot and mocks the ashes of their bones.

They were gods of the highest dignity – gods of civilised peoples – worshipped by entire worlds. All were omnipotent, omniscient and immortal.

And all are dead.

If any of them ever really existed, they were but aspects of the true Pantheon, masks behind which hide the first gods of the universe in all their terrible beauty.

Lorgar has been vociferous in his proselytising of this fact, wearily so.

But he does not know as much as he believes.

Imperial Truth? Primordial Truth?

Both are irrelevant.

There is a god who has raised Himself higher than all the others, mightier than any imagined deity or hell-spawned monster dreamed into being.

He is the Emperor.

My father.

And I have to kill Him.

That *is the only Truth that matters.*

ONE

The Mausolytica
Confraternity
Brothers

THE DEAD OF Dwell were screaming. The Mausolytic Precinct was a place of terror for them now, where the cessation of mortal functions offered no respite from continual torment. A thousand tech-adepts died by the sword before enough had finally been compelled to repair the damage done in the wake of the Sons of Horus's assault, but repair it they had.

The dead of the Mausolytic screamed from dawn till dusk, through the night and across every day since Aximand had captured it in the name of the Warmaster. They screamed in fear, in horror and revulsion.

But most of all they screamed in anger.

Only the Warmaster heard them, and he cared nothing for their anger. His only interest was in what they could tell him of the past; as they had experienced it and as they had learned it.

A vaulted sprawl of colonnaded stone structures that possessed the same scale as the palace of a mighty Terran patrician, was here a repository of the dead and librarium in one. Plain facades of ochre granite shone like burnished copper in the dying sunlight, and the cries of circling seabirds almost made Horus Aximand forget a war had been fought here.

Could almost make him forget that he nearly died here.

The battle for the Mausolytic Precinct had been won by bloody, shoulder-charging bodywork, blade to blade, muscle to muscle. There had been collateral damage of course; machinery destroyed, stasis capsules smashed open and preserved flesh turned to hard leather upon exposure to the unforgiving atmospherics.

Blood still stained its walls in the catastrophic spray patterns of bodies detonated within ruptured personal shields. The ruined corpses of the Compulsories were gone, but no one cared enough to wash away their blood.

Aximand stood at a knee-high wall of sun-blushed stone, one foot on the parapet, forearms resting on his raised knee. The sound of waves far below was peaceful and when the wind blew in from the ocean, the burned metal smell of the port was replaced with the tang of salt and wildflowers. From his vantage point upon the high plateau, the tumbled city of Tyjun was much as it had been when the Sons of Horus made their first landings.

His first impression was that a vast tidal surge had swept along the rift valley and deposited the forgotten detritus of an ocean upon its retreat. There appeared to be no order to the city, but Aximand had long since come to appreciate the organic subtleties of the city's ancient designers.

'It is protean,' he would say, when he found a willing ear, 'a city that thrives on its disregard for clean lines and imposed clarity. The ostensive lack of cohesion is deceptive, for order exists *within* the chaos, which only becomes apparent when you walk its twisting paths and find that your destination has been set from the very beginning.'

Every building was unique in its own way, as though an army

of architects had come to Tyjun and each designed a wealth of structures from the salvaged steel and glass and stone.

The only exception was the Dwellan Palace, a recent addition to the city that bore the utilitarian hallmarks of classical Macraggian architecture. Taller than anything else in Tyjun, it was a domed palace of Imperial governance, a monument to the Great Crusade and an expression of Primarch Guilliman's vanity all in one. It had mathematically precise proportions and though Lupercal thought it austere, Aximand liked the restraint he saw in its elegantly crisp design.

Exquisite statuary of Imperial heroes stood proud around the circumference of the main azure dome and in recessed alcoves running the full height of the central arch. Aximand had learned the identity of every one before they were smashed; Chapter Masters and captains of the Ultramarines and Iron Hands, Army generals, Titan princeps, Munitorum pontiffs and even a few aexactor tithe-takers.

Evening sunlight honeyed the city's rooftops and the Sea of Enna was glassy and still. The water became a golden mirror streaked with phosphor-bright reflections of orbiting warships, the occasional moon and void-war debris falling far out to sea.

The prow of a sunken cargo tanker jutted from the water at the quayside, petrochemical gels frothing its surface with oily scum.

Far to the north, a glowing star clung stubbornly to the horizon, the twin of the sun setting in the south. This, Aximand knew, was no star, but the still burning remains of the Budayan ship school, its orbit degrading with each planetary revolution.

'Won't be long until that impacts,' said a voice behind him.

'True,' agreed Aximand without turning.

'It's not going to be pretty,' said another. 'Best we're gone before then.'

'We should have left here long ago,' added a fourth.

Aximand finally turned from the bucolic vision of Tyjun and nodded to his battle-brothers.

'Mournival,' he said. 'The Warmaster calls for us.'

THE MOURNIVAL. RESTORED.

But then, it had never been lost, just broken awhile.

Aximand marched with Ezekyle Abaddon. In his spiked warrior-plate, the First Captain of the Sons of Horus was more than a head taller than Aximand. His body language was savagely aggressive, cruelly planed features pulled hard over jutting bones. His skull was hairless, save for a glossy black topknot jutting from his crown like a tribal fetish.

He and Abaddon were old hands, Mournival from the time before the galaxy had slipped a gear and turned to a very different hand at the crank. They had spilled blood on a hundred worlds in the name of the Emperor; hundreds more for the Warmaster.

And they had once laughed as they fought.

The two newest members of the Mournival marched alongside their proposers, lunar marks graven upon their helms by the reflected light of Dwell's moon. One was a warrior with a reputation, the other a sergeant who'd earned his during the disaster of Dwell's fall.

Widowmaker Kibre commanded the Justaerin Terminators. One of Abaddon's men and a true son. Where Kibre was seasoned and war-known, Grael Noctua of the Warlocked was new to the men of the Legion. A warrior possessed of a mind like a steel trap, his intellect was likened by Abaddon to a slow blade.

With Kibre's investiture, a potent weight of choler lay to one side of the Mournival. Aximand hoped Noctua's phlegmatic presence would counterbalance it. There had been rumblings at the favour Aximand showed Noctua, but Dwell silenced them all.

With their two newest brothers, Aximand and Abaddon led the

way to the central Mausolytic Hall in answer to the Warmaster's summons.

'Do you think it will be a mobilisation order?' asked Noctua.

Like all of them, he was eager to be unleashed. The war here was long-ended, and but for a handful of forays beyond the system, the bulk of the Legion had remained in place while their primarch sequestered himself with the dead.

'Perhaps,' said Aximand, unwilling to speculate on the Warmaster's motives for remaining on Dwell. 'We will know soon enough.'

'We should be on the move,' said Kibre. 'The war gathers momentum while we stagnate with inaction.'

Abaddon halted their march and placed a hand in the centre of the Widowmaker's breastplate. 'You think you know the course of war better than your primarch?'

Kibre shook his head. 'Of course not, I just–'

'First lesson of the Mournival,' said Aximand. 'Never second guess Lupercal.'

'I wasn't second guessing him,' snapped Kibre.

'Good,' said Aximand. 'Then you've learned something useful today. Perhaps the Warmaster has found what he needed, perhaps not. Maybe we will have mobilisation orders, maybe we won't.'

Kibre nodded and Aximand saw him force his volatile humours into balance. 'As you say, Little Horus. The molten Cthonian core that burns in us all waxes stronger in me than most.'

Aximand chuckled, though the sound was not as he once knew it, the muscles beneath the skin moving in subtly different ways.

'You say that like it's a bad thing,' he said. 'Just remember that fire needs to be controlled to be useful.'

'Most of the time,' added Abaddon, and they moved off again.

They traversed high-vaulted antechambers of fallen pillars and halls of bolt-cratered frescos that had once been battlefields. The air thrummed with the vibration of buried generators and tasted like an embalming workshop. Between murals of cobalt-blue Legion warriors being welcomed with garlands, tens of thousands of names were inlaid on coffered panels with gold leaf.

The interred dead of the Mausolytica.

'Like the Avenue of Glory and Lament on the *Spirit*,' said Aximand, pointing out the fine scriptwork.

Abaddon snorted, not even glancing at the names. 'It hasn't been called that since Isstvan.'

'The necrologists may be gone,' sighed Aximand, 'but it is as it has always been, a place to remember the dead.'

They climbed a wide set of marbled steps, crunching over the powdered remains of toppled statues and emerging into a transverse hallway Aximand had fought the length and breadth of, shield raised, *Mourn-it-all*'s blade high, shoulders squared. Soaked in blood to the elbow.

'Dreaming again?' asked Abaddon, noting his fractional pause.

'I don't dream,' snapped Aximand. 'I'm just thinking how ridiculous it was that an army of men were able to trouble us here. When have we ever faced mortals and found them *bothersome*?'

Abaddon nodded. 'The Chainveil fought in the City of Elders. They delayed me.'

No more needed to be said. That any army, mortal or transhuman, could *delay* Ezekyle Abaddon spoke volumes to their competency and courage.

'But they all died in the end,' said Kibre as they passed beneath a great, funerary arch and moved deeper into the tomb complex. 'Chainveil or ordinary soldiers, they stood against us in the line and we killed them all.'

'That they stood at all should have told us there were was something else waiting for us,' said Grael Noctua.

'How so?' said Aximand, knowing the answer, but wanting to hear it articulated.

'The men who fought us here, they believed they could win.'

'Their defence was orchestrated by Meduson of the Iron Tenth,' said Aximand. 'It's understandable they believed him.'

'Only Legion presence gives mortals that kind of backbone,' continued Noctua. 'With the Tenth Legion's war-leader and the kill teams of the Fifth Legion in place, they thought they had a chance. They thought they could kill the Warmaster.'

Kibre shook his head. 'Even if Lupercal had fallen for their transparent ploy and come himself, he would have easily slain them.'

More than likely Kibre was right. It was inconceivable that a mere five legionaries could have ended the Warmaster. Even with surprise in their corner, the idea that Horus could be brought low by a rush team of blade killers seemed ludicrous.

'He outwitted a sniper's bullet on Dagonet, and he evaded the assassins' swords on Dwell,' said Abaddon, kicking over an engraved urn emblazoned with a splintered Ultima. 'Meduson must have been desperate to think the Scars stood a chance.'

'Desperate is exactly what he was,' said Aximand, feeling the itch where his face had been reattached. 'Just imagine if they had succeeded.'

No one answered, no one could conceive of the Legion without Lupercal at its head. Without one, the other did not exist.

But Shadrak Meduson had failed to lure the Warmaster into his trap, and Dwell had fallen hard.

Against Horus Lupercal's armies, everything fell eventually.

'Why defend the dead at all?' said Kibre. 'Aside from commanding the high ground over an open city, holding the Mausolytica offers no tangible strategic merit. We could have simply shelled it flat, and sent Lithonan's Army auxiliaries in to kill any survivors.'

'They knew the Warmaster would want so precious a resource captured intact,' said Noctua.

'It's a house of the dead,' pressed Kibre. 'What kind of resource is that?'

'Now you're Mournival, why don't you ask him yourself?' answered Noctua. Kibre's head snapped around, unused to being addressed with such informality by a junior officer. Mournival equality was going to take time to bed in with the Widowmaker.

'Tread lightly, Noctua,' warned Abaddon. 'You might be one of us now, but don't think that exempts you from respect.'

Aximand grinned at Abaddon's ire. Ezekyle was a warhound on a fraying leash, and Aximand wondered if he knew that was his role.

Of course Ezekyle knew. A warrior did not become First Captain of the Sons of Horus by being too stupid to know his place.

'Apologies,' said Noctua, turning to address Kibre directly. 'No disrespect was intended.'

'Good,' said Aximand. 'Now give Falkus Kibre a proper answer.'

'The Mausolytica occupies the best defensive terrain in the rift valley, but it's barely fortified,' said Noctua. 'Which suggests the Dwellers valued it highly, but didn't think of it as a military target until Meduson told them it was.'

Aximand nodded and slapped a gauntleted hand on the polished plates of Noctua's shoulder guard.

'So why did the Iron Hands think this place was valuable?' asked Kibre.

'I have no idea,' said Aximand.

Only later would he come to understand that the Dwellers would have been far better demolishing the Mausolytic Halls and smashing its machinery to shards than allowing it to fall to the Sons of Horus.

Only much later, when the last violent spasms of galactic war were stilled for a heartbeat, would Aximand learn the colossal mistake they had made in allowing the Mausolytic to endure.

✠ ✠ ✠

THEY FOUND THE primarch in Pilgrim's Hall, where ancient machinery allowed the Mausolytic's custodians to access and consult the memories of the dead. The custodians had joined their charges in death, and Horus Lupercal commanded the machines alone.

A colossal cryo-generator throbbed with power in the centre of the echoing chamber, like a templum organ with a multitude of frost-limmed ducts emerging from its misting condensers. Smeared charnel dust patterned its base where the White Scars kill team had thrown off their disguises.

Radiating outward from the generator like the spokes of an illuminated wheel were row upon row of supine bodies in stacked glass cylinders. Aximand had logged twenty-five thousand bodies in this hall alone, and there were fifty similar sized spaces above ground. He hadn't yet catalogued how many chambers were carved into the plateau's bedrock.

The Warmaster was easy to see.

His back was to them as he bent over a cylindrical tube hinged out from its gravimetric support field. Twenty Justaerin Terminators stood between them and the Warmaster, armed with photonic-edged falchions and twin-barrelled bolters. Nominally the Warmaster's bodyguard, the Justaerin were a throwback to a time when war-leaders actually required protection. Horus no more needed their strength of arms to defend him than he needed that of the Mournival, but after Hibou Khan's ambush, no one was taking any chances.

As ever, the primarch was a lodestone to the eyes, a towering presence to which it was right and proper to offer devotion. An easy smile suggested Horus had only just noticed them, but Aximand didn't doubt he had been aware of them long before they entered the hall.

Titanic plates of brass-edged jet encased him, the plastron

emblazoned with a slitted amber eye flanked by golden wolves. Horus's right hand was a killing talon, and his left rested upon an enormous mace. Its name was *Worldbreaker*, and its adamantium haft was featureless save for an eagle pommel-stone, its murder head bronze and black.

The Warmaster had the face of a conquerer, a warrior, a diplomat and a statesman. It could be a kindly face of paternal concern or the last face you ever saw.

Aximand could not yet tell which it was at this moment, but on a day like this such ambiguity was good. To have Lupercal's humours unknown to those who stood with him would vex those who might yet stand against him.

'Little Horus,' said the Warmaster as the Justaerin parted before them like the gates of a ceramite fortress.

The uncanny resemblance Aximand shared with his gene-father had earned him that name, but Hibou Khan had cut that from him with a blade of hard Medusan steel. Legion Apothecaries had done what they could, but the damage was too severe, the edge too sharp and his wounded flesh too melancholic.

Yet for all that his face was raw with disfigurement, the resemblance between Aximand and his primarch had, by some strange physiological alchemy, become even more pronounced.

'Warmaster,' said Aximand. 'Your Mournival.'

Horus nodded and studied each of them in turn, as though assessing the alloyed composition of the restored confraternity.

'I approve,' he said. 'The blend looks to be a good one.'

'Time will tell,' said Aximand.

'As it does in all things,' answered Horus, coming forward to stand before the sergeant of the Warlocked.

'Aximand's protégé, a true son indeed,' said Horus with a hint of pride. 'I hear good things about you, Grael. Are they true?'

To his credit, Noctua retained his senses in the face of the

Warmaster's appraisal, but he could not meet his gaze for long.

'Yes, my lord,' he managed. 'Maybe... I do not know what you have heard.'

'Good things,' said Horus, nodding and moving on to take the Widowmaker's gauntlet in his taloned grip.

'You're tense, Falkus,' he said. 'Inaction doesn't suit you.'

'What can I say? I was built for war,' said Kibre, with more tact than Aximand expected.

'More than most,' agreed Horus. 'Don't worry, I'll not have you and the Justaerin idle for much longer.'

The Warmaster came to Abaddon and said, 'And you, Ezekyle, you hide it better than the Widowmaker, but I see you also chafe at our enforced stay on Dwell.'

'There is a war to be won, my lord,' said Abaddon, his tone barely on the right side of rebuke. 'And I won't have it said that the Sons of Horus let other Legions do their fighting for them.'

'Nor would I, my son,' said Horus, placing his talon upon Abaddon's shoulders. 'We have been distracted by the schemes and petty vengeances of others, but that time is over.'

Horus turned and accepted a blood-red war-cloak from one of the Justaerin. He snapped it around his shoulders, fixing it in place with a pair of wolf-claw pins at each pauldron.

'Aximand, are they here?' asked Horus.

'They are,' said Aximand. 'But you already know that.'

'True,' agreed Horus. 'Even when we were without form, I always knew if they were close.'

Aximand saw a rogue glint in Horus's eye, and decided he was joking. Rare were the moments when Horus spoke of his years with the Emperor. Rarer still were insights to the time before that.

'In my more arrogant moments, I used to think that was why the Emperor came to me first,' continued Horus, and Aximand saw he'd been mistaken. Horus was, most assuredly, not joking.

'I thought He needed my help to find the rest of His lost sons. Then sometimes I think it was a cruel punishment, to feel so deep a connection to my gene-kin, only to be set apart from them.'

Horus fell silent and Aximand said, 'They wait for you in the Dome of Revivification.'

'Good, I am eager to join them.'

Abaddon's fists clenched. 'Then we are to rejoin the war?'

'Ezekyle, my son, we never left it,' said Horus.

THE DOME OF Revivification was a vast hemisphere of glass and transparisteel atop the largest of the Mausolytic's stone structures. It was a place of reverence and solemn purpose, a place where the preserved memories of the dead could be returned to life.

Access was gained via a latticework elevator that rose into the centre of the dome. Horus and the Mournival stood at the centre of the platform as it made its stately ascent. Over Kibre's protests, the Justaerin had been left below, leaving the five of them alone. Aximand looked up to the wide opening in the floor high above them. He saw the cracked structure of the crystalline dome beyond, sunset darkening to nightfall.

Slanted columns of moonlight slid over the elevator as it emerged into the dome. A rogue shell had damaged its hemispherical structure, and shards of hardened glass lay strewn across the polished metal floor like diamond-bladed knives. Spaced at equidistant intervals around the outer circumference of the elevator were berths for dozens of cryo-cylinders. None were currently occupied.

Aximand took a shocked breath of frosted air as he saw the demigods awaiting within. He had known, of course, who the Warmaster had summoned, but to see two such numinous beings before him was still a moment of revelation.

One was a being of immaterial flesh, the other stolidly physical.

Horus spread his arms in greeting.

'My brothers,' said Horus, his voice filling the dome. 'Welcome to Dwell.'

RUMOURS HAD REACHED the Sons of Horus of the changes wrought in some of the Warmaster's brothers, but nothing could have prepared Aximand for just how profound those changes were.

The last time he had seen the primarch of the Emperor's Children, Fulgrim had been the perfect warrior, a snow-maned hero in purple and gold plate. Now the Phoenician was the physical embodiment of an ancient, many-armed destroyer god. Serpentine of body and clad in exquisite fragments of his once-magnificent armour, Fulgrim was a beautiful monster. A being to be mourned for the splendour he had lost, and admired for the power he had gained.

Mortarion of the Death Guard stood apart from Fulgrim's sinuous form and, at first glance, appeared unchanged. A closer look into his sunken eyes revealed the pain of recent hurts worn like a ragged mourning shroud. *Silence*, the Death Lord's towering battle-reaper, was serrated with battle-notches, and a long looping chain affixed to its pommel was wrapped around his waist like a belt. Jangling censers hung from the chains, each one venting tiny puffs of hot vapour.

His baroquely fashioned Barbaran plate bore numerous marks of the artificer, ceramite infill, fresh paint and lapping powder. From the amount of repair work, whatever battle he had recently fought must have been ferocious.

As Horus had dismissed the Justaerin, so too had his brother primarchs come unescorted; Fulgrim absent the Phoenix Guard, Mortarion without his Deathshroud, though Aximand didn't doubt both were close. Being in the presence of the Warmaster was an honour, but to be present at a moment when three primarchs came together was intoxicating.

Fulgrim and Mortarion had travelled to Dwell to see Horus Lupercal, but the Warmaster had not come to be seen.

He had come to be heard.

Fulgrim's body coiled beneath him with a hiss of rasping scales, raising him up higher than Mortarion and the Warmaster.

'Horus,' said Fulgrim, each syllable veiled with subtle meaning. 'We live in the greatest tumult the galaxy has known and you haven't changed at all. How disappointing.'

'Whereas you have changed beyond all recognition,' said Horus.

A pair of slick, draconic wings unfolded from Fulgrim's back, and dark pigmentation rippled through his body.

'More than you know,' whispered Fulgrim.

'Less than you think,' answered Horus. 'But tell me, does Perturabo yet live? I'm going to need his Legion when the walls of Terra are brought down.'

'I left him alive,' said Fulgrim. 'Though what has become of him since my elevation is a mystery to me. The… what did he name it? Ah, yes, the Eye of Terror is no place for one so firmly rooted in material concerns.'

'What did you do to the Lord of Iron?' demanded Mortarion, his voice rasping from behind the bronze breather apparatus covering the lower half of his face.

'I freed him from foolish notions of permanence,' said Fulgrim. 'I honoured him by allowing his strength to fuel my ascension to this higher state of being. But in the end he would not sacrifice all for his beloved brother.'

Fulgrim sniggered. 'I think I broke him a little bit.'

'You used him?' said Mortarion. 'To become… *this*?'

'We are all using one another, didn't you know that?' laughed Fulgrim, sliding over the floor of the chamber and admiring himself in broken glass reflections. 'To achieve greatness, we must accept the blessing of new things and new forms of power. I have taken that teaching to heart, and embrace such change willingly. You would do well to follow my example, Horus.'

'The spear aimed at the Emperor's heart must not be pliant, but unyielding iron,' said Horus. 'I am that unyielding iron.'

Horus turned to Mortarion, who didn't even bother to hide his revulsion at what had become of the Phoenician.

'As are you, my brother,' said Horus, coming forward to grip the Death Lord's wrist, warrior to warrior. 'You are a wonder to me, my indomitable friend. If not even the Khan's strength could lay you low, what hope have any others?'

'His fleetness of war is a thing of wonder,' admitted Mortarion. 'But rob him of it and he is nothing. I will reap him yet.'

'And I would see it so,' promised Horus, releasing his grip. 'On the soil of Terra we shall hobble the Khan and see how well he fights.'

'I am your servant,' said Mortarion.

Horus shook his head. 'No, never that. Never a servant. We fight this war so we need be no man's slave. I would not have you exchange one master for another. I need you at my side as an equal, not a vassal.'

Mortarion nodded, and Aximand saw the Death Guard primarch stand taller at Lupercal's words.

'And your sons?' said Horus. 'Does Typhon still bait the Lion's hunters?'

'Since Perditus he has been leading the monks of Caliban a merry dance through the stars, leaving death and misery in his wake,' replied Mortarion with a grunt of amusement that puffed toxic emanations from his gorget. 'By your leave I will soon join him and turn the hunters into the hunted.'

'Soon enough, Mortarion, soon enough,' said Horus. 'With your Legion mustered for war, I almost feel sorry for the Lion.'

Fulgrim bristled that he had received no words of praise, but Horus wasn't done.

'Now more than ever I need you both at my side, not as allies and not as subordinates, but as equals. I hold to the name Warmaster, not because of what it represented when it was bestowed, but because of what it means now.'

'And what is that?' asked Fulgrim.

Horus looked into the Phoenician's aquiline features, alabaster in their cold perfection. Aximand felt the power of connection that flowed between them, a struggle for dominance that could have only one victor.

Fulgrim looked away and Horus said, 'It means that only I have the strength to do what must be done. Only I can bring my brothers together under one banner and remake the Imperium.'

'You always were prideful,' said Fulgrim, and Aximand felt the urge to grip *Mourn-it-all*'s hilt at the Phoenician's tone, but the sword was no longer belted at his side, its blade badly notched and still in need of repair.

Horus ignored the barb and said, 'If I am prideful, it is pride in my brothers. Pride in what you have accomplished since last we stood together. It is why I have summoned you and no others to my side now.'

Fulgrim grinned and said, 'Then what would you have of me, Warmaster?'

'The thing I spoke to in the wake of Isstvan, is it gone from you now? You are Fulgrim once again?'

'I have scoured my flesh of the creature's presence.'

'Good,' said Horus. 'What I say here is Legion business, and does not concern the things that dwell beyond our world.'

'I cast the warp-thing out, but I learned a great many things from it while our souls were entwined.'

'What things?' asked Mortarion.

'We have bargained with their masters, made pacts,' hissed Fulgrim, pointing a sickle blade talon at Horus. '*You* have made blood pacts with gods, and oaths to gods should not lightly be broken.'

'It sickens me to my bones to hear you speak of keeping faith with oaths,' said Mortarion.

The Warmaster raised a hand to ward off Fulgrim's venomous response, and said, 'You are both here because I have need of your unique talents. The wrath of the Sons of Horus is to be unleashed once more, and I would not see it so without my brothers at my side.'

Horus walked a slow circle, weaving his words around Mortarion and Fulgrim like a web.

'Erebus raised his great Ruinstorm on Calth and split the galaxy asunder. Beyond its tempests, the Five Hundred Worlds burned in Lorgar and Angron's "shadow crusade", but their wanton slaughters are of no consequence for now. What happens here, with us, *with you*, is what will make the difference between victory or defeat.'

The Warmaster's words were lure and balm all in one, obvious even to Aximand, but they were having the desired effect.

'Are we to march on Terra at last?' asked Mortarion.

Horus laughed. 'Not yet, but soon. It is in preparation for that day that I have called you here.'

Horus stepped back and lifted his arms as ancient machinery rose from the floor like rapid outgrowths of coral, unfolding and expanding with mechanised precision. A hundred or more glass cylinders rose with them, each containing a body lying forever on the threshold of existence and oblivion.

From previously unseen entrances, a host of weeping techadepts and black-robed Mechanicum entered, taking up positions alongside the gently glowing cylinders.

'By any mortal reckoning, our father is a god,' said Horus. 'And for all that He has allowed His dominion to fall to rebellion, He is still too powerful to face.'

'Even for you?' said Fulgrim with a grin.

'Even for me,' agreed Horus. 'To slay a god, a warrior must first become a god himself.'

Horus paused. 'At least, that's what the dead tell me.'

TWO

Solid roots
Molech
Medusa's fire

A KILOMETRE-HIGH DOME enclosed the Hegemon, a feat of civic engineering that perfectly encapsulated the vision at the heart of the Palace's construction. Situated within the Kath Mandau Precinct of Old Himalazia, the Hegemon was the seat of Imperial governance, a metropolis of activity that never stopped nor paused for breath in its unceasing labours.

Lord Dorn had, of course, wanted to fortify it, to layer its golden walls in adamantium and stone, but that order had been quietly rescinded at the highest level. If the Warmaster's armies reached this far into the Palace then the war was already lost.

A million rooms and corridors veined its bones, from soulless scrivener cubicles of bare brick to soaring chambers of ouslite, marble and gold that were filled with the greatest artistic treasures of the ages. Tens of thousands of robed scribes and clerks hurried along raised concourses, escorted by document-laden servitors and trotting menials. Ambassadors and nobility from across the globe gathered to petition the lords of Terra while ministers guided the affairs of innumerable departments.

The Hegemon had long ceased to be a building as defined by the term. Rather, it had sprawled beyond the dome to become a vast city unto itself, a knotted mass of plunging archive-chasms, towers of office, petitioner's domes, palaces of bureaucracy and stepped terraces of hanging gardens. Over the centuries it had become a barely understood organ within the Imperial body that functioned despite – or perhaps *because* of – its very complexity. This was the slow beating heart of the Emperor's domain, where decisions affecting billions were dispatched across the galaxy by functionaries who had never lived a day beyond the winding circuits of the Palace.

And the Kath Mandau Precinct was just one of many hundreds of such regions enclosed by the iron-cased walls of the mightiest fortress on Terra.

Beneath the cloud-hung apex of the Hegemon's central dome was a secluded rift valley, where the last remaining examples of natural foliage on Terra could be found. So enormous was the dome that varying microclimates held sway at different elevations, creating miniature weather patterns that belied any notions of enclosure.

Glittering white cliffs were shawled with mountain evergreens and brocaded by cascading ice-waterfalls that fed a crystal lake of shimmerskin koi. Clinging to a spur of rock partway up the cliffs was the ruin of an ancient citadel. Its outer wall had long since toppled, and the remains of an inner keep were demarcated by a series of concentric rings of glassily volcanic stone.

The valley had existed prior to the construction of the Palace, and rumour told that it held special significance to the Master of Mankind himself.

One man knew the truth of this, but he would never tell.

Malcador the Sigillite sat at the rippling shore of the lake, deliberating whether to advance steadily on the right or throw caution to the wind in an all-out assault. He had the superior force, but his opponent was much larger than him, a towering giant encased in battleplate the colour of moonlit ice and draped in a furred cloak. Long braids of russet hair, woven with polished gems and yellowed fangs, were pulled back from his face, that of a noble savage rendered marble white in the dome's artificial daylight.

'Are you going to make a move?' asked the Wolf King.

'Patience, Leman,' said Malcador. 'The subtleties of *hnefatafl* are manifold, and each move requires careful thought. Especially when one is the attacker.'

'I'm aware of the game's subtleties,' replied Leman Russ, his voice the throaty threat-rasp of a predator. 'I invented this variant.'

'Then you should know not to rush me.'

Mighty beyond all sense of the word, Leman Russ was a tsunami that begins life far out to sea and builds its power over thousands of kilometres as it draws near the shore. His physical form was the instant before impact, and all who looked upon him knew it. Even when apparently at peace, it felt as though Leman Russ was only holding back some explosive violence with great effort.

A bone-handled hunting blade was belted at his waist; a dagger to one of his post-human scale, a sword to everyone else.

Next to Leman Russ, Malcador was a frail, hunch-shouldered old man. Which was, as time went by, less a carefully cultivated image, more a true reflection of his soul-deep weariness. White hair spilled from his crown and lay across his shoulders like the snow on the towering flanks of Chomolungma.

He might bind his hair up when in the company of Sanguinius or Rogal Dorn, but with Russ the observation of physical niceties were secondary to the matters at hand.

Malcador studied the board, a hexagon divided into irregular segments with a raised octagon at its centre. Each segment was pierced with slots into which were placed the playing pieces carved from yellowed *hrosshvalur* teeth; a mix of warriors, kings, monsters and elemental forces. Portions of the board were movable, able to slide over one another and occlude or reveal fresh segments, and rods set in each side could be rotated to block or open slots. All of which enabled a canny player to radically alter the character of the game at a stroke.

One player had a king and a small band of retainers, the other an army, and as in most such games, the object was to kill the enemy king. Or keep him alive, depending on which colour you chose. Russ always chose to play the outnumbered king.

Malcador removed a hearth-jarl and pushed it towards the octagon where the Wolf King's pieces had gathered, then twisted one of the side rods. Clicking mechanisms rotated within the board, though it was impossible to know for certain which slots had opened up and which had closed until a player had committed to a move.

'Bold,' noted Russ. 'Nemo would say you hadn't given that move enough thought.'

'You were pressing me.'

'And you let yourself be goaded?' mused Russ. 'I'm surprised.'

'There is not the time for deep reflection now.'

'You've made that point before.'

'It's an important point to make.'

'Nor yet is it a time for recklessness,' said Russ, moving his Warhawk and twisting a side rod. Malcador's hearth-jarl fell onto its side as the slot it had occupied was sealed.

'Foolish,' said Malcador, foregoing the opportunity to alter the board to advance an extra piece. 'You are exposed now.'

Russ shook his head and pressed the segment of board before him, rotating it by ninety degrees. As it clicked back into place,

Malcador saw the king's retainers were now poised to flank his army and execute its cardinal piece.

'You say exposed,' said Russ. 'I say *berkutra*.'

'The hunter's cut,' translated Malcador. 'That's Chogorian.'

'The Khan taught me his name for it,' said Russ, never one to take another's virtue for his own. 'We call it *almáttigrbíta*, but I like his word better.'

Malcador graciously tipped his cardinal piece onto its side, knowing there would be no escape from the Wolf King's trap, only a slow attrition that would see his leaderless army scattered to the corners of the board.

'Well played, Leman,' said Malcador.

Russ nodded and bent to lift a wide-necked ewer of wine from beside the table. He held a pair of pewter goblets in his other hand and kept one for himself before handing the second to Malcador. The Sigillite took note of the wine's provenance and raised a curious eyebrow.

Russ shrugged. 'Not everything of the Sons was bitter with sorcery.'

The wine was poured, and Malcador was forced to agree.

'How long until your fleet is battle ready?' asked Malcador, though he had already digested the work schedules of the Fenrisian vessels from Fabricator Kane at the Novopangean orbital yards.

'Alpharius's whelps tried to tear the *Hrafnkel*'s heart out, but her bones are strong and she'll sail again,' said Russ with a phlegmatic grunt. 'The shipwrights tell me it'll be another three months at least before she's void-worthy, and not even Bear's threats are getting them to move faster.'

'Bear?'

'A misnomer that's stuck,' was all Russ would say.

'And the rest of the fleet?'

'Probably longer,' said Russ. 'The delay chafes, but if Caliban's angels hadn't arrived when they did, there wouldn't be a fleet left to rebuild at all. We fill our time though. We train, we fight and prepare for what's ahead.'

'Have you given any thought to the alternative I broached?'

'I have,' said Russ.

'And?'

'My answer is no,' answered Russ. 'It stinks of revenge and last resort.'

'It's strategy,' said Malcador. 'Pre-emption, if you will.'

'Semantics,' said Russ, a warning burr in his voice. 'Don't think to weave linguistic knots around me, Sigillite. I know why you want that planet burned, but I'm a warrior, not a destroyer.'

'A slender distinction, my friend, but if any world's death would turn the Warmaster from his course it would be that one.'

'Perhaps, but that is a murder for another day,' said Russ. 'My fleet's guns will be better directed against Horus himself.'

'So you are set on this course?'

'As the cursed ice-rigger of *bróðirgráta* is doomed to follow the bad star.'

'Dorn would have you stay,' said Malcador, passing the red pieces to Russ. 'You know Terra would be mightier with the Great Wolf lying in wait, fangs bared and claws sharp.'

'If Rogal wants me so much, he should ask himself.'

'He is *in absentia* just now.'

'I know where he is,' said Russ. 'You think I fought my way back from Alaxxes and didn't leave silent hunters in the shadows to see who follows my wake? I know of the intruder ship and I saw Rogal's men take it.'

'Rogal is proud,' said Malcador. 'But I am not. Stay, Leman. Range your wolves on Terra's walls.'

The Wolf King shook his head. 'I'm not built for waiting, Sigillite.

I don't fight well from behind stone, waiting for the enemy to try and dig me out. I'm the executioner, and the executioner lands the first blow, a killing strike that ends dispute before it begins.'

Malcador nodded. He'd suspected this would be Russ's answer, but had to present an alternative nonetheless. He looked up at the highest reaches of the dome, where distant anabatic winds tugged at the clouds. A soothsayer or astromancer might read omens and signs of the future in their form, but Malcador just saw clouds.

'Has the exiled cub been summoned?' said Russ, sitting back and draining his wine as though it were water.

Malcador returned his gaze to Russ. 'You should not call him that, my friend. He faced the Warmaster's decision to betray the Emperor and refused to follow it. Do not underestimate the strength of character that took, strength a great many others singularly failed to show.'

Russ nodded, conceding the point, as Malcador continued. 'The Somnus Citadel's shuttle arrived at Yasu's villa this morning. He approaches the Hegemon as we speak.'

'And you still believe him to be the best?'

'The best?' said Malcador. 'A hard thing to quantify. He is uniquely capable, no doubt, but is he the best? The best what? The best fighter, the best shot, the best heart? I don't know if he is the best of them, but he won't fail you.'

Russ let out a heavy, animal breath and said, 'I've read the one-time slates you gave me, and they don't make for comforting reading. When Nathaniel Garro found him he was a maddened killer, a slayer of innocents.'

'That he survived the massacre at all was a miracle.'

'Aye, maybe so,' said Russ.

'Trust me, Leman, this one stands with us, as straight up and down as any I have known.'

'What if you're wrong?' asked Russ, leaning over the board and toppling his own king. 'What if he goes back to the Warmaster? The things he's seen and done. The things he knows. Even if he is as loyal as you believe, you can't know what will happen when he enters the belly of the beast. You know how much rests upon this.'

'Only too well, old friend,' said Malcador. 'Your life, the Emperor's. Perhaps all of our lives. The Emperor wrought you for a terrible purpose, but a necessary one. If anyone can stop Horus before he gets to Terra, it is you.'

Russ's head snapped up and his top lip curled back over his teeth, like an animal sensing danger. 'He's here.'

Malcador looked down the valley and saw a lone figure cresting the Sigillite's bridge far below. At this distance, he was little more than a speck of steeldust grey against the white of the cliffs, but his poise was unmistakable.

Russ rose to his feet and watched the distant figure approach, regarding him as though he were a wounded hound that might turn on its master at any moment.

'So that's Garviel Loken,' said Russ.

SHIMMERING FLUORESCENT LIGHT filled the Dome of Revivification with the arrival of the cryo-cylinders, and Aximand felt the not unreasonable discomfort at seeing those who were alive and yet ought to be dead. The thought triggered a memory of a dream, a half-heard echo of something best forgotten.

'Who are they?' asked Mortarion, his deathly pallor made even more corpse-like by the glow of the life-sustaining mechanisms of the Mausolytic.

'They are Dwell's greatest resource,' said Horus, as Fulgrim moved through the suspended cylinders with the leathery scrape of unnatural flesh over broken glass. 'A thousand generations of its most brilliant minds, held forever at death's threshold in the final instant of their life.'

Horus waved Aximand forward and he took his place at the Warmaster's right hand. Horus placed the taloned gauntlet on his shoulder guard.

'Aximand here led the assault to take the Mausolytic Precincts,' said Horus with pride. 'At no small personal cost.'

Fulgrim turned to him, and Aximand saw the change in the Phoenician went far deeper than his physical transformation. The narcissism Aximand always suspected lay at the heart of the Emperor's Children's obsessive drive for perfection was rampant in Fulgrim. Nothing he said could be taken at face value, and Aximand wondered if trusting Fulgrim had been Perturabo's downfall. Surely Horus would not make the same mistake?

'Your face,' said the Phoenician. 'What happened to it?'

'I got careless in the vicinity of a Medusan blade.'

Fulgrim reached out with one of his upper arms and took hold of Aximand's chin, turning his head to either side. The touch was repellent and exhilarating.

'Your whole face removed in one cut,' said Fulgrim with grudging admiration. 'How did it feel?'

'Painful.'

'Lucius would approve,' said Fulgrim. 'But you shouldn't have re-attached it. Imagine the bliss of that pain each time you were helmed. And one less of you looking like my brother is no bad thing.'

The Phoenician moved on and Aximand felt a curious mix of relief and regret that the primarch's touch was no longer upon him.

'So you can talk to them?' asked Mortarion, examining the controls of a cryo-cylinder. The tech-adept next to him dropped to his knees, soiled and weeping in terror.

The Warmaster nodded. 'Everything these people knew is preserved and blended with the hundreds of remembrancers and iterators who came to this world after Guilliman restored it to the Imperium.'

'And what do they say?'

Horus made his way to a gently glowing cylinder in which lay the recumbent form of an elderly man. The Mournival followed him and Aximand saw the body within was draped in a red-gold aquila flag, the planes and contours of his features suggesting he was not a native Dweller.

'They try to say nothing,' grinned Horus. 'How the galaxy has changed isn't to their taste. They scream and rage, trying to keep me from hearing what I want, but they can't scream all the time.'

Fulgrim coiled his serpentine lower body around the mechanisms of the cylinder, rearing up and peering through the frosted glass.

'I know this man,' he said, and Aximand saw that he also recognised him, picturing the preserved face as it had been nearly two centuries ago when its owner had boarded the *Vengeful Spirit*.

'Arthis Varfell,' said Horus. 'His iterations during the latter days of Unity were instrumental in the pacification of the Sol system. And his monographs on the long-term benefits of pre-introducing *advocatus* agents into indigenous cultures prior to compliance overtures became required reading.'

'What's he doing here?' asked Mortarion.

'Varfell was part of the Thirteenth's expeditionary forces when they reached this world,' said Horus. 'Roboute gave him much credit for making Dwell's reintegration to the Imperium bloodless. But soon after compliance the old man's heart finally started rejecting the juvenat treatments, and he chose to be implanted within the Mausolytic rather than continue onwards. He rather liked the idea of becoming part of a whole world's shared memory.'

'He told you this?'

'Eventually,' said Horus. 'The dead don't easily give up their secrets, but I didn't ask gently.'

'What do the dead of this world know of gods and their doom?' demanded Fulgrim.

'More than you or I,' said Horus.

'What does *that* mean?'

Horus strolled through the rows of cryo-cylinders, touching some and pausing momentarily to peer at their glowing occupants. He spoke as he walked, as though recounting nothing of consequence, though Aximand saw the studied nonchalance veiled great import.

'I came to Dwell because I recently became aware of several lacunae in my memories, voids where there ought to be perfect recall.'

'What couldn't you remember?' said Fulgrim.

'If that isn't a stupid question, I don't know what is,' grunted Mortarion with a sound that might have been laughter.

Fulgrim hissed in anger, but the Death Lord took no notice.

'I'd read the Great Crusade log concerning Dwell decades ago, of course,' continued Horus, 'though I'd put it from my mind since there hadn't been any conflict. But when I sent the Seventeenth to Calth, Roboute spoke of the great library his highest epistolary had constructed. He said it was a treasure-house of knowledge to rival the Mausolytic of Dwell and its great repository of the dead.'

'So you came to Dwell to see if you could fill the void in your memory?' said Fulgrim.

'After a fashion,' agreed Horus, circling back to where he had begun his circuit of the cylinders. 'Every man and woman interred here over the millennia has become part of a shared consciousness, a world memory containing everything each individual had learned, from the first great diaspora to the present day.'

'Impressive,' agreed Mortarion.

'Hardly,' said Fulgrim. 'We all have eidetic memories. What is there here of value I do not already know?'

'Do you remember all your battles, Fulgrim?' asked Horus.

'Of course. Every sword swing, every manoeuvre, every shot. Every kill.'

'Squad names, warriors? Places, people?'

'All of it,' insisted Fulgrim.

'Then tell me of Molech,' said Horus. 'Tell me what you remember of that compliance.'

Fulgrim opened his mouth to speak, but no words came out. His expression was that of a blank-faced novitiate as he sought the answer to a drill sergeant's rhetorical question.

'I don't understand,' said Fulgrim. 'I remember Molech, I do, its wilds and its high castles and its Knights, but...'

His words trailed off, putting Aximand in the mind of a warrior suffering severe head trauma. 'We were both there, you and I, before the Third Legion had numbers to operate alone. And the Lion? Wait, was Jaghatai there too?'

Horus nodded. 'So the logs say,' he said. 'We four and the Emperor travelled to Molech. It complied, of course. What planet would offer resistance to Legion forces led by the Emperor?'

'An overwhelming force,' said Mortarion. 'Was heavy resistance expected?'

'Far from it,' said Horus. 'Molech's rulers were inveterate record keepers, and they remembered Terra. Its people had weathered Old Night, and when the Emperor descended to the surface it was inevitable they would accept compliance.'

'We remained there for some months, did we not?' asked Fulgrim.

Aximand glanced at Abaddon and saw the same look on the First Captain's face he felt he wore. He too remembered Molech, but like the primarchs was having difficulty in recalling specific details. Aximand had almost certainly visited the planet's surface, but found it hard to form a coherent picture of its environs.

'According to the *Vengeful Spirit*'s horologs, we were there for a hundred and eleven standard Terran days, one hundred and nine local. After we left nearly a hundred regiments of Army, three Titanicus cohorts and garrison detachments from two Legions were left in place.'

'For a planet that embraced compliance?' said Mortarion. 'A waste of resources if ever I heard it. What need did the Emperor have to fortify Molech with such strength?'

Horus snapped his fingers and said, 'Exactly.'

'I'm guessing you have an answer for that question,' said Fulgrim. 'Otherwise why summon us here?'

'I have an answer of sorts,' said Horus, tapping the cryo-cylinder containing Arthis Varfell. 'A speciality of this particular iterator was the early history of the Emperor, the wars of Unity and the various myths and legends surrounding His assumption of Old Earth's throne. The memories of Dwell are untainted, and many of its earliest settlers were driven here by the raging tides of Old Night. What they remember goes back a *very* long way, and Varfell assimilated it all.'

'What do you mean?' asked Fulgrim.

'I mean that some of the oldest Dwellers came from Molech, and they remember the Emperor's first appearance on their world.'

'*First*?' said Fulgrim.

Mortarion gripped *Silence* tightly. 'He had been there before? When?'

'If I'm interpreting the dreams of the dead right, then our father first set foot on Molech many centuries, or even millennia before the wars of Unity. He came in a starship that never returned to Earth, a starship I believe now forms the heart of the Dawn Citadel.'

'The Dawn Citadel… I remember that,' said Fulgrim. 'Yes, there was an ugly, cannibalised structure of ship parts at the end of a mountain valley! The Lion built one of his sombre castles around it, did he not?'

'He did indeed,' said Horus. 'The Emperor needed a starship to reach Molech, but didn't need it to get back. Whatever He found there made Him into a god, or as near as makes no difference.'

'And you think whatever that was is still there?' said Fulgrim with heady anticipation. 'Even after all this time?'

'Why else leave the planet so heavily defended?' said Mortarion. 'It's the only explanation.'

Horus nodded. 'Through Arthis Varfell, I learned a great deal of Molech's early years, together with what the four of us did there. Some of it I even remembered.'

'The Emperor erased your memories of Molech?' said Abaddon, forgetting himself for a moment.

'Ezekyle!' hissed Aximand.

Abaddon's outrage eclipsed his decorum, his choler roused as he sought to vent his anger. Beyond him, the stars were out, casting a glittering light over Tyjun. Stablights from patrolling aircraft swept the city. Some close, some far away, but none came near the skeletal structure of the dome.

'No, not *erased*,' said Horus, overlooking his First Captain's outburst. 'Something so drastic would quickly result in a form of cognitive dissonance that would draw attention to its very existence. This was more a… *manipulation*, the lessening of some memories and the strengthening of others to overshadow the gaps.'

'But to alter the memories of three entire Legions,' breathed Fulgrim. 'The *power* that would require…'

'So, it's to Molech then?' said Mortarion.

'Yes, brothers,' said Horus, spreading his arms. 'We are to follow in the footsteps of a god and become gods ourselves.'

'Our Legions stand ready,' said Fulgrim, febrile anticipation making his body shimmer with corposant.

'No, brother, I require only Mortarion's Legion for this war-making,' said Horus.

'Then why summon me at all?' snapped Fulgrim. 'Why insult my warriors by excluding them from your designs?'

'Because it's not your Legion I need, it's you,' said Horus, spearing to the heart of Fulgrim's vanity. 'My Phoenician brother, I need *you* most of all.'

Aximand's ocular filters dimmed as a stablight swept through the buckled struts of the dome. Stark shadows bowed and twisted.

Everyone looked up.

The dark outline of an aircraft rose up beyond the dome, its engines bellowing with downdraft. A blizzard of broken glass took to the air. Glittering reflections dazzled like snow.

'Who the hell's flying so close?' said Abaddon, shielding his eyes from the blinding glare. More noise, fresh stablights from the other side of the dome.

Another two aircraft.

Fire Raptors. Horde killers that had made their name at Ullanor. Coated in non-reflective black. Hovering, circling the dome. Icons on their glacis shone proudly after months of being obscured.

Silver gauntlets on a black field.

'It's Meduson!' shouted Aximand. 'It's Shadrak bloody Meduson!'

Three centreline Avenger cannons roared in unison. Braying quad guns on waist turrets followed an instant later.

And the Dome of Revivification vanished in a sheeting inferno of orange flame.

THE GAME WAS called hnefatafl, and Loken found himself in the presence of a Titan he'd never expected to see again, much less be sat opposite. He'd met primarchs before, had even talked to some of them without making a fool of himself, but the Wolf King was another entity altogether. Primal force bound to immortal form, elemental fury woven around a frame of invincible meat and bone.

And yet, of all the post-human demigods he had met, Russ gave the impression of being the most human.

Until ten hours ago, Loken had been ensconced within a lunar biodome on the edge of the Mare Tranquillitatis. Since returning from the mission to Caliban, he'd spent most of his time tending to the gardens within the dome, seeking a peace that remained forever out of reach.

Iacton Qruze had brought Malcador's summons, together with his bare, steeldust grey armour, but his fellow Knight Errant had not joined him on the Stormbird to Terra, claiming he had heavy duty elsewhere. The Half-heard had changed markedly since their time together aboard the *Vengeful Spirit*, becoming a sadder, but wiser man. Loken was not sure if that was a good thing or not.

The Stormbird set down by a villa in the mountains beyond the Palace, and a young girl with skin like burnished coal who had introduced herself as Ekata had offered him refreshments. He'd declined, finding her appearance unsettling, like a reminder of someone he'd once known. She led him to a black-armoured skimmer emblazoned with a serpentine dragon. It flew into the heart of the Palace Precincts, beneath the shadow of one of the great orbital plates moored to a mountainside, until coming to land within sight of the vast dome of the Hegemon. He'd climbed the valley alone, pausing only as he reached the Sigillite's bridge as he saw the two figures at the side of the lake.

Malcador sat on a stool at the side of the board and Loken favoured him with a puzzled look.

'You summoned me to Terra just to play a game?'

'No,' answered Russ, 'but play it anyway.'

'A good game is like a mirror that allows you to look into

yourself,' said Malcador. 'And you can learn a lot about a man by watching how he plays a game.'

Loken looked down at the board, with its movable segments, rotating rods and one outnumbered force.

'I don't know how to play,' he said.

'It's simple,' said Russ, moving a piece forward and rotating a slot. 'It's like war. You learn the rules fast and then you have to play better than everyone else.'

Loken nodded and moved a piece forward in the centre. His was the larger army, but he had no doubt that would be of little advantage against the man he suspected had devised the game. He spent the opening moves in what he hoped was an all-out assault, provoking responses from the Wolf King, who didn't even deign to look at the board or appear to give his strategy any consideration whatsoever.

Within six moves, it was clear that Loken had lost, but he had a better idea of how the game was played. In ten moves, his army had been split and its cardinal piece eliminated.

'Again,' said Russ, and Malcador reset the pieces.

They played another two games, with Loken defeated both times, but like any warrior of the Legiones Astartes, Loken was a quick study. With every move, his appreciation of the game was growing until, by the midpoint of the third game, he felt he had a good grasp of its rules and their applications.

This latest game ended as the three before it, with Loken's army scattered and lost. He sat back and grinned.

'Another game, my lord?' he said. 'I almost had you until you changed the board.'

'It's a favourite endgame of Leman's to finish with a bold reshaping of the landscape,' said Malcador. 'But I think we've played enough, don't you?'

Russ leaned over the board and said, 'You don't learn quick

enough. He doesn't learn quick enough.'

This last part was addressed to Malcador.

'He already plays better than I,' said the Sigillite.

'Even the Balt play better than you,' said Russ. 'And they have minds like clubbed *vatnkýr*. He didn't listen to what I told him, he didn't learn the rules fast and didn't play better than everyone else.'

'Another game then,' snapped Loken. 'I'll show you how quick I learn. Or are you afraid I'll beat you at your own game?'

Russ stared at him from beneath hooded brows and Loken saw death in those eyes, the sure and certain knowledge of his own doom. He'd goaded a primarch of notorious unpredictability and saw his earlier impression of Russ being the most human of primarchs had been so very wide of the mark.

He was now about to pay for that mistake.

And he didn't care.

Russ nodded and his killing mood lifted with a wide grin that exposed teeth that looked too large for his mouth to contain.

'He's a lousy player, but I like him,' said the Wolf King. 'Maybe you were right about him, Sigillite. There's solid roots to him after all. He'll do.'

Loken said nothing, wondering what manner of test he had just passed and what had been said of him before his arrival.

'I'll do for what?' he asked.

'You'll do to find me a way to kill Horus,' said the Wolf King.

HORUS KNEW THE capabilities of the Fire Raptor intimately. Its range, weapon mounts, rate of fire. Ullanor had shown just how savage a gunship it was. It had been integral to the victory.

I should be dead.

He breathed in sulphur-hot fumes. Fyceline, scorched metal, burning flesh. Horus rolled onto his side. Hearing damaged. A deadening numbness filled his head with dull echoes. The rasping of a saw. Thudding detonations.

He didn't need his visor display to know how badly he'd been hurt. His armour was battered, but unbreached, though his skin was burned to the bone, his scalp scorched bare. Temperature warnings, oxygen deficiencies, organ damage. He shut them out with a thought.

Clarity. He needed clarity.

Shadrak Meduson!

Autonomic reactions took over. Time and motion became gel-like as Horus pushed himself to his feet. He swayed, concussive shock waves making him dizzy. How bad did it have to get for a primarch to feel dizzy?

Flames surrounded him. The Dome of Revivification was gone, its structure torn away in scything arcs of explosive mass-reactive bolts. Cryo-cylinders lay in shattered ruin. Wet-leather bodies smoked like trail rations.

Horus saw Noctua and Aximand pinned beneath a fallen structural member. The plates of their armour were buckled and split, their helms splintered into pieces. No sign of the Widowmaker or Ezekyle.

'Mortarion!' he shouted 'Fulgrim!'

His brothers? Where were his brothers?

A figure rose from the centre of the dome, painfully bright. Too bright, giving off a radiance that sent a twist of nausea through his gut. Sinuous, winged, many armed.

Beautiful, so very beautiful. Even bleeding sick light from fractures in his essence. He rose like a snow-maned phoenix, rising from the ashes of its immortal rebirth. Horus saw sinews like hawsers in Fulgrim's neck, his black, murderer's eyes now filled with light that was not light.

A howling Fire Raptor swung around, the gimbals of its waist cannons swivelling to track the Phoenician.

Before it could fire, the rear wings peeled back from its body, like the wings of a dragonfly plucked by a spiteful child. Its tail section crumpled, buckling inwards under invisible force.

Fulgrim roared and brought his hands together.

The gunship imploded, crushed to a mangled ball of twisted flesh and metal. Compressed ammunition detonated and the flaming wreckage dropped like a stone.

Despite the flames, Horus felt the icy wind of warp-craft fill the dome. He'd known his brother's transformation had empowered him enormously, but this was staggering. He saw movement in the wreckage beneath the Phoenician.

Mortarion's Barbaran plate was black as char, his pallid face seared the same colour. He leaked blood like a pierced bladder.

Ezekyle and Aximand appeared at their primarch's side. The First Captain's face was a mask of crimson, his topknot burned down to the skull. Strands of it hung over his face, making him look like the victim of a wasting disease. Aximand was shouting, dragging him, but all Horus heard were explosions.

The cloying torpor of near death fell from him.

Noise and fury returned as his senses caught up with the world. The two remaining Fire Raptors were circling, methodically and systematically destroying the dome. Horus saw interlocking trails of high-calibre shells streaking from the prows of the Legion's Fire Raptors. Streams of fire raced downward as the gunships strafed in concert around the dome's circumference.

Nothing could live through so thorough and savage an attack.

I should be dead.

He shook off Aximand's grip and barged through the blazing wreckage of the dome towards Mortarion, immense in his custom Martian plate. Bodies of Dwell's greatest minds snapped beneath his weight.

The Iron Tenth's gunships filled the air with shells again.

He tried to shout, but his throat was a scorched ruin of smoke-damaged tissue. He coughed up ash and seared lung matter.

Explosions detonated prematurely, orange flame and black smoke. Shrapnel and casings fell like hot nails.

I should be dead.

And but for the craft of Malevolus and the Phoenician's power, he would be.

Fulgrim's arms were outstretched, and Horus guessed he had summoned a force barrier or kine-shield. Beads of phosphor-bright ichor ran like sweat down his body. Writhing smoke coated his serpent form as dark radiance spilled from his eyes and mouth.

Whatever he was doing, it was robbing the solid rounds of their potency. Not all of it, but most of it.

Six shells tore into Fulgrim's body, exploding from his spine.

Horus cried aloud as if he had been struck himself. Blood like bright milk spattered Mortarion's armour. It smoked like an acid burn. Fulgrim screamed and the roar of gunfire and explosions swelled in power. The platform of the dome sagged, solid metal warping in the heat of the fire.

'Horus! Bring them down!' gasped Fulgrim. 'Quickly!'

Aximand and Abaddon fired their bolters at the gunships, hoping for a lucky hit. A cracked canopy, a buckled engine louvre. Impacts pummelled the gunships' flanks, but Fire Raptors were built to withstand deadlier weapons than theirs.

Mortarion waded through the wreckage, as unbroken as ever, the black blade of *Silence* unlimbered and trailing a burning length of chain. He roared something in the heathen tongue of his home world as he ran towards the edge of the dome.

The Death Lord hurled *Silence* like an axeman.

The great reaper blade spun and hammered into the heraldic fist upon the nearest Fire Raptor's glacis. Heels braced in the shattered dome, Mortarion hauled on the chain attached to *Silence*'s heel.

The gunship lurched in the air, but the Death Lord wasn't done with it. Its Avenger cannon flensed Mortarion, driving him back. Plates sheared from him, blood arced in pressurised sprays. Flesh melted in the fury of high power mass-reactives.

And still Mortarion pulled on the chain, pulling the screaming gunship closer.

'I've hooked him!' yelled Mortarion. 'Now finish it!'

The pilots fought to escape his grip. The Fire Raptor's engines shrieked in power, but hand over hand, the downed primarch reeled the gunship in like a belligerent angler.

Horus appeared at Mortarion's side, running.

Even in his towering armour he was running. Jumping.

He vaulted onto the shattered remains of a cryo-capsule and launched himself through the air. Hooked by the Death Lord, the gunship was powerless to evade. Horus landed on its prow and knelt to grip the haft of *Silence* as the gunship lurched with the impact of his landing.

He saw the pilots' faces and drank in their terror. Horus never normally gave any thought to the men he killed. They were soldiers doing a job. Misguided and fighting for a lie, but simply soldiers doing what they were ordered to do.

But these men had *hurt* him. They'd tried to murder him and his brothers. They'd lain in wait for an opportunity to behead their enemy. That he'd been foolish enough to believe Shadrak Meduson would only have one plan in place inflamed Horus's humours as much as the attempt itself.

He lifted his right arm, and *Worldbreaker*'s killing head caught the firelight.

The mace swung and demolished the pilot's compartment.

The last Fire Raptor swung around the dome. Seeing him atop

the second gunship and knowing it was doomed, the Fire Raptor's cannons roared.

High explosive, armour penetrating shells ripped along the fuselage of the wallowing gunship, shearing it in two. It exploded in a geysering plume of fire, but Horus was already in the air.

Silence in one hand, *Worldbreaker* in the other, he landed on the back of the last gunship, slewing it around. The Fire Raptor gunned its engines as it tried to shake him from its back. Horus swung *Silence* in a wide arc and split the Fire Raptor's spine.

Still roaring, the gunship's engines wrenched free with a screech of tortured metal. Horus swept *Worldbreaker* around like a woodsman's axe and its flanged head ploughed through the gunship's fuselage, obliterating the pilots and turning the prow to scrap.

The shattered remains fell away as Horus dropped into the dome with both *Silence* and *Worldbreaker* held out at his sides.

An explosion mushroomed behind him.

Horus dropped both weapons and ran to Mortarion. He knelt and reached out to clasp his blood-soaked brother to his burned breast. Mortarion's arms hung limp, tendons ripped from bones and muscles acid-burned raw.

Neither moved, a living tableau of the ashen sculptures of the dead left in an atomic detonation's wake.

One touch and they would crumble to cinders.

'My brother,' wept Horus. 'What have they done to you?'

THREE

The Bringer of Rain
House Devine
First kill

AT FIRST, LOKEN thought he'd misheard. Surely Russ hadn't said
what he thought he'd just said. He searched the Wolf King's eyes
for any sign that this was another test, but saw nothing to convince him that Russ hadn't just revealed his purpose.

'Kill Horus?' he said.

Russ nodded and began packing up the hnefatafl board, as
though the matter were already concluded. Loken felt as though
he had somehow missed the substance of a vital discussion.

'You're going to kill Horus?'

'I am, but I need your help to do it.'

Loken laughed, now certain this was a joke.

'You're going to kill Horus?' he repeated, carefully enunciat-
ing every word to avoid misunderstanding. 'And you need my
help?'

Russ looked over at Malcador with a frown. 'Why does he keep
asking me the same question? I know he's not simple, so why is
he being so dense?'

'I think your directness after so oblique an approach has him confused.'

'I was perfectly clear, but I will lay it out one last time.'

Loken forced himself to listen intently to the Wolf King's every word, knowing there would be no hidden meanings, no subtext and no ulterior motives. What Russ required of him would be exactly as it was spoken.

'I am going to lead the Rout in battle against Horus, and I am going to kill him.'

Loken sat back on the rock, still trying to process the idea of a combat between Leman Russ and Horus. Loken had seen both primarchs make war over the last century, but when it came down to blood and death he saw only one outcome.

'Horus Lupercal will kill you,' said Loken.

Had he named any other individual, Loken had no doubt the Wolf King would have torn his throat out before he'd even known what was happening. Instead, Russ nodded.

'You're right,' he said, his eyes taking on a distant look as he relived old battles. 'I've fought every one of my brothers over the centuries, either in training or with blooded blade. I know for a fact I can kill any one of them if had to... but Horus.'

Russ shook his head and his next words were spoken like a shameful confession, each one a bitter curse.

'He's the only one I don't know if I can beat.'

Loken never thought to hear such a bald admission from any primarch, let alone the Wolf King. Its frank honesty lodged in his heart, and he would take Leman Russ's words to the grave.

'Then what can I do?' he said. 'Horus must be stopped, and if you're going to be the one doing it, then I want to help.'

Russ nodded and said, 'You were part of my brother's inner council, his... what did you call it? The Mournival. You were there the day he turned traitor, and you know the Sons of Horus in a way I cannot.'

Loken felt the import of the primarch's next words before he said them, like the tension in the air before a storm.

'You will go back to your Legion like the *aptrgangr* that walks unseen in the wilds of Fenris,' said Russ. 'Lay a hunter's trail within the rogue wolf's lair. Reveal the flaw to which he is blind, and I can slay him.'

'Go back to the Sons of Horus?' said Loken.

'Aye,' said Russ. 'My brothers all have a weakness, but I believe that only one of his own can see that of Horus. I know Horus as a brother, you know him as a father, and there are none who can bring down fathers like their sons.'

'You're wrong,' said Loken, shaking his head. 'I barely knew him at all. I thought I did, but everything he told me was a lie.'

'Not everything,' said Russ. 'Before this madness, Horus was the best of us, but even the best are not perfect.'

'Horus *can* be beaten,' added Malcador. 'He is a fanatic, and that's how I know he can be beaten. Because beneath whatever horrors drive them, fanatics always hide a secret doubt.'

'And you think I know what that is?'

'Not yet,' said Russ. 'But I'm confident you will.'

Loken stood as the Wolf King's certainty filled him. He sensed the breath of someone standing near him, the nearness of the ghost that finally convinced him to accept Malcador's summons to Terra.

'Very well, Lord Russ, I will be your pathfinder,' said Loken, extending his hand. 'You may have your sights set on the War-master, but there are those within the ranks of the Sons of Horus to whom I owe death.'

Russ shook his hand and said, 'Have a care, Garviel Loken. This isn't a path of vengeance I'm setting you on, nor is it one of execution. Leave such things to the Rout. It's what we do best.'

'I can't do this alone,' said Loken, turning to Malcador.

'No, you cannot,' agreed Malcador, reaching to take Loken's hand. 'The Knights Errant are yours to command in this. Choose who you will, with my blessing.'

The Sigillite glanced down at Loken's palm, seeing the fading echo of a bruise in the shape of a gibbous moon.

'A wound?' asked Malcador.

'A reminder.'

'A reminder of what?'

'Something I still have to do,' said Loken, looking up to the ruined citadel high on the cliff side as the hooded figure of a man he knew to be dead withdrew into its shadow.

Loken turned from Russ and Malcador, following the snaking path that led back down the valley. As he left, the clouds gathered beneath the dome split apart.

And a warm rain began to fall in the Hegemon.

THE BLOOD-RED KNIGHT climbed through the rocky canyons and evergreen highlands of the Untar Mesas with long, loping strides. At nearly nine metres tall, its mechanised bulk simply splintered the lower branches of the towering bitterleaf trees it didn't bother to avoid. Some broke apart on impact, some were sheared cleanly by the hard edges of the Knight's ion shield. A wonder of ancient technology, the Knight was lighter kin to the Titan Legions, a lithe predator to their lumbering war engines.

Its name was *Banelash*, and a crackling whip writhed at one shoulder mount. Upon the other, banked racks of heavy stubber barrels whined with the energy stored in their propellant stacks.

The Knight's hull plates were vermillion and ebony, segmented and overlapping like burnished naga scales. It had reaved the borders between warring states of Molech a thousand years before the coming of the Imperium. The Knight was a predator stalking the mountain forests, seeking dangerous quarry to bring down.

Encased within the pilot's compartment, Raeven Devine, second-born son of Molech's Imperial commander, let the sensorium surround him with graded representations of the landscape. Plugged into *Banelash* via the invasive technology of the Throne Mechanicum, its every motion and stride was his to command.

His limbs were its limbs; what it felt, he felt.

Sometimes, when he rode into the secret canyons to join Lyx and her intoxicated followers, the Knight's heart would surge with memories of its previous pilots; a ghostly parade of wars he'd never fought, foes he hadn't killed and blood he'd never shed.

Its powered whip had belonged to Raeven's great-great-grandfather, who was said to have slain the last of the great nagahydra of distant Ophir.

A golden eagle icon within the sensorium depicted his father's Knight a thousand metres below him. Cyprian Devine, Lord Commander Imperial of Molech, was rapidly approaching his hundred and twenty-fifth year, but still piloted *Hellblade* like he thought he was the equal of Raeven's juvenated sixty-four.

Hellblade was old, far older than *Banelash*, and was said to be one of the original *vajras* that rode the Fulgurine Path with the Stormlord, thousands of years ago. Raeven thought that unlikely. The Sacristans could barely maintain the war machines of Molech's noble Houses without their dour Mechanicum overseers to hand.

What hope would they have had before then?

Darting icons representing House Devine's retainers, beaters and huscarls on skimmer-bikes ranged around his father's Knight, but Raeven had long since outrun them into the mountains' misty peaks.

If anyone was going to slay the beasts, it would be him.

The tracks of the rogue mallahgra pair led into the highest regions of the Untar Mesas, a knifeback range of mountains that effectively divided the world in two. It was rare for the great beasts – once so plentiful on Molech, now hunted almost to extinction – to come within sight of human beings, but as their numbers dwindled, so too did the extent of their hunting grounds.

The last three winters had been harsh, and the springs scarcely less so, with snow blocking the paths through the mountains. Prey animals had been driven down to the warmer lowlands, so it was little wonder the mallahgra were forced to descend from their fissure-lairs upon waking from hibernation.

The settlements crouched in the foothills of the Untar Mesas, scattered strip-mining hives and refining conurbation-stacks mainly, were now within the hunting grounds of a ravenous mallahgra and its mate. Three hundred people were already dead, with perhaps another thirty missing.

Raeven doubted any of those taken were alive, and if they were they'd soon wish they'd died in the first attack. Raeven had heard stories of mallahgra that had devoured their victims over days, a limb at a time.

Bleating petitions sent to the city of Lupercalia – a name of exquisite poor taste in these days of rebellion – begged the Knight Seneschal to sally forth and slay the beasts. Despite the high level of alert imposed on Molech with the Warmaster's treachery, Raeven's father had chosen to lead a hunting party into the Untar Mesas. As much as he despised his father, Raeven couldn't deny that the old man knew the value of his word.

Despite Lyx offering innumerable pledges to the Serpent Gods to end Cyprian's life, they had so far not obliged. Raeven had never really shared his sister-wife's faith in the old religion, only indulging her beliefs for the carnal and intoxicating diversions they provided from the daily tedium of existence.

The path he was following traced the edge of a plunging cliff. Through breaks in the fog and cloud, Raeven could see the plains thousands of metres below. The trees reached almost to the sheer drop, snapped off where the brutish mallahgra had passed.

Their trail was easy enough to follow. Blood stained the ground in slashing arcs and every now and then he saw splintered nubs of discarded bone jutting from the snow. He'd inloaded the bio-sign taken from the latest attack to *Banelash*'s auspex, and it was only a matter of time until he came upon the beasts.

'Sooner than I thought,' he said, emerging onto a widened area of clear ground, and halting his Knight's advance as he saw a huge body lying butchered on the snow before him.

At full height, a mallahgra stood nearly seven metres tall, with bulky simian shoulders and long, muscular arms that could tear an unskilled Knight apart. Their heads were blunt, conical horrors of mandibles, tentacles and row upon row of serrated triangular teeth.

They had six eyes, two forward looking in the manner of predators, two sited for peripheral vision and two embedded in a ridged fold of flesh at the back of its neck. Evolutionary adaptations that made them devils to hunt, but Raeven had always enjoyed a challenge.

Not that this beast offered much in the way of threat.

An ivory-furred adolescent male around five metres tall, it lay on its side with its belly carved open. Thick red blood steamed in the cold, and glistening ropes of pinkish blue intestines pooled around its stomach like butcher's offal. The corpses of a dozen miners lay scattered around the creature's body.

Raeven walked his Knight around the dead beast, keeping one eye on the sensorium for any sign of the female. Bloodied tracks led into the forest farther back from the edge of the cliff.

Before he could resume the hunt, the ground shook as *Hellblade* finally caught up to him. A number of skimmer-bikes followed, as *Banelash*'s sensorium fizzed with static and Cyprian Devine's lined, patrician face appeared on the pict-manifold.

Wanting to get the first word in, Raeven said, 'Glad you could
join me.'

'Damn you, boy, I told you to wait for me!' snapped his father. *'You
aren't Knight Seneschal yet! First kill isn't yours to make.'*

The skimmer-bikes circled the two Knights, several retainers
dismounting to check the miners for signs of life.

'As always, your snap judgement of my actions is entirely
misplaced,' said Raeven, lowering his pilot's canopy to the mallahgra's body and studying the shredded mass of its flanks and
chest. By themselves, none of these injuries were mortal, but each
would have been excruciatingly painful. The wound in its belly
had killed the beast, a disembowelling cut made by something
viciously sharp and with the power to rip through tough hide to
the organs beneath.

Raeven pulled the canopy back to its full height and said, 'I
didn't kill it.'

'Don't lie to me, boy.'

'You know me, father, I'm not shy of taking credit for things
others have done, but this beast didn't fall to me. Look at these
wounds.'

Hellblade leaned over the corpse, and Raeven took a moment
to study his father's ravaged features in the manifold. Cyprian
Devine had eschewed juvenat treatments that were purely cosmetic, only allowing those that actively prolonged his life. In
Cyprian's world, all else was vanity, a character flaw he saw most
evidently in his second son.

Raeven's older half-brother, Albard, had always been Cyprian's favoured son, but a failed attempt to bond with his Knight
forty-three years ago had broken his mind and left him a virtual
catatonic. Kept locked away in one of the Devine Towers, his continued existence was a stain on the ancient name of the House.

'These tears in the beast's flesh are messy, like something your chainsabre would do,' said Raeven as the Devine retainers carried the bodies of the miners to the skimmer-bikes. From the attention one man was getting from a medicae, it appeared there was actually a survivor.

'*The female must have done this,*' declared his father. '*They must have fought over the spoils and she gutted him.*'

'An unlikely explanation,' said Raeven, circling the corpse.

'*You have a better one?*'

'If the female killed her mate, then why did she leave the bodies?' said Raeven. 'No, something drove her from here.'

'*What could possibly drive a female mallahgra from her mate?*'

'I don't know,' said Raeven, lifting one of his Knight's clawed feet and tipping the hulking mallahgra onto its front. 'Something that can do this.'

Bloodied craters punctured the creature's back, each one unmistakably an exit wound of explosive ammunition.

'*It's been shot?*' hissed Cyprian. '*Damn it all. House Kaushik, it's got to be. Those faithless scavengers must have picked up the distress petition and sent their own Knights into the mountains, hoping to steal glory from my table!*'

'Look at these wounds,' pointed out Raeven. 'House Kaushik are little better than Tazkhar savages. Their Sacristans can barely maintain the fusion-powered crankers they favour, let alone anything this powerful.'

His father ignored him and strode towards the tree line where the blood-smeared tracks of the second mallahgra disappeared.

'*Sort out the retainers then follow me,*' ordered Cyprian. '*The female's injured, so she can't have gone far. I'll have her bloody head above the Argent Gate before morning, boy. And if anyone gets in my way, mark my words, I'll have their heads up beside it.*'

Cyprian walked *Hellblade* into the darkness beneath the bitter-leaf canopy, leaving Raeven to deal with mundane business beneath his notice. Raeven turned *Banelash* and declined the canopy towards the circle of skimmer-bikes where the dead miners were being strapped down.

He linked with the vox-servile and said, 'Take the bodies back to whichever hell-hole they were abducted from. Issue standard renumeration for death in service to any dependants and send death notices to the aexactor adepts.'

'*My lord,*' said the senior retainer.

'Out of curiosity, is the survivor saying anything interesting?'

'*Nothing we can understand, my lord,*' said the medicae, one hand pressed to the side of his helm. '*It's doubtful he'll live much longer.*'

'So he's saying *something?*'

'*Yes, my lord.*'

'Don't be an idiot all your life, man,' snapped Raeven. 'Tell me what he's saying.'

'*He's saying "lingchi", my lord,*' said the medicae. '*Keeps repeating it over and over.*'

Raeven didn't know the word. Its sound was familiar, like it belonged to a language he couldn't speak, but was vaguely aware existed. He put it from his mind and turned *Banelash*, knowing his father wouldn't approve of his dawdling with the lower orders.

He walked his Knight into the shadow of the towering bitterleaf tree line. His mood was sour as he followed *Hellblade*'s tracks and the bio-sign of the wounded mallahgra.

One dead beast and another his father was sure to claim.

What a colossal waste of time this hunt had proven to be.

HELLBLADE WAS A bullish machine, without the agility of Raeven's mount, and the trail of broken branches was easy to follow. In many ways, it was the perfect match for Cyprian Devine, a man who lived as though in the midst of a charge.

Cold beams of light shafted through the forest canopy, ivory columns glittering with motes of powdered snow. Raeven followed *Hellblade*'s tracks through the narrow canyons of the forest, emerging onto a windswept plateau. Patches of crushed rock and smeared blood led into a bone-strewn fissure in a cliff ahead.

'Gone back to your lair,' said Raeven. 'That was stupid.'

His father's eagle icon in the sensorium was just ahead, two hundred metres into the fissure, and Raeven remembered the last time *Hellblade* had fought a mallahgra.

It had been on the eve of Raeven's Becoming, a day some forty-odd years ago, but forever etched in his mind. A rogue Sacristan had tried to kill his father by blowing out the cranial inhibitors of a docile mallahgra with an electromagnetic bomb. The pain-maddened beast almost killed Raeven and Albard, but their father had split it in two with a single strike of his Knight's chainsabre, despite taking spars of iron through his chest and stomach in the battle.

But that wasn't the story that caught the people's imagination.

Raeven had stood before the rampaging monster with only his brother's powerless energy sabre held before him, a tiny figure who faced down the beast with no hope of victory. Lyx's carefully placed whispers lauded Raeven's courage and diminished Cyprian's.

Years passed, and Raeven expected to take up his hereditary position, but the old bastard just wouldn't die. Even when Raeven fathered three boys to continue the House name, Cyprian showed no sign of letting the reins of power slip from his grasp.

Denied any power of real worth, Raeven spent the years indulging Lyx in her beliefs, even taking part in some of her cult's rituals when the inevitable boredom took hold. Lyx was an epicurean of the sensual arts – the nights they spent beneath the moons, naked and delirious from envenomed Caeban wine, were certainly memorable, but ultimately hollow compared to ruling an entire world.

A wash of red light through the sensorium snapped him from his bitter reverie, and he immediately brought *Banelash* up to full stride. Threat filters filled the auspex, and Raeven heard the familiar snaps of massed stubber fire.

'Father?' he said into the vox.

'*The beast!*' returned a voice thick with strain. '*It wasn't the other's mate!*'

Raeven pushed *Banelash* deeper into the darkness. Dazzling arc lights unfolded from the upper surfaces of the Knight's carapace, flooding the fissure with light. The sensorium could guide him, but Raeven preferred to trust his own eyes when death lay in wait.

Banelash strained at the edge of his control, a wild colt even after all this time. Raeven was tempted to let it take the lead, but kept his grip firm. The older pilots were replete with tales of men whose minds had been lost when they allowed a mount's spirit to overwhelm them.

Raeven powered the whip and fed shells into the stubber cannon. He felt the heat of their readiness envelop his hands, letting the trip hammer of his heart mirror the thunder of *Banelash*'s reactor.

The fissure was a winding split in the mountains. Its course was thick with debris, rotted vegetation, frozen mounds of excrement and the half-digested remains of dismembered carcasses. Raeven crushed it all flat as he followed the sounds of las-fire and the shrieking roar of a heavy-gauge chainsabre.

He pulled *Banelash* into a widened portion of the fissure, a cavern where the walls almost met high above and all but obscured the sunlight.

The spotlight beams lit a nightmarish sight of the largest mallahgra he had ever seen; fully ten metres tall and broader than any of the largest Knights. Its fur was a piebald mixture of white and russet, and its long arms were absurd with musculature. Blood poured from a wound torn in its side, but this beast cared nothing for such hurts.

Hellblade was down on one knee at the edge of a sulphurous chasm that belched noxious yellow fog. Its right leg was buckled and his father was desperately fending off thunderous blows from the monster's simian arms with the revving edge of his blade. Blood sprayed, but the mallahgra was too enraged to notice.

Raeven lowered his mount's head and charged, uncoiling the whip and letting fly with a burst of stubber fire. High-calibre bolts burned a path across the mallahgra's back and it reared at the suddenness of his attack.

Raeven blanched at the monster's size and the grizzled, ancient texture of its hide. Now he understood his father's last words.

This wasn't the dead adolescent's mate.

It was its mother.

The mallahgra leapt at him, bellowing in outrage. A clubbing arm smashed into *Banelash*'s canopy. Glass shattered and Raeven sucked in a breath of savage cold. The impact was monstrous, and the beast swung at him again. Raeven swayed aside, pulling the ion shield over his exposed canopy to deflect the blow. The mallahgra's blackened claws swept past him, barely a handspan from tearing his face away.

Raeven shucked his gun arm forward and a hurricane of stubber fire strobed the canyon with muzzle flare. Tracer rounds stabbed into the mallaghra's shoulder, setting light to its fur and driving it back. He followed up with a crack from the energy lash that ploughed a bloody trough in its chest.

The mallahgra roared in pain, and Raeven didn't give it a chance to recover. He stepped in close and slammed the hard edge of his ion shield into its face. Fangs snapped and oily blood poured from its ruined maw. The lash cracked again and peeled the muscle from the monster's thigh.

A clawed hand tore at his chest armour, but Raeven batted it away with the barrels of his stubber cannon. He brought the arm back and pumped half a dozen shots into its face, shattering the bone and exploding the eye sited in the side of its skull.

The mallahgra surged towards him, and not even Raeven's gen-hanced reflexes could match its speed. Its corded arms encircled *Banelash*, and began crushing the life out of him.

Hot animal breath doused him in rank saliva and the reek of rotten meat. Raeven gagged at the stench and fought to escape the monster's grip. They stamped back and forth through the cavern like drunken dancers at a Serpent Revel, slamming into walls and dislodging debris from high above. A chunk of rock smashed onto Raeven's shoulder, buckling his pauldrons and shattering his carapace lights. Broken glass rained into the shattered canopy and Raeven flinched as razored fragments sliced his cheeks.

Warning lights flashed on the damaged sensorium. Armour squealed as it reached its maximum-rated tolerances. Raeven brought his knee up into the mallahgra's side, where his whip had previously wounded it. The beast roared, almost deafening Raeven, and its pain gave him the opening he needed.

He slammed his ion shield against the bloodied, heat-fused side of the mallahgra's skull. The monster's grip loosened and Raeven pulled free of its crushing embrace, unleashing a blitzing stream of fire into its chest and head.

Repeated lashes from his energy whip followed each salvo and the mewling beast stumbled away, its lifeblood flashing to red mist in the cauterising heat of gunfire.

Raeven laughed as he drove it back.

He didn't see *Hellblade* surge up on its one good leg behind the mallahgra. All he saw was the fountain of viscous blood as the revving blade of his father's chainsabre exploded from the mal-lahgra's ribcage.

The life fled from its eyes and Raeven felt something caged within his chest for four decades stir at the monster's death, something barbed and hateful and full of spite. The juddering chainsabre caught on the mallahgra's ribs. It spasmed with false life before Cyprian wrenched the blade out through its side in a flood of reeking viscera. The gutted beast toppled into the chasm, and anger filled Raeven as it fell.

He turned *Banelash* to face his father's wounded Knight.

Hellblade crouched at the edge of the chasm, one leg buckled beyond its ability to bear any weight. The Knight had suffered a grievous hurt, but with the ministrations of the Mechanicum and the Sacristans, it would walk again.

'*It died a good death,*' said Cyprian, between heaving breaths and using the end of his stilled blade to remain upright. '*Damn shame the head is gone though. No one's going to believe the size of that thing.*'

'The kill was mine,' said Raeven with cold fury.

'*Now you're being ridiculous,*' returned Cyprian. '*I'm the Knight Seneschal, the right of first kill was always mine. Don't piss your britches, boy, I'll credit you with aiding me. You'll win a share of the glory.*'

'Aiding? You'd be dead if it wasn't for me.'

'*But who ended its life? Me or you?*'

The cage in Raeven's chest unlocked and the barbed thing of hate and ambition that imprinting with the Throne Mechanicum had sought to imprison was freed to stab his soul once more.

'And who will they say ended yours?' hissed Raeven. 'Me or the mallahgra?'

Too late, Cyprian Devine saw the depthless well of venom in his son's heart, but there was nothing he could do to stop what happened next.

Stepping back to plant *Banelash's* clawed foot in the centre of *Hellblade's* chest, Raeven kicked the Knight into the chasm. His father yelled in outrage, and Raeven watched the ancient machine fall end over end. It slammed into a sharp outcropping of rock and broke apart like a confiscated automaton from the Clockwork City beneath a Sacristan's forge hammer.

The remains of *Hellblade* vanished into the sulphurous mist, and Raeven turned away. With every purposeful stride he took from the chasm, the poisonous ambition within him took an ever more defined shape.

Raeven was now Imperial commander of Molech. What would Lyx make of this new development?

Raeven grinned, knowing exactly what she would say.

'The Serpent Gods provide,' he said.

FOUR

Reforged
Filum Secundo
The Seven Neverborn

WHEN THE WARMASTER needed to dominate or awe petitioners he received them in Lupercal's Court, with its towering, vaulted ceiling of muttering shadows, black battle standards, glimmering lancets and basalt throne. But when simply desiring company, the summons was to his private staterooms.

Aximand had come here many times over the years, but usually in the company of Mournival brothers. In his staterooms, the Warmaster could put aside that heavy title for a few precious moments and simply be Horus.

Like most places aboard the *Vengeful Spirit*, it had changed markedly over the last few years. Trinkets taken in the early years of the Great Crusade had vanished, and many of the paintings were now hidden by sackcloth. A vast star map with the Emperor at its heart, and which had covered one entire wall, was long gone. In its stead were innumerable pages of densely wound script, together with fanciful imagery depicting cosmological conjunctions, omega-point diagrams, alchemical symbols, trefoil knots and a central image of an armoured warrior bearing a golden sword and glittering silver chalice.

Those pages had presumably been ripped from the hundreds of astrological primers, Crusade logs, histories of Unity and mythological texts that lay scattered like autumn leaves.

Aximand tilted his head to catch a few of the titles: *He who saw the Deep*, *The Nephite Triptych*, *Monarchia Alighieri* and *Libri Carolini*. There were others, with titles both mundane and esoteric. Some, Aximand noticed, were lettered in gold-leaf Colchisian cuneiform. Before he could read any further, a booming voice called his name.

'Aximand,' called Horus. 'You know better than to stand there like some poxy ambassador, get in here.'

Aximand obeyed, limping past haphazardly stacked piles of books and data-slates towards the primarch's inner sanctum. As always, it gave him a thrill of pride to be here, to know that his gene-father esteemed him worthy of this honour. Of course, Horus always dismissed such lofty nonsense, but that only made these moments more precious.

Even seated and without the encasement of armour, Horus was enormous, a heroic Akillius or Hektor, a cursed Gylgamesh or Shalbatana the Scarlet Handed. His skin was pink and raw with grafts and regeneration, especially around his right eye where the charred ruin of his skull had been exposed. His hair was still bristly with regrowth, but the attack on the Dome of Revivification appeared to have left no permanent scars. At least none that Aximand could see.

In the immediate aftermath of the ambush, the three primarchs had withdrawn to their flagships to heal and recuperate. The Sons of Horus had levelled Tyjun in a spasm of retaliation, murdering its populace and leaving no stone upon another to root out any other attackers.

Five days later, the Warmaster's assembled fleets set sail from Dwell, leaving the planet a smouldering wasteland.

Horus worked at a table encircled by a curtain-wall of books, folded charts, celestial hierarchies and tablets of carven formulae.

From the thickness of its spine and tabular aspect of its pages, the book that currently held the Warmaster's attention was a Crusade log. Even upside down, Aximand recognised the violet campaign badge in the upper corner of the facing page.

'Murder?' said Aximand. 'An old tally, that one.'

Horus closed the book and looked up, a strange irritation in his eyes, as though he had just read something in the log he hadn't liked. Puckered scar tissue pulled at his mouth as he spoke.

'An old one, but still relevant,' said Horus. 'Sometimes you can learn as much, if not more, from the battles you lose as the ones you win.'

'We won that one,' pointed out Aximand.

'We shouldn't have had to fight it at all,' said Horus, and Aximand knew not to ask any more.

Instead he simply made his report. 'You wanted to know when the fleets translated, sir.'

Horus nodded. 'Any surprises I should know about?'

'No, all Sons of Horus, Death Guard and Titanicus vessels are accounted for and have been duly entered in the mission registry,' said Aximand.

'What's our journey time looking like?'

'Master Comnenus estimates six weeks to reach Molech.'

Horus raised an eyebrow. 'That's quicker than he originally calculated. Why the revised journey time?'

'With the Ruinstorm behind the fleets, our esteemed shipmaster tells me that, and I quote: "the path before us welcomes our fleets like a bordello welcomes bored soldiers with full pockets".'

Horus's earlier irritation vanished like a shadow on the sun.

'That sounds like Boas. Perhaps Lorgar's rampage across the Five Hundred Worlds has been more useful than I expected.'

'*Lorgar's* rampage?'

'Yes, I suppose Angron is doing most of the rampaging,' chuckled Horus. 'And what of the Third Legion?'

Aximand was used to swift changes of tack in the Warmaster's questioning, and had his answer at the ready. 'Word comes that they set course for the Halikarnaxes Stars as ordered.'

'I sense a "but" missing from that sentence,' said Horus.

Aximand said, 'But the word did not come from Primarch Fulgrim.'

'No, it wouldn't have,' agreed Horus, waving to a couch set against one wall upon which hung a variety of punch daggers and quirinal cestus gauntlets. 'Sit, take some wine, it's Jovian.'

Aximand poured two goblets of wine from an amethyst bottle and handed one to Horus before sitting on the portion of the couch not obscured by the primarch's reading material.

'Tell me, little one, how are your Mournival brothers?' asked Horus as he sipped some wine. 'Fulgrim's power shielded us from the worst of the gunships' fire, but you...'

Aximand shrugged, also taking a drink and finding its flavour much to his liking. 'Burns and bruises mainly. We'll heal. Kibre acts like it never happened, and Grael is still trying to figure out how the Tenth Legion kept three Fire Raptors hidden for so long.'

'Some dark age tech salvaged from Medusa, I expect,' said Horus. 'And Ezekyle?'

'He's about ready to fall on his sword,' said Aximand. 'You were almost killed, and he blames himself for that.'

'I dismissed the Justaerin, if you remember,' pointed out Horus. 'Tell Ezekyle that if there's blame to be apportioned, the bulk of it's mine. He's not at fault.'

'It might help if that came from you.'

Horus waved away Aximand's suggestion. 'Ezekyle is a big boy, he'll understand. And if he doesn't, well, I know Falkus covets his rank.'

'You'd make the Widowmaker First Captain?'

'No, of course not,' said Horus, lapsing into silence. Aximand knew better than to break it and took more wine.

'I should have known Meduson would have a contingency in case the White Scars failed,' said Horus at last.

'Do you think Shadrak Meduson was on one of those gunships?'

'Perhaps, but I doubt it,' said Horus. He finished his wine and placed the cup to one side. 'But what aggrieves me most is the destruction the Legion unleashed in retaliation. Especially the loss of the Mausolytic. Razing it and Tyjun was unnecessary. So much there still to be discovered.'

'With respect, sir, it had to be done,' replied Aximand. 'What you learned, others could learn. And truthfully, I'm not sorry we burned it.'

'No? Why?'

'The dead should stay dead,' said Aximand, trying not to look over the Warmaster's shoulder at the ornately wrought box of lacquered wood and iron.

Horus grinned, and Aximand wondered if he knew of the dreams that had plagued him before the reattaching of his face. Those dreams were gone now, consigned to history in the wake of his invincible rebirth and rededication.

'I never considered the Dwellers truly dead,' said Horus turning to address the box. 'But even so, a man ought not to be afraid of the dead, little one. They have no power to harm us.'

'They don't,' agreed Aximand as Horus rose from his seat.

'And they don't answer back,' said Horus, hiding a grimace of pain and beckoning Aximand to his feet. With a stiff gait, Horus made his way into an adjacent room. 'Walk with me. I have something for you.'

Aximand followed Horus into a reverentially dim arming chamber, illumined only by a soft glow above the steel-limbed rack supporting the Warmaster's battleplate. Spindle-limbed adepts in ragged chasubles worked to repair the damage done by the Fire Raptors' cannons. Aximand smelled fixatives, molten ceramite and dark lacquer.

Worldbreaker hung on reinforced hooks next to the left gauntlet. The lion-flanked amber eye upon the plastron seemed to follow Aximand as they traversed the chamber. Horus might have died, it seemed to say, but Aximand shook off the sensation of judgement as they approached a high-vaulted forge of smelting and metalworking. The seething glow of a furnace hazed the air.

Only when Aximand followed Horus into the chamber did he see his error. No natural light of a furnace illuminated the forge, but something bright and dark at the same time, something that left a fleeting succession of negative impressions on his retina. Aximand felt corpse breath on the back of his neck and tasted human ash at the sight of a flame-wreathed abomination floating a metre above the deck.

It had once been a Blood Angel. Now it was… what? A daemon? A monster? Both. Its crimson armour was broken, cracked where the evil within it licked outwards in unnatural, eternal flames.

Whoever the legionary within that armour had once been was immaterial. All that remained of him was the scorched prime helix symbol of an Apothecary. It called itself the *Cruor Angelus*, but the Sons of Horus knew it as the Red Angel.

It had been bound and gagged by chains that were originally gleaming silver, but had since been scorched black. Its head went unhelmed, but its features were impossible to discern through the infernal flames, save for two white-hot eyes filled with the rage of a million damned souls.

'Why is *it* here?' said Aximand, unwilling to voice its name.

'Hush,' replied Horus, leading Aximand towards a timber workbench upon which rested implements that looked more akin to surgeon's tools than those of the metalworker. 'The Faceless One's aborted angel has a part to play in our current endeavour.'

'We shouldn't trust anything that came from that scheming bastard,' said Aximand. 'Exile was too easy. You should have let me kill him.'

'If he doesn't take my lesson to heart I may let you,' said Horus, lifting something from the workbench. 'But that's a murder for another day.'

Only reluctantly did Aximand let his gaze turn from the Red Angel, as any warrior was loath to let an enemy fall from sight.

'Here,' said the Warmaster, holding a long, cloth-wrapped bundle before him. 'This is yours.'

Aximand took the bundle and felt the weight of strong metal. He unwrapped it with reverent care, guessing what lay within.

Mourn-it-all's edge had been badly notched in the fight against Hibou Khan, the White Scar's borrowed Medusan blade proving to be more than the equal of Cthonian bluesteel.

'Hard as a rock and hot as hell in the heart,' said Horus, tapping his chest. 'A weapon that's Cthonia to the core.'

Aximand gripped the leather-wound hilt of the double-edged sword, holding the blade out before him and feeling a last part of him he'd not even appreciated was missing now restored. The fuller was thick with fresh etchings that glittered in the daemon-thing's firelight. Aximand felt lethal potency within the blade that had nothing to do with its powered edges.

'I need you and your sword, Little Horus Aximand,' said the Warmaster. 'The war on Molech will test us all, and you're not you without it.'

'It shames me I was not the one to restore its edge.'

'No,' said Horus. 'It honours me that I could do it for you, my son.'

ARCADON KYRO HAD learned a great many things during his time as a Techmarine of the Ultramarines, but the teaching he'd taken most to heart was that no two vehicles were ever wholly alike in temper or mien. Each was as individual as the warriors they carried into battle, and they too had legacies worthy of remembrance.

Sabaen Queen was as good an example of this as he could wish for. A Stormbird of Terran provenance, it had led the triumphal fly-by over Anatolia in the last days before the XIII Legion launched the campaign to reclaim the Lunar enclaves from the Selenar cults alongside the XVI and XVII Legions. Kyro was yet unborn, but felt *Sabaen Queen*'s pride to have been part of the Great Crusade's first true battle.

It was a proud aircraft, haughty even, but Kyro would sooner pilot a prideful craft than a workhorse made resentful by poor treatment. He banked *Sabaen Queen* around the easternmost peaks of the Untar Mesas, dropping his altitude sharply and pushing out the engines as the landscape opened up. The flight from the defence readiness inspection along the Aenatep peninsula had been a long one, and the Stormbird had earned this chance to flex her wings.

With brown hills and golden fields stretching to Iron Fist Mountain on the horizon, Molech resembled a great many of the Five Hundred Worlds, and was dotted with efficient agri-collectives and crisscrossed by wide roads, maglevs and glittering irrigation canals. It had been brought to compliance without the need for war, yet – for reasons unknown to Kyro – still boasted a garrison force numbering in the millions.

Ultramarines boots were still fresh on the ground, newly

deployed as part of a regular rotation of Legion forces between Ultramar and Molech. Vared of the 11th Chapter had returned to Macragge with full honours, passing the *Aquila Ultima* to Castor Alcade, Legate of Battle Group II within the 25th Chapter.

With the Warmaster's host said to be somewhere in the northern marches there was likely little glory to be won on Molech, but few warriors were so in need of glory as Castor Alcade.

Thus far, Alcade's career had been unremarkable. He had assumed the mantle of legate by dint of a service record that showed him to be a warrior of due diligence and requisite ability, but little flair.

Under Alcade's command, Battle Group II had acquired a largely unearned reputation for ill-fortune. Two particular examples in the last thirty years had turned arming-chamber whispers into 'fact'.

On Varn's World, they had fought alongside the Ninth and 235th Companies to crush the greenskin host of the Ghennai Cluster. Alcade coordinated a gruelling flanking campaign, routing the feral greenskin in the highland latitudes before arriving an hour *after* Klord Empion had broken the enemy host comprehensively at the battle of Sumaae Delta.

During the final storming of the cavern cities of Ghorstel, a series of malfunctioning auspex markers saw Alcade's assault through the ventral manufactories misdirected into dead end arcologies. Hopelessly lost in the maze of tunnels, the absence of Battle Group II's companies left Eikos Lamiad and his warriors to fight the bio-mechanical host of the Cybar-Mekattan unsupported.

Lamiad's heroically earned victory cemented an already formidable stature and led to his appointment as Tetrarch of Konor, while consigning Alcade's reputation – through no fault of his own – to self-evident mediocrity.

It was said that the Avenging Son himself had remarked on the matter, saying, 'Not every commander can be the proudest eagle, some must circle the aerie and allow others to fly farther.'

Kyro had his doubts as to the remark's authenticity, but that didn't seem to matter. Those who knew of Alcade's reputation named him 'Second String' – *Filum Secundo* – forgetting that, by its original meaning, the archer's second string had to be just as strong and reliable as the first.

A threat auspex chirruped in Kyro's ear as a mountaintop battery of Hydra anti-aircraft guns unmasked and locked onto the *Sabaen Queen*. He sent a communion pulse, telling the gunners that he was a friendly, and the threat disappeared from the slate.

'The Untar Mesas guns?' inquired Legate Alcade, appearing in the hatchway linking the troop compartment with the cockpit.

'Yes, sir,' replied Kyro. 'A little slow in acquiring us, but I was making them sweat for it.'

'A little sweat now will save a lot of blood when Horus's dogs reach Molech,' said Alcade, strapping himself into the copilot's seat across from Kyro.

'You really think the traitors will come here, sir?'

'Given Molech's location, eventually they must,' said Alcade, and Kyro heard the hope that such an event might come sooner rather than later. Alcade *wanted* war to reach Molech. He had the scent of glory in his nostrils.

Kyro understood glory. He'd earned his share of it. Such an allure was more potent than any Apothecary's opiates. The power of its need was something to be feared, even by transhuman warriors who claimed to be above such mortal weakness.

Alcade scanned the avionics display. His battleplate's onboard systems would already have given him the Stormbird's approximate location, but Ultramarines didn't work with approximates.

'So what's your verdict on the Aenatep peninsula?'

Kyro nodded slowly. 'Fair.'

'That's it?'

'It'll do if all they have to fight are mortals and xenos, but it's not Legion strong.'

'How would you strengthen it?' asked Alcade. 'Give me a theoretical.'

Kyro shook his head. 'In the forge we prefer speculative and empirical – all the potentials and all working actuals. Even the best practical doesn't become empirical until it's been proven combat-effective a significant number of times.'

'A subtle difference,' said Alcade. 'Too subtle for most when the bolts are in the air.'

'That's why Techmarines are so valuable,' said Kyro, bringing them down towards the valley of Lupercalia, a name that must surely be changed in light of the Warmaster's treachery. 'We calculate how things need to be so the commanders in the field don't have to.'

More range-markers and Hydras fixed on them, and Kyro let *Sabaen Queen* dismiss their interrogations with lofty disdain.

'What would we do without our brave brothers in the forge to keep us mere commanders in line?' said Alcade.

Kyro said, 'Good to know you appreciate us, sir.'

'Did you ever doubt it?' grinned Alcade. 'But you didn't answer the question.'

Kyro spared his legate a sidelong glance. As heroic a warrior of the XIII Legion as any, not even transhuman genhancements could smooth out his patrician features or the finely sculpted planes of his cheekbones. His eyes were pale aquamarine, set in skin like weathered birch upon which he wore a waxed beard forked in the manner of the Khan's sons. Perhaps he thought it gave him a rakish, dangerous appearance, but together with his tonsured silver hair, it made him look more monk than warrior.

'I'd bring in another Chapter of the Thirteenth Legion to stiffen its soldiers' backs,' said Kyro. 'Then more artillery. At least three brigades. Maybe some cohorts of Modwen's Thallax cyborgs. And Titans, can't go wrong with Titans.'

'Always so precise,' laughed Alcade. 'I'd ask you the time and you'd tell me how to build a watch.'

'It's why I was chosen to go to Mars,' said Kyro.

Ahead of the Stormbird, Lupercalia gouged into the mountains along a stepped valley of ochre stone. Six kilometres wide at its opening, the valley gradually narrowed as it ascended towards Mount Torger and the Citadel of Dawn, where Cyprian Devine ruled Molech with an admirably stern hand. The city's walled defences were impressive to look at, but archaic and largely value-less against a foe with any real military ability.

Previous Ultramarines commanders had done their best to alter them, employing the primarch's *Notes towards Martial Codification*, but they faced resistance from an intransigent population.

'I sense there's more you want to say,' said Alcade.

'Can I speak freely, sir?'

'Of course.'

'The problem with Molech isn't the emplaced defences or its armed might, the problem is the embedded culture.'

'Give me your theoretical, sorry, speculative.'

'Very well. The way I see it, the people of Molech have been raised on tales of heroic Knights riding out to do battle in hon-ourable contests of arms,' said Kyro. 'Their world hasn't seen real fighting in centuries. They don't know that massed armies of ordinary men with guns is the new reality. Numbers, logistics and planning are the determining factors in who wins and who dies.'

'A grim view,' said Alcade. 'Especially for the Legions.'

'An empirical view,' said Kyro, tapping two fingers to the skull-stamped Ultima on his breastplate. 'Ah, don't mind me, sir, I was always best at envisaging worst-case scenarios. But if you're right and the traitors *do* come to Molech, it's not the Army regiments they'll look to kill first.'

'True, it will be us and Salicar's Bloodsworn.'

'We have three companies, and Emperor alone knows how many Blood Angels are on Molech.'

'I'd say less than half our strength,' said Alcade. 'Vared spoke of Vitus Salicar being a warrior not overly given to the spirit of cooperation.'

'So five hundred legionaries,' said Kyro. 'And hyperbole aside, that's not enough to defend a planet. Therefore the primary burden of defending Molech *has* to fall on the Army regiments.'

'They might be mortals, but there's nearly fifty million fighting men and women on this planet. When war comes to Molech, it'll be bloody beyond imagining, and it won't be ended quickly.'

'But in the final practical, mortals simply can't resist massed Legion war, sir,' said Kyro.

'You don't think nearly a hundred regiments can hold one of the Emperor's worlds?'

'What practical would you give any mortal army resisting Legion forces? Honestly? You know what they call it when baseline humans find themselves fighting warriors like us?'

'Transhuman dread,' said Alcade.

'Transhuman dread, yes,' agreed Kyro. 'We've both seen it. Remember the breach at Parsabad? It was like the blood had frozen their veins. I almost felt sorry for the poor bastards we had to kill that day.'

Alcade nodded. 'It was like threshing wheat.'

'Since when have the noble families of Macragge ever threshed their own wheat?' said Kyro.

'Never,' agreed Alcade, 'but I *have* seen picts of it.'

Approach vectors appeared on the display slates in front of

Kyro. Alcade fell silent as *Sabaen Queen* began its descent to the cavern hangar just below the great citadel at the valley's heart.

The chiming of threat warnings was constant, but Kyro shut them off as he brought the aircraft level with a booming flare of deceleration, followed by the jolt of landing claws meeting the ground.

Alcade unsnapped his restraints and returned to the troop compartment, where fifty Ultramarines sat in banked rows along the aircraft's centreline and fuselage. Kyro powered down the engines, letting the Stormbird reach its own equilibrium before releasing the locking mechanisms on the assault doors.

As the ground crew rushed to tend the aircraft, Kyro unsnapped his own restraints and finished the last of his post-flight checks. He placed a fist over the aquila on the flight console then made the Icon Mechanicum to honour both Terra and Mars.

'My thanks,' he said before ducking into the troop compartment. Armoured in cobalt-blue and ivory, the five squads of Ultramarines were a fine sight indeed, mustered and ready to debark.

The scents of scorched iron, hot engines and venting propellant blew in through the lowered assault ramp, a heady mix that took Kyro back to the forge and the simple pleasure of shaping metal.

Gathering the equipment cases containing his servo-harness, Kyro followed the line warriors down the ramp as landing menials and deck crew readied the Stormbird for her next flight.

Didacus Theron was already waiting for them on the landing strip, and from the look on the centurion's face the news he bore was of a dark hue. A low-born scrambler from Calth, he'd achieved high office within the Legion by virtue of saving the life of Tauro Nicodemus at Terioth Ridge nearly sixty years ago.

'Grim tidings,' said Theron, as the legate approached.

'Speak,' commanded Alcade.

'Cyprian Devine is dead,' said Theron, 'but that's not the worst of it.'

'The Imperial commander is dead and that's not the worst of it?' said Kyro.

'Not even close,' said Theron. 'The Five Hundred Worlds are under attack and the whoreson Warmaster is en route to Molech.'

Icy winds howled over the steeldust hull of the Valkyrie, spiralling in ghostly vortices around its cooling engines. Vapour streamed from the leading edges of its wings and linked tailfin, making it look as though it was still in flight. Loken had instructed Rassuah to keep the engines' fires banked to prevent them icing up completely. Though his armour kept the cold at bay, Loken shivered at the frozen desolation of the mountaintop.

The Urals ran for nearly two and a half thousand kilometres, from the frozen reaches of Kara Oceanica to the ancient realm of the Kievan Rus Khaganate. Ahead, the towering forge spire of Mount Narodnaya was a hazed blur, wreathed in the smoke and lightning of mighty subterranean endeavours.

The riches of these mountains had been plundered by a succession of peoples, but none to match the monumental scale of the Terrawatt Clan. Said to spring from the same root as the Mechanicum, its theologiteks had carved temples into the bones of the Urals during a technological dark age, where they weathered the fury of Old Night in splendid isolation until their very existence became a whispered legend.

When the Terrawatt Clan finally emerged from their lair beneath the *Kholat Syakhl*, it was to find a planet ravaged by wars fought between monstrous ethnarchs and tyrants. As word of the Clan's rebirth spread, petitioners came from across the globe to beg for their ancient wonders, offering bargains, treaties and threats in equal measure.

But only one man came offering more than he sought to take.

He called Himself Emperor, a title the Clan *Aghas* mocked until His vast knowledge of long forgotten technologies became apparent. His willingness to share these lost arts allied the Clan to His banner, and from their archives came many of the weapons that brought Old Earth to Unity. The entombed memory-cores of its eldest Aghas claimed it was *their* technology, not that of Mars, that precipitated the creation of the first proto-Astartes, a claim utterly refuted by the Mechanicum.

Loken saw little evidence of technological wonder here, just a high ridge of black rock swathed in freezing mists and blustering ash clouds expelled from the buried Dyatlov forge complexes. The rocks were bare of vegetation, sharp-edged and utterly inimical to flora of any kind. Loken turned on the spot, seeing nothing but the solitary landing platform upon which sat the Valkyrie.

He checked the slate he carried, its edges already limned with a coating of pale, fibrous dust.

'You're sure this is the place?' he asked.

'I have a hunter's eye, and I've flown from one side of Terra to the other on the Sigillite's business,' said Rassuah, her voice clipped and efficient. 'And I've landed at the Seven Strong Men many times, Garviel Loken, so, yes, I'm sure this is the place.'

'Then where is he?'

'You are asking me?' said Rassuah. 'He's one of yours. Shouldn't you know?'

'I never met him,' said Loken.

'Neither have I, so why do you think I'll know?'

Loken didn't bother to answer. Rassuah was a mortal, but even Loken could tell there was more to her than met the eye. Her augmetics were subtly woven into a physique clearly honed by genetic modification and a rigorous regime of training. Everything about her spoke of excellence. Rassuah claimed to be a simple naval pilot, but smiled as she said it, as if daring Loken to contradict her.

Her inscrutability, skin tone, eye shape and gloss-black hair suggested Panpacific genestock, but she'd never volunteered any information on her heritage, and Loken never asked.

Rassuah had flown him from Old Himalazia to the northern reaches of the Urals to find the first member of Loken's pathfinders, but it seemed that was going to be more difficult than anticipated.

The man Loken had come to find was one of the Sons of Horus and he...

No, he wasn't. He was a Luna Wolf.

He hadn't been part of the Legion when it took that first step on the road to treachery. Not a true son then, but he was a genebrother, and Loken wasn't sure how he felt about that.

Yes, Iacton Qruze was one of his fellow Knights Errant, but he'd served with the Half-heard aboard the *Vengeful Spirit* when things had gone to hell. They had a shared experience of what their lost brothers had done that this warrior could never know.

The wind dropped for a moment, and Loken peered through the stilled clouds of particulate matter, seeing dark outlines like towering giants frozen to the summit. Too tall to be anything living, they were like the heavy columns of some vast temple that had been eroded over centuries of exposure.

He set off towards them, trudging through the wind-blown ash with long strides. The shapes emerged from the clouds, revealing themselves to be far larger than he had suspected, great pillars of banded rock like the megaliths of some tribal fane.

Six of them clustered close together, none less than thirty metres tall, with a seventh set apart like an outcast. Some were narrow at the base, widening like spear blades before tapering towards their peaks. The wind howled through them in a keening banshee's wail that set Loken's teeth on edge.

Static buzzed in his helmet, a side effect of the charged air from the unceasing industry beneath the mountains. Loken heard whistles, clicks and burps of distortion, and what sounded very much like soft breath.

Garvi…

Loken knew that voice and spun around, as if expecting to see his fallen comrade, Tarik Torgaddon, standing behind him. But he was utterly alone; even the Valkyrie's outline growing indistinct in the fog.

He was no longer sure if he'd heard the voice or imagined its existence. It had been an apparition of his murdered friend that had convinced Loken to leave the sanctuary of the lunar bio-dome, a memory that was growing ever fainter, like the fading echoes of a distant dream.

Had that even happened, or was it a reflection of guilt and shame caught in the splintered shards of his tortured psyche?

Loken had been dug from the ruins of Isstvan III a broken shell of a man, haunted by delusions and phantasmal nightmares. Garro had brought him back to Terra and given him fresh purpose, but could any man return from such an abyss without scars?

He took a moment to balance his humours as bleeding whispers of what might have been vox-traffic drifted on the edge of hearing. Loken's breath caught in his throat at its familiarity.

He'd heard this kind of thing before.

On Sixty-Three Nineteen.

At the Whisperheads.

Jubal's horrifying transformation flashed before Loken's eyes like a stuttering pict-feed and his hand dropped to the holstered bolt pistol. He thumbed the catch from its cover. He didn't expect to draw it, but just resting his hand on its textured grip gave him comfort.

Moving through the gargantuan rock formations, the squalling static whined and crackled to the rhythm of the ash storm. Did the pillars amplify the interference or was it a by-product of the hundreds of forge temples below him?

The static abruptly cut out.

'*Do you know where you are?*' said a low voice, its accent guttural and hard-boned with palatal edges and rough vowels.

'Tarik?' said Loken.

'*No. Answer the question.*'

'The Urals,' said Loken.

'*This particular mountain.*'

'I didn't know it had a name.'

'*It's called Manpupuner,*' said the voice. '*I'm told it means* little mountain of the gods *in some dead language. The clans say these are the petrified corpses of the Seven Neverborn.*'

'Are you trying to frighten me with old legends?'

'*No. We were born here, did you realise that?*' continued the voice. '*Not literally, of course, but the first breed of transhumans were made beneath this mountain.*'

'I didn't know that,' said Loken. 'Where are you?'

'*Closer than you think, but you'll have to find me if you want to talk face to face,*' said the voice. '*If you can't manage that, then we'll not speak at all.*'

'Malcador said you would help me,' said Loken. 'He didn't say anything about having to prove myself.'

'*There's a lot that crafty old man isn't saying,*' said the voice. '*Now let's see if you're as good as Qruze says you are.*'

The voice faded into a rising hash of static, and Loken pressed himself against the nearest rock pillar. Smooth where exposed to the wind, pitted where centuries of atmospheric pollutants had eaten away at the rock, the mass of stone was immense and loomed like the leg of a titanic war engine.

He eased his head around its rounded corner, switching between variant perceptual modes. None of the spectra through which his helm cycled could penetrate the fog. Loken suspected deliberate artifice in its occluding properties.

Something moved ahead of him, a half-glimpsed shadow of a cowled warrior with the swagger of complete confidence. Loken stepped away from the rock and gave chase. The brittle shale of the ground made stealth impossible, but that handicap would work against his enemy too. He reached where he thought the shadow had gone, but there was no sign of his quarry.

The mists swelled and surged, and the cragged towers of the Seven Neverborn loomed in the fog as if advancing and retreating. Whispering voices sighed through the vox-static; names and long lists of numbers, tallies of things long dead. Echoes of a past swept away by a cataclysmic tide of war and unremembering.

None were discernible, but the sound struck a mournful chord in Loken. He kept still, filtering out the voices, and trying to hear the telltale scrape of armour on stone, a footstep on gravel. Anything that might reveal a hidden presence. Given the nature of the man he was here to find, he wasn't holding out much hope.

'You've forgotten what Cthonia taught you,' said the voice.

It burbled up through the static in his helm; no use for pinpointing a location.

'Maybe you remember a little too much,' replied Loken.

'I remember that it was kill or be killed.'

'Is that what this is?' said Loken, moving as slowly and quietly as he could.

'I'm not going to kill you,' said the voice. 'But you're here to try and get me killed. Aren't you?'

A flicker of movement in the mist to his right. Loken didn't react, but gently eased his course towards it.

'I'm here because I need you,' said Loken, finally understanding the nature of this place. 'The Knights Errant? This is where you trained them to become the grey ghosts, isn't it?'

'I taught them all,' said the voice. *'But not you. Why is that?'*

Loken shook his head. 'I don't know.'

'Because you are the warrior who stands in the light,' said the voice, and Loken couldn't decide if the words were meant in admiration or derision. *'There's nothing I can teach you.'*

The blurred outline of the cowled warrior stood in the lee of a gigantic stone pillar, confident he went unobserved. Loken held him loose in his peripheral vision, moving as though unaware of his presence. He closed to within five paces. He would never get a better chance.

Loken leapt towards the source of the taunting voice.

The hooded man's outline came apart like ash in a storm.

Over there, Garvi…

Loken turned on the spot, in time to see an umbral after-image of a man moving between two of the Seven Neverborn across the summit. Loken caught a flash of skin, a tattoo. Not the cowled man.

Whose voice was he hearing? Was he chasing ghosts?

The legends of the Neverborn were garish scare stories of outrageous hyperbole like those recounted in *The Chronicles of Ursh*. They spoke about phantom armies of killing shadows, mist-born wraiths and nightmares that clawed their way from men's skulls, but that wasn't what Loken was up against.

Cracks in his memory and a silent hunter were his foes here.

'You're going back, aren't you? To Lupercal's lair.'

Loken didn't waste breath wondering how the nature of his mission could already be known. Instead, he opted to prick his opponent's vanity.

'You're right,' he said. 'And I need your help to get in.'

'Getting in's the easy part. It's getting out that's going to be a problem.'

'Less of a problem if you join me.'

'I don't make a habit of going on suicide missions.'

'Neither do I.'

No reply was forthcoming, and Loken considered his options.

As he saw it, he had two; continue blundering around the mist-shrouded mountaintop while being made to look a fool, or leave empty-handed.

He was being tested, but tests only worked if both participants worked towards a common goal. Loken had already played one game without knowing the rules. The Wolf King had beaten him to learn something of his character, but this felt like someone taking pleasure in belittling him.

If Loken couldn't play by someone else's rules, he'd play by his own. He turned towards the Valkyrie. The aircraft was invisible in the mists, but its transponder signal was a softly glowing sigil on his visor. Abandoning any pretence of searching the mountaintop, he marched brazenly back to the assault carrier.

'Malcador and his agents were thorough in their recruitment of Knights Errant,' said Loken. 'There's no shortage of warriors I can assemble in time to make our mission window.'

Loken heard stealthy footsteps in the shale, but resisted the obvious bait. The Valkyrie emerged from the fog and Loken switched the vox-link to Rassuah's channel.

'Spool up the engines,' he said. 'We're leaving.'

'You found him?'

'No, but put that hunter's eye upon me.'

'Understood.'

The footsteps sounded again, right behind him.

Loken whipped around, drawing his weapon and aiming it in one fluidly economical motion.

'Don't move,' he said, but there was no one there.

Before Loken could react, a pistol pressed against the back of his helmet. A hammer pulled back with a sharp snap of oiled metal.

'I expected more from you,' said the voice behind the gun.

'No you didn't,' said Loken, lowering his own pistol.

'I expected you to try a little longer before giving up.'

'Would I ever have found you?'

'No.'

'So what would be the point?' said Loken. 'I don't fight battles I can't win.'

'Sometimes you don't get to choose the battles you fight.'

'But you can choose *how* you fight them,' said Loken. 'How's that hunter's eye, Rassuah?'

'I have him,' said Rassuah. 'Say the word and I can put a turbo-penetrator through his leg. Or his head. It's your choice.'

Loken slowly turned to face the man he had come to find. Armoured in pitted and scarred gunmetal armour without insignia, he went without helm and his bearded face was matted with dust. A draconic glyph tattoo coiled around his right eye, the mark of the Blackbloods, one of Cthonia's most vicious murder-gangs.

Loken saw rugged bone structure that mirrored his own.

'Severian,' said Loken, spreading his hands. 'I found you.'

'By giving up,' said Severian. 'By changing the rules of the hunt.'

'You of all people ought to know that's how a Luna Wolf fights,' said Loken. 'Understand your foe and do whatever is necessary to bring him down.'

The warrior grinned, exposing ash-stained teeth. 'You think your assassin friend can hit me? She won't.'

'If not her, then me,' said Loken, bringing his pistol up.

Severian shook his head and flipped something towards Loken, something that glittered silver and metallic.

'Here,' said Severian. 'You'll need these.'

Loken instinctively reached up as Severian stepped away from him. 'And I had such high hopes for you, Garviel Loken.'

The mist closed around him like a cloak.

Loken didn't pursue. What would be the point?

He opened his palm to see what Severian had thrown him.

Two gleaming silver discs. At first Loken thought they were lodge medals, but when he turned them over and saw they were blank and mirror-reflective, he understood what they were.

Cthonian mirror-coins.

Tokens to be left on the eyes of the dead.

FIVE

The painted angel
Bloodsworn
Pathfinders

THE HANDHOLD WAS a good one, the stone of the ruined citadel still ruggedly impermeable despite being built on a storm-lashed coastline. It reminded Vitus Salicar of the hard rock of the Qarda Massif on Baal Secundus, the hostile range of rad-peaks called home by the tribe that had birthed him.

Granite-hard and bleached of colour after thousands of years' exposure, the stone of the shattered tower offered plentiful handholds, but few were wider than the breadth of a finger. Salicar had climbed the tower many times, but this was his first attempt at the western facade. Erosion had worn the ocean-facing rock smooth, and truculent winds sought to tear him from his perch.

Clad only in a pair of khaki trews, Salicar's transhuman physique was sculpted and pale, like one of the Adoni of the Grekan temples given life and motion. His muscled back was tattooed with a winged blood drop that writhed with every motion of his ascent. Salicar's arms were marked with similar devices at his deltoids and biceps, with his forearms inked with images of drip-ping chalices and weeping-blood skulls. His hair was blond, long and pulled in a tight scalp lock, his features artistically handsome in their symmetry.

The sea was six hundred metres below him, a surging cauldron of thundering waves breaking against the base of the cliff. The advance of the tide filled deep depressions with foaming white water before its withdrawal revealed blades of rock beneath the surface. To fall would be to die, even for a transhuman engineered to be the perfect warrior by the gene-smiths of the Blood Angels.

And would that not be justice?

Salicar pushed away the troublesome thought and craned his neck back to scan the onward route of his ascent. A lightning strike had split the tower four decades ago, shearing it almost exactly in two. That it still stood was testament to the craft of its ancient builders. The path directly above him was impossible, the stone loose and kept in place only by a miracle of confluent compressional forces. Any ascent by that route would dislodge the entire upper reaches.

His current position at the edge of an arched window opening was tenuous as it was, but Vitus Salicar was not a warrior who refused any challenge once offered. Drazen had risked censure by calling him mad to make an attempt on the western facade, and Vastern told him in no uncertain terms that the Sanguinary Priests would not be held responsible for the loss of his gene-legacy.

So, up wasn't an option, but *across…*

The opening was perhaps six metres wide, too far to jump sideways, but at the apex of the window was an overhanging corbel that might once have supported a long-vanished idol of the Stormlord.

Two metres above, and three to the side.

Difficult, but not impossible.

Salicar braced his legs, bending them as much as he was able, and leapt upwards like an enraged fire scorpion. The stone at his feet cracked with the sudden pressure. It fell from the wall as he jumped, and for a heart-stopping moment, Salicar hung in the air as though weightless.

Images of the shattered bones and pulverised organs Vastern had been all too graphic in describing flashed before his eyes. His arms windmilled for the corbel. One outflung hand scraped the edge of the stone and his fingers clamped down hard. He swung like a pendulum, grunting as the tendons of his arm tore.

Pain was good. It told him he wasn't falling.

He closed his eyes and directed the pain away from his arm, letting it disperse through his body by repeating the mantra of flesh to spirit.

'Pain is an illusion of the senses,' he said through gritted teeth. 'Despair an illusion of the mind. I do not despair, so I shall feel no pain.'

Athekhan had taught him that on Fraxenhold. The Prosperine mental discipline was simple, but effective, and soon worked its magic. The pain faded and Salicar opened his eyes, reaching up with his other hand to curl his fingers around the slender lip of the corbel.

He pulled himself up smoothly, as though performing calisthenics in the gymnasia. He swung his legs onto the narrow corbel and stood upright at the centre of the window's arch. A projecting lip of a pediment above him offered another way onwards, but that route presented no significant challenge. He dismissed it and turned his attention to a portion of stonework further over that had fallen from higher on the tower.

Balanced precariously in a wedge-shaped gap in the wall, it sat on a rocky fulcrum like perfectly balanced scales. Salicar adjudged it wedged tightly enough to support his weight. Without taking the time to second guess himself, he vaulted from his narrow perch and landed on the block.

Right away, he knew he had been mistaken to believe it would support his mass. Though weighing several tonnes, it immediately tipped from position and slid from the wall. Salicar sprang away from the block and rammed his hands into a thin split in the rock above him. Skin tore and blood welled from his hands as he clenched his fists to bear his weight.

The block fell from the wall in a cascade of debris, carrying a wealth of shattered stonework with it. It tumbled end over end before slamming down with a booming explosion of splintered stone and a fifty metre geyser of seawater.

On the black stone quayside at the foot of the tower, heads craned upwards, little more than tiny pink ovals. The colours of their plate allowed Salicar to pick out his sub-commanders: Drazen in vermillion and gold, Vastern in white, Agana in black. The rest of his warriors were plated in Legion crimson, their swords glittering silver in the dying sunlight.

He turned from them and searched for another way onwards, but there was only the lip of the pediment above him. And as much as he desired challenge from this climb, there was no other way that wasn't simply suicide.

Salicar eased one bloodied hand from the rock and grabbed hold of the projecting lip. With his weight borne, he withdrew his other hand and pulled himself up.

From here, handholds were plentiful, and he reached the uppermost course of mighty blocks without undue effort. He stood atop the ruined tower and drew himself up to his full height, a beautiful, painted man of idealised form.

He lifted his hands above his head, looking down at the crashing waves, transient pools and lethal rocks. Death hung in the balance of a heartbeat's miscalculation.

And I might welcome it.

Arms swung down to his side, Salicar leapt from the tower.

THE CITADEL OF the Stormlord had been raised at the northernmost peninsula of the island of Damesek; a forsaken spit of lightning-struck peaks carved from volcanic black stone. The island was all but uninhabited and linked to the mainland only by a fulgurite causeway from the pilgrim city of Avadon.

The citadel and the quay at its base were the only man-made structures on Damesek. The quay remained mostly intact, but the citadel was a ruined holdfast constructed in an earlier epoch around a solitary basalt peak. The pale stone of its construction was not native to the region, and the monumental effort it must have taken the pre-technological inhabitants of Molech to bring it here was beyond belief.

One of the planet's oldest legends told of a mythical figure known as the Stormlord. Where he walked, thunder followed, and his Fulgurine Path had once been a pilgrim route across the landscape. The last portion of that route led to this peak, where the Stormlord had ascended on a bolt of lightning to the celestial ark that brought him to Molech.

Before the dismantling of the Blood Angels Librarius, Drazen had studied a great many such legends in search of the truth behind them, and this was a myth dismissed as allegory by most of Molech's people.

Most, but not all.

A determined cadre of mendicants whose number dwindled with every passing generation still dwelled in the lower portions of the citadel, subsisting on the alms and offerings left by curious folk who came to gawp at the ruins.

Drazen Acorah first laid eyes on the citadel almost two years ago, and had trained here many times with Captain Salicar and

the Bloodsworn. He found much to admire in the malnourished men and women who subsisted in the ruins of this barren
coastline.

Like the Bloodsworn, they cleaved to a duty that appeared to
serve little purpose, but would never dream of abandoning. They
no longer called themselves priests – such a term was dangerous
in this age of reason – but the word was appropriate.

There *was* something tangible in the air here. Not so long ago,
Acorah might have openly called it *ethereal*. But like the azure of
the Librarius he had once proudly worn, words like that had been
cast aside. The citadel's stones whispered of something incredible,
something he had never felt before, and only with difficulty did
he resist stretching out his senses to listen to their secrets.

Eighty-three chosen warriors of the IX Legion fought sparring
bouts under the uncompromising gaze of Agana Serkan, their
black-armoured Warden. These warriors were among the Legion's
best, hand-picked by Sanguinius to stand as his proxies. Commanded by the Emperor Himself, the Blood Angels had sent a
Bloodsworn warrior band to Molech for over a century. As great
an honour as it was to serve a direct command of the Master of
Mankind, its members were distraught at being denied the chance
to fight alongside their primarch against the hated nephilim in
the Signus Cluster.

Acorah shared their dismay, but no force in the universe would
compel him to break his vow of duty. Salicar had accepted a crimson grail filled with the mingled vitae of the previous Bloodsworn
band of Captain Akeldama. Salicar and each of his warriors had
drunk from the grail, releasing their predecessors from their oath
before refilling it with their own blood to swear another.

He put aside memories of his arrival on Molech and walked to
the edge of the quayside. Ocean-going vessels had once braved
treacherous seas to bring pilgrims to this place, but many centuries

had passed since any vessel had taken moorings here.

The mendicant priests that constantly fussed around them parted to make way for him. Fully armoured in his blood-red battleplate, even the tallest of them barely reached to the base of Acorah's shoulder guard. They were in awe of him, but their fear kept them distant and Acorah was glad.

Their fear left a bilious taste in his mouth.

They didn't like that Salicar regularly climbed the tallest tower, but that didn't stop the captain. They couldn't voice their objections in terms of blasphemy or desecration and instead cited the instability of its remains.

Acorah heard one of the mendicants gasp in terror and shielded his eyes as he turned his gaze to the top of the tower.

He already knew what he would see.

Vitus Salicar arced outwards from the summit of the tower, his outstretched arms haloed by the sunset like the pinions of a reborn phoenix.

Acorah blinked as Salicar's body was flickeringly overlaid with vivid imagery: a red gold angel plummeting in fire; a comely youth borne aloft on disintegrating wings; a reckless son careening across the sky on a sun-chariot.

He tasted ash and soured meat, and bit back the urge to let his psyker power move through him as it once had so freely. He spat bile as Salicar plunged into a rocky basin of deep water the surge tide had filled only a fraction of a second before.

The water swept back, revealing his captain kneeling on the black rock between a pair of spear-like stalagmites. Salicar's head was down, and when he stood upright, Acorah saw the same fatalistic expression he had worn since their return from the Preceptory Line.

Before the waters could rush in and fill the pool again, Salicar jogged over to the quayside and sprang upwards. Acorah knelt and grabbed his captain's hand, pulling him up. Denied its bounty, the water boomed angrily against the stonework, showering them both with cold spume.

'Satisfied now?' he asked, as Salicar spat a mouthful of seawater.

Salicar nodded. 'Until the next time.'

'A less understanding man might say you had a death wish.'

'I do not wish death,' said Salicar.

Acorah looked back up the length of the tower.

'Then why do you insist on taking such needless risks?'

'For the challenge, Drazen,' said Salicar, moving off towards the fighting men of the Bloodsworn. 'If I'm not challenged, I grow stale. We all do. That's why I come here.'

'And that's the only reason?'

'No,' said Salicar, but did not elaborate.

Acorah felt the tips of his fingers tingle with the desire to wield powers now decreed unnatural. How easy it would be to divine the captain's true motivations, but another oath bound him against such a course.

They came to where the Legion thralls had placed Salicar's battle armour, a master-worked suit of crimson plate, golden wings and black trim. His swords hung from a belt of tan leather and his gold-chased pistol was mag-locked in a thigh holster. His helm was a jade funerary mask, as empty of expression as an automaton's.

'The mendicants would rather you didn't climb the tower,' he said, as Salicar picked up a towel and began to dry himself.

'They're afraid I'll hurt myself?'

'I think it's more the tower they're concerned with.'

Salicar shook his head. 'It'll outlast us all.'

'Not if you keep knocking bits of it loose,' pointed out Acorah.

'You fuss around me like a fawning thrall,' said Salicar.

'Someone has to,' said Acorah, as Salicar looped a pair of

glittering ident-tags around his neck. Even without his transhuman senses, it was impossible to miss the blood flecks on them.

'Is it wise to keep those?' he asked.

Salicar was instantly hostile.

'Not wise, but necessary. Their blood is on our hands.'

'We don't know what happened that day,' said Acorah, pushing against the nightmarish memory of awakening from a fugue state to find himself surrounded by corpses. 'None of us do, but if there is guilt, it is shared by us all equally.'

'I am captain of the Bloodsworn,' said Salicar. 'If the burden of guilt is not mine to bear, then whose?'

YASU NAGASENA'S MOUNTAINSIDE villa had been extended several times in the last year, with numerous annexes, subterranean chambers and technological additions. It had originally been designed as a place of retreat and reflection, but had become an unofficial base of operations for many of the Sigillite's operatives.

Instead of a place of solace for those who came here, it was often the last place on Terra they ever saw. Nagasena himself was *in absentia* on yet another hunt, and Loken's pathfinders had taken up residence.

The walls of the room at the heart of the villa were covered in wax paper schematics retrieved from the deepest and most secure vaults of the Palace. Hundreds of plans, sections and isometrics depicted one of the mightiest vessels ever adapted to the Scylla-pattern construction schemata.

The *Vengeful Spirit* had formed the core of the Luna Wolves campaigns for two centuries, a Gloriana-class war vessel of such power that entire systems had been cowed by the scale of the devastation it alone could unleash. The precisely inked lines of the plans were covered in hasty scrawls and pinned script paper. Choke points within the superstructure were identified, potential boarding points circled and its regions of greatest vulnerability and strength highlighted with painted brushstrokes. The latter far outnumbered the former.

Shipwrights' plotter tables formed a circle around two warriors of transhuman scale, both engaged in heated debate as to the nature of the vessel they were to infiltrate.

Loken tapped a stylus against the upper transit decks.

'The Avenue of Glory and Lament,' said Loken. 'It's the approach to the strategium. Plenty of companionways and gallery decks connect to it, and it's a natural highway through the ship.'

Loken's companion was clearly of a different mindset, and shook his cybernetic-threaded skull. His bulk was considerable; broader and taller than Loken, but with a noticeable stoop that brought his pallid features to the same level.

His name was Tubal Cayne and he had once been an Iron Warrior.

'Shows how long it's been since you stormed a war vessel,' he said, jabbing a finger at the funnel points along the transverse transits. 'A breach there will require a fight, something I was under the impression you wanted to avoid. Besides, any commander worth his salt will have rapid reaction forces stationed here, here and all along here. Or are you telling me the Warmaster's gone soft in the head as well as mad?'

Despite his primarch's treachery, Loken felt an absurd need to defend him against Cayne's insult. The Iron Warrior had a knack for irritating people with his cold logic and utter lack of empathy. Loken had already stepped in to keep Ares Voitek from strangling Cayne with his servo-arm when he suggested that the death of Ferrus Manus might actually have a positive effect on the Iron Tenth.

He took a deep breath to quell his rising choler. 'The *Vengeful Spirit* has never been boarded,' said Loken. 'It's a battle scenario we never bothered to run. Who'd be insane enough to board the Warmaster's flagship?'

'There's always someone mad enough to try the one thing you've never considered,' said Cayne. 'Just look around you.'

'Then where would you suggest?' snapped Loken, tiring of Cayne's incessant naysaying. He knew his irritation was more directed at himself, for each of Cayne's objections was founded in logic and proper diligence of thought.

Cayne bent to study the schemata again, his eyes darting back and forth and his fingers tracing arcane patterns across the hair-thin lines of the Scyllan architect's quill. Eventually he tapped a portside embarkation bay of a munitions sub-deck on the *Vengeful Spirit*'s ventral aspect.

'The lower deck was always the weakest point in other ships' defences,' said Cayne, sweeping his finger out to encompass the adjacent dormitory spaces and magazine chambers. 'It's not presented to the planet below, so there's only going to be menials down there, gun-crews and whatever dregs have sunk below the waterline.'

'*Other* ships?'

'Ships other than the Fourth Legion,' said Cayne, and Loken felt a tremor of unease at the pride Cayne took when speaking of his former brothers. 'The Lord of Iron knew a warship without guns is a powderless culverin and took steps to protect them.'

Tubal Cayne had come to the Knights Errant from the gaol of Kangba Marwu, one of the Crusader Host who had been garrisoned on Terra as a potent reminder of the Legion hosts fighting in humanity's name. Cayne's evolution of breaching doctrines during the storming of the glacier fortresses of Saturn's rings was still an exemplary model by which orbital strongpoints ought to be taken. His release from the Legio Custodes cells had been Malcador's doing, but had only been approved by Constantin

Valdor after rigorous psy-screens had revealed no trace of traitorous rancour.

Cayne was not the only parolee from Kangba Marwu set to join this pathfinding mission, but he was the only one Loken had met so far. The Iron Warrior had responded to the treachery of Horus with stoic practicality, lamenting his Legion's choice of alignment, while understanding that his place was no longer in their ranks.

'Yes,' nodded Cayne. 'That's your way in.'

Loken traced the route a craft would need to follow to reach the ventral decks and said, 'That means flying through the guns' fire zones. Minefields, sentinel arrays.'

'More than likely, but a small enough craft most likely won't show up on the threat auspex of cannons that size. And if a shell hits us we'll be dead before we even know it. So why worry?'

Loken let out a breath at the thought of flying through a gauntlet of ship-killing ordnance and detection arrays. As plans went, it was a risky one, but Cayne was right. This was the portion of the *Vengeful Spirit* that offered the best way in.

The sound of breath at the doorway forestalled any further discussion. A young girl in a simple cream shift, with gleaming black skin and hard eyes of pale ivory, stood at the open door, her hands clasped demurely in front of her. Loken had assumed she was a servant of Yasu Nagasena, but she carried a holstered pistol at her side at all times. He didn't know what position she occupied within the household, but that she was utterly devoted to the villa's master was beyond question.

'Mistress Amita sent me to tell you that Rassuah is on approach,' she said.

Tubal Cayne looked up. 'The last of us?'

Loken nodded. 'Yes.'

'Then let's see who else is walking into hell,' said Cayne.

✠ ✠ ✠

RUBIO AND VARREN came up from the sparring chambers carved into the rock beneath Nagasena's villa, slathered in oily sweat and making imaginary sword cuts as they debated the merits of gladius over chainaxe. Though both warriors had left their Legion identity behind, their Legion expertise was still invaluable.

The interior courtyard of the villa was a place of peace and quiet reflection. A pool with a fountain in the shape of a coiled serpentine dragon burbled in the centre of gene-spliced plants and artificial blooms. Half a dozen robed servants tended the garden, and honeyed scents filled the air.

'So they're here,' said Varren upon noticing Loken.

The former captain of the World Eaters was bare to the waist, his flesh a tapestry of knotted scar tissue, as if he had been stitched together as part of some hideous experiment in reanimation. Tattoos coiled around the scars and over his shoulders; each one a badge of honour and a memory of killing.

Macer Varren had come to the Sol system at the head of a patchwork fleet of refugees, together with detachments from the Emperor's Children and White Scars. In the treachery that followed, Varren's loyalty had been proven beyond question and Garro had offered him a place within Malcador's Knights Errant.

His companion, Tylos Rubio, had been the first warrior that Garro had recruited, snatched from the war-torn surface of Calth in the moments after the XVII Legion doomed the Veridian star. A warrior of the Librarius whose powers had been shackled by the Decree of Nikaea, Rubio had once again taken up psychic arms against the Warmaster. The loss of the cobalt-blue still troubled him, and Loken knew exactly how he felt – though for very different reasons.

His features were the polar opposite of Varren's; sculpted where the World Eater had been battered into shape, unblemished where Varren was forged by scars. His eyes were heavy with regret and loss, but the nascent brotherhood of the Knights Errant was awakening in him a sense of belonging that had hitherto been absent.

'Where are the others?' asked Rubio, raising a hand in greeting.

'Don't you know?' asked Cayne. 'Aren't you supposed to be psychic?'

'My powers are not parlour tricks, Tubal,' said Rubio, as he and Varren fell into step with Loken and Cayne. 'I do not lightly employ them.'

'Voitek is already on the platform,' said Loken. 'He said the aegis-field needed calibrating.'

'What about the Half-heard?' asked Varren.

'Iacton is–'

'Not on Terra,' finished Rubio.

Varren halted as they reached the fortified entrance of the tunnel cut through the mountain that led to the newly built platforms at the rear of the villa.

'You just said you didn't use your powers unless you needed to,' said Cayne, unlocking the armoured portal and allowing the heavy door to grind into its housing.

'One does not need psychic powers to know when Iacton Qruze is near,' said Rubio. 'He has a presence that far outweighs his belittling epithet.'

With Qruze's permission, Loken had reluctantly explained the old nickname of 'Half-heard' to his fellow Knights. A warrior whose words went unheeded by the vast majority of the Luna Wolves had turned out to have been one of the keepers of the Legion's soul. Qruze's days of being disregarded were over, but the name had stuck and always would.

'So where is he then?' pressed Varren.

'He has a heavy burden elsewhere,' said Rubio. 'One that grieves and shames him, but one from which he will not turn.'

'Just like the rest of us,' grunted Varren.

No one said any more, and they entered the mountain, following a long and winding tunnel bored by industrial-scale meltas. Caged lumen globes were strung from the glass-smooth ceiling, swaying gently in sighs of ventilation.

After a journey of two kilometres, they emerged into a steep-sided shaft cut into the haunches of the mountain – a hundred metres wide and three times that in height. In the centre of the cavernous space was a single landing platform, large enough to take a Stormbird, but not much else.

Kneeling beside an opened bank of machine racks at the foot of the platform was a warrior in identical burnished metal armour to the rest of them. Two articulated limbs at his side worked to sort tools and arrange couplings on a long length of oiled cloth. Another two mechanical arms curled over his shoulders arranging nests of cables and preparing connectors to be reattached.

'Have you not finished yet?' asked Cayne. 'You have had ample time to make the necessary adjustments, and Mistress Rassuah is expected at any minute.'

Ares Voitek did not look up or deign to answer, having now learned to resist Cayne's baiting. He continued working, with all four limbs now embroiled in the guts of the machine. The arms moved with whirring mechanical precision, each one guided by the mind impulse unit attached to the nape of Voitek's neck.

'There,' said Voitek. 'Not even Severian could find this place now.'

Loken looked up as the shimmering aegis-field rippled with energy across the wedge of light above them. He saw no difference in its appearance, but assumed the Iron Hand had improved its performance in ways he wasn't equipped to register. The field's mechanics concealed the platform's location via a blend of refractive fields and geomagnetic scramblers. To all intents and purposes, the entrance of the landing field was invisible.

Voitek stood and the servo-arms arranged themselves across his back and midriff with a clatter of folding metal. Voitek's left arm was a brutal augmetic from the elbow down, gleaming silver and kept lustrous by a regime of polishing that went beyond obsessive.

'If it's that good, will Rassuah be able to find it?' asked Varren.

'She already has,' grumbled Voitek, his voice artificially rendered and grating through a constant burble of machine noise.

'Then let's be waiting for her,' said Loken.

The five warriors climbed a switchback of iron stairs to the raised platform as the aegis-field rippled with the passage of an aircraft. A bare metal Valkyrie assault carrier descended on rippling cones of jetfire, deafening in the close confines of the shaft. The air became hot and metallic as it turned ninety degrees on its axis to land with its rear quarters aligned with the embarkation ramps.

'You got them all?' asked Varren.

'All four,' confirmed Loken.

'Does word come of where we are bound?' asked Rubio.

'Saturn's sixth moon,' said Loken. 'To pick up Iacton Qruze.'

'And after Titan?' said Ares Voitek. 'The Warmaster?'

'We'll learn that when we are assembled,' said Loken as the roar of the Valkyrie's engines diminished and its assault ramp dropped.

Four figures marched from its troop compartment, all in the burnished silver of the Knights Errant and armed with a variety of weaponry. Loken knew them from their data files, but even without that information it would have been child's play to identify the four warriors.

Bror Tyrfingr: tall, slender and hollow-cheeked, with a long mane of snow-white hair and a loping stride. A Space Wolf.

Rama Karayan; keeping to the shadows, shaven headed, sallow

of complexion and dark eyed. Without doubt a son of Corax.

The shaven headed warrior with a forked beard waxed to points could only be Altan Nohai, an Apothecary of the White Scars.

And finally, Callion Zaven. Patrician and haughty, his bearing was a hair's breadth from arrogant. Zaven's gaze swept over the waiting warriors, as though judging their worth. A true warrior of the Emperor's Children.

Loken heard Ares Voitek's vox-grille blurt a hash of static, and didn't need Mechanicum augmetics to translate his bone-deep anger at seeing a warrior from the Legion that had murdered his primarch.

The four new arrivals halted at the base of the ramp, and both groups took a moment to gauge the measure of the other. Loken took a step forward, but it was Tyrfingr who spoke first.

'You're Loken?' he said.

'I am.'

Tyrfingr extended his hand and Loken took it in the old way, palm to wrist. Tyrfingr's other hand shot up and gripped the back of Loken's neck, as if to tear out his throat with his teeth.

'Bror Tyrfingr,' he said. 'You brought the silver wolf to bring down the rogue wolf. That's the best decision you'll ever make, but if I think your roots are weak, I'll kill you myself.'

SIX

Nine-tenths of the lore
Tarnhelm
Adoratrice

THOUGH ITS ORIGINAL purpose had been subverted, the so-called Quiet Order of the Sons of Horus still met in secret. The dormitory halls had once housed thousands of deckhands, but only echoes dwelled here in the normal run of things.

Before Isstvan, a time that no longer held meaning for the Legion, the lodge had met only as often as campaign necessity allowed. It had been an indulgence permitted by the primarch, encouraged even, but always subservient to the demands of war. Now it met regularly as the Sons of Horus learned more of the secret arts.

Close to a thousand warriors gathered in the long, vaulted chamber, an army of sea-green plate, transverse helm-crests and crimson mantles. War-blackened banners hung from the dormitory arches, and bloodied trophies were speared on long pike shafts along the chamber's length. Wide bowls of promethium billowed chemical fumes and orange flame. A slow drum beat of fists on thighs echoed from the walls of stone and steel.

The sense of anticipation was palpable.

Serghar Targost felt it too, but he forced himself to keep his steps measured and his bearing regal. The captain of the Seventh Company was broad and powerful, as were all legionaries, but there was a density to him that gave sparring partners pause when they drew his name in the training cages. His blunt features were not those of a true son, and the old scar bisecting his forehead had been overwritten by a more heinous wound.

An Iron Hands Terminator had struck him in the dying moments of Isstvan V and the impact trauma had almost ended him there and then. The enclosing pressure of his helm had kept the broth of his brain from oozing through the pulverised ruin of his skull. The Apothecaries had sutured the bone fragments together beneath the skin, fixing the largest shards in place with dozens of tensile anchors on the surface of his face.

With Lev Goshen's help, Targost had attached the ebon claws torn from the scaled pelt of a dead Salamander to the protruding ends of the anchors, giving him the spiked features of a madman. He could no longer wear a battle helm, but Targost considered it an acceptable trade off.

Targost moved through the Sons of Horus, pausing now and then to observe their labours. Sometimes he would offer instruction on the precise angle of a blade, the correct syntax of Colchisian grammar forms or the required pronunciation of a ritual mantra.

The air sang with potential, as though a secret symphony existed just beyond the threshold of perception and would soon burst through into life. Targost smiled. Only a few short years ago he would have mocked the absurd poetry of such a sentiment.

Yet there was truth to it.

Tonight would see the lodge change from a fraternity of dabblers into an order favoured by the touch of Primordial Truth.

Everyone here knew it, and none more so than Maloghurst.

The Warmaster's equerry entered the chamber via one of the vertical transit spines, clad in a long chasuble of ermine over his battleplate. Maloghurst gave a respectful nod. No rank structure existed within the Quiet Order, save that of lodge master, and even the Warmaster's equerry had to respect that office.

'Equerry,' said Targost as Maloghurst limped to accompany him.

'Lodge master,' replied Maloghurst, turning to match Targost's pace despite the fused mass of bone and cartilage within his pelvis and lower spine that stubbornly refused to heal. He walked with the aid of an ebony cane topped with an amber pommel-stone, but Targost suspected the equerry's wounding was no longer as debilitating as he made out.

'I doubt there is a more abandoned space aboard the *Vengeful Spirit*,' said Maloghurst with a grin. 'You realise, of course, that the lodge has no more need to hide itself in shadows.'

Targost nodded. 'I know, but old habits, you understand?'

'Absolutely,' agreed Maloghurst. 'Traditions must be maintained. Even more so now.'

Maloghurst had earned the soubriquet, 'the Twisted', for having a mind that wove labyrinthine intrigues around the Warmaster, but the old nickname had assumed a more literal connotation in the opening shots of the war-making on Terra.

The *other* Terra, where the misguided fool who believed himself Emperor had stood against the Sons of Horus.

No, Targost reminded himself, back then the Legion had still been the Luna Wolves, their name not yet reflecting the honour of the warrior that led them. Maloghurst had healed, and despite the poor taste of the old nickname, he desired it kept.

They moved through the throng, and as news of Maloghurst's arrival spread, the warriors parted before them to reveal their destination.

Atop a raised plinth marked with chalked geometric symbols

stood two structural beams welded together to form an 'X'. Chained to the cross was a legionary stripped of his armour with his head fixed in place by a heavy iron clamp across his brow.

Ger Gerradon, late of Tithonus Assault, he'd taken two Chogorian tulwars through the lungs on Dwell, and by the time the Apothecaries got to him his oxygen-starved brain was irrevocably damaged. Nothing remained of the man he had once been, just a drooling meat-form who could serve no useful purpose within the Legion.

Until now.

Sixteen hooded lodge members arranged in a circle around Gerradon held weeping captives taken in the assault on Tyjun. Highborns for the most part, some native to Dwell, some Imperial imports; men and women who'd thrown themselves on the mercy of the Sons of Horus only to find they had none to give. In any conventional war they would be bargaining chips, tools of negotiation, but here they were something altogether more valuable. They sobbed and debased themselves with begging or attempts at bargaining, while others offered their loyalty or things far more precious.

A reverent hush descended on the chamber as Maloghurst and Targost stepped onto the plinth. Maloghurst made a meal out of his step, and Targost shook his head at the equerry's theatrics.

'Let's get this done,' said Targost, holding out his hand.

Maloghurst shook his head. 'You can't simply rush this, lodge master,' he said. 'I know you are all about the fundamentals, but this is not a breach to be stormed. Ritual is everything here, Serghar, the proper order of things must be observed, the right words spoken and the offerings made at precisely the right time.'

'Just give me the knife,' said Targhost. 'You speak the words and tell me when to open their throats.'

The captives wailed and their captors tightened their grips.

Maloghurst produced a long dagger from within his robes, its blade curved and worked from dark stone. Its surface was chipped and crude, like something hacked from the ground by savages, but Targost knew its edge to be sharper than any arming chamber tech could match.

'Is that…' he began.

'One of the blades Erebus crafted?' said Maloghurst. 'No, not *that* one of course, but one like it.'

Targost nodded and took the blade, testing its heft and flexing his fingers on the leather-wrapped handle. It felt *good* in his grip, natural. Made for *him*.

'I like it,' he said and turned to Ger Gerradon.

Like him, Gerradon wasn't a true son, his features bearing a malnourished sharpness from a Cthonian childhood that no amount of genhancing could ever restore.

'A loyal member of the lodge and a ferocious killer,' said Targost. 'A man born for assault duties. It's a blow to the Legion to have lost his sword arm.'

'If I have the truth of it, then Ger will fight alongside his brothers with a new soul within him.'

'What the Seventeenth Legion call a daemon?'

'An old term, but as good a word as any,' agreed Maloghurst. 'Lorgar's sons call their twin flames the *Gal Vorbak*. Ours will be the *Luperci*, the Brothers of the Wolf.'

Gerradon's eyes were open, but unseeing. His lips parted, as though he was trying to speak, and drool spilled onto his chest.

'Nothing of the man we knew remains,' said Maloghurst. 'This will restore him.'

'Then let's get it done,' snapped Targost.

Maloghurst stood before Gerradon, placing a tattooed hand on his scarred chest. Targost didn't remember the Twisted having tattoos, but recognised their provenance. The books Erebus had shown him, the ancient texts said to have been borne to Colchis from Old Earth, had been filled with stanzas of *artes* rendered in the same runic script.

'Be ready with that knife, Serghar,' said Maloghurst.

'Have no fear on that score,' Targost assured him.

Maloghurst nodded and began to speak, but in no language Targost had ever heard. The more the equerry spoke, the less Targost believed it *was* a language in any sense that he could comprehend.

He saw Maloghurst's mouth moving, but the motion of his lips wasn't matching the noise in Targost's ears; like rusted metal grating on stone, a death rattle and a tuneless singer combined.

Targost coughed a wad of mucus. He tasted blood and spat onto the deck. He blinked away a momentary dizziness and tightened his grip on the stone dagger as the bile in his stomach climbed his gullet. Targost's eyes widened as noxious black smoke streamed from the blade. The miasma clung to its edges and Targost felt the weight of murder in the dagger's long existence. The temperature plummeted, his every exhalation visible as a long plume of breath.

'Now,' said Maloghurst and the sixteen hooded warriors pulled the captives' heads back to expose their necks.

Targost stepped towards the nearest, a young man with handsome features and wide, terrified eyes.

'Please, I just–'

Targost didn't let him finish and plunged the smoke-edged dagger deep into his throat. Blood fountained from the grotesque wound. The hooded warrior pushed the dying man forward, and Targost moved on, opening one throat after another with no heed of his victims' horror or last words.

As the last one died, their blood lapped around Targost's

boots and spilled over the edge of the plinth. The chalked symbols drank deeply, and Targost felt a tremor in his hand.

'Mal…' he said as his arm lifted the blade to his own throat.

Maloghurst didn't respond, his lips still twisting in opposition to the unsounds he was making. Targost twisted his head, but the world around him was a frozen tableau.

'Maloghurst!' repeated Targost.

'He can't help you,' said Ger Gerradon.

Targost looked into a face alight with malice and perverse enjoyment of suffering. No longer slack with brain death, Gerradon's features were pulled in a rictus grin. His eyes were milky white and empty, like the unpainted eyes of a doll. Whatever their ritual had drawn from the warp was not Ger Gerradon, but something incalculably old, raw-birthed and bloody.

'Sixteen? That's the best you could do?' it said. 'Sixteen measly souls?'

'It's a sacred number,' hissed Targost, fighting to keep the blade from reaching his neck. Despite the freezing temperatures, sweat ran in runnels down his face.

'To who?'

'To us, the Legion…' grunted Targost. 'We're the Sixteenth Legion, the twin Octed.'

'Ah, I see,' said the warp-thing. 'Sacred to you, but meaningless to the neverborn. After everything Erebus taught you people, you still manage to get it wrong.'

Anger touched Targost, and the blade's inexorable path to the pulsing artery in his neck slowed.

'Wrong? We summoned you, didn't we?'

The thing wearing Gerradon's flesh laughed. 'You didn't summon me, I came back of my own accord. I have so much to teach you.'

'Came *back*?' said Targost. 'Who are you?'

'I'm hurt you don't recognise me, Serghar.'

The smoking edges of the gore-encrusted blade touched Targost's neck. Skin parted before its razor tip. Blood pumped as he pushed it deeper into his neck.

'Who am I?' rasped the daemon. 'I'm Tormaggedon.'

RASSUAH FLEW THE pathfinders from Old Himalazia to Ultima Thule, the outermost structure still considered to be in Terran orbit. Discounting the as yet unfinished Ardent Reef, Ultima Thule was the most recent addition to the inhabited plates that made stately circuits around humanity's birth rock; smaller than the supercontinent of Lemurya, less productive than the industrial powerhouse of Rodinia and without the grandiose architecture of Antillia, Vaalbara or Kanyakumari.

It had been constructed sixty-two years previously, by workers since assigned to distant sectors of the Imperium. Eclipsed in scale and power by its grander brethren, its entry in the Terran orbital registry was little more than a footnote.

Over the course of its life, Ultima Thule had been quietly forgotten by the vast majority of Terra's inhabitants. And where most orbital architects would lament such a fate for their creation, anonymity had always been the goal of Ultima Thule.

Its structure comprised of a pair of matte-black cylinders, five hundred metres in length and two hundred wide, connected by a central orb-hub. No armoured windows pierced its structure and no collision avoidance lights strobed to warn of its presence. Any space-farer lucky enough to catch a glimpse of Ultima Thule could be forgiven for mistaking it for dead orbital junk.

That appearance was deliberately misleading, for Ultima Thule was one of the most sophisticated structures orbiting Terra, its endless suites of auspex quietly monitoring spatial traffic throughout the system.

A docking bay opened on its dark side, remaining visible only as long as it took to retrieve the void-capable Valkyrie. Auspex-hardened blast doors shut behind the assault carrier, and Ultima Thule continued its procession around the planet below as though it had never existed.

Anonymous and forgotten.

Silent and invisible.

Just as Malcador had decreed when he ordered it built.

THE REPOSITORY WAS cool, the air kept at a constant relative humidity and temperature. The more fragile artefacts stored here were hermetically sealed in stasis fields, and Malcador tasted the tang of the recessed power generators.

Crystal-fronted cabinets lit up at his passing, but he spared their contents little notice. A book that had once plunged the world into war, sketches by the Polymath of Firenza the Emperor had – wisely, it turned out – deemed too dangerous for Perturabo to see, the half-formed sculpture of beauty incarnate.

Malcador had lied when he told young Khalid Hassan that these rough formed walls were all that remained of the Sigillite Fortress, but some truths were uncomfortable enough without burdening others with them.

The chamber was smaller than those that surrounded it, and it took Malcador a moment only to reach the stele of Gyptia. It sat on a reinforced timber cradle, the black gloss of its original construction undimmed by the passage of millennia. Lives had been lost to retrieve this fragment of humanity's soul, as was the case with many of the objects stored here.

Malcador closed his eyes and placed his fingertips upon the cold surface of the stone. Granodiorite, an igneous rock similar to granite. Hard wearing, but not indestructible.

Given what it had unlocked in ages past, there was a pleasing symmetry to what it now allowed him to do. Malcador's breathing slowed and the already cooled air chilled yet further.

'My lord,' he said.

Silence was Malcador's only answer, and he feared the holocaust raging beneath the Palace was too fierce, too all-consuming for a reply. *Beneath* wasn't strictly speaking correct, but it was the only preposition that seemed to fit.

Malcador.

The Emperor's voice echoed within his mind, stentorian and dominant, yet familiar and fraternal. Malcador felt its power, even over so immeasurable a distance, but also the effort it was taking to forge the link.

'How goes the fight?'

We bleed out every day, while the daemons grow ever stronger. I do not have much time, my friend. War calls.

'Leman Russ is on Terra,' said Malcador.

I know. Even here, I can feel the Wolf King's presence.

'He brings word of the Lion. Twenty thousand Dark Angels are reportedly bound for Ultramar.'

Why does he not make haste for Terra?

Sweat ran down Malcador's back at the strain of maintaining this connection. 'There are… unsettling rumours of what is happening in Guilliman's domain.'

I cannot see the Five Hundred Worlds. Why is that?

'We call it the Ruinstorm. Nemo and I believe the slaughter on Calth to have been part of an orchestrated chain of events that precipitated the birth of a catastrophic and impenetrable warp storm.'

And what do you believe Roboute is doing?

'It's Guilliman, what do I think he's doing? He's building an empire.'

And the Lion goes to stop him?

'So the Wolf King says, my lord. It seems the warriors of the Lion stand with us after all.'

You doubted them? The First? Even after all they accomplished in the time before the others took up their swords?

'I did,' admitted Malcador. 'After Rogal's secret emissaries to their home world returned empty-handed, we feared the worst. But Caliban's angels came to the Wolves' aid when Alpharius threatened to destroy them.'

Alpharius… my son, what chance did you give my dream? Ah, even when war presses in from all sides, my sons still seek to press their advantage. They are like the feudal lords of old, scenting opportunity for their own advancement in the fires of adversity.

The regret pained Malcador's thoughts.

'Russ still plans to fight Horus eye to eye,' said Malcador. 'He sends my Knights to guide his blade and no words of mine can sway him from his course.'

You think he should not fight Horus?

'Russ is your executioner,' said Malcador tactfully. 'But his axe falls a little too readily these days. Magnus felt it, now Horus will feel it.'

Two rebel angels. His axe falls on those deserving its smile.

'And what happens when Russ takes it upon himself to decide who is loyal and who deserves execution?'

Russ is true-hearted, one of the few I know will never fall.

'You suspect others may prove false?'

To my eternal regret, I do.

'Who?'

Another long pause made Malcador fear his question would remain unanswered, but at last the Emperor replied.

The Khan makes a virtue of being unknowable, of being the mystery that none can answer. Some among his Legion have already embraced treachery, and others may yet.

'What would you have me do, my lord?'

Keep watching him, Malcador. Watch the Khan more closely than any other.

'I HAVE NEVER wanted to fly anything so much in all my life,' said Rassuah.

Looking at the sleek, wedge-shaped craft with its jutting, aerodyne prow, Loken couldn't help but agree with her.

'I'm told it's called *Tarnhelm*,' he said.

'Call it what you want, but if I'm not flying it within the hour, there's going to be blood spilled,' said Rassuah.

Loken grinned at her eagerness. He disliked aircraft on principle, but even he recognised something beautiful in the *Tarnhelm*.

Perhaps because it looked so utterly unlike any other aircraft in the Legiones Astartes inventory. The warcraft of the Legions were designed to be brutal, in appearance as well as effect. Their form followed function, which was to kill as quickly and efficiently as possible. *Tarnhelm*'s sleek lines spoke of an altogether different purpose.

Its basic structure was constructed around a central crew section with bulbous drive pods at the rear that tapered towards the prow and formed the ship's delta-winged shape. Without any pennants or beacons, there was nothing to give any clue to its identity or affiliation.

'What is it?' asked Varren. 'It's not an attack ship or a guncutter; too few armaments. And there's not enough armour for it to be a troop transport. One good hit is going to gut it. I don't understand what it is.'

'This is a craft designed to pass through the stars unseen,' said Rama Karayan, and all eyes turned to look at him, as it was the most any of them had heard him say.

'Why in the world would you want to do that?' asked Callion

Zaven, his expression as confused as Varren's. 'The point of the Legions is to be seen.'

'Not always,' said Altan Nohai. 'What the Khan called a clever fighter is one who not only wins, but excels in winning with ease before the enemy even knows he is there.'

Zaven looked unconvinced. 'Shock and awe becomes a lot harder when no one sees it coming.'

'It's got teeth, mind,' said Ares Voitek, his servo-arms unlimbering to point out the barely visible seams of recessed weapon nacelles and missile pods. 'But as Macer says, it's not an attack ship.'

'It's a *draugrjúka*,' said Bror Tyrfingr.

Seeing the looks of confusion among his fellow pathfinders, Bror shook his head and said, 'Don't you people understand *Juvik*?'

'Juvik?' asked Rubio.

'Fenrisian hearth-cant,' said Tubal Cayne. 'It's a stripped-down, simplified language. No subtlety to it – punchy and declarative, just like the warriors that speak it.'

'Have a care, Tubal,' warned Bror, squaring his shoulders. 'A man could take offence at that.'

That seemed to confuse Cayne. 'I don't see how. Nothing I said was untrue. I've met enough Space Wolves to know that.'

Loken expected anger, but Bror laughed. 'Space Wolves? Ha, I forgot that was your idiot name for the Rout. If I didn't think you were being completely serious I'd rip your arms off. Stay by my side and I'll show you just how subtle a *Space Wolf* can be.'

'So what's a draugrjúka?' asked Loken.

'A ghost ship,' said Bror.

A GREY-ROBED SERVILE with augmetic implants worn around her skull like a tonsure had met the pathfinders in the docking bay, and she now led them aboard the *Tarnhelm*. The vessel's interior was stripped back, with only the barest minimum of fitments that would allow it to carry crew.

Its astropath was kept in sealed cryo-stasis, and its Navigator had yet to be implanted in the tapered cupola on the dorsal section. The long-axis of the ship was a cramped dormitory, with alcoves serving as medicae bays, equipment stowage and sleeping areas. Individual crew compartments were set towards the rear of the craft, with a slender nave reaching from the communal areas of the ship to its tapered prow.

Rassuah made her way towards the bridge, while the rest of the pathfinders stowed their equipment in cunningly arranged lockers and weapon racks.

The Knights Errant had been extant only a short while, too short for any real traditions to bed in, but a custom that had been readily adopted was for each warrior to retain a single artefact from his former Legion.

Loken thought back to the battered metal crate in which he had kept his meagre belongings; the garrotting wire, the feathers and the broken combat blade. Junk to any other eyes than his, but there had been one item whose loss had grieved him.

The data-slate Ignace Karkasy had given him, the one from Euphrati Keeler. *That* had been a treasure beyond value, a record of the time when the universe made sense, when the Luna Wolves had been a byword for honour, nobility and brotherhood. Like everything else he had once owned, it was gone.

He snapped his chainsword into the locker's blade rack, careful to fix it in place. Its blade was fresh from a manufactory city in Albyon and inscribed with a boast that it was warranted never to fail.

Just like the thousands of others forged there.

His bolter was no different, the product of manufactories geared for war on a galactic scale, where the ability to mass-produce reliable weaponry was of far greater importance that any considerations of individuality. Lastly, he placed the mirror tokens Severian had given him into the locker. Loken had thought about throwing them away, but some fatalistic instinct told him that he might yet have need of them.

He closed the locker, watching as the rest of his pathfinders stowed their gear. Tubal Cayne unpacked a piece of surveying gear, a modified theodolite with multiple auspex capabilities, Rama Karayan a rifle with an elongated barrel and oversized sight. Ares Voitek had his servo-harness with its burnished gauntlet icon, and Bror Tyrfingr stowed what appeared to be a leather cestus gauntlet of entwined knotwork with ebon claws like knife blades.

Callion Zaven appeared at Loken's side, opening the locker next to him and slotting home a custom-worked boltgun with a clawed wing motif acid-etched onto its platework. Within the Luna Wolves, such weapons had been for officers, but the killing fields of Murder had shown Loken that many of the warriors in the III Legion wielded heavily embellished armaments.

Zaven saw Loken's attention and said, 'A poor effort, I know. Not a patch on my original bolter.'

'That's not your touchstone?'

'Throne, no!' said Zaven, unbuckling his hand-tooled leather sword belt and holding it between them 'This is my touchstone.'

The sword's handle was tightly wound golden wire, its pommel an ebony talon. The quillons were swept eagle wings with a glittering amethyst mounted at the centre of both sides.

'Draw it,' said Zaven.

Loken did so, and his admiration for the weapon increased tenfold. The weapon had heft, but was incredibly light. The handle and setting had been wrought by human hand, but the blade had never known a smith's hammer. Curved like a Chogorian sweep-sword and milky white, dappling to a jaundiced yellow at its edge, the blade was clearly organic.

'It's a vapour-wraith hewclaw,' said Zaven. 'Cut it from one of their warrior caste on Jupiter after he'd stuck it through my heart. By the time I got out of the apothecarion my Legion had already moved on and I found myself part of the Crusader Host for a time. Disappointing, but it gave me the time to work the hewclaw into a duelling blade. Try it out.'

'Perhaps another time,' said Loken.

'Indeed so,' replied Zaven, taking no offence as he took the sword back from Loken. He grinned. 'I heard how you put down that odious little bastard, Lucius. I wish I'd seen that.'

'It was over quickly,' said Loken. 'There wasn't much to see.'

Zaven laughed, and Loken saw a glint in his eye that might have been admiration or could have been appraisal. 'I don't doubt it. You'll have to tell me about it someday. Or perhaps we might match blades on the journey.'

Loken shook his head. 'Don't you think we have enough enemies before us without looking for them in our own ranks?'

Zaven put his hands up, and Loken was instantly contrite.

'As you wish,' said Zaven, his eyes darting to Loken's equipment case. 'So what did you keep?'

'Nothing,' said Loken, blinking away the after-image of a hooded shadow towards the rear of the compartment. His heartbeat spiked and droplets of sweat beaded on his forehead.

'Come on, everyone keeps something,' grinned Zaven, oblivious to Loken's discomfort. 'Rubio has his little gladius, Varren that woodsman's axe, and Qruze keeps that battered old boltgun. And Cayne has… whatever grubby engineer's tool that is. Tell me, what did you keep?'

Loken slammed his locker shut.

'Nothing,' he said. 'I lost everything on Isstvan Three.'

✠ ✠ ✠

ASIDE FROM THE times he'd been deflowering his half-brother's wife, Raeven had always hated Albard's tower. Situated in the very heart of Lupercalia, it was a grim edifice of black stone and copper sheeting. The city was in a state of mourning, black flags and the entwined eagle and naga banners hanging from every window. Raeven's late father might have been a bastard, but he was at least a bastard who'd earned his people's respect.

Raeven climbed the stairs slowly, taking his time and savouring this culmination of his desires. Lyx and his mother followed behind, as eager as him to consummate this sublime moment.

The tower was kept dark. The Sacristans assigned to Albard's care claimed his eyes could not tolerate light beyond the dimmest lumen. Raeven's spies told him Albard never ventured beyond the tower's top chambers, confined by lunacy and infrequent brushes with moribund lucidity.

'I hope he's rational,' said Lyx, his sister-wife's words seeming to take their cue from Raeven's thoughts as they so often did. 'It won't be any fun if he's lost in madness.'

'Then you should prepare yourself for disappointment,' said Raeven. 'It's a rare day our brother even knows his own name.'

'He will be rational,' said his mother, climbing the steps with wheezing mechanical awkwardness.

'How can you be so sure?' asked Raeven.

'Because I have seen it,' replied his mother, and Raeven knew not to doubt her. That Adoratrice consorts were privy to many secrets was well known all across Molech, but that those of House Devine could witness things not yet come to pass was known only to Lupercalia's Knights.

The Devine Adoratrices had preserved that ability for thousands of years by keeping the genestock of their House from being diluted by inferior bloodlines. It surprised Raeven that Lyx had not seen what his mother had, but the ways of the Adoratrice were not his to know.

Cebella Devine, his mother and Adoratrice Drakaina to his father, was now at least a hundred years of age. Her husband had rejected cosmetic juvenat treatments for vanity's sake, but Cebella embraced them with gusto. Her skin was lifted back over her skull like tightened plastic, fixed in place with surgical sutures to a grotesque headpiece that resembled a device of skull-violating horror.

A hunched pair of biologis servitors followed in Cebella's wake, tethered to her via a series of hissing pipes and feeder tubes. Both were venom-blinded and implanted with numerous monitoring devices and gurgling, hissing cylinders containing gel-nutrients, anti-senescence compounds and restorative cell cultures harvested from vat-grown newborns.

To keep Cebella's brittle bones from undue stresses, an ingenious scaffold of suspensor fields, exo-lattices and fibre-bundle muscles had been surgically bonded with her skeletal structure.

'You'd better be right,' snapped Lyx, straightening her bronze-panelled dress and arranging her hair. 'It'll be pointless if he's no better than a beast or a vegetable.'

Lyx had once been wed to Albard, but her vows had been broken even before he'd put his betrothal ring on her. Though it had been their mother that engineered Raeven and Lyx's relationship, Cebella held a depthless contempt for her daughter that Raeven could only attribute to jealousy of her apparent youth.

'It won't be pointless,' he said, shutting them both up before they could get into one of their all-too-frequent arguments. His mother's sickly flesh contorted with what he presumed was a smile, though it was hard to tell. 'After all this time, I want to see the look in his eyes when I tell him I killed his father.'

'Your father too, and mine,' pointed out Lyx.

Their mother's womb had ejected Raeven mere minutes before

Lyx, but sometimes it felt like decades. Today was such a day.

'I'm aware of that,' he said, pausing just before he reached the upper landing of the tower. 'I want him to see the woman who replaced his own mother on one side, his former wife on the other. I want him to know that everything that was and should have been his is now mine.'

Lyx slipped her arm through his, and his mood lightened. As she had done since they were suckled babes, she knew his moods and needs better than he. To her loving populace, her beauty and body were sustained by calisthenics and subtle juvenat treatments.

Raeven knew better.

Many of his wife's long absences into Lupercalia's hidden valleys were spent undergoing nightmarish chirurgical procedures administered by Shargali-Shi and his coven of androgyne Serpent Cultists. Raeven had witnessed one such operation, a dreadful blend of surgery, alchemy and carnal ritual, and vowed never to do so again. The Ophiolater claimed to channel the Vril-ya, the power of the Serpent Gods once worshipped all across Molech in an earlier age. Raeven didn't know if that was true or not, but the results spoke for themselves. Though nearly sixty-five, Lyx could easily pass for less than half that.

'The serpent moons grow ever fuller,' said Lyx. 'Shargali-Shi will call the Vril-yaal to gather soon.'

He smiled. A six day bacchanalia of intoxicating venoms and writhing hedonism within the hidden temple caverns was just what he needed to lighten the coming burden of planetary command.

'Yes,' he said with a grin of anticipation, and all but bounded up the last few steps.

The entrance vestibule of the topmost chambers was dark, the two Dawn Guard standing sentinel at the onward doorway little more than dark silhouettes. Despite the poor light, Raeven knew both of them; soldiers from his mother's personal detail. He wondered if they'd shared her bed, and judged it more than likely from the conspicuous aversion of their gaze.

They stepped aside as Raeven approached, one opening the door for him as the other bowed deeply. Raeven swept past them and moved through richly appointed antechambers, medicae bays and chambers of observation.

A trio of nervous Sacristans awaited them at the entrance to Albard's private rooms. Each was red-robed, in imitation of their Mechanicum masters, plugged with bionics and rank with sweat and grease. Not quite Cult Mechanicum, but too altered to be thought of as human either. If not for their rote maintenance of the Knights, Raeven would have advocated their elimination years ago.

'My lord,' said a Sacristan Raeven thought was called Onak.

'Does he know?' said Raeven.

'No, my lord,' said Onak. 'Your instructions were most precise.'

'Good, you're a competent Sacristan and it would have irked me to flay you alive.'

All three Sacristans moved aside with alacrity as Raeven pushed open the door. The air that gusted from within was musty and stifling, a fetor of urine, flatus and insanity.

A deep couch with a sagging footstool was set on the edge of a dimmed fireplace that was entirely holographic. Upon the couch sat a man who looked old enough to be Raeven's grandfather. Denied sunlight and the rejuvenating surgeries of his half-brother, Albard Devine was a wretch of a human being, his skull hairless and pale as newly hatched maggots.

Before his mind had snapped, Albard's physique had been robust and stocky, but now he was little more than a drained revenant of parchment-dry flesh sunken over a rack of misaligned bones.

Albard had been cruelly handsome, bluntly so, with the stony harshness people expected of a warrior king. That man was long gone. A gelatinous lesion emerging from the burn scars he'd received upon his maturity leaked yellow pus into his long beard. Clotted with mucus and spilled food the beard reached almost to Albard's waist, and the one eye that stared at the fire was jaundiced and milky with cataracts.

'Is that you, Onak?' said Albard, his voice a tremulous husk of a thing. 'The fire must be dying. I'm cold.'

He doesn't even realise it's a hologram, thought Raeven, and his mother's assurance that his half-brother would be in a state of relative lucidity seemed dashed.

'It's me, brother,' said Raeven, moving to stand beside the couch. The stench of corruption grew stronger, and he wished he'd brought a vial of Caeban root to waft under his nose.

'Father?'

'No, you idiot,' he said. 'Listen closely. It's me, Raeven.'

'Raeven?' said Albard, shifting uneasily on the couch. Something rustled beneath the couch in response to Albard's movement, and Raeven saw the thick, serpentine body of Shesha. His father's last surviving naga shifted position with creaking leathery motion, a forked tongue flicking from her fanged mouth. Well over two centuries old, Shesha was in the last years of life, near blind and her long, scaled body already beginning to ossify.

'Yes, brother,' said Raeven, kneeling beside Albard and reluctantly placing a hand on his knee. The fabric of his coverlet was stiff and encrusted, but Raeven felt the brittle, bird-like bones beneath. A haze of filth billowed from the coverlet, and Raeven felt his gorge rise.

'I don't want you here,' said Albard and Raeven felt a flutter of hope that his half-brother was at least in touching distance of sanity. 'I told them not to let you in.'

'I know, but I have something to tell you.'

'I don't want to hear it.'

'You will.'

'No.'

'Father is dead.'

Albard finally deigned to look at him, and Raeven saw himself reflected in that glossy white, hopeless eye. The augmetic had long since ceased to function.

'Dead?'

'Yes, dead,' said Raeven, leaning in despite the rancid miasma surrounding Albard. His half-brother blinked his one eye and looked past his shoulder, now aware of the presence of others in the room.

'Who else is here?' he said, sounding suddenly afraid.

'Mother, *my* mother,' said Raeven. 'And Lyx. You remember her?'

Albard's head sank back to his chest, and Raeven wondered if he'd drifted off into some chem-induced slumber. The Sacristans kept Albard moderately sedated at all times to keep the ravaged synapses of his brain from causing an explosive aneurysm within his skull.

'I remember a whore by that name,' said Albard as a rivulet of yellowed saliva leaked from the dry gash of his mouth.

Raeven grinned as he felt Lyx's rising fury. Men had endured days of unimaginable agony for far less.

'Yes, that's her,' said Raeven. He'd pay for that later, but more and more he relished the punishment more than the pleasure.

'Did you kill him?' said Albard, fixing Raeven with his rheumy gaze. 'Did you kill my father?'

Raeven looked back over his shoulder as Cebella and Lyx drew closer to better savour Albard's humiliation. His mother's features were unmoving, but Lyx's cheeks were flushed in the light of the holographic fire.

'I did, yes, and the memory of it still makes me smile,' said Raeven. 'I should have done it a long time ago. The old bastard just wouldn't let go, wouldn't hand me what was rightfully mine.'

Albard let out a wheezing exhalation of breath as dry as winds over the Tazkhar steppe. It took a second for Raeven to recognise the sound as bitter laughter.

'Rightfully yours? You remember who you're talking to? I'm the firstborn of House Devine.'

'Ah, of course,' said Raeven, standing and wiping his hands on a silk handkerchief he withdrew from his brocaded coat. 'Yes, well, it's not like our House can be led by a cripple who can't even bond with his Knight, now is it?'

Albard coughed into his beard, a dry, hacking retch that brought up yet more phlegmy matter. When he looked up, his eye was clearer than it had been in decades.

'I've had a lot of time to think, over these long years, brother,' said Albard, when the coughing fit subsided. 'I know I could have recovered enough to leave this tower, but you and Lyx made sure that never happened, didn't you?'

'Mother helped,' said Raeven. 'So how does it feel, brother? To see everything that should have been yours is now mine?'

'Honestly? I couldn't care less,' said Albard. 'You think after all this time I care what happens to me? Mother's pet Sacristans keep me barely alive, and I know I'll never leave this tower. Tell me, *brother*, why in the world would I care what you do any more?'

'Then we're done here,' said Raeven, fighting to keep his anger from showing. He'd come here to humiliate Albard, but the wretched bastard had been hollowed out too much to appreciate the pain.

He turned to face Cebella and Lyx. 'Take the blood you need, but make it quick.'

'Quick?' pouted Lyx.

'Quick,' repeated Raeven. 'The Lord Generals and the Legions have called for a council of war and I'll not start my governorship by having anyone doubting my competency.'

Lyx shrugged and pulled a naga-fang filleting knife from the many concealed folds of her dress as she stood above the shrivelled wraith of her former husband and half-brother.

'Shargali-Shi needs the blood of the firstborn,' said Lyx, dropping to one knee and resting the blade against the side of Albard's neck. 'Not all of it, but a lot.'

Albard spat in her face.

'This may be quick,' she said, wiping her face, 'but I promise it will be agonising.'

SEVEN

The Nameless Fortress
War council
The gift

LOKEN STEPPED ONTO the cold embarkation deck of the orbital fortress. Fixed a hundred kilometres above Titan's surface and swathed in the darkness of its night-side, the bleak station spun gently above an active cryo-volcano. Rassuah had flown the *Tarnhelm* onto its embarkation deck with a light hand at the controls, her every auspex warning that she was bracketed by lethal ordnance.

Vapour rose from the void-cold flanks of the *Tarnhelm*, and Loken sweated in his armour. The deck was enormous, with space enough for great prison-barques to disgorge their human cargo and the custodians of the fortress to render them.

A squad of mortal warriors in gloss-red armour and silver-visored helms awaited him at the base of the ramp, but Loken ignored them in favour of the broadly built veteran standing before them.

Armoured identically to Loken, the warrior's deeply tanned and deeper lined face were well known to him. White hair, kept close-cropped, and a neat beard of the same hue made him look old. Pale eyes that had seen too much were even older.

'Loken,' said Iacton Qruze, his voice little more than a whisper. 'It's good to see you, lad.'

'Qruze,' replied Loken, coming forward to take the old warrior's hand. The grip was firm, unyielding, as if Qruze were afraid to let go. 'What is this place?'

'A place of forgetting,' said Qruze.

'A prison?'

Qruze nodded, as though reluctant to expound on the grim purpose behind the nameless fortress.

'An unkind place,' said Loken, taking in the featureless walls and bleak, institutional grimness. 'Not a place to which the ideals of the Imperium easily cling.'

'Perhaps not,' agreed Qruze, 'but only the young and naïve believe wars can be won without such places. And to my lasting regret, I am neither.'

'None of us are, Iacton,' said Loken. 'But why do we find you here?'

Qruze hesitated, and Loken saw his eyes dart in the direction of *Tisiphone*, the great double-edged sword harnessed across his back.

'Did you bring them?' asked Qruze.

'All but one,' answered Loken, curious as to why Qruze had ignored his question.

'Who didn't you get?'

'Severian.'

Qruze nodded. 'He was always going to be the hardest to convince. Well, our mission just went from almost impossible to nigh suicidal.'

'I think that's the part he objected to.'

'He always was a clever man,' said Qruze.

'You knew him?' asked Loken, and instantly regretted it when he saw a distant look enter Qruze's eyes.

'I fought alongside the Twenty-Fifth Company on Dahinta,' said Qruze.

'The overseers,' said Loken, remembering the hard fought campaigns to cleanse the derelict cities of scavenger machines.

'Aye, it was Severian that got us past the circuit defences of the Silicate Palace to the inner precincts of the Archdroid,' said Qruze. 'He saved us months of grinding attrition. I remember when he first brought word of the–'

Loken was well used to Iacton Qruze's wandering reminiscences, but this was not the time to indulge his fondness for old Legion history.

'We should be going,' he said before Qruze could go any further.

'Aye, you're right, lad,' agreed Qruze with a sigh. 'The sooner I'm away from this damn place the better. Necessity is all well and good, but that doesn't make what we do in its name any easier.'

Loken turned to board the *Tarnhelm*, but Qruze made no move to follow him.

'Iacton?'

'This won't be easy for you, Garviel,' said Qruze.

Instantly alert, Loken said, 'What won't?'

'There's someone here who needs to speak to you.'

'To me? Who?'

Qruze inclined his head towards the red-armoured gaolers, who snapped to attention in escort formation.

'She asked for you by name, lad,' said Qruze.

'Who did?' repeated Loken.

'Best you see for yourself.'

OF ALL THE hells Loken had seen and imagined, few compared to the bleak desolation and hopelessness of this orbital prison.

Every aspect of its design appeared calculated to crush the human spirit, from the grim institutional mundanity of its appearance to the oppressive gloom that offered no respite or any hope that its occupants would ever see open skies again.

Qruze had boarded the *Tarnhelm*, leaving him in the custody of the fortress's gaolers. They moved with precision and appeared to care little for the fact that he was a warrior of the Legions. To them, he was just another detail to be factored into their security protocols.

They marched him through vaulted corridors of dark iron and echoing chambers that still bore faint traces of blood and faeces no amount of cleaning fluid could ever scrub away. The route was not direct, and several times Loken was sure they had doubled back over their course, following a twisting path deeper into the heart of the fortress.

His escorting gaolers were trying to disorient him, make him lose any sense of which way they might have come or in which direction lay the exit. A tactic that might work on ordinary prisoners, already half-broken and desperate, but one that was wasted on a legionary with an eidetic sense of direction.

As they marched down a winding screw-stair, Loken tried to imagine who could be incarcerated here that might have asked for him by name.

It should have been easy; Qruze had said 'she', and he knew few females.

Legion life was an overtly masculine environment, though the Imperium cared little for the sex of the soldiers that made up its armies, flew its starships and facilitated its operation. Most of the women he'd met were dead, so maybe this was someone who'd since learned of his existence. A sister or mother, or perhaps even the daughter of someone he'd once known.

He heard distant screams and the soft echo of weeping. The

sounds had no obvious source and Loken had the unsettling impression of years of misery so intense they had imprinted on the walls themselves.

His guardians eventually led him to a barred chamber suspended over a vault of complete darkness. A number of passageways led from the chamber, each narrow enough for a mortal, but almost claustrophobic for a warrior of his stature. They moved along the rightmost corridor, and Loken detected the unmistakable stench of human flesh and ingrained filth and sweat. But most of all he smelled despair.

His escort stopped at a cell secured by a heavy iron door marked with alphanumerics and what looked like some kind of lingua-technis. It meant nothing to him, as he suspected was the point. Everything about this place was designed to be unfamiliar and unwelcoming.

A lock disengaged and the door rose into the frame with a clock-work ratcheting sound, though none of the guards had touched it. Remote contact with a centralised control room most likely. The guards stood aside and Loken didn't waste any words on them, ducking beneath the lintel and stepping within.

Almost no light penetrated the cell, only diffuse reflections from the corridor outside, but that was more than enough for Loken to make out the outline of a kneeling figure.

Loken was no expert on the female form, but the figure's loose robes gave little in its shape to distinguish it. A head turned towards him at the sound of the door opening, and Loken saw something familiar in its faintly elongated occipital structure.

A faint buzzing sound came from the high ceiling, and a humming florescent lumen disc sparked to life. It flickered for a few seconds before the freshly routed power stabilised.

At first Loken thought this was a hallucination or another vision of someone long dead, but when she spoke, it was the voice he knew from the many hours they had spent in remembrance.

He remembered her as being small, even though most mortals were small to him. Her skin had been so black he'd wondered if it had been dyed, but the sickly light of the lumen disk made it seem somehow grey.

Her skull was hairless, made ovoid by cranial implants.

She smiled, the expression faltering and unfamiliar. Loken guessed it had been a long time since she had need of those particular muscles.

'Hello, Captain Loken,' said Mersadie Oliton.

HACKED FROM THE rock of the mountains long before the I Legion built the Citadel of Dawn, the Hall of Flames was a raked amphitheatre of rulership. In the long centuries since then, a vault had had been built around the amphitheatre, a fortress around the vault and a city around the fortress.

Much had changed on Molech since then, but the Hall retained much of its original purpose. The firstborn scions of House Devine were still ritually burned here and the planet's rulers still made decisions affecting the lives of millions here. It was, however, no longer a place where mechanised warriors settled their honour duels with fights to the death.

Right now, Raeven almost wished it was.

A hail of stubber fire from *Banelash* would make short work of the squabbling representatives and silence their strident voices.

As pleasant a fantasy as that was, Raeven took a deep breath and tried to pay attention to what was going on around him. Enthroned at the centre of the amphitheatre, Raeven held the bull-headed sceptre said to have been borne by the Stormlord himself. The artefact was certainly ancient, but that anything could have survived thousands of years without blemish seemed unlikely.

He dragged his focus back to the five hundred men and women filling the tiered chamber, the senior military officers of Molech. Aides, scriveners, calculus logi, savants and ensigns surrounded them like acolytes, and Raeven was reminded of Shargali-Shi and his Serpent Cult devotees.

Castor Alcade and three grim-faced Ultramarines sat on the stone benches at floor-level across from Vitus Salicar. He too was not alone, with a Blood Angel in red gold to his left, another in black to his right.

Tyana Kourion, Lord General of the Grand Army of Molech, sat motionless in the centre of the next tier in her dress greens, stoic and grim. Colonels from a dozen regiments gathered around her like moths drawn to a beneficent flame. Raeven didn't know them, but recognised Kourion's immediate subordinates.

The heads of the four operational theatres were each seated beneath the sigil denoting one of the cardinal compass points.

Clad in her signature drakescale burnoose and golden eye-mask was Marshal Edoraki Hakon of the Northern Oceanic, and sat along from her was Colonel Oskur von Valkenberg of the Western Marches, whose uniform looked as though he'd slept in it for a month. Commander Abdi Kheda of the Kushite Eastings wore full body armour as though she expected to fight her way back through the jungles to her posting, and finally the Khan of the Southern Steppe, Corwen Malbek, sat cross-legged with a longsword and rifle balanced across his knees.

Behind the four commanders sat hundreds of colonels, majors and captains of the various regiments of the Imperial Army, each clad in their battledress armour. The sheer variety of uniforms had the effect of making the gathered soldiery look like revellers in a gaudy carnival. Until now, Raeven hadn't quite grasped just how many regiments were garrisoned on Molech.

His mother and Lyx were in the great gallery above, already in bitter disagreement over the course he should take.

Lyx spoke of the vision she'd had the night of Raeven's Becoming, of how his actions would decide the course of a great war fought on Molech.

Both claimed the power of foresight, but neither could say with any certainty what those actions would be or in whose favour he would turn the war. Was he to align with Horus, and in so doing be granted dominion of the systems around Molech? Or was it his destiny to fight the Warmaster and win glory and repute in his defeat? Both roads offered hope of fulfilling his sister's prophetic vision, but which to choose?

In addition to the ground forces, Molech boasted a sizeable naval presence, with a fleet of over sixty vessels, including eight capital ships and numerous frigates less than a hundred years old. Lord Admiral Brython Semper appeared to be asleep, though such a feat was surely impossible in so noisy an environment. Uniformed ratings took notes for him, but Raeven suspected Semper would never read them. He had no interest in ground-pounding warfare. If the Warmaster's forces reached Molech's surface, he would already be lost to the void.

Seated apart from the branches of conventional warriors were the Mechanicum contingents, brooding figures swathed in a mix of reds and blacks who each kept to their own little enclaves. Raeven knew more than most of the Mechanicum, but even that was rumour and second-hand gossip culled from his spies among the Sacristans.

In the position of prime importance stood the Mechanicum being designated Bellona Modwen of the Ordo Reductor. The senior Martian Adept was fully encased in gloss-green cybernetic body armour that made her look like a seated sarcophagus. The sinister mech-warrior cohorts of Thallax were hers to command, as was a fearsome array of war machines, tanks and unknowable technologies locked in the catacombs of Mount Torger.

Her magi trained the Sacristans and kept the Knights functional. As such, the Martian Priesthood was a substantial power bloc on Molech and had the right to attend every military conclave, though they seldom exercised that right.

The Mechanicum and the fleet might be keeping their own counsel, but the junior officers of the Army were making up for their absent voices. They loudly hectored the speakers below them, either in complete agreement or to drown out what they saw as rank stupidity.

Raeven couldn't decide which.

Current Right of Voice belonged to the Warmonger of Legio Fortidus, an amazonian looking woman in an oil-stained khaki bodyglove named Ur-Nammu. In heavily accented Gothic, she set out the position of her Legio, which, to Raeven's ears ran thusly.

Princeps Uta-Dagon and Utu-Lerna would not endorse any plan that didn't involve charging the Titans of Legio Fortidus straight at the enemy the instant they landed.

Opinicus, the Invocatio of Legio Gryphonicus, held the view that just because the rest of Legio Fortidus had been wiped out on Mars was no reason for the rest of them to throw themselves on the swords of self-sacrifice.

As Raeven understood it, both Ur-Nammu and Opinicus undertook roughly the same role within their Legios, a form of ambassador between the inhuman Titan princeps and those they must perforce fight alongside.

Their bickering was pointless, for Carthal Ashur, the cruelly handsome Calator Martialis of Legio Crucius, had yet to speak. The lesser ambassadors would eventually defer to him, for the largest Titan on Molech was a Crucius engine, the ancient colossus known as *Paragon of Terra*. Ashur carried the authority of the Princeps Magnus, Etana Kalonice, and if she had been roused from her war-dreams beneath Iron Fist Mountain, then the smaller Legios would undoubtedly fall into line behind her.

The ambassadors of the Legios eventually finished speaking and deliberations moved onto logistical matters: the establishment of supply lines, ordnance depots and stockpiling. Raeven's threshold for boredom – already stretched thin by the hours of debate – was pushed to breaking point by long recitations of supply levels. A dozen aexactor clerks had already spoken, and dozens more stood in line to be heard.

Raeven rose from his throne and hammered the sceptre on the stone floor of the hall, eliciting fearful gasps from the reliquary keepers. He drew his pistol and aimed it at the nearest scrivener and his parchment-spewing data-slate.

'You. Shut up. Right now,' he said, his drawing of the weapon cutting through the droning account of lasrifle power-cell short-ages at the Kushite Preceptory Line. 'All of you listen very carefully to what I'm about to say. I will shoot the next scribe who dares to read an inventory list or stock level. Right through the head.'

The clerks lowered their data-slates and shuffled uncomfortably in place.

'That's what I thought,' said Raeven. 'Right, will someone tell me something of actual bloody importance? Please.'

Castor Alcade of the Ultramarines stood and said, 'What sort of thing are you looking to hear, Lord Devine? This is how wars are fought, with properly emplaced lines of supply and a fully func-tioning infrastructure in place to support the front-line forces. If you want to hold this world against the Warmaster, then these are the things you need to know.'

'No,' said Raeven. 'They're the things *you* need to know. All I need to know is where I will ride into battle. I have an army of scriveners, quartermasters and savants to deal with numbers and lists.'

'The Five Hundred Worlds are burning,' snapped Alcade, 'yet my Ultramarines stand ready to fight and die for a world not their own. Speak like that again, and I'll take every warrior back to Ultramar.'

'The Emperor Himself tasked your Legion and the Blood Angels with the defence of Molech,' said Raeven with a mocking smile. 'You would forsake that duty? I don't think so.'

'You would be wise not to test that theory,' warned Alcade.

'I am the rightful ruler of Molech,' snapped Raeven. 'Military command of this world falls to me, and if I learned anything from my father, may he rest in peace, it's that a ruler needs to surround himself with the best people he can, delegate authority and then not interfere.'

'An Imperial commander can delegate authority,' said Alcade, 'but never responsibility.'

Raeven struggled to control his anger, feeling it twist in his chest like a poisoned blade.

'My House has ruled Molech for generations,' he said with cold hostility. 'I know the meaning of responsibility.'

Alcade shook his head. 'I'm not sure you do, Lord Devine. Responsibility is a unique concept. You can share it with others, but your portion is not diminished. You may delegate it, but it is still with you. Blood has given you command of Molech, and its security is *your* responsibility. No evasion, or wilful avoidance of that fact can shift it to others.'

Raeven forced a mask of composure to settle upon his features and nodded as though accepting the legate's patronising words as wisdom.

'Your words carry the acumen of your primarch,' he said, each word filling his belly with cankerous venom. 'I will, of course, review the recommendations of the tithe-takers in due course, but perhaps this is a time for war stratagems rather than dry lists of numbers and dispute between allies?'

Alcade nodded and bowed in wary agreement.

'Indeed so, Lord Devine,' said Alcade, sitting back down.

Raeven let out a poisoned breath that felt like it was scorching
his throat. He fixed his gaze on Brython Semper, taking a moment
to compose himself and giving the Lord Admiral's aide time to
elbow him in the ribs.

'Admiral Semper, can you tell us how long we have before the
Warmaster's forces reach Molech?'

Dressed in a regal purple frock coat of baroque ornamentation,
Brython Semper stood and fastened his top button. The Lord
Admiral's hair was silver white and pulled into a long scalp lock,
his face a scarred, partially augmetic mask.

'Of course, my lord,' he said, inloading the contents of his aide's
data-slate to his ocular implant. 'The astropathic choirs send word
of impending arrivals of scores of vessels, perhaps as many as
forty or fifty in total. Nor are the approaching craft making any
secret of their arrival. I'm getting all sorts of nonsense about astropaths hearing wolves howling in the warp and ships screaming
their designations. More than likely it's some form of empyreal
distortion or simply reflected vox-transmissions, but it's clear the
Warmaster *wants* us to know he's coming. Though if he thinks
we're a bunch of cowards who'll run screaming at the first sign of
the enemy, he's in for a rude awakening.'

Vitus Salicar interrupted the Lord Admiral before he could
continue. 'It would be a mistake to think that just because you
outnumber the Warmaster's fleet, you hold the upper hand.
Legion void war is a savage, merciless thing.'

Semper bowed to the Blood Angel and said, 'I know full well
how dangerous the Space Marines are, captain.'

'You don't,' said Salicar sadly. 'We are killers, reapers of flesh.
You must never forget that.'

Before the Lord Admiral could respond to the Blood Angel's melancholic tone, Raeven said, 'How soon will the enemy be here?'

Visibly struggling to contain his temper in the face of Salicar's dismissal of his fleet's capabilities, Semper spoke slowly and carefully.

'The Master of Astropaths' best estimate is a real space breach any day now, putting them within reach of Molech in around two weeks. I've already issued a muster order to pull our picket ships back from the system's edge.'

'You won't engage the traitors in open space?'

'Since I am not in the habit of throwing away the lives of my crews, no, I will not,' said Semper. 'As Captain Salicar helpfully pointed out, the warships of the Space Marines are not to be underestimated, so our best course of action is to dispatch a provocateur force to goad the traitors onto the horns of our orbital guns. Our main fleet will remain within the umbra of the orbital batteries on the Karman line. Between the hammer and anvil of our static guns and the warfleet, we can gut the traitor ships before they can land so much as a single warrior.'

Despite his bombastic tone, Raeven liked the cut of Semper's jib and nodded.

'Do it, Lord Admiral,' he said. 'Dispatch the provocateur force and wish them good hunting.'

THE CELL HAD no furniture, not even a bed. A thin mattress lay folded in one corner, together with a chipped night-soil pot and a small box, like a presentation case for a medal.

'You look like you've seen a ghost,' said Mersadie, rising from her kneeling position.

Loken's mouth opened, but no sounds came out.

This was the second dead person he'd seen, but this one was

flesh and blood. She was here. Mersadie Oliton, his personal remembrancer.

She was alive. Here. Now.

She wasn't the same though. The harsh light revealed faded scars tracing looping arcs over the sides and upper surfaces of her diminished skull. Surgical scars. Excisions.

She saw him looking and said, 'They took out my embedded memory coils. All the images and all the remembrances I'd stored. All gone. All I have left of them are my organic memories and even they're beginning to fade.'

'I left you on the *Vengeful Spirit*,' said Loken. 'I thought you must be dead.'

'I would be if it wasn't for Iacton,' replied Mersadie.

'Iacton? Iacton Qruze?'

'Yes. He saved us from the murder of the remembrancers and got us off the ship,' said Mersadie. 'He didn't tell you?'

'No,' said Loken. 'He didn't.'

'We escaped with Iacton and Captain Garro.'

'You were on the *Eisenstein*?' said Loken, disbelief and wonder competing for his full attention. Qruze had said little of the perilous journey from Isstvan, but neglecting to mention Mersadie's survival beggared belief.

'And I wasn't the only one Iacton saved.'

'What do you mean?'

'Euphrati got off the *Vengeful Spirit*, Kyril too.'

'Sindermann and Keeler are alive?'

Mersadie nodded. 'As far as I know, but before you ask, I don't know where they are. I haven't seen either of them in years.'

Loken paced the interior of the cell, raw emotions surging like a chaotic tide within him. Sindermann had been a dear friend to him. A mentor of superlative intellect and a confidante of sorts, a bridge between transhuman sensibilities and mortal concerns.

That Keeler had also survived was a miracle, for the imagist had a real knack for getting herself into trouble.

'You didn't know she was alive?' asked Mersadie.

'No,' said Loken.

'You've heard of the Saint?'

Loken shook his head. 'No. What saint?'

'You *have* been out of the loop, haven't you?'

Loken paused, angry and confused. She was not to blame, but she was here. He wanted to lash out, but released a shuddering breath that seemed to expel a heavy weight of bilious humours.

'I was dead, I think,' he said at last. 'For a while. Or as good as dead. Maybe I was just lost, so very lost.'

'But you came back,' said Mersadie, reaching out to take his hand. 'They brought you back because you're needed.'

'So I'm told,' said Loken wearily, curling his fingers around hers, careful not to squeeze too hard.

They stood unmoving, neither willing to break the silence or the shared intimacy. Her skin was soft, reminding Loken of a fleeting moment in his life. When he had been young and innocent, when he had loved and been loved in return. When he had been human.

Loken sighed and released Mersadie's hand.

'I have to get you out of here,' he said.

'You can't,' she said, withdrawing her hand.

'I'm one of Malcador's chosen,' said Loken. 'I'll send word to the Sigillite and have you taken back to Terra. I'm not letting you rot away in here another minute.'

'Garviel,' said Mersadie, and her use of his given name stopped him in his tracks. 'They're not going to let me out of here. Not for now, at least. I spent a long time in the heart of the Warmaster's flagship. People have been executed for a lot less.'

'I'll vouch for you,' said Loken. 'I'll guarantee your loyalty.'

Mersadie shook her head and folded her arms.

'If you didn't know who I was, if you hadn't shared your life with me, would you want someone like me released? If I was a stranger, what would you do? Turn me loose or keep me imprisoned?'

Loken took a step forward. 'I can't just leave you here. You don't deserve this.'

'You're right, I don't deserve this, but you don't have a choice,' said Mersadie. 'You *have* to leave me.'

Her hand reached up to brush the bare metal of his unmarked plate. Thin fingers traced the line of his pauldron and swept across the curve of the shoulder guard.

'It's strange to see you in this armour.'

'I no longer have a Legion,' he said simply, angry at her wilful desire to languish in this prison.

She nodded. 'They told me you died on Isstvan, but I didn't believe them. I knew you were alive.'

'You knew I'd survived?'

'I did.'

'How?'

'Euphrati told me.'

'You said you didn't know where she was.'

'I don't.'

'Then how–'

Mersadie turned away, as though reluctant to give voice to her thoughts for fear of his ridicule. She bent to retrieve the presentation case from the ground next to the mattress. When she turned back to him, he saw her eyes were wet with tears.

'I dreamed of Euphrati,' she said. 'She told me you'd come here. I know, I know, it sounds ridiculous, but after all I've seen and been through, it's almost normal.'

The anger drained from Loken, replaced by an echoing sense of helplessness. Mersadie's words touched something deep within him, and he could hear the soft breath of a third person, the ghost of a shadow in a room where none existed.

'It isn't ridiculous,' said Loken. 'What did she say?'

'She told me to give you this,' said Mersadie, holding out the case. 'To pass on.'

'What is it?'

'Something that once belonged to Iacton Qruze,' she said. 'Something she said he needs to have again.'

Loken took the box, but didn't open it.

'She said to remind Iacton that he is the Half-heard no longer, that his voice will be heard louder than any other in his Legion.'

'What does that mean?'

'I don't know,' said Mersadie. 'It was a dream, it's not like it's an exact science.'

Loken nodded, though what he was hearing made little sense. At least as little sense as answering a summons to war on the word of a dead man.

'Did Euphrati say anything else?' he asked.

Mersadie nodded and the tears brimming on the edge of her eyes like a river about to break its banks spilled down her cheeks.

'Yes,' sobbed Mersadie. 'She said to say goodbye.'

EIGHT

The Eater of Lives
Confrontation
Hope in lies

THE APOTHECARION DECKS of the *Endurance* were cold, bare metal and reeked of the embalmers' art. Acrid chemicals fogged the air and hissing vats of noxious fluids bubbled on retorts between dull iron slabs, suspended cryo-tubes and racks of surgical equipment.

Mortarion had spent altogether too much time here already in the pain-filled days following the attack of Meduson's sleeper assassins. Swathed in counterseptic wraps and bathed in regenerative poultices like an embalmed king of the Gyptia, his superhuman metabolism had taken only seven hours to undo the worst of the damage.

A squad of Deathshroud Terminators escorted him through the artificially cold space with their manreapers gripped loosely. The primarch's honour guard lightly rocked their outsized scythes from shoulder to shoulder to keep them in motion. Even on the flagship, they were taking no chances.

Frost webbed the canted hafts and the light of organ-harvesters glittered from the ice forming on the blades. Armoured in dusky white armour edged in a mixture of crimson and olive drab, they spread out in a pyramid formation, threat auspex alert for the intruder they knew was somewhere on this deck.

Mortarion went bareheaded, fresh skin grafts flushed with highly oxygenated blood that made him look healthier than he had in centuries. A rebreather gorget still covered the lower half of his face, and gusts of earthy breath sighed from its portcullis-like grille. His sockets were craters cut in a lunar landscape, his eyes nuggets of amberglass.

Silence was clamped to his armour's backplate. He had no need of its edge, the Deathshroud had more than enough to go round. Instead, he carried the Lantern, a colossal Shenlongi pistol, drum-fed and possessed of an energy matrix few beam weapons of comparable size could match.

The Deathshroud spread out as their sweep of the chamber reached the impregnable vault at its end. Sealed with locks of magnificent complexity, the gene-vault was a place of mystery and a repository of the Death Guard's future.

Caipha Morarg, late of 24th Breacher Squad, now serving as Mortarion's equerry, shook his head and put up his bolter as he followed his master into the apothecarion.

'My lord, there's no one here,' he said.

'There is, Caipha,' said Mortarion, his voice the breath of a parched desert wind. 'I can feel it.'

'We've swept the deck from end to end and side to side,' reaffirmed Morarg. 'If there was something here, we'd already have found it.'

'There's still one place to look,' said Mortarion.

Morarg followed the primarch's gaze.

'The gene-vault?' he said. 'It's void-hardened and energy shielded. It's a wonder the damn Apothecaries can get in.'

'Do you doubt me, Caipha?' whispered Mortarion.

'Never, my lord.'

'And have you ever known me to be wrong in such matters?'

'No, my lord.'

'Then trust me when I say there's something in there.'

'Some*thing*?'

Mortarion nodded, and he canted his head to one side, as though listening to sounds only he could hear. The muscles in his face twitched, but with the gorget obscuring his jaw, it was impossible to be certain what expression he made.

'Open the door,' he ordered, and a gaggle of hazard-suited Legions serfs ran to it with pneumatic key-drivers and one-time cipher code wands. They inserted the power-keys, but before any were engaged, a green-cloaked Apothecary approached Mortarion under the watchful gaze of the Deathshroud.

'My lord,' said the Apothecary. 'I beg you to reconsider.'

'What is your name?' asked Mortarion.

'Koray Burcu, my lord.'

'We have just breached Molech's system edge, Apothecary Burcu, and there is an intruder aboard the *Endurance*,' said Mortarion. 'It is behind that door. I require you to open it. Now.'

Koray Burcu wilted under Mortarion's gaze, but to his credit, the Apothecary stood his ground.

'My lord, please,' said Burcu. 'I implore you to withdraw from the apothecarion. The gene-vault must be kept sterile and at positive pressure. This entire stock of gene-seed is at risk of contamination if the door is opened even a fraction.'

'Nevertheless, you will do as I order,' said Mortarion. 'I can do it without you, Apothecary, but it will take time. And in that time, what do you think an intruder might be doing in there?'

Burcu considered the primarch's words and made his way to the gleaming vault door. Numerous key-drivers turned simultaneously under Burcu's direction as he wanded a helix-code unique to this moment and which would change immediately upon the door's opening.

The door split at its junction with the wall and a blast of frozen, sharp-edged air escaped from within. Mortarion felt it cut the skin of his face, relishing the needle-like jab of cold. The door swung wider and the hazard-suited thralls withdrew as the reek of preserving chemicals and frost-resistant power cells tainted the air with bio-mechanical flavours. Mortarion tasted something else on the air, a fetor of something so lethal that only one such as he could authorise its release.

But such things were stored in the deepest magazines, locked away in vaults even more secure than this.

'Touch nothing,' warned Burcu, moving ahead of the Death-shroud as they stepped over the high threshold of the gene-vault.

Mortarion turned to Morarg and said, 'Seal the door behind me, and only open it again on my express order.'

'My lord?' said Morarg. 'After Dwell, my place is at your side!'

'Not this time,' said Mortarion and his meaning was ironclad.

Devotion to duty clamped down on Morarg's next words and he nodded stiffly as Mortarion turned and followed Koray Burcu into the vault. No sooner was Mortarion inside than the heavy adamantium door swung closed.

The space within was a hundred metre square vault of frost-white and gleaming silver. Shielded banks of gurgling cryo-tubes lined the walls, and rows of centrifuge drums formed a central aisle.

Illuminated sigils and runic inscriptions of genetic purity flick-ered on brass-rimmed data-slates, and Mortarion extrapolated mental maps of the gene-code fragments. Here was a collection of mucranoids, there a chemical bath of zygotes that would one day be a Betcher's Gland. Behind them, bubbling cylinders of eyeballs.

Half-formed organs floated in gestation tanks and puffs of vapour from humming condensers filled the air with chill moisture that crunched underfoot in microscopic ice crystals. Koray Burcu claimed the atmosphere within the vault was sterile, but such was not the case. The air vibrated with potential, a thing pressing itself upon the fabric of reality like a newborn in a rupturing birth sac.

Only he could feel it. Only he knew what it was.

The Deathshroud advanced cautiously, and Mortarion sensed their confusion. To them, the vault was empty, no sign of the intruder their primarch said they would find. That they believed their gene-father might be mistaken amused him. What must it be like for a warrior of the Legions to think such a thing?

Much as it was for a primarch, he supposed.

But they could not sense what he could sense.

Mortarion had spent a lifetime on a world where the monstrous creations of rogue geneticists and spirit channelling corpse-whisperers had haunted the fogbound crags of Barbarus. Where monsters truly worthy of the name were wrought into being every day. Had even fashioned a few of his own.

Mortarion knew the spoor of such beasts, but more than that, he recognised the scent of one of his own.

'You see, my lord,' said Apothecary Burcu. 'It's plain to see there's nothing here, so can we all please vacate the gene-labs?'

'You're wrong,' said Mortarion.

'My lord?' said Burcu, consulting a grainy holo floating above his narthecium gauntlet. 'I don't understand.'

'He's here, he just can't show himself yet, can you?'

The primarch's words were addressed to the air, but the voice that answered sounded like rocks grinding against one another in a mudslide and seemed to echo from all around them.

'Meat. Need meat.'

Mortarion nodded, already suspecting that was why he had chosen this place. The Deathshroud formed a circle around Mortarion, warscythes at the ready, sensorium desperately searching for the source of the voice.

'My lord, what is that?' asked Burcu.

'An old friend,' said Mortarion. 'One I thought lost.'

No one ever thought of the Death Lord as being quick. Relentless, yes. Implacable and dogged, absolutely. But quick? No, never that.

Silence was a hard iron blur, and by the time its blade completed its circuit, all seven of the Deathshroud lay slain, simply bisected at their midriffs. An apocalyptic quantity of gore erupted within the vault, a glut of shimmering, impossibly bright blood. It sprayed the walls and flooded the polished steel deck plates in a red tide. Mortarion tasted its bitter tang.

Apothecary Burcu backed away from him, his eyes wide and disbelieving behind the visor of his helm. Mortarion didn't stop him.

'My lord?' begged the Apothecary. 'What are you doing?'

'Something grim, Koray,' said Mortarion. 'Something necessary.'

The air in front of Mortarion looked scratched, a phantom image of a humanoid form etched on an incredibly fine pane of glass. Or a pict-feed with the half-formed impression of a body on it, an outline of something that existed only as potential.

The scratched, hurried impression of form stepped into the lake of blood and gradually, impossibly, the liquid's outward spread began to reverse. Slowly, but with greater speed as the rich fluid of all life was drawn into its ethereal form, a figure began to take shape.

First a pair of feet, then ankles, calves, knees and muscular thighs. Then pelvic bones, a spine, organs and whipping, cording, glistening musculature wrapping itself around a wet red skeleton.

As though an invisible mould were being filled with the blood of the Deathshroud, the powerful form of a towering, transhuman warrior took shape.

Fed and fashioned from the blood of the dead, it was form without the casing of skin. A fleshless revenant with butcher's hocks of meat laced around ossified ribs, hardened femurs and a skull like a rock. Red-rimmed eyes of madness stared out from lidless sockets and though the body was yet freshly made, it reeked of putrefaction. The thing's mouth worked jerkily, rubbery tendons pulling taut as the exposed jawline flexed in its housing of bone.

A tongue, raw and purple, ran along fresh-grown nubs of teeth.

For the briefest instant, the illusion of rebirth was complete, but it didn't last. Flaccid white runnels of decomposition streaked the red meat like fatty tissue, and curls of corpse gas lifted from flesh that wriggled as though infested with feasting maggots. Weeping sores opened across the musculature and purulent blisters popped like soap bubbles to leak viscous mucus.

Glass cracked and warning bells began chiming.

Mortarion looked to his left as, one by one, the bell jars of developing zygotes exploded with uncontrolled growth. Rampant necrosis swelled from algal fronds of stem cells and nascent buds of organs. Veined with black, they grew and grew until the bloated mass ruptured with flatulent brays of stinking fumes.

Chemical baths curdled in an instant, their surfaces frothing with scum and overflowing in glutinous ropes. The centrifuges vibrated as the specimens within expanded and mutated with ultra-rapid growth before dying just as quickly.

Behind the primarch, Apothecary Burcu was desperately trying to manipulate one of the key-drivers while punching in a code that had already been rendered obsolete.

'Please, my lord!' he shouted. 'It's contamination. We have to get out of here right now! Hurry, before it's too late!'

'It's already too late,' said the wet, fleshless thing of glistening organs. Burcu turned and his eyes widened in horror at the sight of an oozing weave of translucent skin coating the monster's body. It grew and thickened over the naked organs, unevenly and in patches, but expanding all the time. Decay claimed the skin almost as soon as it grew, flaking from the body in blood-blackened scabs.

The monster's hand punched out. Its fingers stabbed through Burcu's eye lenses. The Apothecary wailed and dropped to his knees as the monster tore the helmet from his head. Burcu's sockets were ruined craters, gaping wounds in his skull that wept bloody tears down ashen cheeks.

But losing his eyes was the least of Koray Burcu's pain.

His cries turned to gurgling retching. The Apothecary's chest spasmed as lungs genhanced to survive in the most hostile environments were assaulted from within by a pathogen so deadly it had no equal.

The Apothecary vomited a flood of rancid matter, falling onto all fours as he was devoured by his hyper-accelerated immune system. Death fluids leaked from every orifice, and Mortarion watched dispassionately as the flesh all but melted from his bones, like the humans of Barbarus who climbed too high into the poison fogs and paid the ultimate price.

His brothers would be horrified by Burcu's death and his abhorrent murderer, but Mortarion had seen far worse in his youth; the monstrous kings of the dark mountains were endlessly inventive in their anatomical abominations.

Koray Burcu slumped forward and a slurry of stinking black and vermillion spilled onto the deck. The Apothecary's body was no more, a broth of decaying meat and spoiled fluids.

Mortarion knelt beside the remains and ran a finger through the mess. He brought the sludge to his face and sniffed. The biological poison was a planetary exterminator, but to one raised in the toxic hell of Barbarus, it was little more than an irritant. Both his fathers had worked to render his physiology proof against any infection, no matter its power.

'The Life-Eater virus,' said Mortarion.

'That's what killed me,' said the monster, as the regenerating and decaying cloak of skin slithered over its body. *'So that's what the warp used to remake me.'*

Mortarion watched as waxen skin inched over the skull to reveal a face he'd last seen en route to the *Eisenstein*. No sooner was it revealed than it rotted away again, an unending cycle of rebirth and death.

Even bereft of skin, Mortarion knew the face of one of his sons.

'Commander,' said Mortarion. 'Welcome back to the Legion.'

'We go to the killing fields, my lord?'

'The Warmaster calls us to Molech,' said Mortarion.

'My lord,' said Ignatius Grulgor, turning his limbs over to better examine the reeking, living death of his diseased body and finding it much to his liking. 'I am yours to command. Unleash me. I am the Eater of Lives.'

'All in good time, my son,' said Mortarion. 'First you're going to need some decent armour or you'll kill everyone on my ship.'

IT WAS BAD enough when the occupants of the nameless fortress prison had been unknown to Loken, but knowing he had no choice except to leave Mersadie incarcerated cut him to the bone. The cell door closing was a knife in the belly, but she was right. With agents of the Warmaster likely abroad in the solar system, perhaps even on Terra itself, there existed no prospect of her release.

Perhaps his escort sensed the build up of anger in him, for they led him back to the embarkation deck without the needless

obfuscation of the route. As Loken had suspected, his final destination had been close to where the *Tarnhelm* had set down.

The sleek ship sat in a launch cradle, already prepped and ready
to depart. Bror Tyrfingr had called it a draugrjúka, a ghost ship,
and he was right to do so, but not for its stealthy properties.

It carried people who might as well be ghosts, presences that
went unnoticed by all, and – more importantly – whose existence
would never be acknowledged.

 Loken saw Banu Rassuah in the pilot's blister on the arrowhead
frontal section, and Ares Voitek circled the craft with Tyrfingr,
using his servo-arms to point out especially noteworthy elements
of the ship's construction.

Tyrfingr looked up at Loken's approach. His brow furrowed as
though detecting a noisome stench or the approach of an enemy.

His eyes roamed Loken's face and his hand slipped to his holster.

'Ho,' said Tyrfingr. 'There's a man whose icerunner's slipped a
sheet. You found trouble?'

Loken ignored him and climbed the rear ramp to the fuselage.
The central dormitory section was only half full. Callion Zaven
sat at the central table with Tubal Cayne, extolling the virtues of
personal combat over massed escalades. At the far end, Varren
and Nohai compared scars on their bulging forearms, while Rama
Karayan cleaned the disassembled skeleton of his rifle.

Tylos Rubio was nowhere to be seen, and Qruze emerged from
the low-ceilinged passageway leading to the pilot's compartment.

'Good, you're back,' said Zaven, managing to completely mis-
read Loken's humours. 'Perhaps we can actually get out of the
system.'

'Qruze,' snapped Loken, reaching to his belt. 'This is for you.'

Loken's wrist snapped out, and the lacquered wooden box flew
from his hand like a throwing blade. It flashed towards Qruze,
and though the Half-heard was no longer as quick as he once was,

he caught the box a finger's breadth from his chest.

'What's–' he said, but Loken didn't let him finish.

Loken's fist slammed into Qruze's face like a pile-driver. The venerable warrior staggered, but didn't fall, his heartwood too seasoned to be felled by one blow. Loken gave him three more, one after the other with bone-crunching force.

Qruze bent double, instinctively driving forward into the fists of his attacker. Loken slammed a knee into Qruze's gut, then spun low to drive an elbow to the side of his head. Skin split and Qruze dropped to his knees. Loken kicked him in the chest. The Half-heard flew back into the lockers, crumpling steel with the impact. Buckled doors flew open and the stowed gear tumbled to the deck: a combat blade, leather strops, two pistols, whetstones and numerous ammunition clips.

The Knights Errant scattered at the sudden violence in their midst, but none moved to intervene. Loken was on Qruze in a heartbeat, his fists like wrecking balls as they slammed into the Half-heard.

Qruze wasn't fighting back.

Teeth snapped under Loken's assault.

Blood sprayed the bare metal of his armour.

Loken's fury at Mersadie's imprisonment cast a red shadow over everything. He wanted to kill Qruze like he'd never wanted to kill anyone before. With every ringing hammer blow he unleashed, he heard his name being called.

He was back in the ruins, surrounded by death and creatures more corpse than living thing. He felt their claws upon his armour, pulling him upright. He threw them off, tasting the planet-wide reek of decaying meat and the hot iron of expended munitions. He was Cerberus again, right in the heart of it.

Lost to madness on the killing fields of Isstvan.

Spitting breath, Loken swept up the combat blade. The edge

glittered in the subdued lighting, hanging in the air like an executioner awaiting his master's sign.

And for an instant Loken wasn't looking at Qruze, but Little Horus Aximand, the melancholic killer of Tarik Torgaddon.

The blade plunged down, aimed for Qruze's exposed throat.

It stopped a centimetre from flesh, as though striking an unseen barrier. Loken screamed and pushed with every scrap of strength, but the blade refused to budge. The handle froze in his grip, blistering the skin with arctic ferocity before turning it black with frostbite.

The pain brought clarity, and Loken looked up to see Tylos Rubio with his hand extended and wreathed in a haze of corposant.

'Drop it, Garvi,' said a voice, though he could not say for certain to whom it belonged. Loken couldn't feel his hand, the icy touch of Rubio's psykery numbing it completely. He surged to his feet and hurled the blade away. It shattered into icy fragments on the curved fuselage.

'Throne, Loken, what was that about?' demanded Nohai, pushing past him to kneel by Qruze's slumped form. 'You've damn near killed him.'

Qruze demurred, but his words were too mangled by swollen lips and broken teeth to make out. The faces of the warriors around him were pictures in shock. They looked at Loken as they would a lunatic berserker.

Loken went to go to Qruze, but Varren stepped in front of him. Bror Tyrfingr stood next to him.

'The old man is down,' said Tyrfingr. 'Leash your wolf. Now.'

Loken ignored him, but Varren put a hand on his chest, a solid, immovable brace. If he wanted past, he'd have to fight the former World Eater too.

'Whatever this is,' said Varren, 'this isn't the time.'

Varren's words were calmly said, and Loken's anger diminished with every heartbeat. He nodded and stepped back with his fists uncurling. The sight of his brother legionary's blood dripping from his cracked knuckles was the final parting of the curtain, and reason resumed its position at the seat of his consciousness.

'I'm done,' he said, backing away until he reached a wall and slumped down to his haunches. His assault had not exerted him overmuch, but his chest heaved with effort.

'Good. I'd hate to have to kill you,' said Tyrfingr, taking a seat at the table. 'And by the way, you owe me a knife. I spent weeks getting that one balanced properly.'

'Sorry,' said Loken, watching Nohai work on Qruze's ruined face.

'Ach, it's only a blade,' said Tyrfingr. 'And it was Tylos here that broke it with that witchery of his.'

'Me?' said Rubio. 'I stopped Loken from murder.'

'Couldn't you have plucked the blade from his hand?' asked Tubal Cayne, examining the broken fragments of the blade. 'I once saw a psyker of the Fifteenth Legion pluck the blades from an eldar swordsman's hands, so I know it can be done. Or was the Librarius of Ultramar less skilled than that of Prospero?'

Rubio ignored Cayne's jibe and made his way back to his private compartment bunk. Loken pushed himself to his feet and crossed the deck towards Qruze. Varren and Tyrfingr moved to intercept him, but he shook his head.

'I only want to talk,' he said.

Varren nodded and stepped aside, but kept his posture taut.

Loken looked down at Qruze, whose eyes were all but obscured by swollen flesh. Clotted blood matted his beard and purple bruising flowered all across the Half-heard's face. Impressions of Loken's gauntlets were battered into his skin. Nohai was clearing the blood away, but that wasn't making the damage Loken had inflicted look any less severe. Qruze lifted his head at the sound of his approach, seemingly unafraid of further violence.

'How long did you know she was here?' said Loken, the calmness of his voice in stark contrast to the fading colour of his skin.

Qruze mopped his cheek where the skin had split and spat a wad of bloody phlegm. At first, Loken thought he wasn't going to answer, but when the words came, they came without rancour.

'Almost two years.'

'Two years,' said Loken, and his fingers curled back into fists.

'Go on,' said Qruze softly. 'Get it out of your system, lad. Beat me some more if it helps.'

'Shut up, Iacton,' said Nohai. 'And, Loken, step back or I'll seriously reconsider my Apothecary's Oath.'

'You left her to rot in there for two years, Iacton,' said Loken. 'After you'd risked everything to save her and the others. Euphrati and Kyril? Where are they? Are they here too?'

'I don't know where they are,' said Qruze.

'Why should I believe you?'

'Because it's the truth, I swear,' said Qruze, grimacing as Nohai inserted another needle into his skull. 'Nathaniel might have an idea where they are, but I don't.'

Loken paced the deck, angry and confused and hurt.

'Why didn't you tell me?' he asked, as the hulking shape of a gold-armoured warrior appeared silhouetted at the boarding ramp.

'Because I ordered him not to,' said Rogal Dorn.

A SPACE WAS cleared for the primarch of the Imperial Fists, though he declined to sit. Chairs were righted and the debris of the recently unleashed violence cleared away. Loken sat the farthest distance he could manage from Iacton Qruze, a terrible weight of shame hanging around his neck. The fury that had driven him to assault the Half-heard had dissipated utterly, though the lie between them still soured his belly.

Rogal Dorn paced the length of the table, his arms folded across his chest. His granite-hard face was stern, and heavy with duty, as though ill-news still swathed him. His armour's golden lustre was faded, but here on this hidden fortress, nothing of beauty could shine.

'You were hard on Iacton,' said Dorn, and the square tones of his voice reminded Loken of how astonishingly soft it had once been. Soft, yet with steel in its bones. That steel was still there, but all softness had been stripped away.

'No more than he deserved,' replied Loken. He was being churlish, but even genhanced livers took time to purge black bile.

'You know that's not true,' said Dorn, as Ares Voitek set a cutdown fuel canister in the centre of the table. 'Iacton was obeying an order from the Lord Protector of Terra. You would do the same.'

The last sentence was as much challenge as it was statement of fact, and Loken nodded slowly.

The months following Loken's return from Isstvan had shown him the depths of Rogal Dorn's displeasure as he was pared down to the bone for signs of treachery. That Malcador and Garro had vouchsafed him loyal was perhaps all that had saved him from an executioner's blade.

'I recall when I first met you aboard the *Vengeful Spirit*, Garviel Loken,' said Dorn. 'You and Tarik almost came to blows with Efried and... my First Captain.'

Loken nodded, reluctant to be drawn into reminiscence, even with a being as godly as a primarch. He heard the pause where he expected to hear Sigismund's name, and wondered what, if anything, it meant.

Ares Voitek filled the silence by distributing tin cups around the table via his servo-arms and pouring a measure of clear liquid into each one.

'What's this you're giving me, Ares?' said Dorn, as Voitek handed him the first filled cup.

'It's called *dzira*, my lord,' explained Voitek. 'It's what the clans of Medusa drink when there's bridges to be mended between brothers.'

'And you just happened to have some aboard?'

Loken looked at the clear liquid in the cup, smelling all manner of strange mixtures in its chemical structure.

'Not exactly,' said Voitek. 'But there are enough alcohol-based fluids aboard the *Tarnhelm* for someone with a working knowledge of alchymical processes to knock up a viable substitute. Normally a Clan Chief would pass a *piyala* bowl around his warring sons, but I think we can break protocol on that just this once.'

'Just this once,' agreed Dorn and took a drink.

The primarch's eyebrow raised a fraction, which should have told Loken what to expect. He followed Lord Dorn's example and swallowed a mouthful of Voitek's spirit. Its heat was chemical and raw, like coolant drained from the core of a plasma reactor. Loken's body could process almost any toxin and expel it as harmless waste product, but he doubted the Emperor had dzira in mind when conceiving the Legiones Astartes physiology.

The others around the table, Qruze included, drank from their cups. All apart from Bror Tyrfingr and Altan Nohai reacted as though Voitek had tried to poison them, but kept their reactions to coughs and splutters.

Dorn's gaze swept the warriors at the table, and said, 'I know little of Medusan customs, but if the drinking of this dzira has served its clans well, then let its purpose be echoed here.'

Dorn leaned over the table, pressing both palms to its surface.

'Your mission is too important to fail through internal division. Every one of you is here because you have strengths and virtues that have cleft you from your parent Legions. Malcador trusts you, though some of you have yet to earn such from me. I hold deeds, not faith, gut-feelings or the whispers of prognosticators as the sum of a warrior's character. Let this mission be what earns you the boon of my trust. Find what the Wolf King needs, and you will have earned the Sigillite a measure of that trust too.'

'Why were you and Qruze here, my lord?' asked Macer Varren without embarrassment.

Loken saw a conspiratorial glance pass between Rogal Dorn and Iacton Qruze. The Half-heard dropped his gaze, and Rogal Dorn let out a heavy sigh that made Varren wish he'd never asked.

'To kill a man I once held in high esteem,' said Dorn, ever unwilling to shirk from the truth. 'A good man sent to his death by Horus to sap our resolve and unbind the mortar that holds the Imperium together.'

Loken swallowed another mouthful of dzira, and the shame keeping him pinned to his seat receded enough for him to ask, 'My lord, do you know where Euphrati Keeler and Kyril Sinder-mann are?'

Dorn shook his head. 'No, Loken, I do not, save that they are not on Terra. I am as ignorant of their whereabouts as Iacton, but if I had to guess, and I'm loath to guess, I'd say they were somewhere on Rodinia right now. They move from plate to plate, hidden by their followers and aided by deluded fools. There were reports she had been seen on Antillia, then Vaalbara and even around the globe on Lemurya. I hear reports of her sermonising all across the orbital ring, but I suspect a great deal of those are false dissemination to throw the hunters off the scent.'

'Surely one woman isn't worth that effort,' said Cayne.

'Mistress Keeler is more than just *one woman*,' said Dorn. 'This saint nonsense that's sprung up around her is more dangerous than you know. Her words fill malleable hearts with false faith and the expectation of miraculous intervention. She imbues the

Emperor with divine powers. And if He is a god, what need has
He of His people to defend Him? No, the *Lectio Divinitatus* is
just the sort of invented lunacy the Emperor sought to see ended
with Unity.'

'Perhaps her words give people hope,' said Loken.

'Hope in lies,' replied Dorn, folding his arms and stepping away
from the table. His brief time with them was over. The primarch
made his way to the boarding ramp, but turned and said one last
thing before departing for Terra.

'I own only the empirical clarity of Imperial Truth.'

Loken knew those words well.

He'd said them once in the water garden on Sixty-Three Nineteen and many times since in the dungeons of Terra. It could be
no coincidence that Rogal Dorn repeated them here. The memory
of them was a reminder of sundered confraternity, oaths broken
and brothers murdered in cold blood.

'As do I,' said Loken, but Rogal Dorn was already gone.

NINE

Remember the moon
Good hunting
Provocateur

A VAST DOME of coffered glass filled the frontal arc of the *Vengeful Spirit*'s high-vaulted strategium, through which could be seen the inky blackness of Molech's inner planetary sphere. The few visible points of light were fragile reflections on the armoured hulls of starships of all description and displacement. An armada of conquest attended upon the *Vengeful Spirit*, surrounding Lupercal's flagship like prowling pack hunters as they drew the noose on Molech.

Recessed lumen globes bathed the domed chamber in light it had not known since before the war against the Auretian Technocracy. A grand ouslite dais was set at the heart of the strategium, a metre in height, ten in diameter. It had once been part of Lupercal's Court, a meeting table, podium of address and, in times not so long ago, an altar of sacrifice.

To Aximand, it felt like that phase of the Legion's past was simply the first stage of its ongoing transformation; another change he had embraced as surely as he embraced his own autumnal aspect. The last blood spilled on its surface had been that of a supposed ally, an arch schemer and manipulator whose ambitions had finally overstepped his reach.

Erebus the snake, the self-aggrandising, self-appointed prophet of rebellion. Mewling and stripped of flesh and power, the base plotter had fled the *Vengeful Spirit* for destinations unknown.

Aximand was not sorry to see him go.

The bloodied trophies and gory window-dressing that had attended his teachings were also gone, ripped into the void by the impact of a clade killer's burning attack ship. Dark robed Mechanicum adepts and muttering, shadow-draped Thallaxii had restored the strategium to its former glory. Where Imperial eagles once glared down at the assembled warriors, now the Eye of Horus observed proceedings.

The message was clear.

The *Vengeful Spirit* was the Warmaster's ship again, and he its commander. This was a new beginning, a fresh crusade to match the one that had taken them to the very edge of space on a bloodied road of compliant worlds. Lupercal had conquered those worlds once, and he would conquer them again as he forged an *Imperium Novus* from the ashes of the old.

The Mournival stood with their master at the ouslite dais, lenses cunningly wrought into its upper surfaces projecting three-dimensional topography of Molech's close-system space. Maloghurst tapped the surface of a data-slate and updated icons winked to life. More ships, more defence monitors, more minefields, more void-traps, more neutron snares, more orbital defence platforms.

'It's a mess,' said Aximand.

'Lots of ships,' agreed Abaddon with relish.

'You're already thinking of how to get close enough to storm them, aren't you?' said Aximand.

'I already know how,' said the First Captain. 'First we–'

Horus held up a gauntleted hand to forestall the First Captain's stratagem.

'Take pause, Ezekyle,' said Horus. 'You and Aximand are old hands at this, and breacher work barely tests your sword arms. Let's assay the temper of the new blood you've added to the mix.'

Noctua and Kibre straightened as Horus gestured towards the garlanded orb of Molech at the centre of the illumined display.

'You're no strangers to a broil of swords and bolters, but show me how you'd crack Molech's girdle.'

As Aximand expected, it was Kibre who spoke first.

He leaned into the projection and swept a hand out to encompass the orbital weapon platforms with their racks of torpedoes and macro-cannons.

'A speartip right through their fleet to the heart of the guns,' said Kibre. 'An overwhelming assault into the centre, hard and fast, with flanking waves to push their ships into the blade of our spear.'

Aximand was pleased to see Grael Noctua shake his head.

'You disagree?' asked Maloghurst, also catching the gesture.

'In principle, no,' said Noctua.

Horus laughed. 'A politician's way of saying yes. No wonder you like him so much, Mal.'

'The plan is sound,' said Abaddon. 'It's what I would do.'

'Why doesn't that surprise me?' grinned Aximand.

'Then let your little sergeant tell us what he would do,' grunted Abaddon, his veneer of civility worn thin.

Noctua's face was a cold mask. 'Ezekyle, I know I'm new in the Mournival, but call me that again and we're going to have a problem.'

Abaddon's eyes bored into Noctua, but the First Captain was aware enough to know he'd crossed a line. With the Warmaster at his side, Abaddon could afford to be gracious without loss of face.

'Apologies, brother,' he said. 'I'm too long in the company of the Justaerin to remember my manners. Go on, how would you improve the Widowmaker's gambit?'

Noctua inclined his head, satisfied his point had been made, but savvy enough to understand that he had strained the bounds of his new position. Aximand wondered when the Mournival had become so fraught that a warrior needed to watch words to his brothers.

The answer readily presented itself.

Since the two whose names could never be voiced had upset a balance so natural none of them even understood it existed.

Noctua took the data-slate from Maloghurst and scanned its display. His eyes darted between its contents and the holographics. Aximand liked his thoroughness. It matched his own.

'Well?' said Horus. 'Lev Goshen tells me you have a bold voice, Grael. Use it. Illuminate us.'

'The moon,' said Noctua with a feral wolf's grin. 'I'd remember the moon.'

MOLECH'S ENLIGHTENMENT WAS a fast ship, the fastest in the fleet, its captain liked to boast. Given the slightest encouragement, Captain Argaun would extol the virtues of his vessel: a Cobra-class destroyer with engines barely thirty years out of an overhaul and a highly trained and motivated crew.

More importantly, the *Enlightenment* had tasted blood, which was more than could be said for most of Battlefleet Molech's warships.

Captain Argaun had fought xenos reavers and opportunistic pirate cutters operating out of the mid-system asteroid belt for years. He was the right blend of aggression and competence.

And best of all, he was lucky.

'How are they looking, Mister Cairu?' said Argaun, reclining on his captain's throne and tapping out updated command notes on an inset data-slate. Behind him, junior ratings tore off order-scrolls from chattering auto-writers and hurried to carry them out.

'No change in bearing, speed or formation, captain,' replied Lieutenant Cairu from his position overseeing the combat auspex teams. 'Vanguard in force, seven vessels at least. The rest of the fleet is following in a gradually widening gun line with its bulk carriers and Titan landers tucked in behind. Looks like a rolling planetary englobement.'

Argaun grunted and looked up at the viewing bay, a flattened, steel-rimmed ellipse fed positional data by banked rows of implanted servitors.

'Standard Legion tactics then,' he said, almost disappointed. 'I expected more of the Warmaster.'

The rotating sphere of the engagement volume filled the viewing bay, lit with identifier icons and scrolling data-streams. Some captains liked to see open space, but to Argaun's way of thinking, that had always seemed utterly pointless. Given the distances involved in void war, the most a captain might see – if he was lucky – were flickering points of light that vanished almost as soon as they became visible.

He magnified the representation of the battlescape. Signifier-runes had identified most of the vessels in the oncoming fleet.

Death Guard and Sons of Horus.

Neither Legion was noted for subtlety. Both were renowned for ferocity. It was upon this latter characteristic that Admiral Brython's provocateur strategy hinged.

The *Enlightenment* led a racing fleet of six fast-attack vessels, and it was their task to seduce the traitors into the teeth of the orbital platforms.

'There you are,' said Argaun, picking out the crimson sigil

representing the *Vengeful Spirit* and feeling a thrill of anticipation travel the length of his augmetic spine. The *Enlightenment* and its accompanying ships were far beyond the reach of the orbital guns. They were exposed, but Argaun wasn't worried. He'd heard Tyana Kourion say that to see the Legions at war was to witness gods of battle, but that was typical Army nonsense.

In the void, a warrior's prowess counted for nothing.

A lance strike or a torpedo detonation would kill a legionary just as easily as a deck menial, and any captain careless enough to let a Space Marine ship get close enough to launch a boarding action deserved everything they got.

'Time to firing range?'

'Eight minutes.'

'Eight minutes, aye,' said Argaun, opening a vox-link to the rest of the provocateur force.

'All captains, my compliments,' said Argaun. 'Begin your launch sequences for prow torpedoes. Full spread, and good hunting.'

'Torpedoes in the void,' said Maloghurst, watching as holographic salvoes crawled across the plinth's display.

'Time to impact?' asked Horus.

'Do you really need me to tell you, sir?'

'No, but do it anyway,' said Horus. 'They're playing their role, so let's allow them to think we're playing ours.'

Maloghurst nodded and estimated the travel time of the enemy torpedoes. 'I make it ninety-seven minutes.'

'Actually it's ninety-five,' said Horus, steepling his fingers and watching the inexorable unfolding of the battle before him.

'Ninety-five, aye,' said Maloghurst as the battle cogitators confirmed the Warmaster's calculation. 'Forgive me, sir, it's been a while since I've needed to work deck duty. It's not a task for which I have any enthusiasm.'

Horus waved away Maloghurst's apology and nodded in agreement.

'Yes, I've always hated void war over other forms of battle.'

'And yet, as in all forms of war, you excel at it.'

'A commander shouldn't be so far removed from the surging ebb and flow of combat,' said Horus, as if Maloghurst hadn't spoken. 'I am a being wrought for war on a visceral scale, where force and mass and courage are death's currency.'

'I almost miss it sometimes,' replied Maloghurst. 'The simplicity of an open battlefield, a loaded boltgun in my hand and an enemy in front of me to kill.'

'It's been a long time since anything was that simple, Mal.'

'If it ever was.'

'There's truth in that,' agreed Horus. 'There's truth in that indeed.'

ANOTHER TRUTH OF void war was that until warships came together in murderous congress, there was very little to do but wait. The closure speeds of the opposing vanguards were enormous, but so too were the distances between them.

But when the dying began, it began quickly.

Multiple salvoes of ordnance erupted from both vanguard fleets, each torpedo fifty metres in length and little more than a huge rocket booster capped with an extraordinarily lethal warhead. As scores of torpedoes surged from their launch tubes, barrages of armour penetrating shells blasted from prow batteries.

Each volley was silent in the void, but brutalising echoes reverberated through every gun deck like the pounding drumbeats of titanic slave overseers, deafening those not already insensate to the unending clamour.

Glimmering plasma trails intersected between the fleets, then split apart as they hunted for targets.

First blood went to the *Enlightenment*. A spiralling torpedo, launched from its starboard launch tubes by Master Gunner Vord-heen and his seventy-strong munition crew, smashed through the armour plating of the Sons of Horus frigate, *Raksha*.

The impact triggered a secondary engine within the torpedo that hurled the main payload deeper into the guts of its target. Like an arena killer whose blade finds a crack in his opponent's armour, the torpedo ripped through dozens of bulkheads before its primary warhead exploded in the heart of the starship.

Raksha's keel snapped in two and over a quarter of its seven hundred crew members were immolated in a storm of atomic fire. Sheets of armour plating blew out like billowing sailcloth in a storm. Pressurised oxygen burned with brief intensity as compartment after compartment was vented to the void. The debris of the frigate's demise continued moving forward in an expanding cone of tumbling iron, like buckshot from an armsman's shotcannon.

The Imperial destroyer, *Implacable Resolve*, took the next hits, a torpedo to its rear quarter and a lance strike that sheared off its command tower. The vessel broke formation in a veering yaw, spewing a comet's tail of debris and vented plasmic fumes. Without captain or command deck to correct her course, the ship fell from the vanguard until the raging hull fires finally reached the ventral magazines and blew it apart in a seething fireball.

Three more vessels were crippled in quick succession: *Devine Right*, *Cthonia Rising* and *Reaper of Barbarus*. A pair of 'fist-to-finger' impacts penetrated the Imperial vessel's prow armour and a superhot plasma jet roared the length of its long-axis. Gutted by searing fires, *Devine Right* exploded moments later as its weapon stores cooked off. The Death Guard destroyer was reduced to a radioactive hulk and critical reactor emissions that lit up the Imperial threat auspex like a beacon fire. The Sons of Horus frigate simply vanished, dead in the water as its power and life-supporting mechanisms failed in the first instant of impact.

Both vanguards had been savaged, but the traitor ships had taken the worst of the engagement. Four vessels remained battle worthy in the Warmaster's vanguard, though all had taken hits in the opening shots of the engagement.

Their captains were hungry for blood, and they fired their ship's engines, eager to tear into the enemy at close range. Behind them, the fleets of the Death Guard and Sons of Horus followed suit.

Battle would be joined and the dead avenged.

The Imperial ships would learn what it meant to face the Warmaster.

But Battlefleet Molech had no intention of going head to head with a vastly superior fleet. No sooner had the ordnance struck the traitor vanguard than Captain Argaun issued orders to turn the provocateur fleet around. His remaining ships raced back to Molech and the cover of its orbital weapon platforms.

And, just as Lord Admiral Semper had planned, the blooded fleet of the Warmaster gave chase.

'REMEMBER THE MOON, he says,' grunted Abaddon. 'As if any Ctho-nian even took part in that fight.'

Unable to make any sound within the frozen vacuum of the tomb ship, the First Captain's voice sounded in Kalus Ekaddon's helmet over the vox.

He didn't answer. Strict vox-silence protocols were in force, but when had something as trivial as a direct order from the Warmaster troubled Ezekyle Abaddon?

'Remember the moon,' repeated Abaddon. 'For two hundred years, we've tried to forget the moon.'

ON THE FLAG bridge of the *Guardian of Aquinas*, Lord Admiral Bry-thon Semper watched the unfolding engagement in the central hololith with a measured sense of satisfaction. He paced with his hands laced behind his back. A cohort of nine Thallax followed him on hissing, piston-driven legs, the low hum of their lightning guns ruffling hairs on the back of his neck.

At least, he told himself it was their strange weaponry.

Semper didn't like the blank-faced cybernetics, as it always unnerved him to know there was some scrap of a living being within that sarcophagus armour.

Still, at least they didn't speak unless you spoke to them, unlike Proximo Tarchon of the vessel's assigned complement of Ultramarines, who proffered unasked-for tactical advice like he were the one who'd spent most of his life aboard a warship.

Tarchon was only a centurion, for Throne's sake, but still he acted as though the *Guardian of Aquinas* was his own Legion warship.

To the Mechanicum and the fleet, Semper's flagship was an Avenger-class grand cruiser, which captured something of the vessel's majesty, but nothing of its savagery. A part of the *Guardian*'s crew since his recruitment on Cypra Mundi, Brython Semper knew just how ferocious a machine of war it was.

Its mode of attack was not subtle. It owed nothing to finesse and was bloody in the way two starving rats locked in a box was bloody. *Guardian of Aquinas* was a gunboat, a sledgehammer vessel that waited for the enemy line to widen before surging into the gap and unleashing hellish broadsides from multiple gun decks.

'Good hunting indeed, Argaun,' hissed Semper, as the wounded vessels of the provocateur fleet limped back into range of the orbital weapons platforms. 'Gave those traitor bastards a bloody nose and then some. By Mars and all his red blades, you did!'

That was overstating the damage caused by the provocateur fleet, but his lavish estimation of it would fire the blood of his crew. The Thallax straightened at the mention of the Red Planet. In pride or some conditioned reflex, he couldn't tell.

As impressive as Argaun's attack had been, it was just the prelude to the real fight. Semper cast his critical gaze over the disposition of his fleet, and was content.

Forty-two Imperial vessels were spread between three attack formations; a strong centre of frigates and destroyers, with fast-attack cruisers on the flanks. Two Gothics sailed abeam of the flagship, the *Admonishment in Fire* and the *Solar's Glory*. Both had fought in the reclamation of the birth system and, like the *Guardian of Aquinas*, they were linebreakers, armed with broadside lances that were sure to wreak fearful havoc among the traitor ships.

Sailing in the leftmost battlegroup was Semper's mailed fist.

Adranus was a Dominator, and its nova cannon was going to create the gap Semper and the Gothics would rip wide open.

The combined Sons of Horus and Death Guard fleets were in wrathful pursuit of the vessels that had hurt them. As Argaun had communicated, the enemy fleets were moving to englobe Molech, but retained a centre mass to engage the orbital defences and Battlefleet Molech.

Semper saw a textbook planetary assault formation, one any first-year cadet would recognise from the works of de Ruyter, Duilius or Yi Sun Shin.

'They must not think very highly of us to come at us with so basic an attack,' said Semper, loud enough for the deck crews to hear. 'So much for Captain Salicar's fears of us being outfought.'

Yet for all his outward bluster, Semper was under no illusions that the enemy approaching Molech was supremely dangerous. He'd studied the Warmaster's tactics during the Great Crusade. His assaults were brutal, without mercy and the enemy almost never saw their doom coming.

This assault felt almost comically simple and direct.

What was he not seeing?

The Warmaster's fleets would be in range of the orbitals at his back in less than three minutes. The hololith flickered with confirmed firing solutions received from their master gunners.

He'd already authorised captain's discretion for each of the platform's commanders. They knew their trade, and needed no direction from him to punish the traitors.

Yet the nagging doubt that wormed its way into his thoughts at the sight of so basic an assault formation wouldn't go away.

What am I missing?

PLATFORM MASTER PANRIK had a surfeit of weapons aboard the Var Sohn orbital station: torpedo racks, missile tubes, close-range defence cannon, ion shields, mass drivers and battery after battery of macro-cannons.

All were eager to be unleashed.

'Weapon systems at full readiness,' reported the deck officer. 'Command authority transfer on your mark.'

Panrik nodded. They'd achieved full readiness a little slower than he'd have liked. Still within acceptable tolerances, so no sense in making a scene just now.

'Mark,' said Panrik, inserting the silver command ring on his right index finger into the slot on his throne. He turned and subvocally recited his authority signifiers.

Clamps locked his neck in place, and a whirring, rotating connector plug slotted into the mind impulse unit socket drilled through into his spine.

Information flooded him.

Every surveyor and auspex on the great, crescent shaped platform was now his to access. His organic vision faded, replaced with a sensorium suite of approach vectors, closure speeds, deflection angles and targeting solutions.

In a very real sense, Panrik *became* Orbital Platform Var Sohn.

A potent sense of might surged through him. Connection burn

and inload surge made him wince, but it faded as cognition-enhancing stims flooded his thalamus and occipital lobe.

Implanted vents at the back of Panrik's skull opened, allowing the heat generated by his over-clocked brain to dissipate.

'I have command authority, aye,' replied Panrik, alternating between the local auspex and the feed coming in from the attack logisters of the *Guardian of Aquinas*. The enemy fleet was coming in hard and fast, looking to roll straight over the orbital defences and break through before suffering too much damage.

A bold strategy, but a risky one.

Too risky, thought Panrik, glancing down at the staggered line of orbitals and the haze of minefields strung between them like glittering jewels.

Panrik cricked his neck and flexed his fingers.

Weapon systems armed in response.

'Come ahead then,' he said to the advancing fleets. 'Give it your best shot.'

00:12

Aximand watched the mottled grey and green marble of Molech rotate below him. Close, so very close. Ice limned the kinetic bracing and frost webbed the plate of his fellow warriors. For the last sixteen hours, he'd been watching the timer in the corner of his visor count down to zero.

00:09

Inaction didn't suit him. It didn't suit any of them, but he at least had learned to deal with it. Ezekyle and Falkus were prowling hounds who savoured the swift kill. Not for them the patient hunt. In contrast, Aximand was a bowstring that lost nothing of its power by being kept taut. Yet even he'd found this long, frozen vigil testing.

00:05

Noctua, he suspected, could outlast them all.

Aximand almost smiled as he wondered how long it had taken before Ezekyle broke the vox-silence protocol. Not long. He'd be too full of hubris to resist letting his mouth run away from him.

Aximand remembered the tales of the moon's fall.

00:02

He remembered chimeric monsters of the Selenar cults; gene-spliced bioweapons, killing machines of flesh and acid and gibbering insanity. He remembered tales of slaughter. Unrestrained, wild, savage and yet to be tempered by Lupercal's discipline.

But most famous of all was the cry of surrender.

Call off your wolves!

00:00

'Speartip,' said Aximand. 'Light them up.'

'CONTACTS!' SHOUTED THE deck officer.

Panrik had seen them no more than a fraction of a second before, but had disregarded them due to their position behind and below Var Sohn. They were faint, no more than flickers.

They couldn't possibly be hostile.

But they were growing stronger with every passing moment.

'Malfunctioning mines?' suggested the auspex master. 'Or hyper-accelerated debris caught in the flare of a surveyor sweep?'

Panrik didn't need cognition-enhancing drugs to hear the desperate hope in the man's voice. He knew fine well what these returns were. He just didn't know how the hell they'd gotten there.

'Tomb ships! Throne, they're tomb ships!' said the auspex master. 'I've heard of the tactic, but thought it was just a myth.'

'What in the name of Hellblade's balls are tomb ships?'

'Tomb ships,' repeated the auspex master. 'Vessels shot into the void and then completely shut down, emptied of atmosphere and left to fly towards their target. There's no power emissions, so they're virtually impossible to detect until they fire up their reactors. It's also next to impossible to pull off.'

'Clearly not impossible enough,' said Panrik, each dart of his ocular implant shifting fire-priorities. 'Retask batteries Theta through Lambda to low orbit echelon fire. Atmospheric bursts only, I don't want any of our munitions hitting the surface. Ventral torpedo bays recalculate firing solutions and someone get me the Lord Admiral.'

Two ships were right on top of him, a dozen more spread behind the network of orbital platforms. They'd appeared from nowhere, the surveyor returns from their hulls growing stronger as dormant reactors were quick-cycled to readiness and targeting auspex trawled his platform for weak points.

He felt the shudder of point-blank torpedo impacts on the hull through the mind impulse unit link with Var Sohn's surface systems. He grimaced in sympathetic pain. Armour penetrators, not explosive warheads.

The sensorium came alive with hull-breach warnings and system failures as the newly revealed ships lashed them with terrifyingly accurate gunfire.

Var Sohn's defence systems blew apart, one by one.

'They mean to board us,' he said with a sick jolt of horror.

THIS WAS JUST the fight he was bred for.

Head hunched low behind a breacher's shield, moving forward, *Mourn-it-all*'s enhanced edge cutting through meat and bone and armour with ease. The boarding torpedo smoked and howled in the splintered underside of the orbital plate. Melting ice streamed from its superheated hull, and Sons of Horus breachers poured from its interior.

The rapid reaction force sent to intercept them were dead. Exo-armoured mortals. Highly trained and well armoured. Now nothing more than offal and butcher meat scattered like abattoir refuse.

Yade Durso, second Captain of the Fifth Company, together with five warriors in heavily reinforced battleplate and shields formed a wedge with him at its point. Tactical overlays appeared on his visor; schematics, objectives, kill boxes. Another timer. This one even more crucial than the last.

Remember the moon, Grael Noctua had said.

Aximand threw back his head and howled.

And let raw savagery take him.

A FLICKER OF *ignis fatuus* was the first warning. Crackling blue teleport flare arced between the primary stanchions of the Var Zerba orbital plate's command centre. Ear canals crackled in the seconds before a hard bang of displaced air shattered every data-slate within twenty metres of the transloc point.

Ezekyle Abaddon, Kalus Ekaddon and six Justaerin stood in an outward facing ring, their armour glossy and black, trailing vapour ghosts of teleporter flare. A hooded priest of the Mechanicum stood in the centre of the ring of Terminators, a hunched thing of multiple limbs, glowing eye lenses and hissing pneumatics.

The junior officers barely had time to register the presence of the hulking killers before a blitzing storm of combi-bolter fire mowed them down.

'Kill them all,' said Abaddon.

The Justaerin spread out, spewing shots that looked indiscriminate, but were, in fact, preternaturally exact. The Warmaster's orders had been unambiguous. The defence platforms were to be captured intact.

Within moments, it was done.

Abaddon marched to the throne at the heart of the control centre. A mewling wretch sat there, soiled and weeping. His eyes were
screwed shut. As if *that* would save him. Abaddon broke his neck
and wrenched the limp sack of bones from the throne without
bothering to undo the neck clamp. The Platform Master's head
tore off and bounced over the deck before coming to rest by an
armaments panel.

'You,' barked Abaddon, waving the Mechanicum priest forward.
'Sit your arse down and get this thing shooting.'

THE FIGHT THROUGH the Mausolytica had been bloody, but its outcome had, knew Grael Noctua, been a foregone conclusion. The
fight through the heart of Var Crixia was just the same. Its defenders were well trained, well armed and disciplined.

But they had never fought transhumans before.

The Warlocked were eternal, a squad never omitted from the
25th Company's order of battle. Death occasionally altered its
composition, but a line of continuity could be traced from its
current makeup all the way back to its inception.

Noctua fought along the starboard axial, a gently curved transit
way that ran from one tip of the crescent shaped station to the
other. Herringbone passageways branched from the main axial
like ribs, and it was from these raked corridors that the exo-
armoured mortals were attempting to hold them off.

It wasn't working.

Breachers went in hard and fast, running at the low-crouch.
Shields up, heads down, bolters locked into the slotted upper
edge. Braying streaks of miniature rockets rammed down the
main axial, killing anything that dared to show itself. Automated
gun carriages pummelled the advancing legionaries, but were
quickly bracketed and shredded by bolter fire.

Static emplacements unmasked from ceiling mounts and hidden

wall caskets. Grenade dispensers dumped frags and krak bombs. Battleplate withstood the bulk of it. Legion warriors stomped on through the acrid broil of aerosolised blood and yellow smoke.

Noctua advanced behind the wall of shields, bolter pulled in tight to his shoulder. Ahead, a barricade of hard plasteel and light-distorting refractors extruded from a choke point in the corridor. Bulky shapes moved through the haze.

Sawing blasts of autocannon fire punched into shields. Ceramite and steel splintered. Other weapons fired. Louder, harder and with a bigger, more lethal muzzle sound. A legionary grunted in pain as a shot found a gap in the shields and blew out his kneecap.

Mass-reactives.

The shell ricocheted from hardened bone and travelled down the length of the warrior's shin. It detonated at his ankle and obliterated his foot. Trailing the shredded remains on a rope of mangled tendons like a grotesque form of penitentiary ball and chain, the warrior kept up with his fellow shieldbearers.

Over the upper edges of the shields, Noctua saw hints of the defenders. It was like looking through a pane of fat-smeared glass. They were big, bigger than even the largest mortal exo-suit, and Noctua was confused until chance light through the refractors granted him a fleeting impression of cobalt-blue and gold plate. An Ultima rendered in mother-of-pearl.

'Legion foe!' he shouted. 'Ultramarines.'

Another volley of hard, echoing shots. Two of the breachers went down. One with the back of his helm a smoking, ruined crater. The other with his head lolling over his back and his throat blown out to the spine.

The advance faltered, but didn't stop. Legionaries following behind swept up the fallen shields and dressed ranks. One died before he could bring the shield up completely, his shoulders and ribs separated by a pair of bolter shells. Another pitched over without a head as a round slotted neatly through the bolter notch.

Noctua took his turn, bending to grab the shield before it hit the ground. A shot punched the lip of the shield and he felt the blazing edge of the shell score a line across his brow where his Mournival mark was graven.

He slid home his bolter.

'Onwards,' he said. 'We stop, we die.'

Gunshots sounded from one of the herringbone corridors. Stubber fire, cannon blasts and whickering volleys of flechettes.

Pin us in place with Legion forces then overwhelm us with mortal units shooting from the flanks and rear. Clever. Practical.

They could fight their way clear. Retreat, regroup. Find a work-around. But that would take time. Time the fleet didn't have if it wasn't going to be savaged by Var Crixia's guns.

No, retreat wasn't an option.

Suddenly it didn't need to be.

An ululating howl came from one of the herringbone corridors, and a pack of dark-armoured warriors charged into the fray. They moved like sprinting acrobats, using the walls as well as the deck to propel themselves forward.

They hit the barricade like a shell from a demolisher cannon, smashing it to splinters with the ferocity of impact. Some fired bolters and wielded blades, others simply tore into their foes with what looked like implanted claws. Blood arced up in cataclysmic geysers and the savagery was beyond anything Noctua had ever seen. Refractors blew out with squalling shrieks and what had previously been hidden was now revealed.

Noctua had thought his reinforcements to be another squad of the 25th Company, but such was not the case. They were still Sons of Horus, or had been once – their armour was a mix of swamp green, soot black and flaked blood. Some went without helms, their faces protean and scabbed with wounds cut into their faces.

The stench of burned meat attended them, and though the refractors were no more, Noctua still felt as though the air between them was somehow polluted. Inhuman strength, beyond even that of a transhuman, tore the Ultramarines apart. Limbs were rent from shoulder guards, clawed fists punched through plastrons and thickly muscled hearts ripped from splintered rib sheaths.

Noctua watched as one of the smoking warriors twisted a helm from a gorget with the head and spinal column still attached. He swung this like a spike-headed flail, battering another of the XIII Legion to death with it.

The warrior spread his arms wide and roared, his maw a red furnace into hell. Scars covered his neck and cheeks, and he bled toxic smoke from two old wounds in his chest.

Shock pinned Noctua in place.

Ger Gerradon, whose fighting days ended on Dwell.

Noctua's eyes met those of Gerradon, and he saw madness behind that gaze – malignant fire and a soul that burned in its chains. The moment lasted an instant only, and Noctua threw off his horror at what Gerradon had become.

The Ultramarines were dead, no longer a threat.

Time to deal with the enemies that were.

'Come about,' ordered Noctua, and the shields lifted high, their bearers turning on the spot as the warriors behind them pushed past. In one fluid manoeuvre, the entire formation of the War-locked was reversed.

Bolter fire flayed the mortal soldiers, and they baulked in the face of sudden reversal. With their Legion allies dead, the mortals knew that the fight was over, and fled.

It went against the grain to let them go, but this plan was of his devising, and he was already behind. Var Crixia's guns needed to be firing at the right targets.

Noctua turned to see what Ger Gerradon and his warriors were doing, reluctant to let them out of his sight, even for a second.

They were on their knees.

Feasting on the Ultramarines they had killed.

TEN

I want that ship
Warmaster
Stowaway

HORUS RETURNED TO the bridge. As the tomb ships closed on the orbitals, he'd retired to his personal chambers and left the observation of the coming attack to Maloghurst.

The strategium was a large space, airy and vaulted, but with the return of the Warmaster arrayed in the full panoply of battle, it seemed cramped. Nor had he returned alone, Falkus Kibre and twenty of the Justaerin carrying breacher shields came with him.

Kibre's helmet hung at his belt. His face was a picture in rapture. Such a change from the bitter resentment he'd worn when the Warmaster removed him from the assault elements. Now he was going into battle at the Warmaster's side, and no greater honour existed within the Sons of Horus.

'You're still set on doing this then?' asked Maloghurst.

'I want that ship, Mal,' replied Horus, rolling his shoulders in a clatter of plate to loosen the muscles beneath. 'And I'm out of practice.'

'I counsel you again, sir, you should not do this.'

'Worried I'll get hurt, Mal?' asked Horus, lifting *Worldbreaker* from his belt. The haft of the mace was the length of a mortal man. Lethal against a Legion foe, absurd overkill against baseline humans.

'It's an unnecessary risk.'

Horus slapped a mailed fist on the Widowmaker's shoulder, a booming clang of metal that echoed through the strategium like rolling thunder.

'I have Falkus here to protect me,' said Horus, unhooking his battle helm and hauling it down onto his gorget. The lenses flared red as its auto-senses were activated.

Maloghurst felt a tremor of awe travel the length of his twisted spine. Horus was an avenging angel, an avatar of battle incarnate and the master of war. So terrible and powerful. Maloghurst was horrified his quotidian dealings with the primarch had rendered the miraculous almost banal.

'I've sat on the sidelines for too long, Mal. It's time everyone remembered that this fight is my fight. It will be my deeds that ensure it's my name that echoes down through the ages. I won't have my warriors win *my* war without me.'

Maloghurst nodded, convinced the moment Horus had secured his helm. He dropped to his knees, though the movement sent a jolt of searing pain through his fused hips.

'My lord,' said Maloghurst.

'No kneeling, not from you,' said Horus, hauling his equerry to his feet.

'Sorry,' said Maloghurst. 'Old habits.'

Horus nodded, as though people kneeling to him were an everyday occurrence. Which, of course, it was.

'Bloody the *Spirit* for me, Mal,' said Horus, turning and leading the Justaerin to the embarkation deck where his Stormbird awaited. 'I don't expect I'll be gone long.'

✠ ✠ ✠

This is it. This is what I missed.

'Tomb ships,' hissed Admiral Semper, seeing notations on an instructional primer from his cadet days writ large in reality on the hololith. 'Throne, bloody almighty, tomb ships. They're fighting the subjugation of the moon all over again. The thrice damned bloody moon.'

The hololith told a tale of horror. Of a plan in tatters, of arrogance and, ultimately, death.

'If it had been anyone else but the Sons of Horus, I wouldn't have believed it,' whispered Semper. 'Who but the Warmaster would have the audacity to launch a full quarter of his fleet into the void and hope they arrived in time and at the right location?'

Except, of course, the Warmaster hadn't *hoped* the tomb ships would arrive where he needed them. He'd *known*. Known with a certainty that chilled Semper to the bone.

'The orbital platforms are gone,' said his Master of Surveyors, hardly daring to believe the evidence of the hololith. Semper shared the man's disbelief.

'They're worse than gone, the enemy has them,' he replied, watching as the most powerful platforms, Var Crixia and Var Zerba, cracked open the orbitals that the enemy assault forces hadn't seized. Var Sohn had launched – and was still launching – spreads of torpedoes into his hopelessly scattered fleet.

'Is the day lost, Lord Admiral?'

The answer was surely obvious, but the man deserved a considered answer. The Lord Admiral swept his gaze over the catastrophic ruin of what had begun as an ironclad stratagem.

He laughed and the nearby Thallax rotated their torsos at the unfamiliar sound. Semper shook his head. He'd forgotten the first rule of war regarding contact with the enemy.

Semper's rightmost battlegroup was no more. Every vessel gutted by treacherous fire from the captured orbitals. As the warships foundered in the wake of the shocking reversal, the Death Guard surged into them like ambush predators picking off herd stragglers. Alone and overwhelmed, each Imperial ship was brutalised until it was no more than a smouldering ruin.

The crippled hulks were then driven into the gravitational clutches of Molech by snub-nosed ram-ships. Wrecks plunged through the atmosphere. Blazing re-entry plumes followed them down.

Semper had traced the trajectories, hoping against hope that the wrecks would hit the atmosphere too sharply and burn to ash before reaching the surface. Or be too shallow and bounce off, careening into deep space.

But whoever had calculated the angle of re-entry had been precise, and every missile of wreckage was going to strike Molech with the kinetic force of heavy battlefield atomics.

The Sons of Horus swarmed the *Adranus*, its nova cannon useless at close quarters and its broadsides unable to hold off the raptor packs of Thunderhawks, Stormbirds and Dreadclaw assault pods slamming into its flanks.

With its escorts crippled by the orbitals, the Dominator was easy prey and was being gutted by vultures. An ignoble death, a bloody death. The Dominator was going down hard.

Screaming vox blurts told of thousands of Legion warriors and *things* of howling darkness ripping it apart from within. He'd ordered the vox shut off, the screams of the *Adranus*'s crew too terrible to be borne.

Only the centre yet endured.

Admonishment in Fire had been manoeuvring when the first assault teams hit the orbitals. Its captain ordered an emergency burst of the engines which undoubtedly saved her ship. For now. Its lance broadsides had demolished Var Uncad and reduced it to a smouldering ruin.

Solar's Glory was ablaze, but still in the fight. With the destruction of Var Uncad, it had been spared the full force of the fire intended to cripple it. A handful of light cruisers had weathered the swarms of torpedoes, but none were in any condition to take the fight to the traitors. At least six would be dead in the void within minutes, and the remaining four could barely manoeuvre or muster a firing line.

There would be no crossing-the-T this day.

'Yes, the day is lost,' said Lord Admiral Semper. 'The rest is silence.'

FIVE STORMBIRDS FLEW the flaming gauntlet from the *Vengeful Spirit* on an assault run. Four streaked forward to take up position alongside the fifth. They peeled away from the Warmaster's flagship as its vast engines fired, manoeuvring it towards the mighty form of the *Guardian of Aquinas* as it swung in.

The two flag vessels were closing like champions in the crucible of combat, seeking one another out in the midst of slaughter.

It would be an unequal fight. The *Vengeful Spirit* was old and tough, its marrow seasoned and its blackened soul ready to taste blood. Collimated blinks of light streamed between the two ships, high-energy pulse lasers intended to strip shields and ablative coatings of ice.

Deck after deck of guns boomed silently in the void, hurling monstrous projectiles through the space between them. In void terms, the two warships were at point-blank range. Two swordsmen too close to use their main blades and reduced to stabbing at one another with punch daggers.

They moved in opposition like stately galleons, sliding through clouds of molten debris and listing wrecks with impunity. Bright hurricanes of light streamed back and forth, explosions, premature detonations of intercepted munitions, crackling arcs of squalling, scraping void shields. Hull plates buckled and blew out as both ships traded blows like punch-drunk pugilists.

In their wake, streams of molten debris and shimmer-trails of frozen oxygen glittered in the star's light. The escorting Gothics attending the *Guardian of Aquinas* came in hard beside her, the *Admonishment in Fire* and the *Solar's Glory* hurling thousands of tonnes of explosive ordnance at the *Vengeful Spirit*.

The Warmaster's ship shuddered under the impacts, but it was built to take punishment, built to bully its way through harsher storms than this.

The *Endurance* came in low, oblique. Shadowed by burning orbitals and pulsing reactor detonations. Its prow weapons savaged the *Admonishment in Fire* and crumpled its hull as if with a fiery sledgehammer. The stricken ship's gun decks burned and its weapons stuttered in the face of the *Endurance*'s assault.

It kept shooting even as the Death Guard vessel rammed it amidships. Millions of tonnes of iron and adamantium moving at speed had unstoppable momentum. The *Endurance*'s reinforced frontal ram ripped through the weakened armour of its target and drove its grey bulk through the very heart of the *Admonishment in Fire*.

The Gothic simply ceased to exist, its keel shattered and its exposed interior compartments raked by unending broadsides. The wreckage spun away, spiralling clouds of flash-freezing atmosphere blooming from its shorn halves.

The *Solar's Glory*, ablaze and choking on its own blood, had already stopped shooting and its rear quarters vanished in the light of a newborn star. A reactor breach or deliberate overload, it didn't matter. A white-hot sphere of plasma bloomed from the vessel and engulfed the flanks of the *Endurance*.

Almost as soon as the fiery explosion flared to life it began to diminish. An inverted hemisphere was gouged in the *Endurance*'s hull and intense oxygen fires burned with raging intensity before the void snuffed them out.

Any other vessel would have been hopelessly crippled, left wheezing and dying by so grievous a wound. But even more than the *Vengeful Spirit*, the *Endurance* was built to take pain. Damage control mechanisms had already sealed off the ruptured decks and it heeled around to rake the engine decks of the *Guardian of Aquinas*.

Lord Admiral Brython Semper's flagship was a gutsy fighter, and though it was ablaze from prow to stern, it kept hurting its attackers with murderous broadsides. Through burning fire decks, its master gunners whipped their choking crews to load one last salvo, one final shell, one parting broadside.

The *Guardian of Aquinas* was doomed, but the killing blow would not come from without, it would come from within.

TWO OF THE gauntlet-running Stormbirds were obliterated before they began their attack run. Simply swatted out of existence by the blitzing storm of detonations filling the space between the grappling warships. Another had its trajectory fatally altered by the close passage of a torpedo, sending it into the hot zone of laser bursts where it immediately exploded.

The final pair swooped low over the topside superstructure of the *Guardian of Aquinas*. They weaved evasion patterns between close-in defence turrets and barrage lines. Raptors on the hunt, they flew almost suicidally close to the gnarled structure of Semper's flagship.

The hull breach behind the bridge was exactly where it was expected, and both Stormbirds flared their wings as vectored thrust suddenly reversed to match their forward velocity with that of the *Guardian of Aquinas*. Assault ramps opened and streams of heavily armed warriors dropped from their troop compartments.

Terminators, breachers and assaulters. Hard fighters all and equipped to fight in the kind of war Space Marines were bred to win. Brutal, close-quarter, barging, blade work. Blazing scrum-fights of bolters, stabbing blades and full-contact bloodwork.

First into the *Guardian of Aquinas* was the Warmaster.

BOLTER SHELLS HOSED the ten metre transit in horizontal spears of fire. The shooting was disciplined. He'd expect no less from warriors of the XIII Legion. Horus felt the hot breath of near-misses, and the kinetic force of their passage battered the plates of his armour.

Shields hunched before them, scraping the deck, Sons of Horus breachers advanced through the banging fury of the defence. Explosions and gunfire rang from the walls. Metallic coughs of grenade detonations filled its volume with scything shrapnel.

To Horus's left, Falkus Kibre fired his combi-bolter over the edge of his shield. A Terminator hardly needed a shield, but Falkus hadn't brought it for his own protection.

'Maloghurst does love to nanny me,' Horus had advised the Widowmaker in the instant before launching the assault. 'Keep it for yourself.'

Never one to gainsay an order if it stood to keep him alive and safe, Falkus had done just that.

The defenders were coming at them from all sides; Ultramarines to the front, a mix of carapace-armoured storm troopers, Army and skitarii to the flanks. The Justaerin advanced in a salient wedge, pushed out in a segmented formation of bolters, blades and shields.

Chaingun fire pummelled the shields and beam cutters sliced through them in white-edged lines. Even Terminator armour was vulnerable. A powerhouse of armoured might, the only thing that could resist a warrior encased in Tactical Dreadnought armour was an identically equipped warrior.

Or so Horus had thought.

Argonaddu went down, the Hero of Ullanor bisected through the chest by a sizzling beam cutter that left a nasty stink of cauterised meat. His killers struggled to reset their weapon, ratcheting cranks and pumping charge-bellows. Horus raised his gauntlet-mounted bolters, their proportions outlandish to any other, but perfectly suited to his primarch's scale.

A continuous stream of shells briefly linked muzzle flare and target. The beam gunners exploded in a confetti of shredded, scorched meat tissue and volcanic blood.

The skitarii launched an assault into the flanks of their advance. The heavies came first. Combat-augs with grossly swollen musculature who wielded motorised saw blades and polearms with photonic edges.

'Ware left!' shouted Kibre, and the Justaerin on the edge of the formation halted and braced for impact. Skitarii were hellish fighters, chosen for aggressive, almost psychopathic tendencies that could be yoked by cybernetics. These were, if anything, more feral than any Horus had seen.

Warriors of the wasteland, post-apocalyptic killers. Reminiscent of the barbarian tribes Horus had last seen as stasis-preserved specimens of pre-Unity. Bedecked in fanged amulets, furred cloaks and scaled breastplates, they charged like men possessed.

A Terminator was a tank in humanoid form, more a war machine than a suit of armour. Only the very best could adapt to its use and only the best of the best fought alongside the Warmaster. A volley of combi-bolters sawed into the skitarii. A dozen fell, two dozen more came on.

They slammed into the Terminators in a flurry of roaring blades and unsubtle firearms. High-load shells exploded against bonded ceramite and plasteel, caroming from deflective angles and ricocheting wildly.

Kibre waded in among them, shooting the head from the nearest skitarii killer. His shield bludgeoned the next, caving his face to a fragmented pulp of liquid flesh and bone. This was the work Kibre loved best. Batter kills, armour blows. Feeling the blood spray your visor, feeling the bones break beneath your fists.

Horus left him to it and jabbed his clawed fist at Hargun, Ultar and Parthaan.

'Keep the right clear,' he said. 'They'll come from that side next.'

His words were prophetic.

Cloaked in power-fields, ion-bucklers and photon-disruptors, blue-cloaked warriors of the Forlorn Spartaks threw themselves at the Sons of Horus. Despite himself, Horus was struck by admiration for the Spartaks' courage. Transhuman dread could freeze even the bravest warrior in place, but they came anyway.

Ultar swung his rotor cannon to bear and the deafening bray of its spinning barrels filled the transit. Hargun chugged shells from his combi-bolter. Power-fields shrieked under the hammer blow impacts and photon-disruptors were no protection against the detonation of the fat shells.

Parthaan broke formation and closed the distance far faster than anything his size ought to be able to move. A shieldwall could only hold for as long as it remained solid, but rotor cannon and combi-bolter had broken this one open. Parthaan went in head down, like a battering ram, striking left and right with his oversized fist. Crumpled forms were hurled about like refuse, bent in ways no body was meant to bend. They shattered on impact, leaving bright red spray patterns on the wall.

The Spartaks fought a thing that could not be fought, tried to kill he who could not be killed. A dozen fell to Parthaan's fist, then a dozen more. They threw themselves at him as though eager to join their comrades in death. The warrior of the Justaerin waded through blood and bodies, trampling them to gory mud beneath his armoured boots. Gunfire and blades tore at his armour, tearing the ocean green paint from its surfaces, but doing no harm.

On the opposite flank, Kibre's warriors were having a harder time against the skitarii. Cauterised fear centres blunted them to the terror of Terminators. Implanted aggression boosters made them wild. Horus was mildly surprised to see two Justaerin on their knees, armour carved open and wet organs flopping out onto the deck.

He hadn't seen that, hadn't incorporated it into his plans.

After Ullanor, many claimed the title of *Warmaster* was simply a recognition of Horus's rank within the Great Crusade. A bellicose thing, fit only for the purposes of conquest. Something to be set aside when the fighting was done.

To his lasting regret, Horus knew better.

Warmaster was not a title, it was what he *was*.

The flow of battle was music to him, a virtuoso performance that could be read and anticipated like the perfect arrangement of notes. Battle was a chaotic, unpredictable maelstrom of chance, a random imbroglio where death played no favours. Horus knew war, knew battle as intimately as a lover. Horus knew what would come next as clearly as if he had lived it before.

Now.

Parthaan's rampage was ended as a coruscating beam of hyperdense light struck the back of his armour. For an instant it played harmlessly over the blood-matted plate. Then the Justaerin's armour buckled as though an invisible giant was crushing him in its fist. Plates ruptured as a rising whine of building power split the air over Parthaan's screams of agony.

A thunderclap of discharge and Parthaan died as he imploded at the subatomic level, and every particle of his being turned inwards and crushed by its own mass. Shattered plates collapsed as though the man within them had simply vaporised and Horus smelled a stink-wind of misted blood and bone.

A beat as the Justaerin struggled to comprehend what had just happened.

'Ultar!' shouted Horus. 'Rapier platform. Conversion beamer.'

The rotor cannon turned on the gun carriage. Ultar walked his shells into it and reduced it to scrap metal.

'Now they'll come,' whispered Horus and swung *Worldbreaker* from his shoulder. He kept the weapon moving. Even for a being of his stature, it took time to build speed and power with so heavy a weapon.

A warrior with a transverse crest of ivory led the Ultramarines.

A centurion. Visor tags identified him as Proximo Tarchon and Horus assimilated his available service record instantaneously.

Ambitious, honourable, practical.

Gladius, of course. Energised combat-buckler on the opposite arm. Bolt pistol, expected.

Tarchon fired as he ran. The thirty Ultramarines at his back did likewise, maintaining their rate of fire even as they charged.

'Impressive,' said Horus. 'You do my brother much honour.'

Two Justaerin nearest the charging Ultramarines went down, carefully bracketed by the warriors in cobalt-blue. With enough mass-reactives brought to bear, even Tactical Dreadnought armour could be penetrated. Return fire punched half a dozen Ultramarines from their feet. Armour cracked open, flesh detonated.

Horus didn't give the XIII Legion a chance to fire again.

Without seeming to move, he was suddenly among them. *Worldbreaker* swung and three Ultramarines exploded as though siege mines had detonated within their chest cavities. A copious volume of blood wetted the air. The flanged mace swung back again, one-handed. Low on an upward arc. Another four warriors died. Their bodies slammed against the walls with bone shattering force, their outlines punched into the steelwork.

Tarchon came at him, gladius arcing towards his throat.

The haft of *Worldbreaker* deflected the blade. Tarchon kicked him in the midriff, firing his bolter one-handed into his chest. Explosions ripped across the Warmaster's breastplate and the amber eye at its centre split down the middle.

Horus caught the bolter between the talons of his gauntlet. A twist of the wrist and the weapon snapped just behind the magazine. Horus stepped inside Tarchon's guard and took hold of his gorget.

Tarchon stabbed with his gladius. Horus felt blood well from the cut. He lifted Tarchon from the deck as though he was a child and clubbed his fist into the centurion's chest.

The impact drove him back through his men, felling them like corn before the scythe. Horus kept going, sometimes bludgeoning, sometimes disembowelling. Gore boiled on his talons, clotted on *Worldbreaker*. Dripped from the cracked amber eye upon his breast.

He pushed into the Ultramarines. Surrounded on all sides by transhuman warriors. Honourable men who, only a short few years ago, would have called him lord. They might have baulked at his naked ambition, resented his appointment to Warmaster over their own primarch, but still they loved and respected him. And now he had to kill them. They stabbed and shot, undaunted in the face of the might of the demigod in their midst. Blades scored furrows in his armour, bolt shells exploded. Fire and fury surrounded the Warmaster.

Against so many sublime warriors, even a primarch could be brought down. Primarchs were *functionally* immortal, but they weren't invulnerable. People often forgot the difference.

In a fight like this, the skill was to find the moments of stillness, the places between the blades and bullets. A chainblade sailed past his head. Horus removed its owner's. Bolter shells ricocheted from his thigh plate. Horus punched his taloned fist through a warrior's hearts and lungs.

Always in motion, talons and mace killing with every stroke.

Twenty-three seconds later, the transit was a charnel house. Hundreds dead and every drop of blood wrung to paint the walls.

Horus let out a cathartic breath.

He felt someone approach and reined in a violent reaction.

'Falkus,' said Horus. 'Get me the centurion's gladius.'

THE BLAST DOOR to the command bridge was bulging inwards. The first blow had hit it like a Titan's fist. The second buckled the metal and tore its upper corners from the frame. Lord Admiral Brython Semper stood with his duelling sabre unsheathed and the captain's twin-barrelled Boyer held loosely at his thigh.

The upper barrel was an ancient beam weapon – a volkite, some called it – the underslung portion a one-shot plasma jet. It was a Space Marine killer, but could it kill a primarch?

Would he get the chance to find out?

He'd be lucky to get even a single shot off with the Boyer.

Perhaps a hundred people stood with him; surveyor readers, aides, juniors, scriveners and battle-techs, deckhands. None were combat-trained worth a damn. Only a single squad of armsmen with shotcannons and the nine Thallaxii Ferrox had any hope of inflicting real damage.

Banks of acrid smoke filled the bridge, and the only light was from a few stuttering lumens. The hololith had failed, and hydraulic fluids drizzled from ruptured pipework. Nothing remained of the command network. The vox crackled with screams.

'We'll make them pay for this, admiral,' said a crewman, Semper couldn't see who.

He wanted to say something suitably heroic. A valedictory

speech to inspire his crew and earn them an ending worthy of the *Guardian of Aquinas*. All that filled his thoughts were the last words Vitus Salicar had said to him.

We are killers, reapers of flesh. You must never forget that.

The blast door finally tore free of its mounting and fell into the bridge like a profane monolith toppled by iconoclasts. A towering figure was revealed, a giant of legend.

Haloed by flames of murder and dripping with blood.

A mantle of stiffened fur wreathed the war god's shoulders. His armour was the colour of night and gleamed with the fire of dying empires.

Semper had expected a charge, bursts of gunfire.

The god threw something at his feet. Semper looked down.

An Ultramarines gladius, the blade coated in vivid crimson. Its handle was wrapped in red leather. The hemispherical pommel was ivory, inlaid with the wreath-enclosed company number.

'That belonged to Proximo Tarchon,' said the god. 'Centurion of the Ninth Division, Battle Group Two, Legiones Astartes Ultramarines.'

Semper knew he should spit in the traitor's face or at least raise his weapon. His crew deserved to be led into their last battle by their captain. Yet the idea of raising a weapon against a being so perfectly formed, so *sublime*, seemed abhorrent.

He knew he faced a betrayer – an enemy, *the* enemy – yet Semper felt enraptured by his sheer magnificence.

The Warmaster took a step onto the bridge, and it took every ounce of Semper's willpower not to kneel. 'Proximo Tarchon and his warriors faced me without fear, for they were trained by my brother on Macragge, and such men are uniquely skilled at death dealing. But Proximo Tarchon and his warriors could not stop me.'

Semper tried to answer the Warmaster, but he couldn't long hold his gaze and his tongue felt leaden.

'Why are you telling me this?' he managed at last.

'Because you fought honourably,' said the Warmaster. 'And you deserve to know how futile it would be to waste your lives in pointless defiance at this point.'

Semper sensed the paralysing awe he'd felt of the Warmaster diminish in the face of so arrogant a statement. He wished he'd had the chance to return to Cypra Mundi and watch his son grow to manhood. He wished the blast shutters weren't down over the viewing bay so he might see the stars one last time.

He wished he could be the one to kill this god.

Semper lifted his duelling sabre to his lips and kissed its blade. He thumbed the activation clasp on the Boyer gun.

'For the Imperium!' shouted Semper as he charged the Warmaster.

HORUS STOOD IN the midst of carnage. One hundred and eleven people dead in less than a minute. A corpse lay at the Warmaster's feet, divided into long sections by a diagonal stroke of energised talons.

'*Who was he?*' asked Mortarion, his holographic form wavering on the temporary floating disc projector the Mechanicum had rigged. Beyond the Death Lord's image, faint impressions of Deathshroud could be seen, trailing their master like ghosts. The disc maintained a constant distance of three metres from Horus, closer than Falkus Kibre would have liked – even for a hologram – but exceptions had to be made for the primarch's brothers.

'Lord Admiral Brython Semper,' said Horus.

'*A Lord Admiral,*' said the Death Lord. '*Looks like you were right. Our father really does value this world.*'

Horus nodded absently and knelt by Brython's corpse. 'A pointless death,' said Horus.

'He tried to kill you,' pointed out Falkus Kibre, taking position at the Warmaster's right hand.

'He didn't have to.'

'Of course he did,' said Kibre. 'You know he had to. He might actually have surrendered until you said what you did at the end.'

Horus rose to his full, towering height. 'You think I *wanted* him to attack me?'

'Of course,' said Kibre, puzzled the Warmaster would even ask.

'Tell me, then – why did I provoke the Lord Admiral?'

Kibre looked up at Lupercal, and saw a fractional tilt to the corner of his mouth. A test, then. Aximand had warned him that the Warmaster liked to play these little games. Kibre took a moment to marshal his response. Quick answers were for Aximand or Noctua.

'Because the Lord Admiral's name would have been reviled forever if he'd surrendered his vessel,' offered Kibre. 'He'd fought hard and done all that honour demanded, but to surrender would have cursed his line from here till the end of time.'

Mortarion grinned. '*What's this? Insight from the Widowmaker?*'

Kibre shrugged, hearing derision.

'I'm a simple warrior, my lord,' he said. 'Not a stupid one.'

'Which is why I was pleased when Ezekyle put your name forward for the Mournival,' said Horus. 'Things have become complex, Falkus, far more so than I thought. And far quicker. It's good to have a simple man at your side in such times, don't you agree, brother?'

'*If you say so,*' grunted Mortarion, and Kibre smiled. The gesture was so unfamiliar to him he didn't at first know what his facial muscles were doing.

The Warmaster placed a hand on his shoulder and walked him to the command throne of the *Guardian of Aquinas*. The hololith had been returned to life, painting a grim portrait of Molech's future.

'Tell me what my simple warrior sees, Falkus,' said Horus. 'You're

Mournival now, so you need to be more than just a shock trooper. Simple or otherwise.'

Kibre studied the shimmering globe of Molech. He took his time, and it was an effort not to advocate a full drop pod assault immediately. How long was it since he'd had to employ anything other than the directness of breacher tactics?

'The battle for space is won,' said Kibre. 'The weapon platforms are ours, and the enemy ships are crippled or captured.'

'Tell me about the orbitals,' asked Horus.

'They're manoeuvring to new positions, but we can't rely on them.'

'Why not?'

'Molech's adepts will be re-tasking the surface missile batteries to destroy the platforms. We'll take out some before they fire, but they were never intended to resist fire from the ground. At best, we'll get a few salvoes away before the platforms are inoperable.'

'*Hardly worth the effort to capture them,*' said Mortarion.

'A few salvoes from orbit is worth a whole battalion of legionaries,' said Kibre. 'Calth taught the Seventeenth Legion that much.'

'He's right, brother,' said Horus, zooming in from the view of Molech's orbital volume to its planetary zones. Four continental masses, only two of which were inhabited or defended to any degree. One heavily industrialised, the other pastoral.

The Sons of Horus and the Death Guard forces would direct the main thrust of their attack upon the latter continent. Molech's primary seat of command lay within a mountain valley, at a city named for Horus himself, Lupercalia.

The Warmaster jabbed a talon at Lupercalia and traced a route across the continent, over verdant plains, past cities, through mountain valleys, before ending up at a ruined citadel on a storm-lashed island virtually clinging to the coastline.

'The Fulgurine Path,' said Horus. 'That's the road I need to walk, and this citadel is where we'll begin.'

'*And the rest of Molech?*' said Mortarion.

'Unleash your Eater of Lives,' ordered Horus. 'Lay waste.'

LOKEN MOVED DOWN the corridor with Bror Tyrfingr to his left, Ares Voitek to his right. He kept the shotcannon pulled in tight, looking down the unfamiliar iron sight as he moved smoothly into the drive chamber. He hadn't used a weapon like this since his time in the Scout Auxilia, but firing bolt weapons aboard a thin-skinned starship was generally frowned upon.

Tarnhelm wasn't a large ship, so when Banu Rassuah informed Loken she'd detected an unauthorised bio-sign during her final calculations for Mandeville translation, it didn't take long to narrow down the potential hiding places in which a stowaway could be hiding.

While the rest of the pathfinders secured the frontal areas of the ship, Loken, Tyrfingr and Voitek swept back to the drives.

'Someone from that grim fortress orbiting Titan?' asked Voitek, his upper servo-arms clicking with restraint cuffs. 'That Oliton girl you saw?'

Loken shook his head. 'No. It's not her.'

'Then a warp-thing?' offered Tyrfingr. 'Something shat out by the Warmaster's *maleficarum?*'

The former Space Wolf had eschewed a shotcannon in favour of his combat blade and knotted leather cestus gauntlet. Its night-bladed claws tapped on his thigh plate in a rhythmic tattoo.

None of them answered Tyrfingr's question. Each of them knew too much to lightly dismiss such speculation. The drive chamber was the only place left on the ship where anyone could realistically conceal themselves, but so far they had found nothing.

The engine spaces were elliptical in section, with a raised floor and suspended ceiling, flanked on both sides by two enormous cylinders that thrummed with barely contained power. Looped cables encircled narrowed portions of the main drives, and hard-wired calculus-servitors with shimmering eyes mumbled binaric plainsong.

A central nave ended at a communion altar, at which stood the unmoving figure of the nameless Mechanicum adept mono-tasked with overseeing the engine functions.

Sitting cross-legged before the altar was a bearded, tattooed warrior in the unadorned plate of the Knights Errant. He was assembling the components of a bolter he'd spread out on the deck.

Loken lowered his shotcannon as the warrior looked up with a disappointed shake of his head.

'What,' said Loken, 'are you doing?'

'I got bored of waiting for you to find me,' replied Severian.

PART TWO
SONS

ELEVEN

**Screaming
Responsibilities
Invasion**

MOLECH WAS SCREAMING.

It bled magma from a score of wounds gouged by the wreckage dropped from orbit. It burned black where macro-munitions punched through the atmosphere and carved blazing canyons in its crust. Night was banished. The engine plumes of incoming warheads and the explosions of intercepted ones eclipsed the light of the moons.

I have been here before, but I do not remember it.

Little Horus Aximand watched the wreckage of Lord Admiral Brython's fleet fall like continually dividing meteors. They scratched painfully bright parabolas in the sky. They shed blazing debris over tens of thousands of kilometres. The southern horizon was a fiery smudge of distant conflagrations and hard-burning retros. A pall of smoke pressed down on the landscape, underlit by the apocalyptic radiance of city fires.

Strange lightning arced in the clouds, the inevitable by-product of the sheer volume of metal piercing the atmosphere. Wrecked starships were coming down all across Molech, mostly on the industrialised landmass across the ocean. Its coastal embarkation facilities, starports and Army bases were in ruins, and saturation spreads of the Death Guard rad-bombs had rendered much of it uninhabitable for centuries.

There would be no reinforcements coming from that quarter.

The Catulan Reavers secured the Stormbird's landing zone, a rain-lashed harbour in the lee of a partially collapsed tower. Waves boomed against the quay, sending up walls of foaming water.

Coming in ahead of the main invasion force, the Warmaster was exposed and vulnerable. Maloghurst and the Mournival cited the assassination attempt on Dwell as reason enough not to descend to this northern island, a volcanic scrap of rock named Damesek.

Horus had brooked no disagreement.

He would be first to Molech's surface.

Lupercal stood at the base of the tower, resting a bare hand on the pale stone of a buttress. His head was bowed, his eyes closed.

'What do you think he's doing?' asked Grael Noctua.

'Lupercal will tell you in good time,' said Aximand.

'In other words, you don't know,' grunted Kibre.

Aximand didn't bother to answer the Widowmaker, but Abaddon gave him a clout on the back of the head for good measure. The Warmaster craned his neck to see the tower's upper reaches. Aximand did likewise and hoped this rainstorm would topple it into the sea.

Horus grinned and rejoined the Mournival, nodding as though in answer to an unheard question. The lustre of his battle armour had been restored, the amber eye upon its breast made whole once again. Had he not been blockaded on Mars, Urtzi Malevolus would have sought fault with the restoration work, but Aximand could find none. Unconsciously, his hand lifted to the split

Mournival mark on his own helm. The half moon quartered.

'It's the sea, you understand,' said Horus. 'I recall the smell of it. The salt and the faint hint of sulphur. I know I remember it, but it's like someone else's memory.'

He turned on the spot, looking back at the tower, as though trying to picture what it might have looked like in its heyday.

'You know what this is, of course?' said Horus.

'A ruined tower?' said Kibre.

'Oh, it's so much more than that, Falkus,' said Horus. 'I'm almost sorry you can't feel it.'

'It's the tower from Curze's cards,' said Aximand.

Horus snapped his fingers.

'Exactly! Curze and his cartomancy. I told him no good would come of trafficking with arcana, but you know Konrad…'

'I don't,' said Aximand. 'And I count myself fortunate.'

Horus nodded in agreement. 'He is my brother, but I wouldn't choose him as my friend.'

'Sir, why are we here?' asked Noctua. 'I don't understand why we landed on this island when there's plenty of tactically superior beachheads on the mainland. We should have dropped straight on Lupercalia.'

Horus let his hand drift to *Worldbreaker*'s haft.

'You have a fine appreciation of tactical necessity, Grael,' said Horus. 'It's why Little Horus here put your name forward, but you have a lot to learn about people and *why* they do things.'

'I don't understand, sir.'

Horus led Noctua to the tower. He put his new Mournival son's hand on the stone and said, 'Because *He* was here. The Emperor. Everything I learned on Dwell was true. My father came here a *long* time ago and left from this very tower.'

'How can you tell, sir?' asked Abaddon, examining the tower as if it might give up its secrets if he stared hard enough. The First

Captain's scalp was now shaven smooth, his manner still contrite.

'Because I can feel it, Ezekyle,' said Horus, and Aximand had never seen their master so vital, so *alive*. The Warmaster had not felt such a connection to his father since Ullanor, and it was energising him.

Horus closed his eyes again and said, 'A being like the Emperor does not move gently through the world. His passing leaves a mark, and He left a very big bruise when He left Molech.'

Tilting his head back, Horus let the rain wash his skin. It fell in a hard, violent baptismal. Aximand smelled the smoke from the myriad fires, saw the ruddy haze that was this world's red dawn.

Lupercal wiped a hand across his face and turned to Aximand.

'This is where the Emperor left Molech,' he said. 'I mean to follow His steps and find what He took from it.'

TO ROUSE DREAMING gods from their mountain holds was no small thing. The darkness under the earth was cool and the promise of rest seductive. Decades of slumber had made the gods forgetful, but the siren song of war was insistent. Dreams became nightmares. Nightmares became memories. Marching feet, braying horns and thundering guns.

They had been built for war, these engines of destruction, so to sleep away the years was not for them. In red-lit choral chambers, the plainsong of the Legio warhosts was carried to the domed cavern temples of the God-Machines.

Beneath Iron Fist Mountain, holdfast of Legio Crucius, *Paragon of Terra*'s reactor roused itself as the embers of its fury were fanned and ritual connections made to the command casket of Princeps Etana Kalonice. Nine hundred and forty-three adepts attended her revival, one for every year of the God-Machine's existence. They intoned blessings of the Omnissiah for her survival and recited a litany of her victories. Carthal Ashur led the songs of awakening from the inviolate summit of the mountain. Binaric subvocalisation inloaded the horrifying reality of Molech's tactical situation.

At Kalman Point, bastion of Legio Gryphonicus, Invocatio Opinicus added his voice to that of Ashur's, his basso tones soaring and filling the gradually awakening god-engines with the urge to fight.

Farther north in the Zanark Deeps, where Legio Fortidus buried itself in shadowed catacombs, Warmonger Ur-Nammu beat binary drums, her guttural call to arms a paean of loss and savagery. Treachery on Mars had destroyed her Legio's brother engines, and these last survivors were intent on vengeance.

Ten thousand Mechanicum priests fed power to the Legio war engines. Their hearts filled with strength, their armour with purpose and their weapons with the scent of the enemy.

War had come to Molech and the world would soon ring to the tread of the god-engines.

ALIVIA SUREKA DITCHED the groundcar when the floodwater blew its motor. The engine block geysered steam and she swore in a language not native to Molech.

No way it was moving. Looked like she was on foot from here.

She'd keep to the back streets and avoid Larsa's main thoroughfares. Terrified people were fleeing the doomed city and she didn't have time to waste fighting her way through crowds.

Alivia climbed out the car. Ice cold water reached her knees.

And the day had started so well.

One of Molech's principal starports and commercia centres, Larsa sat at the end of a wedge-shaped peninsula a few hundred kilometres north of Lupercalia's white noise. It enjoyed a temperate climate carried over the bay from the jungles of Kush, and was kept fresh with coastal winds from Hvitha in the north.

All in all, Larsa wasn't a bad place to live.

That had been true until this morning, when the burning remains of an Imperial frigate impacted twenty kilometres off the coast. Larsa's littoral regions were underwater now, its commercia halls abandoned, its bustling markets and traders swept out to sea.

A foamed lake of debris and corpses engulfed the harbour, and only the greater elevation of the inland port districts had saved them. Disaster control squads were engaged in a desperate rescue effort to save those who might still be alive down there.

Alivia didn't reckon on them finding anyone.

She'd endured the great flood of antiquity, and while today couldn't compare to that deluge, she knew this was only going to get worse. A second or third wave would be building out to sea, and could be anywhere from minutes to hours away.

She needed to get back to the hab she shared with Jeph and his daughters. They lived on the edge of the Menach district in a hillside tenement along with another two thousand other port workers. Not the most exotic place she'd ever lived, but certainly better than many could hope to afford.

Alivia knew she ought to grab another transport and get the hell out of Larsa. Should have left the minute she heard the Warmaster was coming. Alivia's time was short, but a stab of guilt knotted her gut each time she thought of abandoning Jeph and the girls.

She bore a heavy burden of duty, but now she'd acquired *responsibilities*. Mother. Wife. Lover. Just words she'd thought, cosmetic affectations to enhance her anonymity.

How wrong she'd been.

Alivia captained a pilot tender in the harbour, guiding the cargo tankers from Ophir and Novamatia through the submerged defences of Larsa's approaches. Like everyone else, she'd paused to watch the lights flickering in the night sky. They bloomed and faded like a distant fireworks display. Her first mate said it looked pretty until she snapped that every flash probably meant hundreds of people were dying in battle.

Abandoning the trans-loader she'd been guiding in to port, Alivia immediately put to shore over the protests of her crew. It wasn't logical, but all she could think of was getting home, hoping Jeph had been smart and kept the girls indoors. He wasn't the sharpest knife in the block, but he had a good heart.

Perhaps that was why she needed him.

She'd grabbed the first groundcar she could hotwire and driven like a maniac into the hills. She'd reached the mid-level commercia districts when the darkness was dispelled by the fiery descent of the downed starship. Dauntless-class, she had thought. Alivia didn't bother to watch it hit and drove even harder, knowing what was coming.

The impact tsunami slammed a kilometre and a half into Larsa before the drawback dragged half the city's inhabitants to their deaths. Caught at the farthest extent of the wave's force, Alivia had been slammed around by the flood. Old reflexes honed over the years steered the car through the chaos until its motor eventually died.

Fortunately, she was less than a kilometre from the hab-tenement, so didn't have far to go. Alivia sprinted uphill, the water level dropping the higher she went. The streets were thick with people, some looking down in horror at the drowned coastline, others sensibly packing their belongings.

Alivia pushed on, finally reaching her hab, a mid-level stack of bare plascrete and dirty glass on the edge of the walled starport.

'Clever boy,' she said, seeing the hab shutter pulled down over their ground-floor residency. She ran over and banged her fists on the bare metal.

'Jeph, open up, it's me!' she yelled. 'Hurry, we've got to get out of the city.'

Alivia hit the shutter again, and it rose with a clatter of turning gears and rattling chains. She ducked under as soon as there was enough room and took a quick inventory. Miska and little Vivyen clutched their father's overalls, their sleepy faces lined with worry.

'Liv, what's going on?' asked Jeph, doing a poor job of keeping the fear from his voice. She took his hand and steadied him with gentle stimulation of his pituitary gland to produce a burst of endorphins.

'We've got to go. Now,' she said. 'Get the girls ready.'

Jeph knew her well enough to know not to argue.

'Yeah, sure, Liv,' he said, calm without knowing why. 'Where are we going?'

'South,' said Alivia as Jeph began wrapping the girls in heavy outdoor coats before helping them pull on their boots.

'The cargo-five ready to go?' asked Alivia, bending to retrieve a burnished metal gun-case from a cavity she'd cut in the floor beneath their bed. There was a gun in it, yes, but that wasn't what was most precious to her in there.

'Yeah, Liv, just like always.'

'Good,' she said, stuffing the gun-case into her kit bag.

'This why you always say we got to keep it fuelled?' asked Jeph. 'In case of trouble?'

She nodded and his shoulders sagged in relief.

'You know, I always worried it was so you could get out quick if you ever decided you'd had enough of us.'

Alivia didn't have the heart to tell him both reasons were true.

Miska started crying. Alivia fought the urge to pull her close. She didn't have time for sentimentality. As one of Molech's principal port facilities, Larsa was sure to come under attack from Legion forces. She couldn't be here when that happened.

'Liv, they're saying half the city's underwater.'

'Maybe all of it soon,' she said, her eyes sweeping the room to make sure there wasn't anything else of use they might need on the journey south. 'That's why we need to go right now. Come on.'

'Sure, Liv, sure,' nodded Jeph, hugging the girls tight. 'Where are we going again?'

'We drive south until we hit the agri-belt arterials and hope they've not been bombed to oblivion by the time we get there.'

'Then what?'

'Then we go to Lupercalia,' she said.

FAR TO THE east of Lupercalia, the Knights of House Donar held the Preceptor Line, a grand name for a crumbling curtain-wall that marked the edge of civilisation. West were inhabited cities, east the unchecked jungles of Kush, and beyond that only black-gulfed Ophir.

Immense predator beasts stalked the jungle's humid depths, beasts that had once roamed freely across the land. Centuries of hunting had driven them to the fringes of the world, to hidden mountain fissures, jungle lairs or the arid southern steppe.

Armoured in jade and brass, House Donar boasted seven functional Knights and had kept vigil at the Preceptor Line for thirty generations. That regiments of Belgar Devsirmes and armoured squadrons of the Kapikulu Iron Brigade were also stationed along its length was, in Lord Balmorn Donar's opinion, hardly worth mentioning.

Flocks of azhdarchid, flesh-hungry mallahgra or roaming packs of xenosmilus rarely emerged from the jungle, but when they did, House Donar was there to drive them back with chainsabres, battle cannon and thermal lances.

Lord Donar ducked beneath the lintel of the main curtain-wall, though the rusted iron arch was easily tall enough to accommodate his Knight's bulk. His son's Knight limped after him, one leg stained with oily blood where an azhdarchid matriarch had gored him. Towering, flightless birds with oversized necks and crocodilian beaks, azhdarchid were comical in appearance, but fully capable of wounding a Knight.

As Robard Donar had found to his cost.

Behind the wall, redoubts of dug-in Shadowswords and Baneblades, Malcadors and Stormhammers covered the two Knights as the gate slid shut. Thousands of soldiers mustered on the martial fields, embarking onto armoured transports. The invasion of the traitors had shifted the mobilisation up a gear, but the Preceptor Line had been on a war footing ever since a company of Belgar had been found slaughtered in the jungle.

Dying in the jungle was easy, it had a hundred ways to see a man dead, but something unutterably savage had killed these men. Any number of the jungle beasts might have attacked the men, but what manner of beast would take ident-tags as a trophy?

Just one of many mysteries of the Kushite jungle.

'Walk tall,' ordered Balmorn. 'Don't let these Army dregs see you limping. You're a Donar, for Throne's sake. Act like one.'

Balmorn marched his Knight up a long sloping roadway of scaffolding that led to the widened ramparts. The few functional turrets scanned the jungle. Thermal auspex hunted for targets. Robard followed his father, slower as he compensated for the buckled joints of his leg.

'Foolish of you to get caught out like that,' said Balmorn, as his son finally reached the ramparts and braced his Knight's piston-driven leg against an adjacent blockhouse with no roof.

'How could I have known the azhdarchid were going to stampede?' snapped Robard, tired of his father's baiting. 'We were lucky to get away at all.'

A gaggle of Sacristans scurried towards the damaged Knight, but

Robard warned them off with a bark of his hunting horn.

'Luck's got nothing to do with it, lad,' said Balmorn, rotating his upper body to take in a full panorama from their elevated perch.

It wasn't pretty.

The sky painted a gloomy picture for Molech. Furnace orange and coal black burned in every direction. The wind carried the stench of burned stone, heated steel and fyceline. Electromagnetic storms raged over the fertile landscape and flashes of orbital weapon detonations mushroomed on every horizon. Balmorn didn't like to think how big explosions had to be for him to see them all the way out on the Preceptor Line.

As he looked over the jungle canopy, a growing illumination bathed the clouds pressing down on the jungle canopy.

'What's that?' asked Robard. 'Another bombardment?'

Lord Donar didn't answer, watching as thousands of black objects streaked from the clouds and arced over the eastern horizon.

'Too slow to be orbital munitions,' he said. 'And too regimented to be wreckage.'

'They're too fast and steeply angled for assault carriers,' said Robard. 'What *are* they?'

'They're drop pods,' said Lord Donar.

THREE OF OPHIR'S fuel silos were ablaze.

A lake of flaming promethium engulfed the city's southern outskirts and was slowly spreading north. The city's Mechanicum adepts had locked the pumping stations into emergency shutdown. No flames jetted from the vent towers and the ever-present heartbeat of drilling rigs had stilled.

A coaling station at the eastern tip of the continent on the far side of the Kushite jungle, Ophir lay nine thousand kilometres east of the Preceptor Line. Cargo tankers from across the ocean paused here to gorge on the promethium wells before continuing around the northern coastline to the commercia distribution hub of Hvitha or the starports at Loqash and Larsa.

No one called Ophir by its given name. Once it had been called the City of Gold, but centuries of exhaust gases, promethium discharge and oily runoff that stained every structure with a persistent black residue had earned it another name. The soldiers of the Karnatic Lancers knew it as 'the city without shadows'.

Lieutenant Skander of Seventh Brigade had been enjoying a particularly erotic dream when the alarm klaxons went off. Instantly awake, he bounded upright and grabbed his flak jacket from the footlocker at the end of his bed. He could feel the pulse of void shield generators beneath him. Hydra batteries were firing, the rhythmic thud of their shells unmistakable, even through reinforced plascrete.

Skander dragged on his boots and snapped on his shoulder rig, holstering his bolt pistol and checking the safety. He grabbed his sword belt as he ran to the main vehicle hangar. There wasn't much use for a sword in a Stormhammer, but he'd sooner go into battle naked than leave his blade behind.

Five hundred Karnatic armoured vehicles filled the chamber, a mix of Chimera variants, Malcador-pattern assault tanks, Minotaurs and a few superheavies. Each flew pennants bearing the emerald and silver pyramid of lances. His own vehicle was a Stormhammer dubbed *The Reaper*. Drivers, gunners and enginseers swarmed their vehicles. Shell loaders and fuel trucks sped through the cavernous space.

Distant explosions shook the chamber. Dust fell from the vaulted roof. The planetary assault every Army grunt had fully expected the fleet to spectacularly fail to prevent was now upon them.

An enormously augmented enginseer in oil-stained robes

implemented manoeuvre operations quickly and methodically, multiple limbs directing the optimal deployment order. Tanks rolled from their berths, and the throaty bellow of their engines was music to his ears.

Sergeant Hondo waved to him from the front cupola as he ran over. Skander had long believed Hondo lived in the tank, and this only seemed to confirm that suspicion.

'Guess the admiral got beat,' said Hondo over the din of sirens.

'And you're surprised *why*?' replied Skander, hauling himself up the crew ladder to the colossal tank's roof. 'Where's Vari?'

'Already in place, lieutenant,' Vari replied from the cramped driver's compartment. Skander scrambled onto the tank's forward twin battle cannon turret and dropped into the commander's hatch. Helmet on, he plugged in to the onboard attack-logister.

Information cascaded; deployment rates, ammunition levels, core temperature and hull integrity.

All in the green.

The enginseer gave them clearance, but before Skander could give the order to move out, something powerful struck the subterranean hangar.

The chamber roof split wide open.

Colossal chunks of sheared plascrete slammed down throughout the chamber. Dust-smeared pillars of sunlight stabbed inside. A squadron of Baneblades was flattened by debris, their hulls smashed open like toymaker's models.

Skander was slammed forward as a falling chunk of rock struck his helmet. Blood ran down his face and he blinked away tears of sudden pain. Static fogged his visor. He tore the helmet off. It was useless now, split down the middle.

The noise and confusion was unbelievable. The regiment's tanks in the hangar's centre had taken the worst of the barrage, pulverised by hundreds of tonnes of debris and high explosives.

Detonations ripped across the ready line as follow-on shells found their marks in exposed Malcadors and Chimeras. The main roadway was engulfed in flames, burning pools of fuel spewing thick black smoke. Regimental pennants burned in the fires.

The heat from an exploding Minotaur rolled over him, and Skander looked up through the smashed roof of the hanger to see a sky red with flames and black with smoke. Once a refuge for his tanks, the hangar was now a deathtrap.

'Get us out of here!' he shouted and *The Reaper* lurched forward as Vari fed power to the engines. A clattering, screeching howl of protest told him they'd sheared a track in the barrage. They were ripping the hangar floor apart, but that was the least of Skander's worries.

Something hammered down in the flaming heart of the hangar, a pair of tapered oblongs. Pale steel and scorched black with re-entry burn. Scalding exhaust vapour billowed from burned out retros. Locking bolts blasted off and the shielded sides of the drop pod dropped like unfolding prop-drives.

Powerful figures emerged from two of the pods, giants in pale armour bearing a spiked skull icon on their shoulder guards. The warriors of the Death Guard waded through wreckage and rubble, but weren't slowed.

A towering figure in battle armour of bare metal, brass and ivory stepped from his drop pod and into the blazing ruin of the hangar. A giant come to rend their flesh and grind their bones. Framed by fire and a billowing cloak of fibrous mesh, the primarch of the XIV Legion bore a great scythe that shimmered with corpse-light.

Mortarion was attended by cowled Terminators in slab-like armour. They too carried oversized scythes and unquestioningly followed their liege-lord into the fire. Sprays of gunshots reached out to the Death Guard, sparking from impenetrable plates. Shells burst among them, but they marched through their fury without pause.

Their guns were firing. Explosive rounds slaughtered the tank crews who'd survived the initial shelling, pulping them to shredded meat mass. Another pod slammed down behind the first wave. Then another, and another. They fell in pairs, one after the other, each reverberating impact bearing more Death Guard.

The Reaper tried to turn towards Mortarion, but with a snapped track, that wasn't happening any time soon. Skander engaged his commander's override, slewing the twin battle cannon turret around. Men were screaming over the fires and continuous sound of falling masonry.

The primarch of the Death Guard saw him, and Skander almost let go of the controls as he stared into the face of his executioner – pale skinned, with the coldest eyes he had ever seen.

He heard the familiar double reverberation of shells ramming home in the breech. A hiss of locking mechanisms and the whine of accelerator drives.

'Throne, yes,' he hissed, mashing the firing trigger.

All three hundred and twenty tonnes of *The Reaper*'s armoured might rocked under the enormous recoil. The twin muzzle flashes all but blinded him. The conjoined pressure waves punched the air from his lungs and the thunder of discharge blew out his eardrums.

Skander fought to take a breath, concussed by the simultaneous detonations of point-blank battle cannon shells. He blinked away after-images as a rain of plascrete dust rained down. Acrid smoke fogged the air, slashed by cherry red fyceline fires.

He dragged in hot, metallic breath and shouted for a reload, though he knew no one would hear and they'd not get another shot off. Skander ducked down into the Stormhammer, cupping his hands over his mouth.

'Reload! Reload! Throne, give me one more shot at that bastard!'

He repeated his order. He had no idea who was still alive inside *The Reaper*. Until the main gun was loaded, all Skander could directly control was the cupola's point-defence gun. It wasn't a twin battle cannon turret, but it would have to do.

Skander rose up and saw the cloaked figure of the Death Lord standing on his tank. Mortarion's armour looked to have been tenderised by a forge hammer and his cloak was a ragged scrap. The primarch was a grotesque waxwork, a flesh-slick deathmask.

'One shot's all you get,' gurgled Mortarion, swinging *Silence* and carving Skander and his Stormhammer apart.

SIMILAR STORIES PLAYED out all across Molech.

The air defence batteries were completely overwhelmed. Two Legion fleets in close orbit were an impossible force to defeat, and the punishing broadsides turned entire regions of Molech into glassy deserts.

Mount Torger was targeted by a mass impact of bunker penetrators, and not even its many point defences could keep the holdfast of the Ordo Reductor from being gutted by an inferno. Fires raged beneath the mountain, fires that would burn for another seventy years before finally bringing it down.

Goshen, Imperatum and the twin fortress cities of Leosta and Luthre were bombed, as were the coastal cities of Desqua and Hvitha. Known as the City of Winds due to its location at the farthest extreme of the Aenatep peninsula, Hvitha all but fell into the ocean as the rock upon which it was built crumbled under the weight of the barrage.

A red rain fell on Khanis, molten iron and micro-debris falling from the fighting in orbit like burning bullets.

People out in the open went up like vent flares, instantly ablaze. They screamed until the heat sucked the air from their lungs. They ran for shelter, but the molten rain soon ate through the canvas awnings and corrugated roofs.

With the bombardment finished for now, the fleets opened their embarkation decks and wave after wave of the Warmaster's invasion force launched into the upper atmosphere.

They arced down like grains of sand running through a philosopher's fingers; Stormbirds and Thunderhawks, Fire Raptors and Storm Eagles. Coffin ships and bulk landers. Shoals of matte-black Army transports. Armoured trans-loaders and munitions carriers.

Alert horns howled in every city.

Molech was screaming.

TWELVE

Breakout
Decapitation
Twin Flames

A TIDAL WAVE of ocean green crashed onto the beaches at Avadon, but this one didn't recede, it just kept pushing higher. An armoured fist of firepower and transhuman endurance, this was to be a breakout achieved at maximum speed.

Two hundred Sons of Horus Land Raiders led the speartip's thrust.

No grace, no finesse, just a thunderous hammer blow to the heart.

Edoraki Hakon, Marshal of the Northern Oceanic, awaited Lupercal's army with a line of strongpoints, deep trenches, six full regiments of Army and a company of dug-in superheavies. Her defences lined the coastal cliffs and encircled the landward end of the causeway. If the Sons of Horus wanted to reach the mainland, they were going to have to fight their way off Damesek.

Quite why a tactician as superlative as Horus would establish a bridgehead on an island that's only viable egress point was a slender causeway was beyond her understanding.

It made no sense, but that was what the Warmaster had done.

No one in her command staff could adequately explain Horus's reasoning, but the opportunity to punish the traitors for their mistake was there for the taking.

Holst Lithonan's artillery companies on the island's high bluffs had spent the night duelling with Hakon's guns, and the Marshal had reluctantly been forced to withdraw her heavier pieces as dawn's light crept over the horizon.

Freed from suppressive battery fire, traitor guns dumped barrage after barrage of shroud missiles on the Imperials. Banks of glittering electromagnetic fog spewed from spinning shells, breaking firing solutions and disrupting carefully calibrated range-finders.

While Imperial gunners struggled to penetrate the occluding mist, Sons of Horus Land Raiders raced along the last stretch of the causeway to the mainland. Scorpius Whirlwinds sent arcing streams of missiles ahead of them. Their warheads wrecked the emplaced tank traps and ripped up fields of entangling razorwire in a storm of subterranean explosions.

The first Land Raiders slammed down off the causeway into a fury of heavy autocannons, crew-served weapon mounts and emplaced lascannons. Hakon's superheavy tanks crashed back in their berms as volleys of battle cannons and demolishers added their thunder to the day. Siege mortars and bombards, culverin and howitzers coughed their explosive loads skyward.

The end of the causeway vanished in an earthshaking blizzard of explosions. Deafening hammer blows slammed down, one after the other. So quick and so continuous they merged into one unending concussive procession of detonation. Energy weapons boiled ocean waves to geysers of steam. High explosives churned the beach into hurricanes of glassy shrapnel.

The air reeked of salt and burning metal. Seared meat and blood.

Twenty Land Raiders died instantly. Cored and twisted inside out, they slewed around like disembowelled grazer beasts. Sons of Horus legionaries spilled from the smoke-belching wrecks. Blistering crossfires cut them to pieces. Oxy-phosphor warheads seared the agonised cries from their lungs. Armour shredded and disassembled. Flesh vaporised.

Hakon's remaining artillery lobbed explosives onto the causeway, hoping to deny the tanks on the beach reinforcements and strangle the breakout at birth. Atlas recovery tanks by the dozen drove wrecks into the ocean as modified Trojans worked nonstop to keep the causeway viable; nothing could be allowed to slow the flood of troop carriers onto the mainland.

More Land Raiders plunged into the maelstrom. Another half dozen, then a dozen more, spreading out as they hit the shell-torn beach. They ground over the corpses of their Legion brothers, finding cover in blood and fuel-filled craters. Return fire blitzed uphill.

The Scorpius barged past gutted Land Raiders, peeling left and right at the causeway's end. Rotating launchers unleashed rippling salvoes of warheads at the linked strongpoints. Three exploded in quick succession, brought down by implosive warheads that blew out their structural members.

Storm Eagles and Thunderhawks roared overhead, missiles and shells streaming from their wing and nose mounts. Sheets of fire blossomed along the Imperial line, but Edoraki Hakon's regiments were dug in well, and dug in deep.

Hydra batteries slewed to follow the aircraft. Manticore batteries locked their targeting cogitators onto engine flares. Sky-eagle missiles and rapid firing autocannon shells stitched the sky. Half a dozen gunships were brought down in quick succession, smashing into the cliffs like faulty triumphal fireworks.

Sons of Horus bolters punched spiralling contrails through the shroud smoke. Their missiles arced over and slammed down on gun emplacements. Solid hits were announced by mushrooming flares of white light. Dreadnought talons moved through the heart of the attack like giants. Assault cannons too heavy even for a legionary brayed, and rocket after rocket streaked from rotary launchers.

Whickering storms of gunfire, missiles, energy weapons and gouts of flame burned back and forth across kilometres of beach.

The dead and dying were crushed beneath the roaring tracks of the Land Raiders. Rhinos followed them to the assigned high water mark, and the icy sand was churned to gritty, red paste.

THE LAND RAIDER rocked on its tracks as a nearby explosion slammed it to the side. Aximand gripped tight to a stanchion as the heavy vehicle pitched forward into a crater. Its engine roared as it clawed its way out the opposite side. The assault carrier's armour attenuated most of the noise of battle, but the thrumming bass note of the percussive shock waves were thudding with increasing regularity and force.

'Getting closer,' said Yade Durso, line captain of Fifth Company.

'Getting worried?' Aximand asked.

'No,' said Durso, and Aximand believed him. It took more than emplaced strongpoints, companies of superheavies and regiments of Army to rattle a veteran like Durso.

Aximand's subordinate turned something over in his hand, dextrously moving it between his fingers like a sleight of hand barker.

'What's that?'

Durso looked down, as though unaware of what he'd been doing.

'Nothing,' he said. 'Just an affectation.'

'Show me.'

Durso shrugged and opened his palm. A golden icon on the end of a chain to be worn around the neck. The Eye of Horus shone red in the light of the compartment.

'Superstitious, Yade?'

'Turns out I can be now, Little Horus,' said Durso.

Aximand nodded, conceding the point. Not so long ago, such behaviour would have been grounds for censure. Now it seemed only natural. Aximand looked back at his warriors, ten Sons of Horus bearing heavy breacher shields and multi-spectral helmet attachments. Each warrior's armour bore Cthonian gang sigils etched into the plates. Their bolters were decorated with kill markings and grisly trophies hung from every belt.

The Quiet Order had reinstituted the old practices of the home world. Serghar Targost, his throat bound in counterseptic wraps, had advocated the reinstatement of Cthonian iconography and the Warmaster had agreed.

'I thought we were done with savage totems,' he said.

'Just like the old days,' said Durso. 'It's good.'

'But these *aren't* the old days,' snapped Aximand.

Durso shook his head. 'You really want to get into this now?'

'No,' said Aximand, strangely disquieted at the new tribalistic mien of his warriors. He had thought that with Erebus gone, the XVI Legion was to re-establish itself. It seemed it had, just not in the image he'd expected. Edges worn smooth by centuries of compliance were being made rough again.

Aximand patched his helmet's visual link to the Land Raider's external pict-feeds.

There wasn't much to see.

Shroud bombs blanketed the shale beaches and granite cliffs ahead of them in waves of electromagnetic distortion. Flattened tank traps ghosted from the fog alongside acres of shell-ruined razorwire. Static fizzed the display as muzzle flares from cliff-top artillery fired. Seconds later, the Land Raider shook from a nearby impact of high explosive shells. The vehicle juddered over the wreckage of something that might once have been a Rhino.

Aximand silently urged the driver to hurry up.

The Dwell campaign had spoiled him. The urgent, body slamming fury of that fight was a throwback to the earliest days of the Great Crusade, when the Legions were still developing their modus operandi. It had been a testing time, re-learning lessons taught by wars that were only just evolving from the hell of techno-barbarian tribes hacking at one another in two amorphous hosts of flesh and sweat.

New weapons, new technologies, new transhuman physiques and new brothers to fight alongside. It was one thing to build a Legion, another to learn how to *fight* as a Legion.

'Ten seconds,' called the driver.

Aximand nodded, checking the load on his bolter and moved *Mourn-it-all*'s scabbard at his shoulder. Full load, and just right. Just like last time. He shifted on the ready line. He rolled his shoulders and pulled his shield in tight. He clenched and unclenched his jaw.

'Five seconds!'

The pitch of the engine increased, the driver wringing another few dozen metres for the warriors he carried. An explosion rocked the vehicle up onto one track. It landed flat with a crashing boom of grinding stone and protesting metal.

'Go, go, go!'

The Land Raider came to a grinding halt. The assault ramp hammered down and a roaring crescendo of noise rammed inside. Explosions, gunfire, screams and metal banging on metal. The volume on the world spun into the red.

Aximand heard a breath at his ear and shouted, 'Kill for the living, and kill for the dead!'

The old war cry sprang unbidden from his lips as he charged into the maelstrom.

His warriors roared in answer.

THANKS TO LYX, Raeven had marched *Banelash* almost into the ground to get to Avadon, but right now wished he hadn't bothered. She had woken him in the night, leading him to believe that some carnal adventure was in the offing, but instead she'd offered him entrails and prophecy.

'The Great Wolf comes to Avadon,' she'd said, dumping the warm, wet handful of organs in his lap. 'His throat will bare when the twin wolves of fire are upon you. Cut it and the White Naga of legend will come to you with revelation.'

Raeven gagged on the stench of rotten meat, ready to push her away when he saw her eyes were milky white and without pupil. His mother's had done that when he was young and what she'd said always came true. Instead of beating her, he asked, 'Horus? Horus will be at Avadon?'

But she'd gone limp and neither salts nor slaps could rouse her.

Over Tyana Kourion and Castor Alcade's misgivings, Raeven had immediately mustered his household and marched north to Avadon with ten of his Knights. Two of his sons came with him, Egelic and Banan, while his middle son, Osgar, remained in Lupercalia to retain a ruling presence.

And after a full night's gruelling march around the spur of the Untar Mesas, and over unending vistas of agricultural land...

Nothing.

Their honourable machines waited like common footsoldiers, awaiting word from Edoraki Hakon on when they might deploy. Denied a place in the order of battle by that humourless Army sow sent spasms of disgust along his spine.

Banelash reacted to his anger by pawing the ground with its clawed feet. Its threat auspex bathed his sensorium in red, and its weapons powered up with a whine of servos. Nearby Army reserve forces backed away from the Knights as their warhorns blared.

'*We should be over that ridge, father,*' said Egelic, Raeven's oldest son. '*Why are we not fighting?*'

'*Because outsiders have taken Molech,*' hissed Banan, Raeven's youngest. '*When the Imperium came, they cut our House's balls off.*'

'Enough,' snapped Raeven. Banan was almost thirty and should know better, but his mother doted on him and denied him nothing. His manners were boorish, his arrogance as monstrous as his sense of entitlement.

He reminded Raeven a lot of his younger self, except Banan had none of the charm and charisma he'd had to carry off arrogance and make it look like confidence.

But in this case, Banan was also right.

'Come with me,' he said, marching from the area they'd been apportioned and striding through the trenchlines and redoubts. Approaching the forward edge of battle, Raeven linked to the battle cogitators in Edoraki Hakon's command bunker. Inloading data swarmed the sensorium, and *Banelash* growled in anticipation.

It could smell the blood and hear the crash of gunfire. This was war, *real* war, a chance to test itself against a foe more interesting than a rogue mallahgra or a pack of xenosmilus. Raeven felt the echoes of all the warriors who'd piloted *Banelash* before him, heard the mingled whispers of their battle hunger pump through his body like a shot of 'slaught.

Raeven doubted he could have turned back even if he wanted to.

He strode through the jumble of ammo depots, Trojans, artillery pits and rear echelon troops. His Knights followed behind, boasting of the enemies they would kill. The ground rose sharply towards the front and the sky raged as though a phantasmagorical storm blazed like gods in battle in the heavens.

Insistent warnings sounded in the sensorium, tagged with Marshal Hakon's personal signifier. He ignored them and pushed on, striding on to the edge of the cliff.

The end of the causeway was half a kilometre distant, and the space between it and the cliffs was a shattered graveyard of twisted metal and fire. A hellscape of blazing craters, scores of wrecked tanks and hundreds of dismembered bodies.

Thousands of giant warriors pushed forward behind heavy breacher shields. Against small-arms fire and even medium gauge weapons they offered effective protection, but against the kinds of guns Hakon had trained on them, they just weren't up to the job. Each advance left a trail of bodies, limbless corpses and tributaries of blood to fill craters with red lakes.

Raeven had never seen so many Space Marines, hadn't even conceived there could be so many at all. *Banelash* tugged at his mind, urging him to commit, to ride out in glory and smash one of those advancing shield-wedges apart.

'*Come on, father,*' urged Banan. '*Let's break them! Smash each one apart in turn until we roll the entire line up.*'

He wanted to give the order. Oh, how he wanted to give that order.

'Yes, we could break one, probably two, maybe even three of the shieldwalls, but that will be all,' he said, feeling *Banelash*'s ire at his refusal to ride. 'Then we would be overwhelmed by the artillery and dragged down by infantry. An ignoble death. Hardly knightly.'

His Knight sent a spasm of neural feedback through his spine at his resistance, and Raeven winced at the severity of it. When he opened his eyes, they were immediately drawn to an up-armoured Land Raider as it smashed through a rockcrete tidal wall, slamming down on bollard tank traps and crushing them beneath its weight.

A banner streamed from the rear of both track guards, each bearing a rearing wolf insignia. Gunfire sparked from the Land Raider's armour and Raeven saw the direct hit of a lascannon strike its flank where the right-side sponson had been sheared off. It should have blown a hole right into the vehicle.

Instead, the energy of the shot dissipated at the moment of impact and a bloom of fire enveloped the tank, setting the twin wolf banners ablaze.

'Flare shield,' he said, recognising similar tech to the ion shields of *Banelash*.

His throat will bare when the twin wolves of fire are upon you.

'Lupercal,' said Raeven.

THE DECK BENEATH Grael Noctua shuddered with impacts, rounded arrowheads forming in the plates beneath his boots. The Thunderhawk was a utilitarian design, a workhorse craft that had the virtue of being quick and easy to manufacture.

It was also, relatively speaking, disposable.

Which was scant comfort to the men being carried within it.

Squatting by the rear ramp with the bulky weight of a jump pack smouldering at his back, Noctua felt every impact on the gunship's hull. He heard every snap of tension cables and creak of press-bolted wings as the pilot made desperate evasion manoeuvres.

Streams of gunfire reached up to the gunship, weaving through the air as the gunners tried to anticipate its movement. Flak pounded the air like drumbeats. Six warriors dropped as armour-piercing shells ripped up through the fuselage and split them like humanoid-shaped bags of blood.

The line of tracer fire intersected with the starboard wing. The engine took the brunt of the impact, then the aileron sheared off.

'On me!' shouted Noctua.

The jump light was still amber, but if they didn't get off this doomed bird, they were going down with it. The Thunderhawk slipped sideways through the air, heeling over to the side as the starboard engine blew out.

He bent his legs and pushed himself out and down, pulling his arms in tight to his sides. He didn't look back to see if his men were following him. They were or they weren't. He'd know when he hit the ground.

He felt the explosion of the Thunderhawk above him. He hoped its burning carcass wasn't about to fall on him. He grinned at what Ezekyle and Falkus would make of that. Three Thunderhawks went up in flames, probably more. It didn't matter. Everyone knew the aircraft were expendable. Assault legionaries filled the sky.

He ignored them and fixed his attention on the uprushing ground.

His battle-brothers on the beach were embroiled in a quagmire of shelling and interlocking fields of fire. The black shale of the beach reminded Noctua of the massacre on Isstvan V, but this time it was the Sons of Horus doing the dying.

Noctua angled his descent towards the objective given to him by Lupercal himself. The arrangement of strongpoints, trenches and redoubts was exactly as the Warmaster had predicted.

Mortals. So predictable.

An icon in the shape of the new moon, matching the one etched on his helm, overlaid a heavily fortified strongpoint. Layered in outworks, protected by point-defence guns, it was defended by hundreds of soldiers and its placement in the line.

Noctua swung his legs down so he was falling boots first. A pulse of thought fired the jump pack with a shrieking hurricane of blue-hot fire. He'd specially modified the intake/outlet jets to scream as he fired it.

His hurtling descent slowed. Noctua landed with a crash of

splitting stone. His knees bent and the burners of his jump pack scorched the strongpoint's roof. Seconds later the crash of boots on stone surrounded him. By the time he freed the two melta charges from his plastron, he counted twenty-six further impacts.

More than enough.

He slammed the meltas down to either side and bounded back into the air, firing a short burst from the jump pack. His warriors followed suit and no sooner were they in the air then fifty-eight melta bombs exploded virtually simultaneously.

Cutting his burners, Noctua drew his sword and bolt pistol and dropped through the smoking ruin of the strongpoint's roof. The upper level was utterly destroyed, a howling, screaming mass of dying flesh. He dropped onto the floor below, crashing through its weakened structure and landing in the centre of what had once been a projector table.

Stunned mortals surrounded him with faces like landed fish. Mouths opened in terrified, uncomprehending 'O' shapes. He leapt among them, sword cutting three officers down with a single sweep as he shot two more in the face. Before the corpses hit the floor he was moving. Powerful impacts smashed through the ceiling, spilling rock dust and iron beams into what had, only moments before, been a fully functioning command centre.

Dust-covered statues of warrior gods rose up from the debris and slaughtered every living person within reach. Bolter rounds exploded flak-armoured bodies like over-pressurised fuel canisters. Arterial spray painted the walls in criss-crossing arcs. Roaring chainblades hewed limbs and spines, made jigsaws of flesh.

Noctua saw a pair of blank-helmed, piston-legged Thallaxii detach from sentinel alcoves at each of the cardinal entrances. Lightning guns fired, buckling the air, but Noctua rode his jump pack over the coruscating blast. He landed between the Thallaxii, beheading one with his sword, exploding the other's with an executioner's bolt-round.

Two more were felled by a mob of Sons of Horus, another pair shot down before they'd taken a single step. Noctua braced himself against a bank of hissing valves and crackling cogitator domes. His jump pack fired, leaving a canyon of scorched flesh in his wake. He came down at the sprint, driving his heel into the chest of the remaining Thallax as he landed.

It slammed back into the wall, the Lorica Thallax unit shattering like glass and spilling the steel-encased spinal cord and skull to the rubble-strewn floor. The last of them swung its plasma blaster around and managed a snap shot that cut a searing groove in his shoulder guard.

Angry now, Noctua carved his sword down through its shoulder.

The blade tore free from its pelvis, and the stricken cyborg died with a burst of machine pain and flood of stinking amniotics.

Noctua rolled his shoulders, irritated the cyborg *thing* had managed to get so close to him. The flesh beneath was burned, and only now did he feel the pain of it. Thinking of pain, he looked down to see a rolled steel reinforcement bar jutting from his thigh and a Thallax combat blade buried in his plastron.

The latter hadn't penetrated his armour, but the rebar went right through from the front of his leg to the back. Strange that he hadn't felt it. He yanked it out, watching the blood flow for a moment, enjoying the novel sensation of being wounded.

He tossed the bar and nodded to his Master of Signal.

'Get the beacon set up,' he ordered, pointing to the centre of the ruined hololithic table. 'There seems appropriate.'

Noctua heard a wheezing breath and looked down to see that one of the stronghold's command staff was still alive. A dying woman with an ornamented laspistol. Archaic and over-elaborate, but then Imperial officers did so like to embellish their wargear.

Clad in a drakescale burnoose and a golden eye-mask like some desert raider, Noctua saw rank pins on the breast of the uniform beneath. He hadn't bothered to study the military hierarchy of Molech's armed forces as Aximand had, but she was clearly high on the food chain. The burnoose was soaked in blood, and the mask had come loose, hanging over one cheek and exposing a withered, disease-wasted eye.

Still enjoying the feeling of pain, Noctua spread his arms.

'Go on then,' he said. 'Take your best shot.'

'My pleasure,' said Edoraki Hakon, and put her volkite shot right through Grael Noctua's heart.

THE DIN OF battle pounded Aximand like Contemptor fists. Detonation shock waves battered him, solid impacts shook his shield. Constant shellfire made every step perilous. Unimaginable volumes of blood pooled in the base of craters. The passage of fighting vehicles had ground it into sticky red mortar.

Scything blasts of heavy bolters and autocannons tore across the beach. The shields of the Sons of Horus line bore the brunt of the incoming fire, but not all of it. Legion warriors were falling in greater numbers than Aximand had known since Isstvan.

They marched over the dead, scorched plate cracking beneath them and pulped corpses sucking at their feet as they advanced. Apothecaries and serfs dragged away those too wounded to fight. There was little point in such mercies. A Space Marine too wounded to keep going was a burden the Legion could do without.

Let them die, thought Aximand.

Land Raiders overtaking them on either side threw up sprays of gritty black sand and sprays of stagnant blood. Revving gun platforms on tracks blitzed shells and smoking casings. A Dreadnought with one arm missing staggered in circles as though looking for it. Missiles streaked overhead, breath was snatched from lungs by the overpressure.

The air tasted of overworked batteries and smelting steel, burned meat and opened bowels.

The Imperial line was invisible behind a twitching bank of gun-smoke. Muzzle flare from hundreds of weapon slits flickered like picter flashes at a parade. Explosions painted the sky, and weeping arcs of smoke told where dozens of gunships had died.

'Tough going,' said Yade Durso, his helmet cracked down the middle by an autocannon impact on his shield that had slammed it straight back in his face. Blood welled in the crack, but the eye lenses had survived.

'It'll get tougher yet,' he answered.

Something fell from the sky and broke apart as it cartwheeled down the beach, shedding structure and bodies in equal measure. Aximand thought it was a Stormbird but it exploded before he could be sure.

Another gunship crashed. A Thunderhawk this time. It went in hard, nose first. A fan of hard, wet shale sprayed out before it like bullets. A dozen legionaries dropped, killed as cleanly as if by sniper fire. A sharp-edged shard smashed Aximand's visor. The left lens cracked. His vision blurred.

The gunship's wing dipped and ploughed the shale, flipping the aircraft over onto its back. The other wing snapped like tinder as it careened along the sand, coming apart with every bouncing impact. The spinning, burning wreckage crashed into a knot of Sons of Horus and they vanished in a sheeting fireball as its engines exploded. Turbine blades flew like swords.

'Lupercal's oath!' swore Aximand.

'Never thought I'd be glad to be a footslogger in an assault,' said Durso, lifting the golden icon tied to his shield grip.

Aximand shook his head. 'No,' he said. 'Look.'

The three Land Raiders before them looked like they had

been struck by the fists of a Titan's demolition hammer. One was entirely gutted, a blackened skeleton that held only molten corpses. A handful of warriors staggered from the second. Their armour was black – originally so, not scorched by the fires.

'Aren't the Justaerin with the First Captain?' said Durso, recognising the heavy plates of the Terminators.

'Not all of them,' said Aximand.

The third Land Raider's lupine pennants were ablaze, and it had been split open by a ferocious impact.

Horus was down on one knee, his taloned hand pressed to the side of his Land Raider, as though mourning its passing. Blood slicked one side of his dark battleplate and a length of pipework pierced his side like a spear.

'Lupercal,' said Durso, awed by a single warrior in the midst of such industrial-scale slaughter. But *what* a warrior.

'Sons of Horus!' shouted Aximand, pushing onward. 'Rally to me!'

Smoke billowed from the Land Raider's interior. Twisted warriors stepped through it, their bodies on fire. The lenses of their helms shone the bleached white of bone left in dusty tombs.

Not Justaerin, something far worse.

What had Maloghurst called them?

Luperci, the Brothers of the Wolf.

Serghar Targost had called them something else as the narthecium servitors finally removed the sutures holding his throat together.

Twin Flames.

Now Aximand knew why. Their armour was utterly black. Not painted black like the Justaerin and not from the vehicle's destruction, but from the infernal warpfires burning within them.

Ger Gerradon was first out. Aximand could still picture the two swords plunging into his chest, the lake of blood that formed around him as he bled out on the floor of the Mausolytic. Gerradon cared nothing for the fires lapping his armour. Nor did the seven other figures clambering from the wreckage.

Sons of Horus formed up on Aximand, a hundred warriors at least. He couldn't be sure because of the smoke. Each legionary saw what he saw. The Warmaster *threatened*.

The Mechanicum had proofed Lupercal's vehicle against all but a Titan's fury, and every piece of intelligence suggested that none of the Imperial Legios had any gross-displacement engines yet in the field. So what had done this?

The answer wasn't long in coming.

They rode out of the smoke, articulated giants in crimson and gold, banners streaming gloriously from their segmented carapaces. The ground shook with the pounding beat of their clawed feet and the ululating skirl of their hunting horns.

Crackling lances and screaming swords held before them, the Knights of Molech charged the Warmaster.

THIRTEEN

Beacon
Cornered wolf
I made this

HE DREW IN a lungful of hot, metallic air. It burned to breathe, but the alternative was worse. His head pounded and it felt like someone was pressing a steel needle through his left eyeball. His chest hurt, and felt like someone was pressing something considerably larger than a needle through it.

'Get up,' said a voice.

Grael Noctua nodded, though the gesture sent the needle deeper into his brain.

'Get up,' repeated Ezekyle Abaddon.

Noctua opened his eyes. Imperial strongpoint. Interior burned and ruined. *I did this*. There was a drop assault and I killed some Thallax. He didn't think there had been a squad of gloss-black Terminators filling the shattered command centre.

Corposant danced over the titanic plates of their dark armour and Noctua tasted the ice metal flavour of teleport flare.

'The beacon did its job then?' he said.

'About the only thing you managed to get right,' said Abaddon, directing his warriors with sub-vocal Cthonic argot. 'The Imperial line's already rolling up now the Justaerin are here.'

Noctua rolled onto his side, the effort of drawing air into his lungs making him sweat. He pushed himself upright, almost retching with the effort. Upright at last, but unsteady on his feet, Noctua immediately understood the problem. His heart had been destroyed.

The dying woman. The officer. Her pistol had been something more than just a laspistol. Something *considerably* more than just a laspistol. He looked down and saw the neat, cauterised hole burned through his plastron and into his chest. He knew if he picked up the rebar that had been jammed in his leg, he'd be able to thread it through the hole in his chest and out through his back without effort.

'She shot me,' he said. 'The bitch shot me.'

'From what I hear, you let her,' said the First Captain, shaking his head. 'Stupid. I'm behind schedule. And now Kibre will likely roll up his flank first.'

Noctua sought the dying woman, but she was already dead. Her head lay at an unnatural angle to her shoulder because that was about all that was left of her after the impact of mass-reactives to the chest.

'You got away lightly,' he said.

Abaddon took hold of Noctua's shoulder guard and spun him around. The First Captain's Terminator armour gave him a head of height advantage. Noctua looked up into eyes that were like those of a wolf on the hunt, and whose prey was in danger of slipping away.

'Get your men back in the fight,' said Abaddon, 'or I'll finish what she started.'

'Yes, First Captain,' said Noctua.

✠ ✠ ✠

THE KNIGHTS BORE down on the Warmaster, and Raeven had never felt so sure, so righteous in the anticipation of a kill. His arms burned hot with the readiness of his stubber cannons and the crackling energy arcs of his whip.

The warriors who'd ridden to glory before *Banelash* was his screamed at him, crowding his senses with their echoing war shouts. He heard their voices, a chorus of wordless fury. None of them had ever claimed so grand a kill, and they all wanted to feel what Raeven felt.

He channelled their skill and power, used it.

Banelash was the tip of the wedge, the lance thrust aimed at the Warmaster's heart. Egelic and Banan held tight to his flanks. Heads lowered, ion shields held out over their hearts.

Reaper chainblades pulled back to strike.

He loosed a wild laugh. He was Imperial commander. The first kill was his to make, and *what* a kill it would be.

Warriors whose armour looked to be on fire surrounded Horus, but the strangeness of the sight gave Raeven no pause. His sensorium told him more warriors were en route to rescue their leader. They would be too late.

He clenched his fist and a blazing stream of high-energy lasers pumped from his shoulder mount. Four of the black warriors were all but incinerated. The Land Raider was sawn in half.

Horus rose to his feet, and even though he went helmed, Raeven could imagine the fear in his eyes. *Banelash* cracked its whip and the Warmaster was catapulted into the wrecked Land Raider. Purple arcs of lightning flared from his shoulder and chest as he struggled to rise.

The floating cross hairs of Raeven's gunsight centred on the amber eye at the Warmaster's chest.

'Got you,' said Raeven as he unleashed the furious power of the weapon he'd saved just for this moment, his thermal lance.

✠ ✠ ✠

BLITZING SPEARS OF sun-hot light enveloped Lupercal, but when
Aximand blinked away the pinwheeling after-images, he saw only
darkness around his lord and master. The Luperci clung to the
Warmaster like devotees beseeching an ascending god to stay.

They howled and Aximand felt the day's heat snatched away.

Time slowed. Not the way it sometimes did in the heat of battle.
Not like that at all. In fact, it didn't *slow* so much as stop.

The world possessed the quality of timelessness, as though time
never had, never would and never *could* exist here. Galaxies might
swirl into being and spin themselves to extinction and it would
be the blink of an eye. A blowfly could beat its wings and it would
take an eternity to complete the motion.

It bled from the black warriors surrounding the Warmaster, as
though they drew from some unfathomable well within them. Or
maybe some dreadful power reached *through* them and allowed a
measure of its world to seep into this one.

The bolts of killing power from the Knight's armaments passed into
the Luperci. And vanished. Swallowed whole as though the Twin
Flames had become dark windows to another realm of existence.

And then it was over, and Aximand stumbled as the flow of
time caught up to him and the world snapped back into focus.
He steadied himself on his shield, his heart straining as though
pinned in a suit of skin too small for him.

'What...'

It was all he managed before the Luperci broke their embrace
with the Warmaster. Rivulets of black fire clung to Lupercal's
armour, but he was alive.

The Knight leading the charge paused, stupefied that its target
wasn't dead. Its weapons lifted to rectify that upset, but the fractional pause had already cost it its one advantage.

And a fraction was all that Horus needed.

☩ ☩ ☩

I should be dead.

Nerve endings on fire. Pain. Pain like he'd never known.

Even the attack on the Dome of Revivification hadn't been as bad. Burns and physical trauma he could endure, but the barbed fires of the Knight's whip sawed at his nerves like gleeful torturers.

I should be dead.

No time to reflect that he wasn't. Deal with the pain. Force it down into the pit. Endure it later.

Mal and Targost's Luperci had saved him. No time to wonder how. Retreat was not an option. He had been hurt and needed to hurt back. Aximand and the Fifth Company were en route. This would be over before they reached him.

Horus looked up at the charging Knights.

I am alive, and that was your only chance.

The Luperci streamed from him, a flock of raptors loosed from the rookeries of his armour. Far faster than anything living ought to move. Where they had clung to him was marked by burns. Frost burns. Horus followed them, swinging *Worldbreaker* around his head.

The first Knight took a backward step, and Horus laughed.

'Afraid now?' he bellowed.

Screaming vox chatter filled his helmet. He tore it off and threw it away.

Luperci swarmed the legs of the Knight, climbing and vaulting. Hand over hand, gripping the lips of segmented plates. They tore as they climbed, snapping connector cables, ripping out servos and coupling rods. Ger Gerradon climbed fastest and punched a clawed fist into the pilot's compartment. The Knight's whip snapped, flagellating itself to shake him loose. More Knights advanced, flanking the leader.

Get close. Get inside their reach.

Chugging cannons thundered, muzzle flare churning the

ground to powder. Solid rounds chased Horus, but he put the first Knight between him and its fire. Stubber shells ripped across the lead Knight's carapace and thermal lance mount. The weapon exploded.

Another Knight body slammed the first, crushing two more of the Luperci who howled as they died. It rammed its ion shield into its leader's carapace, sending the last of them hurtling through the air. Glass and lubricant drizzled like tears.

The revealed pilot was a darkly handsome man with a cruel smile.

Horus laughed. *You still think you can kill me.*

He dived as the Knight's foot stomped down. Horus rolled to his feet and ripped his taloned gauntlet through a knot of pneumatics at the Knight's ankle joint. It staggered, gyroscopic servos screaming as they fought to keep the war machine upright.

A third and a fourth Knight were moving into firing positions. More jostled for position behind them.

Keep moving. Don't let them pin you in place.

Horus was the lone wolf among the fold, weaving between the legs of his attackers. But the creatures of this fold could crush him, burn him and gut him. Stamping feet pounded the ground flat. Roaring chainblades wider than a Javelin speeder stabbed around him. The energy whip of the lead Knight cracked and fused a three metre trench of glass in the sand.

Horus scrambled onto the claw mechanism of a Knight's splayed foot. He gripped the ribbed cabling at its ankle and bent his legs. From a crouch, he leapt as high as he could. *Worldbreaker* swung and a knee joint exploded. The Knight's leg buckled and it took a drunken step, every stabilisation system powerless to keep it upright.

The Knight crashed down, its armour crumpling, the carapace split open. Flames engulfed the downed machine as the power

cells of its weapon mount exploded. Horus saw the pilot screaming inside the canopy as he burned to death.

Another Knight went down, its upper torso detonating in a
cherry red fireball. Horus felt a wash of heat that had nothing to
do with its destruction. A squadron of three Glaives roared over
the black beach, their insanely powerful volkite carronades rippling in a haze of recent discharge.

The huge tanks were Fellblade variants, ruinously demanding
of resources and expertise to produce. Only with great reluctance
had Mars approved the implementation of a Legion tank bearing such a weapon. The Luna Wolves had been among the first
Legions to receive the Glaives, a further sign of the Emperor's
favour.

More tanks appeared behind them, superheavies all. Two
squadrons of Shadowswords and the cousins of the Glaive, the
Fellblades themselves. Searing beams stabbed from volcano cannons and accelerator turrets crashed back with armour-piercing
shells. The noise was deafening. Echoing booms were thrown
back from the cliffs.

Three Knights were all but obliterated, a pair of molten legs and
a pair of weapon mounts all that remained. A fourth threw its
ion shield up just quick enough to deflect the full force of a high-
density shell that nevertheless ripped its entire arm and most of
its shoulder away.

The Knights were monstrously outgunned and they knew it. The
hunting horn of the lead Knight loosed an ululating blast and
they fled back the way they had come. Humbled and broken, they
left half their number dead and ruined.

Horus drew in a breath of fyceline-scented air, letting the exer-
tion and stress of the fight drain from him. Oily sweat ran down
his ruddy face and pooled in blood-caked grooves in his armour.
His body was running hot to re-knit his flesh. Keeping a body at

such a high pitch was exhausting. Even for a primarch.

He heard the clatter of armour as warriors formed up around him, shields rammed into the sand in a makeshift defensive work. He already knew there was no need.

The battle was already won.

A trailing vox-bead dangling from his gorget after he'd thrown away his helmet told him as much. Noctua's decapitation strike had broken the centre and most likely killed the senior enemy officer. Teleporting Justaerin and the Catulan Reavers were clearing the trenches with Ezekyle and Kibre showing no mercy.

With the defence line's abandonment, thousands of armoured vehicles moved up the bloody beach; Land Raiders, Fellblades, Rhinos, Sicarans and finally the Chimeras of Lithonan's auxiliaries. Predators of all types followed them, together with recovery tractors, scout tanks and Trojan resupply vehicles.

Apothecarion troops swarmed the battlefield, gathering the wounded as the smoke of bombardment was blown out to sea. Fires burned from the multitude of wrecks littering the coastline.

'A heavy cost,' said Horus as Aximand approached and drove his shield into the sand. He coughed and there was blood in his mouth.

'Sir!' said Aximand. 'Sir, are you hurt?'

Horus shook his head before realising that, yes, he *was* hurt. Badly hurt. He reached out and steadied himself on Aximand. The last time he had been surrounded by his warriors and almost fallen it had ended badly for everyone.

'I'm fine, Little Horus.'

They both knew it was a lie, but agreed upon it anyway.

'Taking on ten Knights?' said Aximand. 'Really?'

'I killed one and the rest fled at the sight of me.'

'More like the sight of the Glaives and Shadowswords,' said Aximand.

'Careful,' said Horus, increasing the pressure on Aximand's arm a fraction. 'If I was being ungenerous, I might think you were belittling this victory.'

Aximand nodded, heeding Lupercal's warning and said, 'You're sure you're fine?'

'I'm better than fine,' said Horus. 'I won.'

THE BLACK SAND of Avadon's coastline had reminded Grael Noctua of Isstvan V, but the promethium fires lining the roadway from the beach and the reviewing stand built at its edge was pure Ullanor. Night had fallen, but the sky was still cut by phosphor-bright trails of wreckage coming down from orbit.

Storm Eagles and Fire Raptors circled overhead, like hunting birds eager to be loosed once more.

Perched on a narrow peninsula, Avadon was swathed in darkness, with only the moon's reflected radiance in the ocean to limn its hard edges. The lights of the city's hab-towers, Legion monuments and commercia were all extinguished, its thousands of inhabitants clinging to the dark and hoping the Legion would pass them by.

An army of conquest had landed on Damesek, and it was forming up around Avadon, preparing to advance south across the continent's agricultural heartland towards Lupercalia. Seeker and reconnaissance squads were already in the wind, and intelligence on the disposition of Molech's hundreds of thousands of soldiers was flooding back to Legion command.

The Mournival accompanied the Warmaster as he marched between ranked up companies of the Legion. Hasty repairs made him magnificent again, though none were battle-worthy. He walked with a slight limp, imperceptible to most eyes, but to Noctua's calculating gaze it was blindingly obvious.

The reviewing stand was just ahead, built from the ruins of the defensive line's demolished strongholds. Six Deathbringer War-lords towered behind it, four in the graphite and gold of Legio Vulcanum, two in Vulpa's rust and bone. Moonlight reflected from the heavy plates of their armour. Weapon mounts vented exhaust gases like hot, animal breath.

Twenty-six Titanicus engines had landed at Damasek – eleven from Vulcanum, six from Interfector, four from Vulpa and five from Mortis, the largest concentration of Titans that Noc-tua had seen since Isstvan III. The ten Reavers stood like vast monuments in Avadon's outer manufactorum districts, while six Warhounds stalked the edges of the muster fields like wary guard dogs.

'Reminds me of the Triumph,' said Ezekyle, approvingly.

'That's the idea,' replied Lupercal.

'Aren't triumphs usually held *after* a campaign?' asked Noctua, and the First Captain shot him an angry look. The delay his wounding at the hands of a mortal had caused Ezekyle was some-thing the First Captain wasn't going to forget in a hurry.

'Unless you're one of the Phoenician's rabble,' said Kibre.

'It's symbolic, Grael,' said Horus. 'When we left Ullanor it was as the Emperor's servants. When we leave Molech we will be our own masters.'

Something in the Warmaster's tone told Noctua that wasn't the whole truth, but a warning glance from Aximand advised against pursuing the matter. He nodded and hid a grimace of pain as it felt like someone was plunging an ice cold blade into his chest.

'Grael?' said Horus, pausing and giving him a sidelong glance.

'It's nothing,' he said. 'My own fault.'

'No argument there,' grunted Ezekyle.

Horus nodded and they resumed their march.

The Apothecary who'd treated Noctua at battle's end had all but demanded he remove himself from the order of battle and submit to heart-implantation surgery. Noctua had refused all but the most basic attention.

He forced himself to keep up, feeling the cold blade of pain twist deeper into the empty cavity within his chest. Feeling another's eyes upon him, Noctua turned his gaze from the Warmaster to the warriors lining his path.

Ger Gerradon grinned at Noctua in a way that made him want to put a fist through his face. Fully helmed Luperci with static-filled eyes surrounded Gerradon, many more than Noctua had seen during the assault on Var Crixia.

How far had Maloghurst and Targost gone in seeking volunteers to become hosts for these flesh-eating warp killers?

Gerradon looked over his shoulder and raised his eyebrows.

You will be one with us soon, the look said.

Neverborn.

Unburdened...

'Did you know you and this city share a name, Ezekyle?' said the Warmaster, as they approached the reviewing stand. Noctua turned from Ger Gerradon and tried to shake the thought that he was looking at his future.

'We do?' asked the First Captain.

'Abaddon, I mean. Ezekyle was said to be an ancient prophet, though it seems he might simply have been a witness to Old Earth's first encounters with xenoforms. I've found several mentions of an Abaddon,' he said. 'Or Apollyon or Avadon, depending on whether you're reading the *Septuagint* or the *Hexapla*. Or was it the *Vulgate*? So many versions, and none of them can agree.'

'So who was Abaddon?' asked Kibre. 'Or don't we want to know?'

Horus paused at the foot of the steps to the reviewing stand.

'He was an angel, Falkus,' said Horus. 'But don't let the term mislead you. Back then, angels were soaked in blood, the right hand of a vengeful god who sent them into the world of men to lay waste and kill in his name.'

'Sounds just like you,' said Aximand, and they all laughed.

Horus ascended to the stand, but the Mournival didn't follow. This was their place, invisible in the wings while Lupercal basked in adulation. Noctua took a moment to look out over the assembled legionaries.

The Warmaster's sons stretched as far as the eye could see. At least sixty thousand Space Marines. By conventional reckonings of numbers, it was a paltry force with which to conquer a world.

But this was the XVI Legion, the Sons of Horus, and this was more than enough. It was practically overkill.

The Warmaster took centre stage, *Worldbreaker* and his talon raised high. The Deathbringer Warlord Titans loosed deafening blasts from their warhorns and the thousands of legionaries pumped their fists in the air at the sight of Lupercal.

'From a world of darkness, I did bind daemons and death-doers in the form of wolves.'

Horus swept his maul down and night became day as the Reaver Titans surrounding Avadon opened fire with every one of their weapon systems. They rained down a continuous barrage of lasers, rockets and plasma until the city and all living things within were consumed in a fiery holocaust.

Vox-links broadcast the Warmaster's voice through the horns of the Titans, and his pronouncement shook Noctua's bones.

'So perish all who stand against me.'

'IACTON,' SAID LOKEN, standing at the door to *Tarnhelm's* crew compartment. Since entering the warp, the Knights Errant spent most of their days gathered around the long table, swapping exploits and expertise. Ares Voitek was repeating a story of his Legion's assault on a nomadic fleet of xenos and humans. His servo-arms described the manoeuvres of several starships.

The story petered out as they saw Loken.

'Garviel,' replied Qruze. 'If you've come to finish the job, I'll not stop you, lad.'

'I might,' said Bror Tyrfingr.

'I'm sorry I missed it the first time,' sniggered Severian.

Loken shook his head. 'I'm not here to fight you.'

'Then what do you want?'

'To live up to the words I said to Callion Zaven.'

The former Emperor's Children legionary looked up at the sound of his name, his attention momentarily diverted from the polishing of his hewclaw blade.

'What did you say to him?' asked Qruze.

'I told him that we had enough enemies before us without looking for them in our own ranks.'

'Then why did you almost kill Iacton?' asked Cayne.

'Shut up, Tubal,' said Varren, replacing bladed teeth on his axe that hadn't lost a fraction of their lethal sharpness.

'What?' said the former Iron Warrior. 'It's a valid question.'

'Not the point,' replied Ares Voitek.

Qruze nodded and swung his legs out from beneath the table to face Loken. Aboard ship, the legionaries went without armour, and Loken saw the corded strength within the Half-heard's frame like tempered steel or seasoned heartwood. He wore a sleeveless bodyglove and tan fatigues tucked into knee-high black boots.

His face bore little trace of Loken's assault, just a slight discolouration of the skin around his right eye.

'Good words,' said Qruze. 'Hard to live up to when trust is in such short supply, eh?'

'For what it's worth, I'm sorry,' said Loken, taking a seat at the table.

Qruze waved away his apology and poured himself a beaker of water. He poured Loken a drink, which he accepted. 'I've been waiting for that beating ever since I found out you were alive, lad.'

'There's just one thing I don't understand,' said Loken.

'Just one?' grunted Qruze. 'Then you've a better grasp of things than me. What is it you don't understand?'

'If Lord Dorn told you to keep Mersadie's existence secret, why did you tell me about her on the prison fortress?' asked Loken. 'You could have just boarded *Tarnhelm*, and I'd have been none the wiser.'

'Secrets have a way of coming out,' said Altan Nohai. 'In that place, in that time, it was right that Iacton spoke.'

Qruze nodded. 'I'd gone to Titan with Lord Dorn to kill a man.'

'Who?'

'Solomon Voss, you remember him?'

Loken nodded. 'I never met him, but I had heard the name around the *Vengeful Spirit*.'

'A good man. Too good. I think that's why Lupercal kept him around for so long before sending him back to us. Voss had done nothing wrong, but we couldn't let him live. Horus knew that, knew it would weigh heavily on whoever swung the blade. And like Altan says, secrets have a habit of coming out. The bigger they are the more likely they'll come out just when you don't want them to.'

'What does Solomon Voss have to do with Mersadie?'

Qruze leaned over the table and rested his arms on the table.

'I'm going to be very clear so there's no misunderstanding,' he said. 'We few are heading back to face the Warmaster. The chances of us making it back alive are virtually irrelevant. I thought you deserved to know she was still alive before we left.'

Loken sat back, his face stony. 'Will Lord Dorn kill her too?'

'I think he considered it.'

'What stopped him?' asked Rubio.

'You're the maleficarum,' said Bror Tyrfingr. 'You tell us.'

Rubio shot Bror an irritated glance, but Ultramarian virtue kept him from trading insults with the Fenrisian.

'Compassion,' said Zaven, setting down his sword. 'Not a virtue I'd expected from the Lord of the Fists, but perhaps he's not as hewn from stone as we all thought.'

Qruze said, 'It pained the primarch to execute Solomon Voss, more than you know. Another tally to add to Lupercal's butcher's bill. More blood on his hands.'

They lapsed into silence until Loken withdrew the presentation case Mersadie had given him. He placed it on the table and slid it across to Qruze.

The Half-heard recognised it and eyed the case warily.

'What's that?'

'I don't know. Mersadie said I had to give it to you.'

'Well, open it for Throne's sake,' said Varren, when Qruze made no move to touch the box. 'Don't keep us all in bloody suspense.'

Qruze flipped open the case and frowned in puzzlement. He lifted out a pressed disc of hardened red wax affixed to a long strip of yellowed seal paper.

'An Oath of Moment,' said Tubal.

'It's mine,' said Qruze.

'Of course it's yours,' said Bror. 'Loken just gave you it.'

'No, I mean it's *mine*,' said Qruze. 'I made this, back in the day. I know my own seal work when I see it.'

'To what action does it oath you?' asked Tubal Cayne.

Qruze shook his head. 'No action. It's blank. I made this in the days leading up to the Isstvan campaign, but I was never oathed for that fight.'

'Did you give it to Mersadie?' asked Loken.

'No, it was in my arming chamber,' said Qruze, turning the seal over in his gnarled hands. 'Did Mistress Oliton say anything about why I was to have this?'

'She said to remind you that you were the Half-heard no longer, that your voice would be heard louder than any other of the Legion.'

'What does that mean?' asked Ares Voitek.

'Damned if I know,' said Qruze. 'Garviel? What else did she say?'

Loken didn't answer, staring at the suggestion of a hooded shape in the shadows he knew none of the others would see. The figure shook his head slowly.

'Nothing,' he said. 'She didn't say anything else.'

FOURTEEN

Apollo's Arrow
Engine kill
Elektra complex

OPHIR BELONGED TO the Death Guard. Its refineries, mills and pro-methium wells were now slaved to the will of Mortarion and the Warmaster's Mechanicum cohorts. The fires had been contained, the damage repaired, and within ten hours of the XIV Legion's assault, Ophir's infrastructure was fully functional.

Squadrons of tankers were assembled, filled with precious fuel for the fleets of Land Raiders, Rhinos and battle tanks rumbling on cracked permacrete aprons. Ten thousand Legion warriors stood ready to march westward to the fields of battle, but there was a problem.

Nine thousand kilometres of dense jungle.

Nine thousand kilometres of rocky crags, undulant hills, ridged spines and plunging river basins. Like the *Arduenna Silva* of Old Earth, Molech's generals believed the jungles of Kush to be utterly impenetrable and thus only an ancient curtain-wall warded against assault from that axis. Its local name was the Preceptor Line. Orbital augurs revealed negligible Imperial presence upon it.

But where the generals of Old Earth had been proved wrong, those of Molech were right to believe the jungles an impassable barrier. The terrain was bad enough, but killer beasts dwelled in its steamy interior; roving azhdarchid flocks, territorial mallahgra or predator packs of xenosmilus.

And those were the least of the great monsters rumoured to dwell in the jungle's dark heart.

A SOLITARY RHINO drove out from the hundreds of Death Guard vehicles rumbling at the jungle's edge. Unremarkable in appearance, its hull was old and scarred with damage. Its cupola-mounted bolters were missing, and the heraldry of the Death Guard looked to have been burned off in the fighting to seize Ophir. It passed between the high towers raised to keep watch on the jungle and vanished from sight.

The lone vehicle followed the line of an old hunting trail once used by House Nurthen until the last of that line had been slain when a bull mallahgra tore his Knight apart during mating season. Overgrown and unfavourable to anything other than a tracked vehicle, the trail was just about practicable.

The sound and vibration of its engine couldn't help but attract attention. A pack of spine-backed xenosmilus stalked the Rhino, a muscular blend of sabre-tooth and crocodile, with chameleonic fur and a voracious appetite for flesh.

The pack leader was a monstrous beast with spines like spears and fangs like swords. It matched the Rhino in bulk, and its hide rippled with dappled shadows of the jungle and fleeting shafts of sunlight. As the Rhino followed the trail along the edge of a rocky slope, the pack sprang its trap. Three beasts ran in from the side. They shoulder-barged the Rhino, clawing its hull and gouging the metal with yellowed claws.

The pack leader leapt from hiding and paws like sledgehammers bludgeoned the vehicle from the trail. It tipped onto its side and rolled down the slope into what had once been a river basin.

Now it was a killing floor.

The rest of the pack charged in, tearing at the upturned Rhino and peeling its armour back like paper. Before they could completely wreck the vehicle, an enlarged hatch slammed open in its side and a bulky figure stepped onto the dry basin.

Encased in a fully sealed exo-suit intended for the internal maintenance of plasma reactors – and which had been the precursor to Terminator armour – the figure was snapped up in the pack leader's jaws.

Hook-like teeth deep in the beast's jaws sawed into the layered adamantium and ceramite. Heavy plates groaned, but the monster didn't taste flesh. Roaring in anger, the xenosmilus swung its head and threw the figure at a tumble of boulders. Rock split, but the armour held firm.

The Rhino's occupant rose smoothly to his feet as if being flung around like a rag doll by enormous predators was of no consequence to him. The pack abandoned the Rhino and formed a circle. Caustic saliva dripped from their jaws.

The armoured warrior reached up and snapped open a complex series of locking bolts and vacuum seals. He removed his helmet and dropped it to the ground. The revealed face was in constant flux between life and death, the skin rotting to carrion meat and restoring itself between breaths.

'Pack hunters?' said Ignatius Grulgor. 'Disappointing. I was hoping for some of the bigger beasts.'

The xenosmilus didn't attack. Their spines stood erect as they smelled the corruption on this prey-thing. Bad meat even the scavengers wouldn't touch.

The tall reeds surrounding Grulgor died first, a spreading

wave of death that turned the ground black with rotted vegetation. He exhaled toxins, plagues, bacteria and viral strands
once banned in an earlier age, but which man's greed had
allowed to endure.

His every breath turned the air into a lethal weapon.

The pack leader collapsed, coughing necrotic wads of dissolving lung matter. The flesh melted from its bones in an
instant, a time-lapsed pict-feed of decay run in fast forward.
The pack died with it as Grulgor extended the reach of the Life-
Eater, growing exponentially stronger with his every breath
that wasn't breath.

The jungle was dying around him. Trees collapsed into decaying mulch in a heartbeat. Rivers curdled to dust and vegetation
to gaseous ooze.

He was ground zero, patient zero and every vector imaginable.

His touch was death, his breath was death and his gaze was
death. Where he walked, the jungle died and would never know
growth again.

Ignatius Grulgor was the Life-Eater given sentience, a walking
pandemic. A god of plague to rival the Nosoi of Pandora's folly
or the terrible Morbus of the Romanii.

What had once been impenetrable jungle was dissolving like
ice before the flamer. Thousands of hectares sagged and flowed
around Mortarion's reborn son like melting wax.

Ignatius Grulgor retrieved his helmet and returned to the Rhino,
which now sat in a morass of cancerous vegetation. His warp-
infused flesh was easily able to right the vehicle and its tracks
slammed down on a sopping carpet of purulent matter.

Where before he could see barely ten metres in any direction,
now the horizon receded into the distance as he spread his rampant corruption to its farthest extent.

Ignatius Grulgor climbed back into the Rhino and continued

driving west over a pestilential wasteland of decay.

Fifty kilometres behind, the Death Guard followed.

THE FLOOR OF Noama Calver's Galenus was awash with blood, spilling from side to side with every manoeuvre her driver was forced to make. Constructed from an extended Samaritan chassis, the interior of the Galenus was equipped with a full surgical suite and twenty casualty berths.

Every one of those berths was filled twice over. About a third of the soldiers they carried were dead. Kjell kept urging her to ditch the corpses, but Noama would sooner throw herself out the back than abandon her boys like that. Her surgeon-captain's uniform was supposed to be pale green, but was soaked in blood from the chest down. Ruby droplets dotted lined mahogany skin that was too pale from too little sleep and too many long days in the medicae wards. Eyes that had seen too many boys die were heavy with regret and remembered every one of them.

The Galenus Mobile Medicus was a heavy tracked vehicle as wide and long as a superheavy. But unlike pretty much every other superheavy she knew, it had a decent kick to its engine. That could usually get the wounded out of harm's way, but there were still plenty of things that could move faster than them.

Nothing she could do about that, so instead she concentrated on the matter in hand.

She and Lieutenant Kjell had pulled the soldier from the wreck of a Baneblade whose engine exploded ninety kilometres south of Avadon. Tags said his name was Nyks, and his youthful eyes reminded her of her son serving off-world in the 24th Molech Firescions.

Those same eyes begged her to save his life, but Noama didn't know if she could. His belly had been opened by a red-hot shell fragment and promethium burned skin slithered over his chest like wet clay.

But that wasn't what was going to kill him. That particular honour would go to the nicked coeliac artery in his abdomen.

'He's not gonna make it, Noama!' shouted Kjell over the roar of the engines. 'I need help over here, and this one might actually live.'

'Shut up, lieutenant,' snapped Noama, finally grasping the writhing artery. 'I'm not losing this one. I can get it.'

The glistening blood vessel squirmed in her grip like a hostile snake. The Galenus rocked and her grip slackened for a fraction of a second.

'Damn it, Anson!' she shouted as the artery slid back into the soldier's body. 'Keep us level, you Throne-damned idiot! Don't make me come up there!'

'Trying, ma'am,' said Anson over the vox, *'but it's kind of hard travelling at this speed and with all this traffic.'*

Hundreds of vehicles were fleeing the carnage at Avadon, heading for the armed camp forming six hundred kilometres south around Lupercalia. Regiments from bases along the edges of the Tazkhar steppe and the hinterlands of the east around the Preceptor Line were already congregating on Lupercalia, with more on the march every day.

All well and good. Assuming they made it that far.

Scuttlebutt from vox-fragments and the lips of wounded men said enemy Titans were pursuing them. Noama put little faith in such talk. More than likely the rumours were typical grunt pessimism.

At least she hoped so.

'Are we going to make it, captain?' asked Kjell.

'Don't ask me such stupid questions,' she snapped. 'I'm busy.'

'The Sons of Horus are going to catch us, aren't they?'

'If they do I'll be sure to let you know,' said Noama.

She'd heard a man with no arms and legs claim the Titans of

the three Legios were on the march to save them, but didn't know whether that was a dying man's fantasy or the truth. Knowing what she knew of the things men and women said in their most pain-filled moments, Noama inclined to the former.

'Get back here, you slippery little bastard,' said Noama, pressing her fingers into the soldier's body. She grasped for the artery. 'I can feel the little swine, but it's making me work for it.'

Her fingers closed on the torn blood vessel, and hair-fine suture clamps extruded from her medicae gauntlet to seal it shut.

'Got you,' she said, pinning the artery in place with deft twists of her fingertips. Noama stood straight and, satisfied the worst of the boy's life-threatening injuries was dealt with for now, brought over the implanted nursing servitor with a sub-vocal command.

'Seal him up and wrap those burns in counterseptic gels,' she said. 'I'm not getting the bleeding stopped just for him to die from a damned infection, you understand? Right, now watch his blood pressure too, and let me know if he starts spiking. Clear?'

The servitor acknowledged her orders and set to work.

Noama moved onto the next hideously wounded soldier.

'Right,' she said. 'Been in the wars have we?'

THE TWIN WARLORDS of Legio Fortidus strode from the gloomy caverns of the Zanark Deeps side by side followed by the last of their Legio. Princeps Uta-Dagon's force numbered two Warlords and four Warhounds. On most battlefields that would be enough firepower to easily carry the day.

Against the force on Uta-Dagon's threat auspex it would be spitting in the eye of the tempest.

When word had come of the civil war on Mars, Uta-Dagon had assumed his Titanicus brothers would be at the heart of the fighting, standing with those loyal to the Emperor. Only later, as more details emerged of the catastrophe engulfing the Red Planet, had the truth emerged.

They were all that remained of Legio Fortidus.

In the end, though, it changed nothing.

Molech was at war, and the architect of his Legio's doom was before him.

Uta-Dagon floated within his amniotic casket within the head section of *Red Vengeance*, the Warlord Titan he had piloted for eighty years and whose name he had changed after a vivid waking dream in the Manifold. His sister-princeps, Utu-Lerna, had likewise been compelled to rename her engine, a Warlord whose new designation was *Bloodgeld*.

Uta-Dagon had long since sacrificed his organic eyes to the service of the Legio, but *Red Vengeance*'s auto-senses interpreted the sky a vivid crimson.

<A good sky to die beneath,> said Utu-Lerna, reading his thoughts through the Manifold as she so often did. Twins whose cords had been cut in the rains of Pax Olympus, their birth was seen as auspicious. And so it had proved when both were taken as babes by the Collegia Titanicus.

<*Red Vengeance* and a red sky.>

<For the Red Planet,> finished Utu-Lerna.

Burning starships streaked the sky. Had his brothers on Mars seen skies like this before they died? He hoped so, for it had been under such a sky the Legio had been born, fighting in the Dyzan Valley against the resurgent Terrawatt Clan.

<I see them, brother,> said Utu-Lerna. *Bloodgeld*'s warsight was keener than that of *Red Vengeance* and Uta-Dagon had learned to trust his twin's interpretations of her engine's senses.

Moments later Uta-Dagon saw them too. Fifteen engines on the static-laced horizon, striding south in pursuit of the survivors of Avadon. A great column of armoured vehicles swarmed the

Titan's feet. Scavengers following apex predators.

In three minutes or less, the enemy Titans would be in range of the retreating Imperial forces. Thousands would die unless the pursuers could be given a more tempting target.

Uta-Dagon heard an intake of breath behind him and twisted his withered form around in the fluid-filled casket. Ur-Nammu had seen them too, her almost human face underlit by the soft glow of the threat auspex. Like Uta-Dagon, the Warmonger was Mechanicum. She was not engine-capable, yet had chosen to die with her brothers and sisters.

<You should not be afraid, Ur-Nammu,> said the princeps. <Today we will join our brothers in death.>

'I do not fear death, my princeps,' said Ur-Nammu, before correcting herself and presenting her answer in the Manifold. <I fear that I will be of no help to you in the coming fight.>

<Your presence here honours me,> said Uta-Dagon. <You are what others in the Titanicus call an *executor fetial*, since you can move between the Legios freely. You have no need to die in my engine.>

<Where else would I wish to die?> asked Ur-Nammu and the simple honesty of her cant needed no reply.

The princeps returned his attention to the approaching battlescape, its vector contours and salient features forming in the interface within his skull. Manifold records quickly identified the traitor engines.

Reavers: *Dread Wake*, *Hand of Ruin* and *Myrmidion Rex* of Legio Mortis; *Silence of Death* and *Pax Ascerbus* of Legio Interfector, dubbed the Murder Lords after Isstvan III. *Nightmaw* of Legio Vulcanum.

Warhounds: *Kitsune* and *Kumiho* of Legio Vulpa, *Venataris Mori* and *Carnophage* of Vulcanum.

And then the Warlords: *Mask of Ruin*, *Talismanik*, and *Anger's*

Reward, also of Vulcanum. *Xestor's Sword* and *Phantom Lord* of Legio Mortis.

Data on the enemy engines flowed around Uta-Dagon, engagements fought, engine kills, maintenance profiles and damage records. In a straight up fight, such details could mean the difference between victory and defeat. Here they were unnecessary. The chance to perhaps do a little more damage before being destroyed.

<They see us, brother,> said Utu-Lerna.

<Flank speed,> ordered Uta-Dagon, and his Mechanicum priests drove the reactor to a higher pitch. *Red Vengeance* increased its pace, thunderous footfalls cracking the ground and smashing maglevs where there wasn't enough clearance to avoid them.

Uta-Dagon felt intense heat swell his phantom limbs as his weapon systems spooled up to fire. His right arm was the searing power of a volcano cannon, his left the clenched fist of a hellstorm cannon. He felt the passage of scores of missiles moving through his body of iron and sinew to the launchers at his carapace.

<Warhounds moving to circle us, sister.>

<They think us pitiful, brother.>

<Shall we disabuse them?>

<No, let us play the crippled Legio they think us,> said Utu-Lerna, with what he could hear was a grin on her wraith-like face.

<You always did have the best ideas, sister,> said Uta-Dagon.

IT CALLED ITSELF the *Teratus*, though the Manifold of *Red Vengeance* had identified it as *Pax Ascerbus*, a Reaver of Legio Interfector. Blood was its new oil, the sentience of a million warp scraps its marrow and its corrupt machine-spirit was a howling, warp-stitched thing of murder-lust.

With four Warhounds at its feet, it strode with grim purpose

towards Legio Fortidus. *Talismanik* and *Phantom Lord* marched at
its back, and the *Teratus* dredged power from its every system to
keep ahead of the larger engines. They howled at it to slow its
advance, to let them dispatch the doomed Legio, but the *Teratus*
ignored them.

The engines of Fortidus were running at barely half power,
woken too soon and without the proper consecration. Too long
at rest had reduced their reactor fires to embers. Void shields were
still sparking from emergency ignition and their walk was the
leaden shuffle of a condemned man en route to his execution.

The Warhounds circling the two Warlords were poor specimens.
Wary, where they ought to be aggressive. Keeping close to the
larger engines where they should be duelling with their opposite
numbers.

<Enfeebled half-engines,> it said, and the moderati flesh-things
roosting in the weapon compartments flinched at the scrapcode-
laced barbs in the cant. <The death of their Legio has broken
them. Killing them will be mercy.>

He sent his own Warhounds out to engage the Fortidus Scout
Titans with a pulsed order through the Manifold. Warhorns braying, the eager pups surged forward. They wove in and out of each
other's path, eager to claim the first kill.

The *Teratus* increased its stride, unconsciously trying to match
the pace of the smaller engines. The gap between it and the following Warlords grew wider.

Ranging fire snapped between the Scout Titans. The *Teratus*
ignored it. A baring of fangs, nothing more. Warnings shimmered
at the edge of its perception. Power surges, fusion warnings. Emis-
sion flares. At first they made no sense.

Then, with a sudden pulse of awareness, he realised how it had
been misled, its own sense of righteous superiority causing it to
see what it wanted to see.

Neither of the Fortidus engines was as enfeebled as they first appeared. Their reactors surged to life with high-volume plasma injections. A terminally risky manoeuvre that would end a reactor's useful life in one final sunburst of searing brilliance. Weapon systems blazed with power and opened fire in the same instant.

Kitsune and *Kumiho* suffered first. Shrieking salvoes of Hellstorm fire stripped them of their void shields. Pinpoint volcano cannon shots incinerated their princeps' compartments and left their thrashing limbs pawing the earth. *Venataris Mori* and *Carnophage* scattered at the first barrage of shots, but not fast enough. *Venataris Mori* fell with a leg blown off and *Carnophage* ploughed a hundred metre furrow with its canopy as its gyros overcompensated for its princeps' desperate evasive manoeuvres.

<Engine kill!> blared the Manifold with open-vox transmission from Legio Fortidus. The *Teratus* screamed and its moderaticreatures howled in pain. It bled power from propulsion to the forward void shields. Too little, too late.

While the Warlords of Fortidus were killing the *Teratus*'s Scouts, theirs were sprinting forward, heads down and weapons blazing. Jackals hoping to bring down a land leviathan. Turbo fire, gatling fire and streaking missiles stripped the *Teratus*'s void shields in squalling flares of discharge.

But Scout Titans didn't take on a Battle Titan and live.

The *Teratus* turned the gatling blaster on its nearest attacker. Warhounds were fast and agile, but nothing could outrun gunfire.

A storm of incendiary shells burst its voids and staggered it in a ferocious cannonade. Stripped of its shields and speed it was dead in the water. A shock-pulse of melta reduced its princeps canopy to subatomic slag.

Self-guiding missiles streaked from the *Teratus*'s upper carapace and swatted another Warhound into the ground. Its legs flailed as it tried to right itself. The *Teratus* slammed its vast foot down.

The Warlord's enormous bulk crushed it flat.

The *Teratus* fed on the death scream of its victim, drawing the binaric energy into its corrupted Manifold. Its horns blasted a triumphal roar. Its shields were failing, peeled back by niggling fire from the two remaining Warhounds. The Reaver took a backward step as a combined barrage of Hellstorm cannon from the advancing Warlords blew out the last of its protection.

Warhounds were consummate lone predators, but they were also superlative pack hunters. They darted in, weapons punishing the Reaver's vulnerable rear section. The armour on its reactor housing began peeling back.

Warning sigils flashed through its mind. Coolant leaks, plasma venting. It took another backward step, knowing it needed to link with the Warlord Titans it had tried so hard to outpace. Its right leg locked up, fused by repeated fire from the two Warhounds. The joints and servos there were on fire, and no amount of damage control would free it.

The *Teratus* watched the two Warlords of Legio Fortidus close.

It felt their weapons lock *Pax Ascerbus* in their sights, felt the power that had infused it in the blood-soaked hangar temples flee its iron flesh.

It locked its own weapons in return.

<Come,> said the *Teratus*. <We die together.>

THE THREAT OF two Warlords in the flank now became too serious to ignore, and the traitor Titans broke off their pursuit of Avadon's defenders to crush the Imperial engines.

Leaving the blazing corpses of the *Teratus* and the Warhounds in their wake, *Red Vengeance* and *Bloodgeld* limped into the teeth of *Talismanik, Phantom Lord, Myrmidion Rex* and *Mask of Ruin.*

In the end, it took another three hours for the last engine of Legio Fortidus to fall.

Red Vengeance and a red sky.

For the Red Planet.

CEBELLA DEVINE HAD long since lost any pleasure she might once have taken in tormenting her stepson. Albard's hope had died first, then his expectation of death. He knew they could keep him alive indefinitely.

The nightmare of his continued existence eroded his sanity to the point where her icily constructed barbs fell on deaf ears. She would have killed him long ago, but a firstborn son carried the bloodline. Shargali-Shi's treatments would only work with the vital fluids of the bloodline.

Cebella dismissed the Sacristans at Albard's door.

Some intimacies were for a mother alone.

The holographic fire burned in the hearth, casting its fictive heat and illumination around the gloomy chamber. She had come here so often she could pick out individual flame shapes and tell how long remained before the cycle would repeat.

She turned from the phantom light as a line of blood teared in the corner of her eye. Brightness hurt, and only regular injections of complex elastins and glassine meshes within her eyeballs allowed her to see at all. The droplet ran down the drum-tight skin of Cebella's face, but she didn't feel it. Her skin had been grafted, stretched and injected so many times it was deadened to virtually all sensation.

The stench within Albard's chambers was undoubtedly noisome, but like her tactile perceptions, her olfactory senses had also atrophied. Shargali-Shi had promised to restore and enhance her faculties, and each procedure brought her closer to the perfection she had once possessed.

The silver of her exo-skeleton glittered in the firelight, and Albard looked up from his chair of furs and putrescence. Saliva leaked from the side of his mouth and matted his unkempt beard, but his organic eye was clearer than it had been for a long time.

Raeven's visit had galvanised him.

Good. She had need to vent the pain of her grief upon another.

A blunt, wedge-shaped head rose from behind Albard's chair and a forked tongue tasted the air. Shesha, her former husband's naga. It hissed and sank back to its slumbers, as decrepit and useless as its current master.

'Hello, Cebella,' said Albard. 'Is it that time already?'

'It is,' she replied, kneeling beside him and placing her augmetic-sheathed hands on his lap. The encrusted filth on his coverlet revolted her. It looked like he'd soiled himself, and for once she was glad she could no longer smell things.

'Where's Lyx?' he asked, his voice cracked and brittle. 'It's normally her that plays the vampire.'

'She is not here,' said Cebella.

Albard gave a dry, hacking cough that turned into snorts of laughter.

'Standing at her husband's side as he fights for Molech?'

'Something like that,' said Cebella, producing a trio of amethyst vials and a hollow naga fang from the folds of her dress.

Albard's wheezing laughter died at the sight of the vials, and had it not carried the risk of ripping the skin all the way to her ears, Cebella would have smiled.

She moved the coverlet aside to reveal Albard's scrawny, wasted legs. Pressure sores and puncture marks ran the length of his inner thigh, the skin around them scabbed and raw.

'Are the Sacristans cleaning these?' she asked.

'Scared I might get an infection and poison you?'

'Yes,' she said. 'The bloodline must be pure.'

'Even the word *pure* sounds dirty in your mouth.'

Cebella lifted the naga fang and pressed it to what little meat remained in Albard's leg. The skin dimpled like cured vellum, and purpled veins stood out like roads on a map.

Albard leaned forward, and the movement was so unexpected that Cebella flinched in surprise. It had been years since she'd seen her stepson move more than the muscles of his face. She hadn't been sure that he *could* move at all.

'Lyx usually taunts me with Raeven's exploits,' said Albard, and there was a mocking edge to his tone that made Cebella want to cut his throat here and now. 'Aren't you going to do the same?'

'You said it yourself, your brother fights for Molech,' she said, her voice flat.

'No, no, no,' sniggered Albard. 'The way I hear it, my stepbrother left two of his sons dead at Avadon. Terrible shame.'

Cebella surged forward, scattering the jars. Blood or no blood, she was going to kill him. She'd drain him dry from the jugular.

'My grandsons are dead!' she yelled, blood-laced spittle flying as the skin at the corners of her mouth split. Her hand snatched for his neck.

'Wait,' said Albard, staring over her shoulder. 'Look.'

Cebella turned her head as Albard's hand pressed something beneath his coverlet. The holographic fire exploded with blinding radiance, and Cebella screamed as the light stabbed into her delicate eyes like hot needles.

'Shesha here doesn't have any venom left to blind you,' hissed Albard. 'So this will have to do.'

Cebella clawed at her face. Red tears streaked her cheeks and she tried to rise. She had to get away, had to have her Sacristans take her to Shargali-Shi's hidden valley.

Albard's hand rose from his coverlet and gripped hers.

Cebella looked down in surprise, seeing Albard through a gauzy veil of red. His grip was firm, unyielding. Her flesh cracked, and stinking blood oozed between his fingers.

'Your grandchildren?' continued Albard. 'The midwife should have strangled those inbred freaks with their still-wet cords. They're no better than the beasts we once hunted… you're all monsters!'

She struggled in his grip. The taut skin ripped along her forearm. Anger overcame her shock and she remembered the naga fang in her other hand. She brought it around and stabbed for where she thought his neck would be.

The fang stabbed into his shoulder, but so swathed was he in furs that she doubted it pierced his husked flesh. She fought to pull away, but madness gave Albard strength. Shocking, unfamiliar pain bloomed as the skin of her arm split all the way to her shoulder. It sloughed from the muscle beneath, like a débutante consort slipping off an opera glove.

Horror pinned her in place as Albard dropped the sheath of skin he'd torn from her arm. He gripped her by the skeletal frame of the exo-suit – using her weight for leverage, he hauled himself to the edge of his chair with a grimace of ferocious effort.

The fire dimmed and she saw something glitter in his other hand.

A blade of some kind. A scalpel? She couldn't tell.

Where had Albard obtained a scalpel?

'Lyx enjoys my pain,' said Albard as if she'd asked the question out loud. 'She knows just how to hurt me, but she's not too thorough in gathering up her little toys.'

The scalpel sliced down in two quick slashes.

'I learned a lot about suffering from my bitch wife,' said Albard. 'But I don't much care about your suffering. I just want you to die. Can you do that for me, whore-mother? Can you just *please* die?'

She tried to reply, to curse him to an eternity of pain, but her mouth was full of liquid. Bitter, rich, metallic liquid. She lifted the naga fang as if she might yet slay her murderer.

'Actually, I lied,' said Albard, slicing the scalpel neatly through the tendons of her wrist. The fang clattered to the floor as her hand went limp. 'I *do* care about you suffering.'

Cebella Devine slumped back onto her knees, convulsing as her arteries pumped litres of blood into Albard's lap. The exosuit twitched and spasmed as it struggled to interpret the signals coming from her dying brain.

Eventually it stopped trying.

ALBARD WATCHED THE life flee Cebella's blood-limned eyes and let out a dusty sigh that he had been keeping inside for over forty years. He pushed his stepmother's corpse from his lap and gathered his strength. It had almost been too much to fight her. He was little better than a cripple, and only hatred had given him the strength to kill her.

Looking down at the dead body, he blinked as – just for a moment – he saw the carcass of a mallahgra. Steel struts of armature became bone, furred robes became animal hide. Cebella's too-tight skinmask was the scarab maw of the mountain predator that had taken his eye and cursed him to this augmetic that filled his skull with constant static burr.

Then she was Cebella again, the bitch who had murdered his own mother and replaced her. Who had birthed two unwanted siblings and poisoned them both against him with talk of old gods and destiny. He should have killed her the moment she first came to Lupercalia and insinuated herself into House Devine.

His lap was sticky with her blood. It smelled awful, like bad meat or milk left to curdle in the sun. It was the smell of her soul, he decided. It had made her a monster, and once again it seemed as though her outline blurred, becoming the mallahgra of his nightmares.

Albard dropped the scalpel onto his stepmother's body and

cleared his throat. He spat phlegm and brown lung gunk.

'Get in here!' he shouted, as loudly as he could. 'Sacristans! Dawn Guard! Get in here now!'

He kept shouting until the door opened and his mother's pet Sacristans warily pushed open the door. Their half-human, half-mechanised faces were not yet incapable of registering surprise, and their eyes widened at the sight of their mistress lying dead before the fire.

Two armed soldiers of the Dawn Guard stood at the doorway. Their expressions were very different to those of the Sacristans.

He saw relief and knew why.

'You two,' said Albard waving a hand at the Sacristans. 'Kneel.'

Ingrained obedience routines saw them instantly obey, and Albard nodded to the two soldiers behind them. In the instant before he spoke, he saw them not as mortals, but as towering knights of House Devine. Armoured in crimson and bearing glorious pennants from their segmented carapaces, he saw himself reflected in the glassy canopy.

Not as the half-man he was, but as a strong, powerful warrior.

A god amongst men, slayer of beasts.

Albard pointed at the kneeling Sacristans.

'Kill them,' he ordered.

The Sacristans raised hands in supplication, but twin las-bolts cored their skulls before they could speak. Their headless bodies slumped onto the stone-flagged floor next to Cebella.

Albard waved the two soldiers – *or were they heroic knights?* – forwards. It seemed that their steps were surely too heavy to be those of mortals.

'Strip that witch of her exo-suit,' said Albard. 'I'm going to need it.'

FIFTEEN

The Cave of Hypnos
White Naga
Angel of fire

A NEW LAND Raider had been found for the Warmaster. Equipped with a flare shield, layered plates of bonded ceramite with ablative ion disruptors, shroud dispensers and frag-launchers, the Mechanicum had repeated their claim that it was proof against all but the weapons of a battle engine.

Horus let Ezekyle kill sixteen of them to remind them of the last time they had made that boast.

The Land Raider idled in the foothills of a mountain chain known as the Untar Mesas. Thousands of armoured vehicles surrounded it, connected together in laagers to form miniature fortresses. The Lord of Iron himself would have approved of the defences arranged around the Warmaster.

An unbroken chain of supply vehicles – tankers, ammo carriers and Mechanicum loaders – stretched back to the coast. Warhounds prowled the line of supply like watchful shepherds, and two Warlords in the colours of Legio Vulcanum stood sentinel over the Warmaster.

Horus climbed into the hills with the Mournival arranged around him in a tight circle. Farther out, Terminators of the Justaerin slogged uphill, looking more like relentless machines than living beings encased in armour.

Ger Gerradon's Luperci were out there too, unseen in the darkness. Horus could feel their presence like a scratch on the roof of his mouth. Invisible, but impossible to ignore.

A sky the colour of disturbed sediment swirled overhead, and smoke curled from wrecked orbital batteries and missile silos on the mountaintops. Lightning split the night, a sky-wide sheet that silhouetted the jagged teeth of the mountain. Rain fell in a deluge. A hundred new waterfalls spilled from the cliffs. Horus knew grander peaks than these, but viewed from this perspective it seemed like they were the tallest he had ever seen. It looked like they might snag the moon at its passing.

Fire Raptors and Thunderhawks flew overhead through static-charged clouds. Their engines were distant burrs over thunder that sounded like artillery. Energy discharges from the fighting in low orbit had wreaked havoc in the planet's atmospherics. A cascade effect of violent tempests was spreading all over Molech. Horus knew those storms were only going to get worse until a final apocalyptic event cleared the last of it.

'It's madness to stop like this,' said Abaddon, his armour streaked with rainwater and moonlight. 'We're too exposed. First the gunships on Dwell and then those Knights. It's almost like you're *trying* to put yourself in harm's way. It's our job to take those kinds of risks.'

'You've known me long enough to know I am not cut from that kind of cloth, Ezekyle,' said Horus. 'I am a warrior. I cannot always sit back and let others shed blood for me.'

'You're too valuable,' pressed Abaddon.

'We have been down this road before, my son,' said Horus,

letting all four of them understand that this was his final word on the subject.

Abaddon let the matter go, but like a hunting hound with the scent of blood in its nostrils, Horus knew he'd be back to that particular argument before long.

'Very well, but every moment we delay, the deeper the bastards can dig in,' said Abaddon.

'You still believe this world matters?' asked Noctua, as breathless as a mortal. Horus paused and listened to Grael's heartbeat through the rain. His secondary heart was still catching up to the level of his original, and his circulation likely wouldn't ever be as efficient as his supra-engineered biology required.

'What do you mean *matters*?' said Abaddon.

'I mean as a military objective, something to be won in battle then held and consolidated.'

'Of course,' said Abaddon. 'Molech is a stepping stone world. We control it and we control the Elliptical Way, easy access to Segmentum Solar's warp routes and the bastions worlds of the Outer Systems. It's a precursor world to the assault on Terra.'

'You're wrong, Ezekyle,' said Aximand. 'This invasion has never been about anything as prosaic as territory. As soon as we win this fight, we'll abandon Molech. Won't we, my lord?'

'Yes, Little Horus,' said the Warmaster. 'Most likely we will. If I'm right about what the Emperor found on Molech, then it won't matter what worlds we hold. All that's going to be important is what happens when I face my father. That's always been at the heart of this.'

'So why are we fighting as if we give a damn about Molech?' asked Kibre. 'Why wage a ground war at all?'

'Because what we will take away will be worth more than a hundred such rocks,' said Horus. 'You have to trust me on this. Do you trust me, Falkus?'

'Of course, sir.'

'Good, then no more questions,' said Horus. 'We should reach the cave soon.'

'What cave?' said Aximand.

'The cave where the Emperor made us forget Molech.'

THE WOMAN'S HARD-WEARING fatigues suggested a port-worker, maybe a rigger. Hard to be sure with the amount of blood covering them. Her chest rose and fell in stuttering hikes, every breath a victory. She'd been brought to Noama Calver's Galenus by a weeping man with two children in tow. He'd begged Noama to save her, and they were going to give it a damn good try.

'What happened to her?' asked Noama, cutting the woman's bloodied clothes away.

The man didn't answer at first. Sobs wracked his body and tears flowed down his open, earnest face. The two girls were doing a better job of holding it together.

'I can do more for her if I know what happened,' said Noama. 'Tell me your name, you can do that, can't you?'

The man nodded and he wiped his snot and tear streaked face with his sleeve like a child.

'Jeph,' he said. 'Jeph Parsons.'

'And where are you from, Jeph?' said Noama.

The woman moaned as Kjell began cleaning her skin and attaching bio-readout pads. She tried to push him off, strong for someone so badly hurt.

'Easy there,' said Kjell, pressing her arm back down.

'Jeph?' asked Noama again. Keep your eyes on me.'

He was looking at the brutalised flesh of his wife's body, seeing the blood dripping from the gurney. The woman reached up and took his hand in hers, leaving red marks on his wrist. She was a strong one, saw Noama, badly hurt but still able to offer comfort to those around her.

Jeph took a deep breath. 'Her name's Alivia, but she hates that. Thinks it sounds too formal. We all call her Liv, and we came from Larsa.'

The Sons of Horus had landed in force at Larsa, wiping out the Army forces stationed there in one brutal night of fighting. The port facilities were now in enemy hands, which could only be a bad thing.

'But you got her and your children out,' said Noama, 'that's good. You did better than most.'

'No,' said Jeph. 'That was all Liv. She's the strong one.'

Noama had already come to that conclusion. Alivia had the lean, wolfish look of a soldier, but she wasn't Army. She had a faded tattoo on her right arm, a triangle enclosed in a circle with an eye at its centre. Blood covered the words written around the circle's circumference, but even if it hadn't they were in a language Noama didn't recognise.

She'd caught shrapnel in the side, some glass in the face. Nothing that looked life-threatening, but she was losing a lot of blood from one particular wound just under her ribs. The readouts on the slate didn't paint a reassuring picture of her prognosis.

'We joined a column of refugees at the Ambrosius Radial,' said Jeph, the words pouring from him now the dam inside had broken. 'She thought she'd got out of Larsa quick enough, but the traitors caught up to us. Tanks, I think. I don't know what kind. They shelled us and shot us. Why did they do that? We're not soldiers, just people. We had children. Why did they shoot at us?'

Jeph shook his head, unable to comprehend how anyone could open fire on civilians. Noama knew just how he felt.

'She almost did it,' said Jeph, his head in his hands. 'She almost got us out, but there was an explosion right next to us. Blew off her door and... Throne, you can see what it did to her.'

Noama nodded, digging around in the wound below Alivia's ribs. She felt something serrated buried next to her heart.

A fragment of shrapnel. A big one. The volume of blood coming from the wound meant it had probably sliced open her left ventricle. With a proper medicae bay it would be a simple procedure to save Alivia, but a Galenus wasn't the place for such complex surgery. She looked up at Kjell. He'd seen the bio-readouts and knew what she knew. He raised an eyebrow.

'I have to try,' she said in answer to his unvoiced question.

The import of the words went over Jeph's head and he kept speaking. 'They killed everyone else, but Liv drove that cargo-five like it was an aeronautica fighter. Threw us all around the cab with tight turns, hard brakes and the like.'

'She drove you out of an attack by enemy tanks?' said Kjell, making his impressed face as he sorted out the instruments they'd need to cut Alivia open and get to her heart. 'That's a hell of a woman.'

'Just about blew the engine out,' agreed Jeph, 'but I guess that's why she wanted a 'five. They're not max-rated riggers, but their engines pack a punch.'

Noama placed an anaesthesia mask over Alivia's mouth and nose, cranking up the delivery speed. The rate of blood loss meant they had to be quick.

'You got your children out,' she said. 'You saved them.'

Alivia's eyes opened and Noama saw desperation there.

'Please, the book... it says... have to... get to... Lupercalia,' she gasped into the mask. 'Promise me... you'll get us... there.'

Alivia took Noama's hand and squeezed. The grip was powerful, urgent. Conviction and courage flowed from it, and the need to make Alivia's last wish a reality was suddenly all that mattered to Noama. It only relaxed when the gas began to take effect.

'I'll get you there,' she promised, and knew she meant it more than she'd meant anything in her life. 'I'll get you all there.'

But Alivia didn't hear her promise.

IN THE DECADES since Molech's compliance, something large and predatory had made its lair in the cave. Bones lay scattered by an entrance large enough for a Scout Titan, and not even the rain could cover the stench of partially digested remains. The earth at the cave mouth was a sopping quagmire, but blurred impressions of clawed feet wider than a Dreadnought's crossed and recrossed.

'What made these, sir?' said Aximand, kneeling by the tracks.

Horus had no answer for him. The tracks were from no beast he remembered from Molech, though given the fractured recall of his time on this world that shouldn't have surprised him.

And yet it did.

The Emperor hadn't *erased* his memories, only manipulated them. Greyed some out, blurred others. He knew the indigenous beasts of Molech. He'd seen their heads mounted on the walls of the Knightholds, had studied their images and dissected corpses in illuminated bestiaries.

So why did he not recognise these tracks?

'Sir?' repeated Aximand. 'What are we going to find in there?'

'Let's find out,' said Horus, pushing aside his doubts and marching into the darkness. The Justaerin's suit lamps swept the wide entrance, and the claws of Horus's talon shimmered with blue light as he followed them inside. Strobed shadows painted heavily scored walls. Abaddon went next, then Kibre, Aximand and Noctua.

The cave corkscrewed into the mountain for perhaps a hundred metres, lousy with distorted echoes and strangely reflected light. As tall as a processional on a starship, the passage shimmered with rainwater seeping through microscopic cracks in the rock. The shifting beams caught falling droplets and shimmering rainbows arced between the walls.

They paused as the low, wet growl of something large and hungry was carried from deeper in the tunnels. Territorial threat noise.

'Whatever that is, we should leave it alone,' said Kibre.

'For once I'm in total agreement with you, Falkus,' said Noctua.

'No,' said Horus. 'We go on.'

'I knew you were going to say that,' said Abaddon.

'And if we run into whatever that is?' asked Aximand.

'We kill it.'

The Mournival drew closer to Horus, each with a bladed weapon and firearm drawn. Moisture drizzled the air. It pattered on armour plates and hissed on powered blade edges.

'You know what it is, don't you?' said Aximand.

'No,' said Horus. 'I don't.'

The sounds of animal breath rasping over dripping fangs came again. It drew Horus on even as some primal part of his brain told him that whatever lurked in the darkness beneath the mountain was something not even he could defeat.

The thought was so alien that he stopped in his tracks.

The intrusion to his psyche was so subtle that only a thought so incongruous to his self-image revealed its presence. It didn't feel like an attack though, more an innate property of the cave.

Or a side effect of whatever had happened here.

Horus pressed on, the passageway eventually widening into a rugged cavern thick with dripping stalactites and blade-like stalagmites. Some ran together in oddly conjoined columns, wet and glistening like malformed bones or mutant sinews.

A stagnant lake filled the centre of the cavern, its surface a basalt mirror. Rotted vegetation, festering dung and heaps of bone taller than a man were heaped at the water's edge. The ambient temperature dropped by several degrees, and plumes of breath feathered before the Warmaster and his sons.

Horus's skin tingled at the presence of something achingly familiar yet wholly unknown. He'd felt something similar at the base of the lightning-struck tower, but this was different. Stronger. More intense. As though his father were standing just out of sight, hidden in the depths and watching. Shadows stretched and slithered as the beams of the Justaerin's lamps swept around the chamber.

'I have been here before,' he said, removing his helmet and hooking it to his belt.

'You remember this cavern?' said Aximand as the Mournival and Justaerin spread out.

'No, but every fibre of my body tells me I stood here,' said Horus, moving through the chamber.

Light refracting through the translucent columns and crystalline growths imparted colour to the walls: bilious green, cancerous purple, bruise yellow. They were standing in the guts of the mountain. Literally. A chamber of digestion. A suitlight played over the lake, holding steady enough for Horus to picture it as a low-hanging moon.

Not Molech's moon, but Terra's moon, as though the lake wasn't a body of water at all, but a window through time. He'd sat with his father on the shores of the *Tuz Gölü* and skimmed rocks at the image of the moon and for a moment – just a fleeting moment – he could smell its hypersaline waters.

The light moved on and the water was just water. Cold and hostile, but just water.

With a growing sense of purpose, Horus made his way towards the water's edge. Shadows where no shadows ought to be stretched over the walls, and a thousand muttering voices seemed to rise from the water. He glanced back at the Mournival. Could they hear the voices or see the shadows? He doubted it.

This cave was not entirely of this world, and whatever was

keeping it anchored was fraying. Just by being here he was tugging on its loose threads. The image of bones and sinews returned, something organic, the architecture of the mind.

'That's what you did here,' he said, turning on the spot. 'You cut through the world here and reshaped us, made us forget what we'd seen you do…'

'Sir?' said Aximand.

Horus nodded to himself. 'This is the scab you left behind, father. Something this powerful leaves a mark, and this is it. The bruise you left behind when you shaped your lie.'

The frayed edge pulled a little more. The scab peeled back.

Ghost shapes moved through the cavern, given life by his picking at the wound in the angles of space and time. Each was numinous and smudged, like figures seen through dirty glass. They were indistinct, but Horus knew them all.

He walked among them, smiling as though his brothers were here with him now.

'The Khan stood here,' said Horus as the first figure stopped and took a knee on his left. A second figure knelt to his right.

'The Lion over there.'

Horus felt himself enveloped in light, cocooned by its cold illumination. He'd retraced the steps he'd taken almost a century ago without even knowing it.

Horus moved back, detaching from a rendering of his own body in ambient light. Like his spectral primarch brothers, his radiant doppelgänger knelt as a figure approached from across the lake. Gold fire and caged lightning; the Emperor without His mask.

'What is this?' demanded Abaddon, his bolter raised and ready to fire. The figures were only now becoming visible to them. Horus waved their weapons down.

'An imprint left over from days past,' he said. 'A psychic figment of a shared consciousness.'

The ghost of his father walked over the surface of the lake, wordlessly repeating whatever psycho-cognitive alchemy he had wrought to reshape the pathways in the minds of his sons.

'This is where I forgot Molech,' said Horus. 'Maybe here is where I will remember it.'

Aximand raised his bolter again, aiming it at the numinous being on the water. 'You said that thing is an echo? A psychic imprint?'

'Yes,' said Horus.

'Then why is it boiling the lake?'

THE CHIRURGEON'S METALLIC fingers trembled as they applied yet another flesh-graft to Raeven's right arm. The skin from pectorals to wrist was pink and new like a newborn's. The pain was intense, but Raeven now knew that physical suffering was the easiest pain to endure.

Edoraki Hakon's death meant the task of keeping the thousands of soldiers who'd escaped Avadon alive had fallen to him. Legio Fortidus had won the retreating Imperial forces a chance to properly regroup in the wooded vales of the agri-belt. With luck and a fair wind, they should link with forward elements of Tyana Kourion's Grand Army of Molech outside Lupercalia in two days.

Coordinating a military retreat was hard enough, but Raeven also had to deal with an ever-growing civilian component. Refugees were streaming in from the north and east. From Larsa, Hvithia, Leosta and Luthre. From every agri-collective, moisture-farm and livestock commercia.

Borne in an armada of groundcars, cargo carriers and whatever motive transport could be found, tens of thousands of terrorised people had been drawn to Raeven's ragamuffin host.

He'd welcomed the burden, the role so consuming it kept him from dwelling on the loss of his sons. But with the threat of immediate destruction lifted, Raeven's thoughts turned inwards.

Tears flowed and grief-fuelled rages had seen a dozen aides beaten half to death. A hole had opened inside him, a void that he only now recognised had been filled by his sons.

He'd never known joy to compare to Egelic's birth, and Osgar's arrival had been no less wonderful. Even Cyprian cracked a smile, the old bastard finally pleased with something Raeven had done.

Banan had struggled to enter the world. Birth complications had almost killed him and his mother, but the boy had lived, though he had ever been a brooding presence in the feast halls. Hard to like, but with a rebellious streak Raeven couldn't help but admire. Looking at Banan was like looking in a mirror.

Only Osgar now remained, a boy who'd displayed no aptitude or appetite for knightly ways. Against his better judgement, Raeven had allowed the boy to follow Lyx into the Serpent Cult.

The chirurgeon finished his work and Raevan looked down at the crimson, oxygenated flesh of his arm. He nodded, dismissing the man, who gratefully retreated from Raeven's silver-skinned pavilion. Other chirurgeons had been less fortunate.

Raeven rose from the folding camp-seat and poured a large goblet of Caeban wine. His movements were stiff, the new flesh and reset bones of his chest still fragile. *Banelash* had been badly damaged, and the repercussions of the Knight's hurt were borne by his body.

He swallowed the wine in one gulp to dull the ache in his side. He poured another. The pain in his side dimmed, but he'd need a lot more to dull the pain in his heart.

'Is that wise?' said Lyx, sweeping into the tent. She'd arrived from Lupercalia that morning, resplendent in a crimson gown with brass and mother-of-pearl panels.

'My sons are dead,' snapped Raeven. 'And I'm going to have a drink. Lots of drink in fact.'

'These soldiers are looking to their Imperial commander for leadership,' said Lyx. 'How will it look if you tour the camp stumbling around like a drunk?'

'Tour the camp?'

'These men and women need to see you,' said Lyx, moving close and pushing the wine jug back to the table. 'You need to show them that House Devine stands with them so that they will stand with you when it matters most.'

'House Devine?' grunted Raeven. 'There practically isn't a House Devine any more. The bastard killed Egelic and Banan, or didn't you hear me tell you that when you got here?'

'I heard you,' said Lyx.

'Really? I just wanted to be sure,' snapped Raeven, turning and throwing his goblet across the pavilion. 'Because for all it seemed to affect you, I might as well have been talking about a particularly good crap I'd had.'

'Horus slew them himself?'

'Don't say that name!' roared Raeven, wrapping a hand around Lyx's neck and squeezing. 'I don't want to hear it!'

Lyx fought against him, but he was too strong and too enraged with grief. Her face crumpled and turned a livid shade of purple as he squeezed the life out of her. He'd always thought of her as fundamentally ugly, even if her outward appearance suggested otherwise. She was broken inside, and the thought sent a spasm of loathing through him. He was just as broken as her.

Perhaps they both deserved to die.

Maybe so, but she'd go first.

'My sons were to be my immortality,' he said, almost spitting in her face as he pushed her back against the pavilion wall. 'My legacy was to be the honourable continuance of House Devine, but the bastard Warmaster has put paid to *that* dream. My sons' armour rusts on Avadon's beach, and their bodies lie rotted and unclaimed. Food for scavenger birds.'

He felt something sharp at his groin and looked down to see a hooked naga fang pressed against his inner thigh.

'I'll slice your balls off,' said Lyx, pressing the needle-sharp point hard against his leg. 'I'll open your femoral artery from your crotch to your knee. You'll empty in thirty seconds.'

Raeven grinned and released her, stepping away from his sister-wife with a grunt of amusement. Colour returned to her face and he was sure that the excitement he saw in her eyes was mirrored in his own.

'Cut my balls off and House Devine really is finished,' he said.

'A figure of speech,' said Lyx, massaging her bruised throat.

'Anyway, your womb will be as barren as the Tazkhar steppe by now,' said Raeven as Lyx poured them both a drink.

He shook his head and took the goblet she offered him. 'We make a pair don't we, sister dearest?'

'We are what our mother made us,' replied Lyx.

He nodded. 'So much for your talk of turning the tide.'

'Nothing has changed,' said Lyx, putting a hand out to stroke the pink flesh of his neck. He flinched at her touch. 'We still have Osgar, and he knows full well the importance of the continuance of the House name.'

'Shargali-Shi is more of a father to that boy,' said Raeven, only now understanding what a mistake it had been to allow him anywhere near the Serpent Cult. 'And from what I hear, he has no interest in taking just one consort nor becoming father to a child. He won't be the one to keep the Devine name alive.'

'He doesn't have to be a *father*, so long as he puts a child in the belly of a suitably pliant consort,' said Lyx. 'But that's a talk for when this war is concluded.'

Raeven nodded and accepted more wine. He felt a calming fuzziness at the edges of his perception. Wine and pain-balming chems were a heady mixture. He struggled to remember what they'd been talking about before their lover's tiff.

'So do you think I'm still the one whose actions will turn the tide of this war?'

'If anything, I'm even more certain of it,' said Lyx.

'Another vision?'

'Yes.'

'Tell me.'

'I saw *Banelash* in the heart of the great battle for Molech. In the shadow of Iron Fist Mountain. The tread of war gods shakes the earth. Flames surround the Knights of Molech. Death and blood breaks upon *Banelash* in a red tide and you fight like the Stormlord himself.'

Lyx's eyes misted over, cloudy with psychic cataracts.

'A battle to end all battles rages around your Knight, yet no blade, no shell, no enemy can lay it low. And when the appointed hour comes, the mightiest god on the field is slain. Its fall is a rallying cry, and all about scream the Devine name!'

The opaqueness of Lyx's eyes faded and she smiled, as though a great revelation had just been revealed to her.

'It's here,' she said, breathless with excitement.

'What is?' said Raeven, as the air turned chill.

'The White Naga.'

'It's here? Now?'

Lyx nodded, turning around as though expecting to see the avatar of the Serpent Cult within Raeven's pavilion.

'The blood sacrifice made at Avadon has brought its divine presence into the realms of men,' she said, taking his hand. 'The deaths of our sons has earned you the right to speak with it.'

'Where is it?'

'In the forest,' said Lyx.

Raeven snorted at the vagueness of her reply. 'Can you be more specific? How do I find it?'

Lyx shook her head. 'Ride *Banelash* into the forest, and the White Naga will find *you.*'

IT MOVED FASTER than anything Horus had ever known.

Faster than an eldar blade-lord, faster than the megarachnids of Murder, faster than thought. Its body was mist and light, sound and fury.

A Justaerin was the first to die, his body split down the middle as though he'd run full tilt into a bandsaw. His body emptied of blood and organs in a heartbeat.

Horus moved before anyone else, slashing his taloned gauntlet at the glittering light. His claws cut empty air and a golden fist slammed into his stomach. Doubled over, he saw Aximand shooting. The Widowmaker hunted for a target.

Noctua was down on one knee, clutching his chest. Abaddon ran to his side, a long-bladed sword held low. Stuttering muzzle flare lit the cavern in strobing bursts. Suit lights swayed and danced. Hard volleys of mass-reactives shattered crystalline growths, blew out fist-sized lumps of calcified stone. The Justaerin moved to interpose themselves between their attacker and the Warmaster.

Noctua fired from his knees. Kibre added his combi-bolters to the sweeping barrage, not aiming, just firing.

They hit nothing.

The cavern was suddenly gloriously illuminated. An angel of fire, with swords of lightning held outstretched. Faceless, remorseless, Horus recognised it for what it was. A sentinel creature, a final psychic trap emplaced by the Emperor to destroy those who sought to unpick the secrets of His past.

Horus could barely fix on the beast.

Its radiance was so fierce, so blinding. Its swords unleashed forking blasts of lightning, and Aximand was hurled across the cavern. His smoking body slammed into a wall. Stone and armour split. Horus knew the impact trauma was enough to break his spine.

Coruscating blue swords lashed out like whips. Abaddon dived to the side, his pauldron sheared clean away. A portion of the First Captain's shoulder remained inside, and bright blood sheeted his arm. One of the Justaerin took a step towards his downed captain before remembering his place.

The creature turned its gaze upon the Terminator. The warrior staggered. The combi-bolter fell from his grip as he struggled to tear off his helmet. His screams over the vox were agonised. Liquid light writhed in the joints of his armour, spilling out in blistering streams of white-green fire.

Horus shucked his taloned gauntlet, slamming shells into the breech of the inbuilt bolters. He often spoke of the murder-haruspex of Cthonia that led him to the weapon in an arming chamber of a long-dead warlord. That wasn't entirely accurate, but the truth was for Horus alone. The gauntlet's baroque craftsmanship was unmatched, and though Horus had been little more than a callow youth at the time, the gauntlet fitted his blood-scabbed hand as though fashioned just for him.

A two metre tongue of flame blazed from the weapon. The recoil was savage, but Urtzi Malevolus had built his armour well and suspensor compensators kept it on target. Scads of light flew from the angel like molten steel. Torn from its body, its essence dimmed, dissolution turning it to vapour in seconds.

It shrieked and the air between it and Horus buckled with concussive force. The last Justaerin flew apart, shattering like an assembly diagram of something vastly complex. His skeleton and internal biology atomised in a flash burn of intense light.

Horus flew back, as though lifted by a hurricane. He came down hard in the water, its freezing temperature ramming the breath from him with an explosive fist. His mouth filled with black water. Throat muscles reacted instantly to seal his lungs and shift breathing to secondary respiratory organs.

He spat black mouthfuls and rose from the water in time to see Abaddon pinned in place by blazing tridents of lightning. Light poured from the First Captain's mouth. Kibre's gunfire sprayed the angel of fire, surrounding it in swarms of phosphor embers. Enough mass-reactive shells to put down a bull-grox achieved precisely nothing against the blazing sentinel.

Horus marched from the lake, whips of fire arcing from his talon. Noctua plunged his sword into the angel's back. The blade melted in an instant and Noctua cried in pain, clutching his ruined hand. Aximand crawled towards the fight, spine cracked, legs useless.

Horus didn't bother to shoot the angel. He killed the power to his talons with a thought. Its essence was godly and mortal weapons were useless. He reached for his only other option.

The angel spun to face him, releasing Abaddon from its crackling barbs. The First Captain fell to his front, broiled near death by divine fire.

The angel descended on Horus, wings of bright flame erupting from its back. The swords of lightning became elongated claws. Furnace heat blazed from its body.

Horus stepped to meet it.

He swung *Worldbreaker* in an upward arc, like a hammer thrower from an ancient age. A weapon forged by the Emperor's own hand, *Worldbreaker* was a gift from a god. Its killing head buried itself in the flaming body of the angel.

Only one thing could end this creature, and that was the power that had birthed it.

The angel exploded. Streamers of fire arced from its death like blazing promethium. It shrieked as the power binding it to this place was shattered. By the time the Warmaster's maul had completed its swing, the angel was no more.

Its scream lingered long, echoing throughout the mountain, all across Molech and through uncounted angles of space and time. The embers of its sun-hot core drifted to the cavern floor like grave-bound fireflies.

And with its death, Horus remembered Molech.

He remembered everything.

SIXTEEN

Flagship
Exogenesis
Infiltration

EVEN AFTER EVERYTHING that had happened, the betrayal, the massacre and all that came later, the sight of the *Vengeful Spirit* still had the power to take Loken's breath away. She was monstrous and beautiful, a gilded engine whose only purpose was to destroy.

'We should have known it would end this way,' he whispered, as the image of his former flagship shimmered on the slate.

'What do you mean?' asked Rassuah.

'We set out from Terra to make war,' said Loken. 'That's all. Sigismund was right. The war will never be over, but what else should we have expected when we crossed the stars in ships like that?'

'It was a crusade,' said Rassuah. 'And you don't set out to reclaim the galaxy with kind words and good intentions.'

'Ezekyle had a similar argument with Lupercal before we reached Xenobia. He wanted to make war with the Interex straight away. The Warmaster told him that the Great Crusade had evolved, that since the human race was no longer on the edge of extinction the nature of the Crusade had to change. *We* had to change.'

'Change is hard,' said Rassuah. 'Especially for people like us.'

Loken nodded. 'We were created to fight, to kill, and it's hard to change what you were born to do. But we were capable of so much more.'

He sighed. 'Whatever else we might have achieved, we'll never get the chance. From now on there is only war for us.'

'It's all there is for any of us,' said Rassuah.

THEY'D TRANSLATED INTO Molech's system space on the very inner edge of the Mandeville point. A risky manoeuvre, but with a ship as fine as *Tarnhelm* and a pilot of finesse, it was worth the risk.

The approach to Molech was made in near silence, with *Tarnhelm*'s systems running at their lowest ebb. A brief burst of powerful acceleration during a moment of sunspot activity hurled the stealth ship towards Molech. Momentum would do the rest.

In the three days since, the pathfinders had spent their time in solitary reflection, preparing their wargear and running through individual preparations. For Rubio that involved meditation, for Varren and Severian the obsessive dismantling and reassembly of weaponry. Voitek and Qruze played Regicide every hour, while Callion Zaven honed the monomolecular edge of his hewclaw blade. Alten Nohai spent his time teaching Rama Karayan a form of martial art that looked curiously peaceful. Only Bror Tyrfingr was restless, pacing the deck like a rutting stag in mating season.

Loken spent the time alone, trying to ignore the shadowed suggestion of a hooded figure in the corner of his bunk-alcove. He knew it wasn't there, that it was just a memory given form, but that didn't make it go away.

It spoke to him, though he knew the words were all in his mind. *Kill me. When you see me, kill me.*

✠ ✠ ✠

'SHE'S BEEN HURT,' said Qruze, as the wallowing form of the *Vengeful Spirit* hovered over the table. He pointed to blackened portions of the hull, impact craters along the spinal fortresses and sagging buttresses made molten by concentrated laser fire. 'Someone made her pay for victory.'

'It was a scrappy fight,' said Varren, pointing out the drifting wrecks of numerous light cruisers and orbital platforms. 'They got up close and bloody.'

The image of the Warmaster's flagship was being projected by the device Tubal Cayne had brought. A compact logic engine of some kind, around the size of a small ammo crate. Loken had watched the former Iron Warrior run a portion of the device over the Scyllan shipwrights' plans in Yasu Nagasena's villa.

Those schemata were now displayed in three-dimensional holographic form, every structural member and compartment rendered in the finest detail. The image flickered as inloads from *Tarnhelm*'s forward surveyors updated the ship's appearance from what had been built to what was approaching.

Tubal Cayne made adjustments to the device, zooming in on various parts of the ship with an architect's precision. Too quick for the rest of them to follow his working, the former Iron Warrior hunted out weaknesses in the structure, gaps in the defences for them to exploit.

'Anything?' asked Tyrfingr, tapping his fingers on the table.

'Ventral spine on the portside looks good,' said Severian.

'If you want to die,' replied Cayne.

'What?' said Severian, his voice low and threatening.

'Look at the internal structure beyond,' said Cayne, highlighting a section of transverse bracing. 'The *Vengeful Spirit* is Gloriana-class, not Circe. We'd pass too close to a main transit arterial. There will be automated defences here, here and here, with warden-sentinels at these junctions.'

'I could get past them.'

'But you're not doing this alone, are you?'

Severian shrugged and sat back. 'Where would you suggest?'

'As I told Loken, the lower decks are always the weakest point in most ships' defences. Just as I suspected, it's not presented to the planet below.'

'So?' asked Varren.

'You people,' said Cayne with a shake of his head. 'So fixated with putting an axe in someone's head.'

'I'll put one in *your* head soon,' said Varren.

'Why? I am simply telling you of a better way to infiltrate our target.'

'Explain how,' said Loken.

Cayne zoomed in on the lower decks, to a portion of the hull ravaged by torpedo impacts and broadsides. From what Loken remembered of those sections, Cayne was showing them dormitory spaces and magazine chambers.

'These areas on a Scylla-pattern Gloriana were designed for menials, gun-crews and whatever Iagan has sunk to the ship's bowels,' said Cayne. 'They are not Legion spaces, so it is highly unlikely any repair work has been undertaken.'

'That one,' said Rama Karayan, pointing to an impact crater in the shadow of a collapsed deflector array. Almost invisible, even to Cayne's device, it was a deep gouge in the *Vengeful Spirit*'s flank. 'A wound easily large enough to allow *Tarnhelm* entry.'

'A good choice, Master Karayan,' said Cayne.

'Exload that to Rassuah,' said Loken.

'I already have,' replied Cayne.

RASSUAH LET CAYNE'S device and the motion of *Tarnhelm* guide her, allowing the ship to feel its way through the maze of destroyers, frigates, system monitors and orbital patrol boats. Cayne's device was plugged into the ship's avionics panel and was plotting a constantly updating route.

The traitor fleet was enormous, many hundreds of vessels moored at high anchor. The bigger ships kept themselves geo-stationary, but didn't otherwise move. The light cruisers and destroyers were the ones Rassuah needed to worry about. They patrolled the void above Molech, vigilant hunters and guard dogs all in one. Threat auspex lashed orbital space in search of prey. Even if a search sweep passed right over the *Tarnhelm*, Rassuah didn't think they'd sniff out the stealthy infiltrator.

But in case the enemy got lucky, she ghosted the *Tarnhelm* between scads of orbital junk, keeping as many drifting wrecks between her and the hunters as possible.

Just the kind of delicate, hyper-intricate flying only one schooled and augmented by the surgeons of the clade masters could achieve. Even so, a fine sheen of perspiration beaded her brow.

'You let me know the instant any of those destroyers so much as changes a micron of its course,' she said.

Cayne nodded, but gave her a look of patronising indulgence.

She didn't know exactly what his device was, but Cayne asserted it could pick a path through even the most densely lay-ered defences, and so far it hadn't let them down. Retroactively emplaced mines, electromagnetic pulsars and passive auspex had been seeded through high orbit, but the device had sniffed every one of them out and provided course corrections to avoid them.

When she'd asked him where it had come from, all he had said was that it was a confection designed by the Lord of Iron in one of his more introspective moments. She'd laughed at that, telling him she hadn't figured his primarch being one prone to introspection.

He had looked at her strangely and said, 'The more powerful and original a mind, the more it will incline towards solitude.'

Leaving her with an assurance that the device would function perfectly well without him, Cayne returned to the crew spaces and Ares Voitek had taken his place. While Rassuah would pilot the ship, Voitek would crew its weapons. Any significant weapons' fire would likely announce their presence as surely as a vox-hail, but better to be prepared. Voitek had plugged into the console, his senses meshed with the passive auspex.

'Servitor-crewed one-shot,' he said picking up the active surveyors of a torpedo with an implanted servitor to fire it upon detection of a target. 'Nine hundred kilometres high on your ten.'

'I see it,' said Rassuah, angling their course to avoid its arc of coverage.

'Overlapping sentinel array dead ahead,' said Voitek.

'Can you burn out its auspex with a tight-focus volkite beam?'

'I can. Generating micro-burst solution.'

'Ares, wait,' said Rubio, appearing at the hatch behind them, his face lined with effort. 'Don't shoot it.'

'Why not?' asked Voitek. 'I have a perfect firing solution.'

'Destroy it and you will alert our enemies.'

'I don't intend to destroy it, simply blind its main auspex.'

'It's not the auspex you need to worry about.'

'We take this one down and we open the largest gap,' explained Voitek. 'The only time these things register with the command ship is when they detect something. Its going dark won't be noticed.'

'Open fire and you'll find out just how wrong it's possible to be,' said Rubio. 'There is a corrupt Mechanicum sentience onboard, something analogous to a Thallax, but tasked only with maintaining a link in an auspex chain. Break that chain and the enemy will know of our presence.'

'We need that gap,' said Rassuah. 'Cayne's toy can only find a way to the *Vengeful Spirit* if there's a gap.'

Rubio nodded and closed his eyes. 'I will give you your gap, Rassuah. Be ready, Ares. Shoot when I give the word.'

Witchlight hazed Rubio's eyelids, and his crystalline hood pulsed with corposant. Rassuah felt the hairs on the back of her neck rise. Rubio's eyes darted back and forth, as though following a tortuous maze where one wrong turn meant disaster. His lips parted and a breath of frozen mist sighed out.

'Shoot,' he said. 'Now.'

Rassuah didn't see anything happen. Voitek's control of the weapons was via an implanted servo-arm and the volkite beam was too quick and too precise. Even so, she held her breath.

Rubio opened his eyes, but his hood still glowed. His skin was pale and he looked like he'd just eaten something unpleasant.

'What did you do?' asked Rassuah.

'I implanted an image of dead space within its polluted mind,' said Rubio. 'Voitek destroyed its eyes, but it is seeing what I want it to see. It believes it is still part of the auspex chain.'

'How long will it believe that?'

'As long as I keep the image strong in its consciousness,' said Rubio, holding firm to the door stanchions. The strain of holding false thoughts in a deviant cyborg's mind was taking its toll.

Cayne's logister chimed as it registered a newly opened gap and offered up a path. Rassuah was already easing *Tarnhelm* through with a twitch of manoeuvring jets.

'Fly steady, and fly smooth,' cautioned Rubio.

'It's the only way I fly,' Rassuah assured him.

The *Vengeful Spirit* loomed ahead of *Tarnhelm*, a vast edifice of black metal, two hundred kilometres and closing. Rassuah shivered at the sight of the Warmaster's flagship, as though it were a voracious oceanic predator and they a bleeding morsel swimming heedlessly towards it.

Everything about the *Vengeful Spirit* was threatening.

Each gun port was a snarling maw, every cloistered broadside array a serrated cluster of gargoyles and daemons. The huge amber eyes on its flanks, none smaller than a hundred metres across, were actively staring at her. The blade of its prow was an assassin's dagger whose sole purpose was to cut her throat.

Rassuah tried to shake off the creeping horror of the vessel. Throne, it was just a starship! Steel and stone, an engine and a crew. She whispered clade mantras to clear her thoughts. She fixed on *Tarnhelm*'s displays and controls, but always found her gaze drawn back to the *Vengeful Spirit*'s hellforged eyes.

The impact crater yawned before *Tarnhelm* like a gateway to the abyss, a black hole into the unknown.

'Starships have machine-spirits, yes?' asked Rassuah.

Voitek looked up from the console, his half-machine face showing puzzlement at the timing of her question.

'A gift of the Omnissiah, yes,' he said at last. 'Every complex machine has one bestowed upon it at the moment of its activation. The larger the machine, the greater the spirit.'

'So what kind of spirit does this ship have?'

'You know its name, what do you think?'

'I think that any ship built to rule over a world of toxins and murder has a spirit best avoided.'

'And yet we must fly into the heart of this one,' said Voitek as the *Vengeful Spirit* swallowed the *Tarnhelm* whole.

THEY MET ON an island at the centre of an artificial lake. Reflected moonlight wavered on its gently rippling surface. The location spoke of earlier times in the Legion's history, before ritual had replaced tradition. When things had been simpler.

Now it seemed that even that simplicity had been a lie.

A flaming spear rammed into the ground at the centre of the island burned with orange light, bathing the features of those assembled in a ruddy glow of health that belied their true condition.

Abaddon's skin was waxy with regenerative balms and fresh-grafted skin. Noctua now boasted a clicking augmetic for a right hand, while Aximand was supported by a spinal armature while his shattered vertebrae regrew. Only Falkus Kibre had fought the angel of fire and emerged unscathed.

Maloghurst stood with the Mournival, for once looking like the least wounded among them. Ger Gerradon and his growing band of Luperci also gathered to hear of the invasion's next phase.

'We have achieved great things, my sons, but the hardest fight is yet to come,' began Horus, circling the burning spear and placing a hand over the amber eye at his chest. 'The enemy mass before us, an unbroken host of men and armour stretching all the way to Iron Fist Mountain. Armies from all across Molech are gathering, but they will not stop us from reaching Lupercalia.'

Aximand stepped from the circle.

Of course it would be Aximand. He would have fought the coming battle a hundred times already in his head. Of all his sons, Little Horus Aximand was the most fastidious, the most conscientious. The one whose thoughts came closest to his own.

'The numbers do not favour us, my lord,' said Aximand.

'Numbers aren't all that decide a battle,' pointed out Kibre.

'I know that, Falkus, but even so, we're outnumbered nearly fifty to one. Perhaps if the Death Guard fought with us...'

'Our brothers of the Fourteenth Legion are poised to be the anvil upon which the hammer of the Sons of Horus will break the Imperials,' said Horus.

'They'll be with us for the coming fight?' said Aximand. 'We can count on that?'

'Have you ever known Mortarion's sloggers to fail?' said Horus.

Aximand nodded, conceding the point. 'What are your orders?'

'Simple. We fight for the living and kill for the dead. Isn't that what you say?'

'Something like that,' grinned Aximand.

'What's at Lupercalia?' asked Abaddon, his voice forever burned down to a scorched rasp. 'What did you learn from the thing in the cave's death?'

Horus nodded and said, 'I remembered why the Emperor came here, what He found and why He didn't want anyone else to know about it. Lupercalia is where I'll find what we need to win this long war.'

'So what did it show you?' asked Aximand.

'All in good time,' said Horus. 'But, first, I have a question for you, my sons. Do any of you know how life began on Old Earth?'

No one answered, but he hadn't expected them to; the question too far beyond their usual sphere of interaction.

'Sir?' said Maloghurst. 'What does that have to do with Molech?'

'Everything,' said Horus, enjoying this rare moment to be a teacher instead of a warrior. 'Some of Earth's scientists believed life began as an accidental chemical reaction deep in the oceans around hydrothermal vents. A chance energy gradient that facilitated the transformation of carbon dioxide and hydrogen into simple amino acids and proto-cells. Others believed life came to Earth by exogenesis, microorganisms entombed deep in the hearts of comets travelling the void.'

Horus walked to the edge of the lake, his warriors parting before him. He knelt and scooped a handful of water in his palm. He turned to face his sons and let it spill between his fingers.

'But that's not where you and I came from,' said Horus. 'As it turns out, our dream didn't begin on Earth at all.'

THIS WAS A part of the ship Loken had never visited. But even if he had, he doubted he would have recognised it. The *Tarnhelm* sat canted at a shallow angle on a buckled plate exposed to the void. Landing claws held it tight to the deck, and Rassuah kept the engines at their lowest pitch.

Loken led the pathfinders from the ship and into the cratered section of the *Vengeful Spirit*, his armour gusting puffs of exhaled breath. Feathers of vapour bled from the heat of his armour's backpack. The sound of his breathing filled his helmet as he crossed the ruptured chamber.

'Rassuah, once we're inside, take *Tarnhelm* out and follow our progress via the armour locators as best you can,' said Loken. 'And keep close to the hull. If this goes bad, we'll need a quick evacuation.'

'*You want me to keep my hunter's eye in?*' asked the pilot.

'As best you can.'

'*Count on it,*' said Rassuah, signing off.

Infinite space stretched behind him, an unending black tapestry of emptiness and points of aeons-old light. Before him was the vessel where he'd known his greatest joys and deepest woes.

He was back on the *Vengeful Spirit* and didn't know how to feel.

The best and worst of his memories had been shaped in its arming chambers and companionways. He'd known his greatest friends and seen them become his most terrible enemies. Loken felt like a murderer at the scene of his crime, or a tortured shade revisiting the place of his death.

He'd known that returning here would be difficult, but actually being here was something else entirely.

A hand pressed against his left shoulder guard. He'd proudly borne the heraldic icon of the Sons of Horus there. Now it was a blank space, burnished grey.

'I know, lad,' said Iacton Qruze. 'Strange to return, eh?'

'We called this ship home for the longest time,' said Loken. 'The memories I have...'

Qruze tapped a finger to his temple.

'Remember her as she was, not the beast they've turned her into. Everything began on this vessel and everything will end on it. Mark my words, lad.'

'It's just a ship,' said Severian, moving over the crumpled deck. 'Steel and stone, an engine and a crew.'

Qruze shook his head and followed Severian.

Loken felt old eyes upon him. He told himself it was just his imagination and set off after Qruze. He followed the rest of the team deeper into the cavern blown in the side of the ship.

By the look of its walls it had once been a dormitory space. Now it was an empty void. Every loose piece of apparatus had been explosively vented into space by whatever weapon had torn through the ship's hull.

'Transverse impact,' said Ares Voitek, pointing out tear lines and direction of blast shear. 'This was a lucky hit, a torpedo brought down by point-defence guns and spiralling away.'

'I wonder if it felt lucky to the people inside,' said Altan Nohai. 'Lucky or not, they still died.'

'They were traitors,' said Varren, pushing past. 'How does it matter how they died? They died, that's enough.'

'They died screaming,' said Rubio, a hand pressed to the side of his helmet. 'And they'd been screaming for a very long time.'

The pathfinders spread out, moving to where the nearest interior bulkhead was still intact. Voitek moved across the wall, his servo-arms tapping and clicking along the bulkhead as though searching for something.

'Here,' he said. 'There is atmosphere on the other side. Cayne?'

'Setting up now,' said Cayne.

He placed the same device he'd used to thread the maze of seeded defences surrounding the *Vengeful Spirit* at Voitek's feet. A detachable wand connected via a coiled cable snapped out and he panned the wand up and down.

'You are correct, Master Voitek,' he said, consulting a softly glow-ing slate on his device. 'A passageway, sealed at one end by debris. The shipwright's plans indicate there is a way through in the other direction, a sub-transit that leads up to an ammunition runnel-path for a lower gun deck.'

'Will it get us deeper into the ship?' asked Loken.

'I already said it would,' said Cayne. 'Aren't you familiar with the layout of sub-decks on the gunnery levels?'

'No, not particularly.'

Cayne shook his head as he packed up his device and slotted the wand back home. 'You Luna Wolves, it's a wonder you were able to find your way around at all.'

Severian drew his combat blade. 'I can kill him if you want,' he offered.

'Maybe later,' said Loken.

Severian shrugged and leaned forward to scratch a symbol onto the wall, an angular rune of vertical and crosswise lines.

'You know *futharc*?' said Bror Tyrfingr, looking over Severian's shoulder. 'How do you know futharc?'

'What's futharc?' asked Loken.

'Battle sigils,' said Severian. 'Scouts of the Space Wolves – sorry, the *Vlka Fenryka* – use them to guide follow-on forces through void-hulks and the like. Each symbol gives the main host infor-mation about what's ahead, the best routes to take. That sort of thing.'

'You didn't answer my question,' said Bror Tyrfingr.

'The Twenty-Fifth Company served with your lot more than once,' said Severian, finishing his script. 'A wolf named Svessl taught it to me.'

'Something he'll regret if I ever see him,' grunted Bror.

Qruze and Rama Karayan moved past Bror and Severian. They

began unfolding a blocky series of struts and portable generators from a series of narrow crates that might once have contained rockets for a missile launcher.

This was Karayan's area of expertise, and he quickly set up what looked like a framed template of a door. With Voitek's assistance, Karayan hooked his construction to a generator and wound a crank until a gem-light on its side turned green.

Karayan pressed a snap-covered activation switch. A shimmer of liquid energy bloomed around the frame's inner edges, spreading until it filled the enclosed space like the surface of a soap bubble. It rippled, filmy with rainbow colours.

'Integrity field established,' said Karayan. 'Safe to breach.'

Voitek nodded and his servo-arms reached through the field to grip projections on the bulkhead.

'Breaching now,' said Karayan as precision melta-cutters on the back of the frame burned with short-lived, but ferocious intensity. They sliced through the bulkhead instantaneously, and Ares Voitek yanked the cut slab of metal back through the integrity field.

'We're in,' said Varren.

SHOCK GREETED THE Warmaster's pronouncement. Disbelief and confusion. Aximand felt the ground beneath him turn to shifting sand at the truth of the Warmaster's words.

'Don't you feel it, my sons?' continued Horus. 'Don't you feel how special Molech is? How singular among all the worlds we have won it is?'

Aximand found himself nodding, and saw he wasn't the only one.

Lupercal walked in a circle, jabbing a fist into his palm with every sentence.

'At the dawn of the great diaspora, the Emperor travelled here in humble guise and found the gateway to a realm of immortal gods.

He offered them things only a god-in-waiting could offer, and they trusted Him. They gave Him a measure of their power, and with that power He wrought the science to unlock the mysteries of creation.'

Horus was radiant as he spoke, as though he had already ascended to a divine plane of reality.

'But the Emperor had no intention of honouring His debt to the gods. He turned on them, taking their gifts and blending them with His genecraft to give birth to demigods. The Emperor condemns the warp as unnatural, but only so no other dares wield it. The blood of the immaterial realm flows in my veins. It flows in all our veins, for as I am the Emperor's son, you are the Sons of Horus, and the secret of our genesis was unlocked upon Molech. The gateway to that power is in Lupercalia, far beneath the mountain rock. Sealed away from the light by a jealous god who knew that someday one of His sons would seek to surpass His deeds.'

And finally Aximand understood why they had come here, why they had expended such resources and defied all military logic to follow in the footsteps of a god.

This would be the moment they rose to challenge the Emperor with the very weapons He had kept for Himself.

This was to be the apotheosis of them all.

KARAYAN AND SEVERIAN led the way, moving into the tangled mess of the corridor beyond the integrity field. Loken and Qruze went next, followed by the others in quick succession. The corridor was dark and cluttered with smashed metal. Only the faint glow of helmet lenses and the occasional spark from fusing machinery lit the way. Debris littered the deck. Ruptured pipes drizzled the air with moisture and vapour.

Loken's auto-senses tasted it as the stagnant water in a bleak mountain tarn. He heard static like a rasp drawn over stone. Whispers lingered.

The Seven Neverborn. The Whisperheads. Samus. Samus is here…

Loken shook his head to clear the unbidden thought, but it was lodged like a splinter worming its way deeper into his flesh. He saw Rubio reach out a steadying hand to the wall, then flinch as though it were red hot.

Loken focused on Callion Zaven's back, imagining how it would look blown open with a mass-reactive or chewed up by a chainsword. He wondered if Zaven's death scream would echo with perfect pitch as he died.

'Loken?' said Altan Nohai. 'Is something wrong? Your heart-rate is elevated.'

'I'm fine,' said Loken, the image of murder lingering like the taste of blood. 'This place, it's hard being back.'

If the Apothecary heard the lie, he gave no sign. Loken pressed on, hearing the soft breath at his shoulder that he couldn't possibly be hearing.

They moved down the corridor, reaching a junction of dripping echoes and tangled cabling hanging from the ceiling spaces. Blue sparks spat from a crumpled junction box. An Eye of Horus had been crudely painted on the wall in white. Drip lines made it look as though it was weeping milky tears.

'Cayne, which way?'

'As I said, straight on and up the stairs at the end.'

Severian was already moving, bolter pulled in tight. It looked as though his body was utterly still from the waist up. The barrel of his weapon never wavered, never so much as drifted a millimetre from his eyeline.

Moving silently in power armour was a trick only a few could manage, but Severian and Karayan elevated it to an art form. If anything, Rama Karayan moved with even less apparent effort than Severian, mirroring his path as they pushed ahead.

Loken felt clumsy in comparison, every echo of his footfalls sounding like the stomping tread of a Dreadnought. He could see that the others felt the same way.

The scrape of a blade behind him set Loken's teeth on edge, like an Apothecary's saw grinding through bone. In deference to Bror Tyrfingr's displeasure, Severian left the marking of their path to the warrior of the Rout. It would be his gene-sire making this future assault, and the symmetry was pleasing.

Iron stairs were just where Cayne had said they would be, and the pathfinders climbed to one of the ventral gun decks. The top opened into a high-ceilinged chamber of acoustic baffles that sagged from the walls in wadded lumps and filled the air with drifting particulates. Another Eye of Horus on the wall. Loken reached out to touch it. The paint was still wet.

Shielded from the guns' pressurised venting of superheated propellant by heavy mantlet shutters, the ammunition runnel-path was a sunken roadway ten metres wide behind the ranked-up guns. In battle, a constant stream of flatbed gurneys would ride the rails, distributing shells to the macro-cannon batteries and hauling discarded casings to the smelters.

The guns were silent, but chains rattled in enormous windlasses and the rumble of magazine elevators set the air vibrating. The sour smell Loken had tasted earlier returned, stronger this time. The voices scratching at the edge of hearing like animals left out in the rain became clearer.

'What *is* that?' said Zaven.

'You hear it?' asked Loken.

'Of course, it's like a part-tuned vox in another room,' said Zaven. 'It keeps saying the same thing over and over.'

'What are you hearing?' asked Rubio urgently.

'I don't know exactly,' said Zaven. 'It's gibberish. *Maelsha'eil Atherakhia*, whatever *that* means.'

'No, it's not words at all,' said Varren. 'It's screaming. Or maybe someone's trying to chop a chainaxe through adamantium.'

'That's what you hear?' said Tubal Cayne. 'Getting hit on the head all those times must have damaged the aural comprehension centres of your brain.'

Rubio put himself between Cayne and Varren. His psychic hood flickered with light, though none of it was of his doing.

'What do you hear?' demanded Rubio.

'The noise of a gun deck,' said Cayne. 'What else would I hear?'

Rubio nodded and said, 'Be thankful you are a man of pure reason, Tubal Cayne.'

'What's going on, Rubio?' said Loken.

The psyker turned around, addressing them all. 'Whatever you think you're hearing, it's not real. Low-level psychic energy is simmering beneath the surface. It's like background radiation, but within the mind.'

'Is it dangerous?' said Nohai. 'I'm showing elevated adrenal levels and combat responses in every single one of you.'

'Because he just told us we're under the effect of maleficarum!' hissed Bror Tyrfingr, baring his canines.

Macer Varren unhooked his axe, finger hovering over the activation stud. The noise of its chained teeth would be heard for hundreds of metres in all directions.

Rubio's fists clenched and ghostlights danced in the crystalline matrix of his hood. The whispering in Loken's helmet drifted away, as if carried on a stiff breeze. Soon it was gone, leaving only the percussive hammering of the gun deck. He let out a breath.

'What are you doing?' Tyrfingr asked Rubio.

'Shielding you all from the psychic bleed-off that permeates this ship,' said the psyker, and Loken heard the strain in his voice. 'Everything you hear from now on will be the truth.'

The thought gave Loken no comfort.

SEVENTEEN

Beasts of Molech
Mission-critical
No perfection without imperfection

THE HORIZON HAD been burning for days. Jungle fires were nothing new, but in all his life, Lord Balmorn Donar hadn't seen anything to match the scale of this conflagration. Worse, the leading edge of the blazing jungle was no more than a day away at best.

'Is it the Death Guard?' asked Robard, marching his Knight onto the wall to join his father. The leg of Robard's Knight had been repaired, but it was a patch-job by second-rate apprentices. With the main axis of enemy advance coming from the north, the Preceptor Line had been stripped of its Mechanicum adepts and most of its Sacristans. Every one of them had been seconded to Iron Fist Mountain to service the God-Machines of Legio Crucius.

'It can't be the Death Guard,' he said. 'It can't be *anyone*. Even the most potent fire-throwers, chem-flayers or rad-bombs would take months or years to cut a viable path without destroying your own army.'

'Then what is it?'

Lord Donar took his time before answering. His sensorium

rendered the sky as a flat black smudge, but sometimes – just for a fraction of a second – it broke apart into buzzing static, like an unimaginably vast swarm of flies.

'I don't know, boy,' he said at last, 'but I'm damn sure it isn't a fire.'

'My thermal auspex says otherwise,' said Robard. 'So do the wall guns.'

'Aye, but the readings are spiking hard then dying away almost to nothing before repeating the cycle,' pointed out Lord Donar. 'I'm not a bloody expert, but even I know fires don't behave like that. I don't know *anything* that behaves like that.'

'So what do we do?'

'What we always do, boy,' said Lord Donar. 'We hold the Line.'

The beast packs hit the wall an hour later.

THE AZHDARCHID CAME first. The fleetest of the great beasts, they raced ahead of the black tide engulfing the jungle. Their long necks were scaled and feathered, their crocodilian beaks stretched and snapping in animal panic.

The wall guns opened up when they came within a thousand metres of the Preceptor Line. The noise was tremendous, even encased within the armour of a Knight. Lord Donar filtered out their cries and watched the flocks charge through a streaming hurricane of rotor cannon fire. Heedless of the carnage, the loping, flightless birds screamed as the shells cut them down without mercy.

At six hundred metres, the seven Knights of House Donar opened fire. Battle cannon shells left five metre craters and flying, disassembled bodies in their wake. Stubber cannons carved bloody trenches through the horde. Scores fell, trampled to pulp by those behind them. The killing ground was a quagmire of blood-soaked earth and unrecognisable meat. The air misted red, tasted of metal shavings.

Xenosmilus packs came next, hundreds of the monstrous quad-rupeds charging for the wall in snarling desperation. The guns pulped them. Flesh and bone shredded in thousands of bloody explosions. Basilisks and Medusa of the Kapikulu Iron Brigade lobbed shells over the wall with their gun barrels at maximum elevation.

Seismic shock waves and pulverising overpressure from close-range detonations shook the wall and the facing stonework split with sharp cracks. Entire swathes of the Preceptor Line visibly sagged.

Massacre wasn't a big enough word to encompass the slaughter, but the rampaging flocks soon found gaps where the Preceptor Line's wall guns were non-functional. Too close for the artillery to engage, streams of the predator beasts surged towards the wall.

'With me!' shouted Lord Donar, striding to cover the gaps. He rolled his shoulders, and the Knight responded. Weapons charged, ammo-hoppers engaged. Solid slugs rammed into breeches. Tar-geting icons snapped into focus. Too many to choose from. Too many targets to miss. Lord Donar felt the Knight's spirit and all its previous pilots' thrill at the nearness of death.

Other nobles gave names to their Knights, but to House Donar it was the man inside that counted. A machine might have glori-ous history, but pair it with a below-par warrior and no amount of glory would matter.

Lord Donar counted at least two hundred azhdarchid, twice that many xenosmilus. More beasts than he'd seen in his life. The snapping, hooting, cawing packs were actually trying to claw and bite their way through the wall. What was behind them that could be so bad as to drive them to annihilate themselves like this?

A black miasma oozed from the tree line, a bank of questing smoke. All the world's insect life come to watch the killing.

No time to ponder, there was fighting to be done.

The azhdarchid were trapped at the base of the wall, screeching and battering themselves to destruction at its corpse-heaped base. The xenosmilus packs were climbing the wall like besiegers, iron-hard claws digging into the crumbling, cracking stonework and hauling their enormous bodies up its angled facade.

Lord Donar picked out a milling pack at the base of the wall and unleashed a one-two punch from his battle cannon mount. Twin explosions mushroomed. Mangled bodies tumbled through the air, burned unrecognisable. His stub-cannon raked side to side, snatching roaring beasts from the wall. Corpses slithered downward to join the ever-growing heap of dead animals at its base.

A turret to his right blew out as a pair of imperfect shells exploded prematurely. The shattered oblong of blackened metal tumbled down the wall in flames. More turrets were falling silent as their ammo reserves ran dry.

'Cover the gaps!' ordered Lord Donar. 'Robard! You take it.'

His son's Knight strode out to the crumbled portion of the wall where the smoking base of the turret still sat. Bracing one leg on the wall, Robard leaned out and stabbed his thermal lance into the hordes. A screech of magma-hot air exploded among the azhdarchid, vaporising at least nine of them. His stubber flensed the wall.

But for every dozen beasts they killed, twice that came behind them. A never-ending stream of monsters was abandoning the disintegrating jungle. Death at the hands of Imperial guns was preferable to facing what had driven them from their lairs. The black miasma was *dissolving* the thick-boled trees, reducing them to decayed mulch.

The xenosmilus were on the ramparts. Their heavy paws were bloody, their claws all but torn out by the climb. Lord Donar decapitated a beast with a single shot.

'Too close for battle cannon!' shouted Robard.

'Perfect for reaper work!' answered Lord Donar, striding his machine over to the thickest concentration of beasts surging onto the battlements.

His reaper blade roared to life, six metres of razor-toothed chainsaw. The first beasts over the wall were cut in half with a single sweep. Dismembered corpses were hurled twenty metres by the blade's spinning teeth. A return stroke tore broken merlons from the wall. Lord Donar could fight like this all day. Let every beast of the jungle come. He would kill them all.

The Knights roved the wallhead. Stubbers fired dry or until their barrels grew too hot to shoot. Reaper blades cut down anything that reached the wall. The killing was mechanical. Death delivered by machine to animal like robot slaughtermen in an abattoir.

Robard's reaper blade was clogged with bone and annealed flesh, so he used his thermal lance as a club. His mass was a weapon too, crushing foes beneath clawed feet. He was alone. And surrounded.

But the beasts pushing past him didn't turn and attack his vulnerable rear. They dropped to the esplanade, running pell-mell to put as much distance between them and the wall. Squads of Devsirmes opened fire on them, but only a handful of beasts were brought down.

Lord Donar turned his Knight around in time to see the blackened, rotting edges of the jungle smashed apart as the mallahgra arrived. The simian giants bounded towards the wall in long, fist-dragging leaps. Their beetle-like heads were lowered like battering rams.

'Luthias, Urbano, the gate! Now!' ordered Lord Donar. 'Robard, the wall is yours, don't lose it, boy!'

The two named Knights turned from the hewing at the ramparts and followed their lord.

A pair of xenosmilus vaulted onto Urbano's back and fouled the workings of his reaper blade long enough for another six to gain the walls and drag him down. Weapons sill firing, Urbano was pulled over the rampart. Lord Donar and Luthias strode through the fighting towards the gate.

The Kapikulu's few remaining Malcadors assumed dug-in firing positions either side of the gateway. Weapon teams of Belgar Devsirmes occupied elevated sangars and sandbagged pillboxes.

Small-arms fire stabbed at the walls. Las-rounds, missiles and heavy bolters. Inconsequential compared to the Knights' weapons.

Lord Donar and Luthias reached the gate just as the first mallahgra hit. The metal deformed, then deformed again and again. One after another, the mallahgra combined their superior mass to smash the gate from its mounting though it must surely have shattered the bones in their shoulders and necks. Hinges the size of Earthshaker cannon barrels tore from their mountings as the gate finally gave in to the pressure.

A tide of grey-furred giants rammed through the gate, all muscle, fangs and fury. Lord Donar shot the skulls from the first two with a burst of stubber shells. Luthias vaporised the three behind them with his thermal lance. The Malcadors shredded flesh and turned the gateway into a solid volume of gore.

Lord Donar fired until his stubber burned through his reserve ammo-hoppers. He'd seen Tyrae's icon go dark. His death went unwitnessed and, with another Knight's loss, more and more of the beasts were gaining the ramparts.

The battlements were lost. A tide of rampaging monsters was spilling over the wall.

Luthias died as a pair of rearing mallahgra smashed open his carapace and cut him in half with razored stumps of claws. Lord Donar waited for them to turn on him, but the gigantic creatures simply kept on going, pounding away from the wall.

Only then did Lord Donar notice what he should have seen from the beginning of this assault. The beasts were not the danger. They weren't attacking the Preceptor Line as a military force, they were attacking because it was in their way. He should have opened the damn gate long ago.

'All forces, stand down,' ordered Lord Donar. 'Get out of their way. House Donar, to me!'

It went against the grain to allow beasts to go unmolested, but to fight here was to die. Something worse was coming, something they had to have numbers to fight. The last four Knights stepped aside, taking what cover they could as an avalanche of jungle creatures swarmed the wall and fled the battlefield.

Soldiers of the Kapikulu and Devsirmes were still dying, crushed in the stampede, but Lord Donar could do nothing for them. He kept his Knight pressed tight to the inner face of the wall. It shamed him that the Preceptor Line had been breached, but there had been no chance of holding it. The beasts would likely take refuge in the mountain caves at the edge of the Tazkhar steppe. Those that didn't would be eliminated by Abdi Kheda's Kushite Eastings if they travelled farther west or north.

It took another hour before the tide of jungle creatures was ended. The last beasts were poor specimens indeed, crippled, aged and diseased things. The Devsirmes shot them as they passed, and those shots were mercy kills.

The Preceptor Line was in ruins – the gateway was choked with dead animals and entire sections of the wall were breached from close-range artillery blasts.

Only one scaffold ramp still offered access to the wall, and Lord Donar climbed it warily, hearing every creak of timber and groan of over-stressed metal. The top of the wall was a shattered ruin of broken stumps where protective merlons had once offered protection. Its entire complement of turrets had been destroyed, or were without ammunition.

Straight away, Lord Donar saw none of that would matter.

The Kushite jungle was gone, wiped out entirely.

Six hundred million hectares of lush vegetation were now an unending morass of necrotic black ooze. Lord Donar knew only one weapon that could comprehensively destroy life with such speed.

The black miasma at the edge of what had once been a jungle of incomparable depth and fecundity began dissipating like night before the dawn. His sensorium broke up into buzzing static as what looked like a trillion flies lifted from the ocean of decay beyond the walls.

Lord Donar punched the canopy release and let the segmented hood of his Knight fold back into its carapace. The stench hit him first, a paralysing reek of spoiled meat, dung and polluted earth.

As the miasma continued to lift, Lord Donar saw an army of invasion grinding its way through the decaying remains of the jungle. Enormous fuel tankers bearing the golden heraldry of the Ophir promethium guilds stretched to the horizon where striding Titans moved with ponderous steps.

Led by a virtually wrecked Rhino, a host of fighting vehicles and giant artillery pieces threw up great clods of black mud from their tracks as they advanced on the wall. Marching grimly alongside them were thousands of Legion warriors in plate that had once been a pale ivory, but which was now plastered with filth and decaying matter.

At the head of the army was an armoured giant in a matted cloak of scraps and iron. His face was a leering skull gagged by a bronze mouthpiece and he bore a reaper blade of such scale that it seemed possible he had hacked the jungle down single-handedly.

Lord Donar saw scores of monstrous culverins and wide-mawed

artillery pieces fed enormous breacher shells. His heart hardened as he turned his Knight about and made his way from the wall.

'Father?' said Robard, as Lord Donar reached the ground.

'Knights of House Donar,' he said. 'March with me.'

Lord Balmorn Donar strode through the gate, his Knights quick to follow him through the corpse-choked gateway.

The Knights stood before the impossible army of the Death Guard. Grumbling superheavies took aim at them with Titan-killing weaponry; volcano cannons, plasma blastguns and accelerator cannons. The overkill was ridiculous. Target locks appeared on Lord Donar's auspex, too many to count.

Enough weaponry to kill a dozen Knight Houses were trained upon them and the wall they had spent their lives defending. Lord Donar's guns were empty and useless. Only his reaper blade was still viable, and he would match it against the whoreson master of the Death Guard.

'Only one order left to give,' said Robard.

'Charge!' shouted Lord Donar.

WITH THE LOWER gun deck marked, the pathfinders moved deeper into the *Vengeful Spirit*. They kept to the runnel-path, hugging the walls when baying servitors stalked past above. They moved when distant rumbles obscured the sounds of their passing.

From the gun deck they followed Cayne's directions, moving out into dimly-lit arterials. They threaded a path towards structural hubs where a torpedo or macro-cannon impact would do the most damage and areas where practicable boardings into wide staging areas could be effected. Bror Tyrfingr marked such places in futharc, and Ares Voitek planted hidden locator beacons with encrypted Imperial triggers to guide assault boats and torpedoes.

Loken was ostensibly the leader of the mission, but he moved in a daze, still struck by the incongruity of being aboard the *Vengeful*

GRAHAM MCNEILL

Spirit. The lower decks were unfamiliar to him and yet curiously welcoming. Oft-times he would hear a whisper at his shoulder that would direct him without recourse to confirmation from Cayne's surveyor machine.

He saw more of the graffiti Eye of Horus, and each time Loken saw the paint was still sticky, as though there was someone just ahead of Severian marking their onward route. Like portraits in a gallery, each Eye seemed to follow him, as though the ship itself were silently watching foreign organisms moving within its body.

I see you. I know you…

He wondered if anyone else saw them.

Qruze looked at him strangely, as though aware something wasn't right. Loken heard the soft sigh of breath, *real* breath, not the hiss of exhalations through a helmet grille. The breath of an old friend. Rubio was shielding them from the psychic emanations permeating the ship. What then did that make this?

Auditory hallucinations caused by the trauma of Isstvan or a dead friend aiding him? Latent psychosis or wishful thinking?

Garvi…

Loken saw a drifting figure at the junction ahead.

Mechanicum, black robed and hooded with augmetics. Cables trailed from the tech-priest's spine, and a host of blue-eyed servo-skulls orbited his transparent skull. A retinue of hunched, dwarf servitors followed him, chattering in binaric spurts and burps. The skulls spun to face them. Their eyes flared cherry red.

Rama Karayan dropped and pulled his bolter to his shoulder. Its sight was linked to his visor. The weapon coughed a three-round burst, far softer than any bolter had a right to sound. The lone tech-priest dropped silently, crumpling in on himself like a building undergoing controlled demolition.

Two of his accompanying retinue died in the same burst.

Before the other servitors could react, Severian was on them.

His combat blade stabbed. Once, twice, three times.

The servo-skulls floated above the corpses, held fast by a web of cables and copper wires. The light in their eyes stuttered. Severian sawed through something under the tech-priest's hood. Oily fluid sprayed and the floating skulls fell to the deck.

He waved the rest of the pathfinders forward.

'Clear the junction,' he ordered.

They hauled the bodies out of sight and packed them into a darkened alcove farther down the corridor. Voitek's servo-arms stripped a panel and loose debris from the roof spaces to conceal them.

'Gunnery overseer,' said Varren, pulling back the hood.

Loken didn't see how he could know that. The corpse's skull was little more than a gruel-filled bowl of detonated brain matter and machine fragments. A gold vox-grille hung from the flapping lower jaw, and iron teeth fell out as Varren let go.

'Not like any I've seen,' said Severian.

'We had ones like this on the *Conqueror*,' said Varren, tapping a crude, electrode-spiked implant still attached to a scrap of skull and trailing numerous bare cables into the detritus of its brain.

'Hardwired with motivational barbs. Deck guns don't reload as quickly as they ought to? The pain centres of the brain get a jolt. A battery misses its target? Double jolt. Miss again and the brain's flash-burned to vapour. Gets a warship's gun-crews highly motivated.'

'The Luna Wolves never needed such things,' said Qruze, disgusted.

'This isn't a Luna Wolves vessel any more.'

'Did those servo-skulls send an alarm signal?' asked Rubio.

'That depends on whether Karayan's shot broke the noospheric link before they could exload a warning,' said Voitek.

'Is there any way to know for certain?' asked Loken, looking up into the silent stare of another painted Eye of Horus.

Voitek tapped the tech-priest's ruined skull. 'Not any more.'

'His absence will soon be noted,' said Tubal Cayne. 'Regardless of whether the tech-priest or his skulls sent an alarm or not.'

Qruze shook his head. 'By the time it's noticed we'll be long gone.'

'Then let's not waste the time in between,' said Loken.

THE DEEPER THE pathfinders penetrated the *Vengeful Spirit*, the stronger the sensation of an invisible member of their team grew in Loken's mind. He paused often, using the guise of checking corners and their back trail to see if he could see their phantom accomplice. He felt no threat from the presence, even as he understood it indicated a deeper malaise within his psyche.

Dark service stairwells brought them onto metal gantries and vaulted chambers hung with distant, flapping things that might have been banners but probably weren't. Some bore stitched Eyes, and Loken tried not to look at them.

They avoided contact where possible, killing only when necessary. Severian's combat blade and Karayan's silenced bolter did most of the work, but Callion Zaven's hewclaw blade was wetted, and Voitek's servo-arms permanently closed the throats of many a laggardly deckhand. Those they killed were uniformly human or cyborgised menials. The deep regions of the ship were rarely visited by Legion warriors and the pathfinders made full use of that small advantage.

Time passed slowly, the diurnal cycle that provided the illusion of day and night aboard a starship no longer in place. Hours became days in *Vengeful Spirit*'s deep spaces. They measured time by the sourceless chants of unseen choirs and the machine noises of pipework and ducts. To Loken, it sounded like the distant parts of the ship whispering to one another, passing messages and exchanging frightful secrets.

Scattered lumen strips, furnace lights and isolated chambers where skeletal inhabitants of the lower decks gathered in islands of flare-light were all that illuminated the lower decks. Bells tolled constantly, klaxons blared, and screeching Mechanicum adepts in tattered black robes set the pace of work for their wretched charges with whips and crackling prods.

'It's time we breached the upper decks,' said Bror Tyrfingr, as Tubal Cayne halted their progress to update his plotter with fresh measurements. 'We've roamed below the waterline long enough.'

'The higher we go, the more we risk exposure,' said Qruze.

'And encountering Legion forces,' added Karayan.

'Bring them on,' said Varren. 'It's about time my axe split some traitor skulls.'

'That axe of yours will be heard all the way to the strategium,' said Altan Nohai. 'As soon as the Sons of Horus are aware of our presence, this mission is over.'

'We're not here to fight,' Loken reminded Varren. 'We're here to mark the way for the Sixth Legion to assault.'

'Then it's time to mark mission-critical targets,' insisted Bror. 'Main gun batteries, Legion arming chambers, reactor spaces, command and control nodes. And once we mark them, we move forward. The Wolf King isn't above a bit of subtlety and misdirection, but he won't come at the Warmaster from the shadows. He'll come at him head on, fangs bared.'

After facing Leman Russ across the hnefatafl board, Loken was inclined to agree, but the thought of heading into more familiar spaces within the ship was an unappealing prospect.

'You're right, Bror,' he said. 'It's time to show why we were chosen for this mission. We need to mark this vessel's jugular, ready for the Wolf King to tear out. We're going higher into the *Vengeful Spirit*.'

✠ ✠ ✠

ANOTHER VOX-INTERRUPT TRIED to cut across *Banelash*'s sensorium, but the echoes of its former pilots dissipated it before it could reach him. Just like him, they did not care to hear Tyana Kourion's demands for him to return to the battle-line.

The Grand Army of Molech was assembling in the hills north of Lupercalia, stretching eastwards from the rugged haunches of the Untar Mesas to Iron Fist Mountain. With thousands of armoured fighting vehicles, hundreds of thousands (if not more) soldiers, battery after battery of artillery and two Titan Legions mobilising to fight, the Lord General could surely manage without one Knight.

He'd searched the upland forests for days now, climbing through rugged crags and mossy valleys to find the White Naga. His initial thrill of being on the verge of something miraculous had faded almost as soon as he'd left camp. The divine avatar of the Serpent Cult had singularly failed to manifest before him, and his patience was wearing thin.

He'd chosen a direction at random, marching his Knight from camp with purposeful strides. The damage the Warmaster had inflicted was still there, a bone-deep hurt that would never go away, a permanent reminder to rival that of the loss of his sons. Being connected to *Banelash* via his spinal implants made their loss seem remote, disconnected, as though it had happened to someone else.

Tragic, yes, but ultimately bearable.

That remoteness would end as soon as he disconnected, and he entertained the wild idea of never removing himself from *Banelash*. Ludicrous, of course. Prolonged connection with the machine-spirit of a Knight filled a pilot's brain with foreign memories, unrelated data junk and sensory phantoms.

To remain within a Knight for too long was to embrace madness.

As crazed as it was, the idea had taken root and could not be dislodged.

Raeven's mouth was parched and his stomach growled. He hadn't eaten before leaving camp, and wine soured in his belly. Recyc-systems filtering his waste were allowing him to continue without food and water, but he could already feel toxins, both physical and mental, building throughout his body.

If the White Naga didn't reveal itself soon, he wouldn't survive to return with any divine boon. The thought of dying alone in the deep forest amused him momentarily. How ludicrous an end it would be for a Knight of Molech. He would become a statue of iron and desiccated flesh, standing alone and forgotten for thousands of years. He imagined debased savages of a future epoch discovering him and coming to worship at his corpse as though *Banelash* were an ancient pagan altar.

He blinked as the sensorium flickered and stretched like poured syrup. The images it displayed were not externally rendered by machines, rather they were mental projections, controlled stimulations of his synapses to trigger a visual representation of the auspex returns.

Then Raeven saw it wasn't the sensorium that was faulty.

It was the landscape that was twisting.

Normally the display was a monochromatic thing, stripped bare for clarity in battle, but now it erupted with sensation. The trees blossomed with new life and incredible growth. Flowers sprouted where he walked and their perfume was intoxicating and almost unbearably sweet. Colours with no name and sounds hitherto unheard assailed him. Raeven saw circulatory systems in every blade of grass, unblinking eyes on every leaf, a history of the world in every rock.

Every colour, every surface became unbearably sharp, excruciatingly real and swollen with vital potential. It was too much, a sensory overload that threatened to burn out the delicate connections within his mind. Raeven gasped, nausea stabbing his gut.

If it hadn't already been empty, he would have puked himself inside out.

Banelash staggered in response, an iron giant lumbering like a drunk. The Knight's bulk smashed writhing branches apart and dislodged rippling boulders. Its energy whip lashed out, felling centuries old trees that shrieked as they fell. The rain-slick ground offered no purchase, as though it *wanted* him to fall, and Raeven fought to keep the Knight upright.

To fall so far from help would be death, but the thought no longer amused him. He wrestled with the controls as the overwhelming ferocity of the world's hyper-reality cut him open and pared him back to the bone.

'Too much,' he screamed. 'It's too much!'

'There is no such thing as too much!'

The power of the voice stripped the blinking leaves from the trees for a hundred metres and set Raeven's mind afire like an aneurysm. The armourglass canopy of his Knight cracked and he screamed as blood filled his right eye.

He finally righted his staggering Knight.

And saw the divine.

'The White Naga,' he gasped.

'One of my many names. I am the Illuminator, the beginning and the end, the ontological ideal of perfection.'

Without conscious thought, *Banelash* knelt before the godly being. The White Naga shimmered with light, a sun come to Molech in corporeal form with a heat so savage it would burn him from existence in the blink of an eye.

'Here,' wept Raeven. 'Throne, you're here...'

Amorphous clouds of scented musk attended it, together with the sound of mirrors shattering in their unworthiness to reflect such beauty. Its manifestation was wondrous and inconstant, a tapestry of writhing, winged serpentine imagery.

'Your blood sacrifice brings me to Molech, Raeven Devine.'

Its many arms reached for him, beckoning him. Raeven wanted nothing more than to bring his Knight to its feet and lose himself in its embrace. To surrender to beauty was no surrender at all.

A last shred of human instinct restrained him, screaming that to submit to the White Naga would bind him to its service forever.

And would that be so bad...?

Its every incarnation was burned and reborn, as though it ever sought to reach a pinnacle of perfection. A starburst of ice-white hair haloed eyes the colour of indulgence.

Raeven wanted to speak, but what could he say to a god that would not be trite?

'Speak and do as you wish, Raeven Devine. That is the whole of the law. You are free to throw off the shackles of those who chain your will and confine your desires. All must be free to indulge in every excess! Wring every moment of sensation and you draw closer to perfection.'

Raeven struggled to follow its words, each one a hammer blow against the inside of his skull.

'Mankind was once free, Raeven, well-born and living with honour. That freedom intrinsically lead to virtuous action, but the Imperium has shackled your species. And so constrained, your noble natures fight to remove that servitude, because men will always desire what they are denied.'

The message was so simple, so pure and clear that it amazed him he hadn't grasped it on his own. The barbed anger he'd felt before the Ritual of Becoming twisted in his gut, a powerful knot of painful disgust that misted his eyes with tears.

And as though filtering lenses had dropped over his eyes, Raeven saw through his tears to what lay beyond the White Naga's veil.

Bloated and serpentine, it was no creature of the divine, but a hideous monster straight from the ancient bestiaries. A loathsome snake of iridescent scales and draconic wings, grasping arms and a grotesque face at once beautiful and repugnant.

'What are you?' cried Raeven.

It heard his horror and its glamours dug their claws deeper in his mind. The image of a godlike avatar warred with the bestial *thing* he knew it to be.

'*I am your god, your deliverer. I will lead you to glory!*'

'No,' said Raeven, feeling the White Naga's powerful will wrapping around his own like a constrictor. He held to the barbed hatred in his heart, and the White Naga cried out as they tore at its presence.

'You don't offer freedom,' said Raeven, forcing each word out through the narcotic musk surrounding the creature. 'You offer enslavement. It's a lie, a damned, filthy lie!'

The musk surged with intoxicating power, and Raeven felt the monster's rage like a physical force. It battered him towards submission. Whatever the White Naga truly was, it reared up on its coiled serpent body to face him through *Banelash*'s canopy.

'*What is more foolish than denying the perfection of an all-embracing being? There can be no creed, no leader, no faith that is as harmonious, perfect and finished in every respect as I. What madness would cause you to reject me?*'

Raeven felt the walls of his resistance crumbling and fought to hold onto the heart of his sense of self. The image of the monster was slowly overlaid with the beauty of a god. Desperate survival instincts threw up a fragment of the tedious classes on aesthetics he'd been forced to endure in his youth.

'There is no such thing in the world as perfection!' he screamed, dredging his memories for the teachings of his boyhood tutors. 'If a thing were perfect, it could never improve and so would lack true perfection, which depends on progress. Perfection *depends* on incompleteness!'

The White Naga's hold on him slipped. Just for a second, a *fraction* of a second. It was enough for him to look into its eyes and see the yawning abyss of madness and ego that thought nothing for a single other living being, and cared only that they fall to their knees and adore it.

Raevan clenched his fist and *Banelash* coiled its energy whip.

With a cry of rage, horror and anguish he swung.

The whip cracked, its photonic length slashing down through the White Naga's powerfully muscled shoulders. Milky light spurted from the wound, as though the creature was formed from hyper-dense liquid under intense pressure.

A wing crumpled, torn like tissue, and its upper arm spun away like a broken tree branch. The whip tore through the creature's torso and its anguished screams were those of a god whose most fervent believer has turned against it.

The White Naga – or whatever damned *thing* it truly was – lurched away from *Banelash*. Shock twisted its once beautiful features and made it ugly. Worse than ugly, the furthest extreme of loathsomeness wrought into being. Its repellent form fuelled Raeven's towering sense of injustice.

Raeven shucked his other arm and felt the heat of his thermal lance engage. He rarely employed the lance, its killing power too swift and sure for his liking. But that was exactly what he needed right now. The White Naga surged in anger, its ruined body bleeding radiance from the galaxy of stars in its chest.

One wing hung from its muscular back, and its right side was a crumpled, molten mass of lightning-edged flesh where its arms hung limply at its side.

Raeven burned the thermal lance through its chest.

And ran.

EIGHTEEN

Eventyr
Torments
Deaths overdue

EVERY BUMP IN the road was exquisitely transferred up through the suspension of the Galenus to send jolts of pain into Alivia's side. Her chest hurt abominably, and the fresh grafts in her chest pulled painfully every time she shifted position on the gurney.

Still, she knew she was lucky to be alive.

Or at least lucky it hadn't been worse.

'You need more pain balms?' asked Noama Calver, the surgeon-captain, seeing her pursed lips.

'No,' said Alivia. 'I've slept for altogether too long.'

'Sure, just let me know if you need any though,' she said, missing Alivia's meaning. 'No need to suffer when there's a remedy right here.'

'Trust me, if it gets too bad, you'll be the first to know.'

'Promise?'

'Hope to die,' said Alivia, crossing her heart with her hand.

Noama smiled with matronly concern. She squeezed Alivia's arm as though she were her own daughter, which was exactly the emotion Alivia had planted in her mind. Noama Calver had a son serving in an off-world Army regiment and her concern for his wellbeing ranked only slightly higher than the wounded men under her care.

Alivia didn't like using people this way, especially good people who might have helped her if only she'd asked. Getting to Lupercalia was too important for her – *for them* – to take any chances that Calver might not have helped.

Kjell had been even easier. A good man, he'd joined the Medicae out of a desire to stay away from the front lines – little realising that medics were often in the thickest fighting without a weapon. The Grand Army of Molech was preparing to meet the Warmaster's army in open battle, so it had been child's play to ease his thoughts towards heading south to Lupercalia.

Noama moved down the Galenus, checking on the other wounded they carried. Every one of them ought to be back with their units, but they'd kept quiet when Noama ordered her driver, an impressionable boy named Anson who just wanted to get back to Lupercalia to see a girl called Fiaa, to drive away from the fighting.

Too easy.

Jeph lay stretched out on a gurney farther down the Galenus, snoring like an engine with a busted gear. She smiled at the softening of his features, hating herself for making him care for her so much. She'd had enough of time alone, and there were only so many years a girl could spend on her own before company, *any* company, was infinitely preferable. She knew she should have left him back in Larsa the minute the starship crashed, but he wouldn't have lasted another hour without her.

Honestly, back in the day, would you have looked twice at him?

An easy enough question to answer, but it wasn't that simple.

There'd been complications. Two complications to be exact.

Miska and Vivyen sat playing a board game called *mahbusa* with a number of ebony and ivory counters. She'd taught it to them a few months back. An old game, one she'd learned in the counting houses of the Hegemon, though she suspected it was older even than that compact city of scribes.

The girls had been suspicious of Alivia at first, and rightly so. She was an intruder in their world. A rival for their father's affections. But she'd won them over with her games, her kindness and her fantastical stories of Old Earth's mightiest heroes and its magical ancient myths.

No one told a story quite like Alivia, and the girls had been captivated from the beginning. She hadn't even needed to manipulate their psyches. And quite without realising it, Alivia found herself cast in the role of a mother. It wasn't something she'd expected to relish, but there it was. They were good girls; cheeky, but with the charisma and wide eyes to get away with it.

Alivia knew Jeph wasn't the reason she'd gone back to the hab, it had been for Miska and Vivyen. She'd never even considered being a mother, wasn't even sure it was possible for someone like her. She'd been told she had greater concerns than individual lives, but when the first impacts hit Larsa, Alivia had understood how foolish she'd been to blindly accept that.

Every part of her mission was compromised by having attachments. She'd broken every rule she'd set herself when she first came to Molech, but didn't regret the decision to become part of their family. If John could see her now, he'd laugh in her face, calling her a hypocrite and a fraud. He'd be fully justified, but she'd still kick him in the balls for it and call him a coward.

Vivyen looked over at her and smiled.

Yes, definitely worth it.

The girl got up from her box seat and came over to Alivia with a hopeful look in her eye.

'Who's winning?' asked Alivia.

'Miska, but she's older, so it's okay.'

Alivia smiled. *Okay*. One of Oll's words. Another thing she'd taught them. They said it in the scholam, where the other children looked strangely at its unusual sound.

'I can teach you a few moves if you like,' said Alivia. 'I was taught by the best. Could give you an edge.'

'No, it's okay,' said Vivyen, with all the earnestness of a twelve-year-old. 'I do lots of things better than her, so it's good she has this.'

Alivia hid a smile as she saw Miska make a face behind Vivyen's back and make a gesture her father wouldn't approve of.

'Are you all right?' said Alivia, as Vivyen climbed onto the gurney. 'It's been pretty hard since we left Larsa, eh?'

Vivyen nodded. 'I'm fine. I didn't like it when the tanks were shooting at us, but I knew you'd get us out in one piece.'

'You did?'

'Yes.'

Alivia smiled. A child's certainty. Was there anything surer?

'Will you read me a story?' asked Vivyen, tapping the gun-case tucked in tight next to Alivia. Even wounded, she hadn't let herself be parted from it.

'Of course,' said Alivia, pressing her thumb to the lock plate and moving it in a way she kept hidden from the girl. She opened the case, feeling over her Ferlach serpenta to the battered storybook she'd taken from the *Odense Domkirke* library. Some people might say stolen, but Alivia liked to think she'd rescued it. Stories were to be told, not for sitting in an old museum.

The longer she owned the book, the more she wondered about that.

A dog-eared thing, its pages were yellowed and looked to be hundreds of years old. The stories inside were much older, but

Alivia had made sure the book would never fall apart, never fade and never lose the old, fusty smell of the library.

Alivia opened the book. She knew every story off by heart and didn't need to read from the page. The translation wasn't great, and what she read often didn't match the words written down. Sometimes it felt like the words changed every time she read it. Not by much, but just enough for her to notice, as though the stories liked to stretch and try new things every once in a while.

But the pictures – woodcuts, she thought – were pretty and the girls liked to ask questions about the strange looking people in them as she read aloud.

Vivyen pulled in close, and Alivia hissed as the synth-skin bandage pulled taut again.

'Sorry.'

'It's okay,' said Alivia. 'I've had worse.'

Much worse. Like when the guardian angel died, and Noama thought she'd lost me when my heart stopped…

She ran a finger down the list of stories. 'Which one do you want to hear?'

'That one,' said Vivyen, pointing.

'Good choice,' said Alivia. 'Especially now.'

'What do you mean?'

'Nothing, never mind. Now do you want me to read it or do you have any more questions?'

Vivyen shook her head and Alivia began.

'Once there was a very wicked daemon, and he made a looking-glass which made everything good or beautiful reflected in it seem vile and horrible, while everything worthless and bad looked ten times worse. People who saw their reflections ran screaming from their distorted faces, and the daemon said this was very amusing.

'And when a pious thought passed through the mind of anyone looking in the mirror it was twisted around in the glass, and the daemon declared that people could now, for the first time, see what the world and mankind were really like. The daemon bore the looking-glass everywhere, till at last there was not a land nor a people who had not been seen through this dark mirror.'

'Then what did he do?' asked Vivyen, though she'd heard this story a dozen times or more.

'The daemon wanted to fly with it up to heaven to trick the angels into looking at his evil mirror.'

'What's an angel?'

Alivia hesitated. 'It's like a daemon, only it's good instead of evil. Well, most of the time.'

Vivyen nodded, indicating that Alivia should continue.

'But the higher the daemon flew the more slippery the glass became. Eventually he could scarcely hold it, and it slipped from his hands. The mirror fell to Earth, where it was broken into millions of pieces.'

Alivia lowered her voice, leaning fractionally closer to Vivyen and giving her words a husky, cold edge.

'But now the looking-glass caused more unhappiness than ever, for some of the fragments were no larger than a grain of sand and they blew all around the world. When one of these tiny shards flew into a person's eye, it stuck there unknown to them. From that moment onward they could see only the worst of what they looked upon, for even the smallest fragment retained the same power as the whole mirror. A few people even got a fragment of the looking-glass in their hearts, and this was very terrible, for their hearts became cold like a lump of ice. At the thought of this the wicked daemon laughed till his sides shook. It tickled him so to see the mischief he had done.'

Miska had come over by now, drawn by the rhythmic cadences of Alivia's voice and the skill of the ancient storyteller. With both girls tucked in next to her, Alivia told the rest of the story, of a young boy named Kai whose eye and heart were pierced by a sliver of the daemon's looking-glass. And from that moment, he became cruel and heartless, turning on his friends and doing the worst things he could think of to hurt them. Ensnared by a wicked queen of winter, Kai was doomed to an eternity imprisoned upon a throne of ice that slowly drained him of his life.

But the parts they loved the most were the adventures of Kai's friend, a young girl named Gerda who always seemed to be just about the same age as Miska and Vivyen. Overcoming robbers, witches and traps, she found her way at last to the lair of the winter queen.

'And Gerda freed Kai with the power of her love and innocence,' said Alivia. 'Her tears melted the ice in Kai's heart and when he saw the terrible things he had done, he wept and washed the sliver of the daemon's mirror from his eye.'

'You forgot the bit about the word Kai had to spell,' said Miska.

'Ah, yes, mustn't forget that bit,' said Alivia. 'The ice queen had given her oath that if Kai could solve a fiendishly difficult puzzle to spell a special word, then she'd let him leave.'

'What word was it?' asked Vivyen.

'A very important word,' said Alivia with mock gravitas. 'A word that still echoes around the world today. All the way from Old Earth to Molech and back again.'

'Yes, but what *is* it?'

Alivia flipped to the end of the story and was about to speak the word she'd read a hundred times. In the original language it was *Evigheden*, but that wasn't what was on the page now.

'Liv?' asked Miska, when she didn't answer.

'No, that can't be right,' said Alivia.

'What is it?' said Vivyen. 'What's the word?'

'*Mord*,' said Alivia. 'It's Murder.'

✠ ✠ ✠

THE MAIN WAR tent of the Sons of Horus was hot and humid, like a desert after the rains. Thick rugs of animal fur were spread across the ground, weapon racks lined the billowing fabric walls and a smouldering fire burned low in a central hearth. Like the halls of a plains barbarian chief or one of the Khan's infrequent audiences, it was bare of the comforts that might be expected of a primarch.

Horus stood at the occidental segment of the firepit, reading from a book bound in human skin. Lorgar claimed that corpses from Isstvan III provided its binding and pages, and, for once, Horus had no reason to doubt him.

Symbolism, that was the word his brother had used when he'd asked why a book already bleeding with horror needed to be bound so unwholesomely. That was something Horus understood, and he had arranged the others sharing the taut angles of his war tent accordingly.

Grael Noctua stood to attention across from him in the oriental aspect of the soul and breath of life. Tall and proud despite the injuries he had suffered on Molech, his augmetic hand was almost fully meshed with his nervous system, but a void still existed where his heart once beat.

Ger Gerradon stood in the septentrional aspect of earth, his porcelain-white doll's eyes reflecting none of the firelight. Birth, life, death and rebirth were his aspect. Facing the leader of the Luperci in the meridonal position of fire was the floating figure of the Red Angel. Both stared at one another with crackling intensity, immaterial monsters bound to mortal flesh.

One a willing host, the other a willing sacrifice.

The book had enabled Horus to learn much of the Red Angel's origins on blood-soaked Signus Prime. Just as it had allowed him to pass the rites of summoning to Maloghurst.

The words Horus spoke were not words as such, but harmonics

resonating in an alternate plane of existence like musical notes or a key in a lock. Their use reeked of black magic, a term at which Lorgar sneered, but the term fitted better than his Colchisian brother knew.

With each couplet, the chains encircling the Red Angel pulled tighter. All but one. Its armour creaked and split still further. Hissing white flame licked at the cracks. The chain encircling its skull melted away, dribbling from its mouth in white-hot rivulets.

'Is that wise?' asked Noctua as the Red Angel spat out the last of its binding.

'Probably not, Grael, but needs must.'

The Red Angel turned its burning eye-sockets upon Horus.

'I am a weapon, Horus Lupercal, the agonies of a thousand damned souls distilled into a being of purest rage,' it said. *'And you keep me bound with chains of cold iron and ancient wards? I hunger to slay, to maim, to wreak havoc on those that once called this shell brother!'*

Its words were like hooked barbs drawn through the ear. Anger bled from the daemon, and Horus felt himself touched by its power.

'You will have your share of blood,' said Horus.

'Yes,' said the Red Angel, sniffing the air and licking its lipless face with a blackened tongue. *'The enemy host musters before you in numbers uncounted. Millions of hearts to devour, an age of suffering to be wrought upon bones of the dead. A wasteland of corpses shall be the playthings of the letters of blood.'*

Noctua turned to Ger Gerradon and said, 'Are all warp-things so ridiculously overwrought?'

Gerradon grinned. 'Those that serve the lord of murder do enjoy some bloody hyperbole, certainly.'

'And who do you serve?' asked Horus.

'You, my lord,' said Gerradon. 'Only you.'

Horus doubted that, but this wasn't the time for questions of loyalty. He required information, the kind that could only be harvested from beings not of this world.

'The death of my father's sentinel in the mountain has revealed many things to me, but there are still things I want to know.'

'All you need know is that there are enemies whose blood has yet to be shed,' said the Red Angel. *'Unleash me! I will bathe in an ocean of blood as deep as the stars.'*

'No,' said Horus, unsheathing the claws within his talon and turning to stab them through the chest of the Red Angel. 'I need to know quite a bit more than that, actually.'

The Red Angel screamed, a blast of superheated air that billowed the roof of the war tent. The chains creaked and spat motes of flickering warp energy. Cracks spread over the daemon's face, as though the flames enveloping it now had licence to consume it.

'I *will* extinguish you,' said Horus. 'Unless you tell me what I want to know. What will I find beneath Lupercalia?'

'A gateway to the realm beyond dreams and nightmares,' hissed the unravelling daemon, cracks spreading down its neck and over the plates of its armour. *'A ruinous realm of madness and death for mortals, the uttermost domain of misrule wherein dwell the gods of the True Pantheon!'*

Horus pushed his claws deeper into the Red Angel's chest.

'Something a little less vague would be better,' said Horus.

Despite its agony, the Red Angel laughed, the sound dousing the last flames in the firepit. *'You seek clarity where none exists, Warmaster. The Empyreal Realm offers no easy definitions, no comprehension and no solidity for mortals. It is an ever-shifting maelstrom of power and vitality. What you seek I cannot give you.'*

'You're lying,' said Horus. 'Tell me how I can follow my father. Tell me of the Obsidian Way that leads to the House of Eyes, the

Brass Citadel, the Eternal City and the Arbours of Entropy.'

The Red Angel bared its teeth at Ger Gerradon in a blast of fury. The chains binding its arms creaked. The links stretched.

'You betray your own kind, Tormaggedon! You name what should not be named!'

Gerradon shrugged. 'Horus Lupercal is and always was my master, I serve him now. But even I don't know the things you know.'

'The Obsidian Way is forbidden to mortals,' said the Red Angel.

'Forbidden doesn't mean impossible,' said Horus.

'Just because the faithless Forethinker walked the road of bones does not mean you can follow Him,' hissed the Red Angel. *'You are not Him, you can never be Him. You are His bastard son, the aborted get of what He was and will one day be.'*

Horus twisted his talons deeper, feeling only a hollow space of scorched organs and ashen flesh within.

'You cannot end me, mortal!' cried the daemon. *'I am a thing of Chaos Eternal, a reaper of blood and souls. I will endure any torments you can devise.'*

'Perhaps you can, but I didn't devise these torments,' said Horus, nodding towards the flayed-skin book. 'Your kind did.'

Horus spoke words of power and the Red Angel screamed as the spreading black veins thickened and stretched. Smoke streamed from its limbs, coming not from its fires, but the dissolution of its very essence.

'I have your attention now?' asked Horus, clenching a taloned fist within the Red Angel's body. 'I can tear your flames apart and consign every scrap of you to oblivion. Think on that when you next speak.'

The Red Angel sagged against its chains.

'Speak,' it hissed. *'Speak and I will answer.'*

'The Obsidian Way,' said Horus. 'How can it be breached?'

'*As with all things,*' snarled the daemon. '*In blood.*'

'Now we're getting somewhere,' said Horus.

THE RED ANGEL fell slack in its chains and Horus withdrew the crackling claw from the daemon's body. Slithering black ichor dripped from the blades and squirmed into the earth around the firepit like burrower worms.

'Did you get what you needed?' asked Gerradon.

Horus nodded slowly, flexing his talons. 'I believe I did, Ger, yes. Though I can't help thinking I should have got it from you.'

Gerradon shifted uncomfortably, perhaps understanding that being summoned to Lupercal's war tent was not the honour he might have imagined.

'I don't follow, my lord.'

'Yes you do,' said Horus. 'As I understand it, you are brother to the Red Angel. You are both children of Erebus, one birthed on a world of blood, the other on a world of fire.'

'As in the mortal world, there are hierarchies among the never-born,' said Gerradon. 'To my lasting regret, a being wrought on a daemon world by a dark prince of the warp is more exalted than one raised by a mortal.'

'Even a mortal as powerful as Erebus?'

'Erebus is a deluded whelp,' spat Gerradon. 'He believes himself anointed, but all he did was open a door.'

'And that's the crux of it, isn't it?' said Horus, circling Gerradon and letting his talon blades scrape across the Luperci's armour. 'You can't come into our world unless we let you. All the schemes, all the temptations and promises of power, it's all to get into our world. You need us more than we need you.'

Gerradon squared his shoulders, defiant now.

'Keep telling yourself that.'

'Why didn't you tell me what it knew?'

'I told you why.'

'No, you spun a plausible lie,' said Horus. 'Now tell me the real answer or I'll get to the *really* interesting couplets in that book of horrors.'

Gerradon shrugged. 'Very well. It was a rival. Now it's not.'

Horus sheathed his talons, satisfied with Gerradon's answer. He turned from the daemon-things and approached Noctua, who'd stood as immobile as a statue throughout this process of daemonic interrogation.

'There's a lesson for you here in the proper application of power,' said Horus. 'But that's not why I summoned you.'

'Then why am I here, sir?' asked Noctua.

'I have a special task for you, Grael,' said the Warmaster. 'You *and* Ger actually.'

Noctua's face fell as he understood that his task would keep him from the coming battle. He rallied a moment later.

'What would you have me do, my lord?'

Horus put a paternal hand on Noctua's shoulder guard.

'There are intruders aboard my flagship, Grael.'

'Intruders?' said Noctua. 'Who?'

'A prodigal son and two faithless cowards who once fought as your brothers,' said Horus. 'They lead a rabble of that troublesome Sigillite's errant fools into the heart of the *Vengeful Spirit.*'

'I will find them,' promised Noctua. 'And I'll kill them.'

'Very good, Grael, but I don't want them *all* dead.'

'You don't?'

'Kill the others if they give you trouble,' said Horus, 'but I want the prodigal son alive.'

'Why?' asked Noctua, forgetting himself for a moment.

'Because I want him back.'

✠ ✠ ✠

Iron Fist Mountain dominated the eastern skyline, and farther south, a black smudge on the horizon spoke of distant fires somewhere around the Preceptor Line. A vast assembly of Imperial might – *his* army – filled the agri-plains north of Lupercalia.

Raeven pushed *Banelash* forward, staggering as toxins in his blood distorted his perception of the Knight's sensorium. It swayed and crashed with phantom images of winged serpents, hideous, fanged mouths and eyes that burned with the fury of rejection.

The thought of what he had almost given into made him sick.

Or was it the thought of what he'd given up?

He no longer knew nor cared.

Raeven walked his Knight towards the thousands of armoured vehicles, scores of regiments and entire battalions of artillery below. A thousand shimmering banners guided him in, regimental pennants and company battle flags, muster signs and range-markers.

House banners streamed from the carapaces of assembled nobility: Tazhkar, Kaushik, Indra, Kaska, Mamaragon. Others he didn't recognise or couldn't make out. Their Knights dwarfed the Army soldiers, but they were a long way from being the biggest, most destructive killers on the field.

A dozen war engines of Legio Gryphonicus and Legio Crucius strode through designated corridors to take up their battle positions. Mighty. Awe-inspiring.

But all dwarfed by the immovable, man-made mountain at the centre of the line.

An Imperator Titan, *Paragon of Terra* was a towering fortress of adamantium and granite, a mobile citadel of war raised by long-cherished artifice and forged in blood and prayer. A temple to the Omnissiah and a destroyer god all in one, the Imperator was the central bastion upon which each wing of the army rested.

The black and white of the Legio were the heraldic colours of Princeps Etana Kalonice, whose Mechanicum forebears had piloted the first engines on Ryza.

The heat from its weapons hazed the air, and Raeven blinked away tears of exhaustion.

Connection fatigue made his bones ache, made every part of him ache. Broken glass ground in his joints and the stabbing pain behind his eyes was like something trying to burrow out from the centre of his brain. Fluids recycled around his body many more times than was healthy had kept him alive, but were now poisoning him.

A patrolling squadron of scout Sentinels found Raeven staggering from the tree line overlooking the army. They turned heavy flamers and multi-lasers on him, and he readied his own weapons in response before the proper protocols were issued and returned.

'Get me to the Sacristans,' wheezed Raeven.

HE LOST TRACK of time. Or it slipped away from him.

Either way, he remembered falling from *Banelash*'s opened carapace, rough hands – *metal hands* – lifting him down and carrying him to his pavilion.

Lyx was waiting for him, but the hurt look in her eyes only made him smile. He liked hurting her, and couldn't think why. She asked questions he couldn't or wouldn't answer. His answers made no sense anyway.

Needles stabbed his flesh. Toxic blood was siphoned from him and fresh litres washed in. Pain balms soothed his ground glass joints, smoothed his rough edges.

Time fractured, moved out of joint. He heard angry voices and chattering machines. He actually *felt* fluids moving through him, as though he was a great pumping station over the promethium wells at Ophir. Sucking up immense breaths of fuel and spitting it out into the great silos.

The image of himself as a vast pump pleased him.

No, not a pump – an engine. An agent of change that drove the lifeblood of the planet around its myriad systems. Infrastructure as circulatory system.

Yes, that was the metaphor he liked.

Raeven looked down. *His arm was dark iron, a pistoning length of machinery thick with grease and hydraulic fluids. Promethium coated his arms and he imagined sitting up as it gushed from his mouth in a flaming geyser. His other arm was a writhing pipe, plunging deep into the ground and gurgling with fluids pumped up from the depths of the planet.*

He was connected to Molech's core…

The enormity of that thought was too much and his stomach rebelled. That one man could be so intimately connected with the inner workings of an entire world was a concept beyond his grasp. *His mind plunged into the depths of the planet, streaking faster than light, past its many layers until shattering through the core and emerging, phoenix-like from the other side…*

Raeven gasped for air, gulping in swelling lungfuls.

A measure of clarity came with the oxygen.

Lofty metaphors of planetary connection and bodily infrastructure diminished. With every breath, Raeven's awareness of his surroundings pulled a little more into focus. His mouth tasted of metal and perfume, dry and with a mucus film clinging to the back of his throat.

Raeven was no stranger to mind-expanding narcotics. Shargali-Shi's venoms had allowed him to travel beyond his skull often enough to recognise the effects of a powerful hallucinogen. He'd had his share of balms too. Hunting the great beasts took a willingness to suffer pain, and Cyprian had beaten an acceptance of pain into him as a child.

The balms he could understand, but hallucinogens?

Why would the Sacristans administer hallucinogens?

'What did you give me?' he asked, knowing at least one Sacristan was nearby. Some Medicae staff too most likely from the sound of low voices, shuffling footsteps and the click of machinery.

No one answered.

'I said, what did you give me?'

'Naga venom mixed with some potent ergot derivative,' said a voice that couldn't possibly be here. Raeven tried to move his head to bring the speaker into his line of sight, but there was something wrong.

'Can't move?'

'No, why is that?'

'That'll be the muscle relaxants.'

A hissing, clanking sound came from behind Raeven and he rolled his eyes to see an old man looking down at him. The face he didn't recognise at first, clean shaven and greasy with healing agents.

But the voice, ah, no mistaking *that* voice.

Or the hissing, clanking exo-suit encasing his wasted limbs.

'I'm still hallucinating,' said Raeven. 'You can't be here.'

'I assure you I am most definitely here,' said Albard Devine, his one good eye fluttering as though finding it difficult to keep focus. 'It's taken forty years, but I'm finally here to take back what's rightfully mine.'

His stepbrother wore clothes several sizes too large for him. They hung from his bony frame like rags. The laurels of an Imperial commander were pinned to his lapel.

'You can't do this, Albard,' said Raeven. 'Not now.'

'If not now, then when?'

'Listen, you don't need to do this,' said Raeven, trying to keep the panic from his voice. 'We can work something out, yes?'

'Are you *actually* trying to bargain for your life?' laughed Albard, a wheezing, racking cough of a sound. 'After all you stole from me, all you did to me? Forty years of torture and neglect and you think you're going to talk your way out of this?'

'That exo-suit,' said Raeven, stalling for time. 'It's mother's isn't it?'

'Cebella was your mother, not mine.'

'She's not going to like that you're wearing it.'

'Don't worry, she doesn't need it any more.'

'You killed her?' said Raeven, though he'd already come to that conclusion. Death was the only way Cebella Devine would be parted from her exo-suit. But he needed more time; for the Dawn Guard to realise there was a snake in their midst, for Lyx to return.

Someone, anyone.

'I cut your mother's throat,' said Albard, leaning close enough for Raeven to smell his corpse breath. 'She bled out in my lap. It was almost beautiful in its own way.'

Raeven nodded, and then stopped when he realised what he'd done.

Either Albard didn't notice or didn't care that he'd moved, too lost in the reverie of his stepmother's murder. The muscle relaxants were wearing off. Slowly. Raeven wasn't going to be wrestling a mallahgra anytime soon, but surely he'd be strong enough to overcome a cripple in an exo-suit?

'Where's Lyx?' asked Raeven. 'Or did you kill her too?'

'She's alive.'

'Where?'

'She's here,' said Albard, leaning down to adjust the medical table on which Raeven was lying. 'Trust me, I don't want her to miss out on what's going to happen next.'

Someone moved behind Raeven and the table rotated on its central axis, bringing him vertical. A restraint band around his waist kept him from falling flat on his face. A pair of Dawn Guard stood at the entrance to the pavilion, and a gaggle of Sacristans worked at the machines supposedly restoring him to health.

His heart sank at the sight of the armoured soldiers. Their loyalty was enshrined in law to the scion of House Devine, and with Albard abroad from his tower, they were his to command.

The men flanked Lyx, her hands fettered and her eyes wide with incomprehension. A gag filled her mouth and tears streaked her cheeks.

'What's the matter, Lyx?' said Albard, lurching with the unfamiliar gait of the exo-suit. 'The future not playing out as you planned it? Reality not matching your visions?'

He ripped the gag from her mouth and threw it aside.

She spat in his face. He slapped her, the metal encasing his hand tearing the skin of her cheek. Blood mingled with her tears.

'Don't you touch her!' shouted Raeven.

'Lyx was my wife before she was yours,' said Albard. 'It's been a long time, but I seem to remember her liking that sort of thing.'

'Look, you want to be Imperial commander, yes?' said Raeven. 'You're wearing the laurel on your lapel, I see that. Fine, yes, fine, you can be commander, of course you can. You're the firstborn son of Cyprian Devine. The position's yours. I give you it, have it.'

'Shut up, Raeven!' screamed Lyx. 'Offer him nothing!'

Raeven ignored her.

'Be Imperial commander, brother. Lyx and I will leave, you'll never hear from us. We'll go south, over the mountains to the Tazkhar steppe, you'll never see us again.'

Albard listened to the rush of words without expression. Eventually he held up his hand.

'You're offering me what's already mine,' said Albard. 'By right of birth and, well, let's just call it right of arms.'

'Shut your mouth, Raeven!' howled Lyx, her face beautiful in her tears and pain. 'Don't give him anything! He killed our son!'

'Ah, yes, didn't I mention that?' said Albard.

Every molecule of air left Raeven's body. As surely as if a pneumatic press had crushed him flat. He couldn't breathe, his lungs screamed for air. First Egelic and Banan, and now Osgar. Grief warred with anger. Anger crushed grief without mercy.

'You bastard!' screamed Raeven. 'I'll kill you! I'll hang your entrails from the Devine Towers. I'll mount your head on *Banelash*'s canopy!'

'I don't think so,' said Albard, pressing a hand down on Raeven's chest. 'The drugs coursing around your body came from Osgar's supply. Such a good boy, he always came to visit his poor deranged uncle in his tower. Kept me informed of the comings and goings around Lupercalia, how Shargali-Shi's devotions to the White Naga were spreading to his cousins in the Knights.'

Seeing Raeven's horror at the mention of the Serpent Cult's avatar, Albard grinned. The resemblance to a leering skull was uncanny.

'He didn't say that every one of your Knights is a devotee of the Serpent Cult?' said Albard. 'Didn't mention that they were no longer loyal to you, but to the cult? No? Well, you always did see Osgar as the runt of the litter, didn't you? No taste for fighting, though I'm given to understand he was a hellion in the debauches.'

Raeven tried to struggle against his bindings, but even with the tiny control he'd regained, it wasn't enough.

'Osgar even smuggled stimms and the like past Cebella's Sacristans from time to time. Such a shame I had to kill him. As much as he had a fondness for indulging his insane old uncle, I don't think he'd forgive me killing both of you. And I think you'll agree that your deaths are *long* overdue.'

'You can't do this,' pleaded Lyx. 'I am the Devine Adoratrice, I saw the future. It can't end this way! I saw Raeven turn the tide of the war, I *saw* him!'

'You're wrong, Lyx,' said Albard, 'Osgar told me you never actually saw Raeven in your visions. You saw *Banelash*.'

Albard nodded to the Dawn Guard holding Lyx.

The soldier forced her to her knees and placed the barrel of his bolt pistol against her head.

'I saw–' Lyx began, but a gunshot abruptly ended her words.

'No!' bellowed Raeven as Lyx fell forward with a smoking crater in the back of her skull. 'Throne damn you, Albard! You didn't have to do that... no, no, no... you didn't... please no!'

Albard turned from Lyx's body, and drew a hunting knife from a leather sheath at his waist.

'Now it's your turn, Raeven,' he said. 'This won't be quick, and I promise it will be agonising.'

NINETEEN

Casualties of war
The order is given
The Stormlord rides

THE TRANSIT WAS thick with bolter shells. They spanked from projecting stanchions and blasted portions of the walls away. Across
from Loken, Qruze ducked back into cover and ejected the magazine from his weapon. The barrel drooled smoke and heat.

Qruze slapped a fresh load into the weapon. He shouted to
Loken.

'Get in the damn fight!'

Loken shook his head. This was all wrong.

More shots filled the corridor leading to the armoury. A security
detail of Sons of Horus – together with a number of Mechanicum adepts – were inside, hunkered behind a bulwark designed
to prevent an enemy from seizing the stockpile of ammunition,
weapons and explosives.

A grenade detonated nearby. Fragments of hot iron pinged from
his armour. A few embedded. None penetrated.

'Loken, for Cthonia's sake, shoot!' shouted Qruze.

The bolter in his hands felt like a relic dug up by the Conservatory.

Something fascinating to look at, but whose purpose was alien and unknown. He could no more bring the gun to bear than he could understand the mechanisms of the machine that crafted it.

'Loken!'

THE PATHFINDERS HAD encountered the Sons of Horus en route to mark the armoury for a tertiary torpedo strike. Guiding futharc sigils had been scraped into the wall, warning assault teams away, and they'd paused for Tubal Cayne to divine a path towards a nearby ordnance signum array.

Severian and Karayan were scouting potential routes when the Sons of Horus had marched straight into the radial hub.

The watch sector had been Loken's, but he'd missed them.

He hadn't heard them or even been aware of their approach.

Lost in contemplation of a painted Eye of Horus on the opposite bulkhead and trying not to listen to the scratch of voices at the periphery of hearing.

The first he'd known of the enemy was when their sergeant called out, demanding identification. Stupid, he should have shot first.

Mutual surprise was all that saved the pathfinders.

Neither force had expected to encounter the other. The fleeting shock was just enough time for Loken to raise the alarm.

The Sons of Horus regrouped down the radial corridor towards the armoury as Altan Nohai and Bror Tyrfingr had opened fire.

'Contact!' reported Cayne.

QRUZE LEANED OUT and fired a short burst.

'Come on, Loken,' he shouted between bursts. 'I need you with me to go forward!'

The hard bangs of bolter fire and the chugging beat of an emplaced autocannon filled the transit with a storm of solid rounds. Ricochets bounced madly from the walls. A shell fragment deformed the metal beside Loken's helmet.

He gripped his bolter, his grip threatening to crush the stock.

This isn't right.

The Sons of Horus were traitors, the Warmaster the *Arch*-traitor.

But these are your brothers. You accepted their brotherhood, and swore to return it as a brother.

'No,' he hissed, slamming the bolter against the faceplate of his helmet. 'No, they're traitors and they deserve to die.'

You are a Son of Horus. So is Iacton. So is Severian. Kill them and kill yourself if you would damn all of Lupercal's lineage!

Loken fought to keep the voice out.

The vox crackled.

'Go when you hear us,' said Severian.

ASSAULTING AN ARMOURY was a sure-fire way to end up facing some extremely potent ordnance, but what choice did they have?

'Tubal? Only two ways in or out?' shouted Qruze.

Cayne nodded, sweeping through layers of deck schematics. 'Yes, according to the extant plans.'

'Both covered?'

'Voitek and Rubio are blocking the other one,' said Varren, not shooting, but ready with his chainaxe.

'So they're not getting out,' said Qruze. 'But they'll be voxing for help right now.'

'Voitek is employing a vox-jammer,' said Cayne, zooming in on the image of their current location.

'How long before the adepts burn through it?' asked Zaven, firing down the transit to the armoury. 'And is anyone else even slightly concerned that we're shooting *into* an armoury?'

'Eighteen seconds till burn through,' answered Cayne. 'So long as you don't hit anything sensitive in there we should be fine.'

'Sensitive?' said Bror. '*Hjolda!* It's a bloody armoury, everything's sensitive!'

'On the contrary, I think you'll find–' began Cayne, but Qruze shut him up.

'Stow it,' said Qruze, glancing over at Loken. 'Everyone keep shooting and be ready.'

'You said the armoury has only two exits?' said Zaven.

'Yes,' confirmed Cayne.

'So how's Severian getting in?'

'READY?' SAID SEVERIAN.

Karayan nodded and Severian set the timer for two seconds.

They rolled aside as the graviton grenade detonated with a pulse of energy that made him sick to his stomach. An orb of anomalous gravitational energy swelled to a diameter of exactly a metre and increased the local mass of steel girders and air-circulation units within the reinforced ceiling void a thousand-fold.

A sphere of ultra-dense material compacted in on itself like the heart of a neutron star and fell into the armoury with the force of an Imperator Titan's footfall.

Karayan was first through the hole, dropping into the armoury like a weighted shadow. Severian followed him an instant later. He landed at the edge of the crater punched in the deck and brought his bolter up.

The enemy reacted to the intruders in their midst quicker than Severian would have liked. They were Sons of Horus, what else could he expect? Severian put a bolt into the nearest, displacing and ripping a burst through another. Return fire chased him.

Karayan favoured knifework. His non-reflective blade found the gap between a sergeant's helmet and his gorget. He plunged and twisted. Blood sprayed. He moved on, diving, rolling, using the walls and floor. His knife killed the Mechanicum adepts.

Chemical fumes misted the air. Floodstreams painted the walls with brackish, oily fluids.

Severian took a knee and pumped another three shots out.

Two legionaries dropped, the third brought an energised buckler around in time to deflect the bolt. Severian's surprise almost cost him his life. The warrior was too bulky, had too many arms.

Forge lord. Manipulator harness.

He leapt at Severian, a photonic combat blade on a mechanised limb arcing for his neck. Severian threw up his bolter and the blade carved through it. Slowed enough for his armour to take the hit. A second and third arm snapped at his helm and shoulder. Severian barged forward, elbow cracking into the forge lord's faceplate.

Company colours said Fifth; Little Horus Aximand's lot.

They rolled on the deck, grappling. Fighting like the murdergangs of Cthonia in the pits. Knees, elbows, heads; weapons all. The forge lord had more than him and his were harder. Claws tore chunks from Severian's battleplate. A plasma cutter seared a fire-lined groove in the deck plate a finger breadth from his head.

Severian rammed his helmet into his opponent's visor. Lenses cracked. Not his. The blade skittered over the armoury floor, its edge fading without a grip.

He rolled. A boot crashed into his helmet. He rolled again.

Ignition flare. A blur of blue-edged light.

Pain and blood. Lung burping itself empty through his plastron.

Severian hooked an elbow around the forge lord's flesh and blood arm and twisted. Pain shot through to his spine, but the arm snapped with a satisfying crack of tinder.

The forge lord grunted in momentary pain. A manipulator claw slammed into Severian's face. He ripped the knife from the broken manipulator arm and hacked the claw from the harness. Black oil and lubricant sprayed him. It tasted of malt vinegar.

The forge lord's spewing binary made the muscles in his armour spasm. Severian shoulder checked his opponent, stabbing the hissing blade into his neck and chest. He cut connector cables and mind impulse unit links. The servo-arms went limp, dead weight now. A bolter shell impacted on the underside of his shoulder guard. Fired from the floor. He spun around and stamped down on a helmet, crushing it like an ice sculpture.

The forge lord came at him again, but without his threshing, clawed arms he was no match for Severian. Too many hours in the armoury, not enough in the arming cages. Severian spun around the clumsy attack and twisted one of the limp servo-arms. He jammed it in the small of the forge lord's back and manually triggered the plasma cutter. Blue-hot light exploded from the forge lord's helm lenses. He screamed as superheated air burned its way out of him.

Severian dropped the smoking corpse in time to take a bolt-round in the chest. Thousands of fiery micro-fragments stabbed into his chest through the wound torn by the energised blade. The impact and explosion hurled him back against a rack of bolters. They clattered around him, fresh-oiled and pristine.

He grabbed one. Unloaded, of course. No quartermaster ever stored his weapons fully loaded. Severian tried to stand, but the bolt shell had punched him empty of breath. A traitor legionary swung his bolter to bear while drawing his chainsword.

Efficient, thought Severian as the bolter fired.

Severian was looking down the barrel and even in the moment of seeing the muzzle flare, he knew he should already be dead. Then he saw the spinning round hovering in the air before him. A web of pale lines, like frosted spiderwebs, coated the round.

+Move!+ hissed a voice in his head. *Rubio.*

Severian dived to the side and the round blew apart the weapon rack behind him. His would-be killer stared in astonishment and took aim again. An explosion lifted him from his feet. Blood misted the air, arcing in a fan from his shattered chest. Gunfire suddenly filled the armoury, multiple sources and directions. The deafening roar of a chainaxe. Severian grabbed a fallen magazine and slammed it hard into his new bolter.

'Clear!' shouted a voice. *Tyrfingr*.

'Clear!' *Qruze*.

'Grenades, Iacton? *Really*?' *Tubal Cayne*.

Severian grinned. Breath sucked back into his remaining lung and secondary organs. Pain came with it and he pursed his lips.

'You lot took your bloody time,' he said as Ares Voitek approached and offered him a hand up. Severian took it and hauled himself to his feet. Gunsmoke fogged the armoury, the stink of bolter propellant. Armoured bodies opened like cracked eggs lent their meaty, metallic, oily odour to the space.

'Only four seconds from your breach,' said Ares Voitek.

'That all?' said Severian, gratefully putting his arm around the former Iron Hand's shoulders. 'Could have sworn it was longer.'

'That's combat for you,' said Voitek. 'Unless you're an Iron Hand with internal chrons. Then you know *exactly* how long has elapsed since the commencement of an engagement.'

'I'll take your word for it.'

'Nohai!' shouted Qruze. 'Quickly, Zaven and Varren are down!'

THEY SEALED THE armoury and carried the wounded from the site of the battle. Nobody would miss the signs of fighting, but at least they could keep the bodies from being discovered for a while. Cayne swiftly navigated forgotten passageways and corridors in search of somewhere isolated and secure.

They tried not to leave a trail of blood.

The chamber Cayne led them to was filled with wrecked tables and chairs, its walls covered in water-damaged murals and obscene graffiti. Some seemed oddly familiar to Loken. The scale of the furnishings and its abandoned nature told him it had once been a retreat for mortals, but he could think of no reason why he might have come to a place like this.

Nohai went to work on Varren and Zaven. Rubio offered his aid, and Nohai gratefully accepted it. Both fallen warriors were badly hurt, but of the two, Zaven's wounds were the more serious.

'Will they make it?' asked Qruze.

'In the apothecarion, yes. Here, I don't know,' said Nohai.

'Do what you can, Altan.'

Loken sat with his back to a long bar, toying with a set of mildewed cards marked with swords, cups and coins. He'd known someone who'd played an old game of the Franc with such cards, but couldn't focus on the face. A man? Yes, someone of poetically low character and unexpectedly high morals. The name remained elusive, frustratingly so for a transhuman warrior with a supposedly eidetic memory.

He felt eyes upon him and looked up.

Tubal Cayne stood beneath an obscene mural rendered in anatomically precise detail – thankfully, time and water damage had obscured the offending portions. Cayne sat with one hand on his device, the other resting on the grip of his bolter.

'What?' said Loken.

'You are finding it onerous being here, Loken,' said Cayne.

'Is that a question or a statement?'

'I have not yet decided. Call it a question for now.'

'It's strange,' admitted Loken, slipping the cards into a pouch at his waist. 'But there's little left of the ship I knew. This vessel bears the same name, but it's not the *Vengeful Spirit*. Not the one I knew. This is a twisted reflection of that proud ship. It's unpleasant, but no more than I'd expected.'

'Truly? I had concluded you were experiencing significant

psychological difficulties. Why else would you not take part in the fighting at the armoury?'

Loken was immediately on guard, but forced down an outright denial. He stood and brushed water droplets from his armour.

'This used to be my home,' he said, walking slowly towards Cayne. 'Those Sons of Horus used to be my brothers. It shames me that they are now traitors.'

'It shames us all,' added Qruze from a booth across the room where he was cleaning his bolter.

'Speak for yourself,' said Severian, who sat on the long bar etching kill-notches into his vambrace with his newly acquired photonic combat blade. The punctured lung made his words breathy.

'No,' said Cayne. 'That is not it. If it were, I would expect to see the same psychological markers in Iacton Qruze and… wait, what *is* your full name, Severian?'

'Severian's all you need to know, and even that's too much.'

'You did not fire a single shot, Loken,' said Cayne. 'Why not?'

Loken was angry now. He rose to his feet and crossed the chamber to stand in front of Cayne. 'What are you saying, that I'm not up to the task? That you can't rely on me?'

'Yes, that is exactly what I am saying,' answered Cayne. 'You are showing all the hallmarks of severe post-traumatic damage. I have been watching you ever since we boarded the *Vengeful Spirit*. You're broken inside, Loken. I urge you to return immediately to the *Tarnhelm*. Your continued presence is endangering the mission and all our lives.'

'You need to back off,' said Severian, spinning his combat blade around to aim its glittering tip at Cayne.

'Why? You of all people know Loken is unfit for this mission.'

Loken slammed Cayne back against the mural.

He pressed a forearm hard against Cayne's throat.

'Say that again and I'll kill you.'

To his credit, Cayne was unfazed by Loken's attack.

'This only further proves my point,' he said.

Qruze appeared at Loken's side and put a hand on his shoulder.

'Put the gun away, lad.'

Loken frowned. 'What are you talking about?'

He looked down and saw he had his bolt pistol pressed against Cayne's chest. He had no memory of drawing the weapon.

Bror Tyrfingr eased Loken's arm from Cayne's throat.

'Hjolda, Loken,' said Bror. 'There'll be plenty more people trying to kill us soon enough without you doing the job for them.'

'Do you regret leaving the Sons of Horus?' asked Cayne. 'Is that it? Is that why you came on this mission, to return to your former master's side?'

'Shut up, Tubal,' snapped Bror, baring his teeth.

'I do not understand why you all wilfully ignore Loken's damage,' said Cayne. 'He attacks Qruze at Titan, he fails to fight against his former brothers, potentially costing the lives of two of our team. And now he holds a gun on me. We are at a mission-critical stage of our infiltration, and Loken cannot continue. I am not saying anything the rest of you haven't thought.'

Loken stepped back from Cayne and holstered his pistol. He looked around at the rest of the pathfinder team.

'Is he right?' he demanded. 'Do you all think I'm unfit to lead this mission.'

Qruze and Severian shared a look, but it was Varren who answered, limping over from where he'd been patched up by Altan Nohai. The former World Eater's chest was a perforated mass of bolter impacts and bloodstains. Skin packs and sealant grafts were all that kept his innards where they belonged. His skin was oily with sweat as his genhanced body burned hot with healing.

'We have a leader,' said Varren. 'I shed blood with Nathaniel and Tylos to bring Loken back from Isstvan. Any warrior who lived through that slaughter deserves our respect. He deserves *your* respect, Tubal. Malcador and the Wolf King thought Garviel Loken fit for this mission, and I'll not gainsay them. Nor should you.'

Cayne said nothing, but gave a curt nod.

'Is this the will of the group?'

'It is,' said Bror Tyrfingr. 'If any man deserves a chance to strike back at the Warmaster, it's Loken.'

'You are making a mistake,' said Cayne, 'but I will say no more.'

Altan Nohai appeared at Varren's side, his arms slathered in blood to the elbows.

'Zaven?' asked Qruze.

Nohai shook his head.

THE BATTLE OF Lupercalia began, as the industrialised wars heralding the first collapse of Old Earth once had, with a pre-dawn barrage. Fifty-three newly landed artillery regiments with over twelve hundred guns between them shattered the day with thunderous fire from upraised Basilisks, Griffons and Minotaurs.

Heavier guns waited in artillery depots for the general advance, the Bombards and Colossus, the Medusas and the Bruennhilde. Their guns were unsuited for long range barrages, and would follow the mechanised infantry to pound the Imperial ridge in the moments before the final escalade.

Army regiments sworn to the Warmaster advanced in wide convoys behind a creeping barrage of high explosives and a glittering screen of shroud bombs. Tens of thousands of armoured carriers daubed with the Eye of Horus and bearing icons of unnatural provenance roared towards the enemy. Battle tanks bore hooked trophy racks of corpses, and one glacis in five bore a chained prisoner from Avadon.

Hideous Mechanicum constructs of dark iron, clanking legs, spiked wheels and bulbous, insectile appearance marched with feral packs of skitarii keeping a wary distance.

A tide of armour and flesh roared over the wide expanse of the lowland agri-belts. The continent's breadbasket of arable land, gold and green from horizon to horizon, was churned to ruin beneath their biting tracks. Totem carriers on flatbed transporters bore beaten iron sigils on swaying poles amidst hundreds of robed brotherhoods.

Self-anointed with bloodthirsting titles, their chants and rhythmic drumbeats were carried on unnatural winds to the waiting Imperial forces.

Perhaps half of the Titan engines of Vulcanum, Mortis and Vulpa followed the dread host. The Interfector engines were nowhere to be seen. The battle with Legio Fortidus had cost the Warmaster dearly. His Legios held the advantage of numbers, but the Imperials had an Imperator Titan and scores of Knights. A Knight was no match for a Titan, but only a fool would ignore their combined strength.

Tyana Kourion watched the advance of the Warmaster's army from the flattened crescent ridge fifteen kilometres away. She leaned back in the cupola of her Stormhammer superheavy, panning her magnoculars from left to right. Eschewing battle dress, she wore her ceremonial greens. Though they were uncomfortable and hot, her entire regiment had chosen to emulate her defiance to keep her from standing out to enemy snipers.

'A lot of them, ma'am,' said Naylor, her executive officer. He sat in the secondary turret at the rear of the vehicle, scrolling through reports coming in from the flanking observation posts.

'Not enough,' she said.

'Ma'am?' said Naylor. 'Looks like plenty to me.'

'Agreed, but where are the Sons of Horus?'

'Letting the poor bloody mortals take the brunt of it.'

'Perhaps,' said Kourion, unconvinced. 'More than likely getting us to expend munitions on sub-par troops. It galls me to waste quality rounds on turncoat dross.'

'It's either that or let them roll over us,' pointed out Naylor.

Kourion nodded. 'The Legion forces will show themselves soon enough,' she said. 'And until then we'll make these scum pay for their lack of loyalty.'

'Is the order given?'

'The order is given,' said Kourion. 'All units, open fire.'

YADE DURSO KEPT the Stormbird low, hugging the mountain rock of the Untar Mesas. Imperial fighters from the mountain aeries of Lupercalia duelled the vulture packs in screaming dogfights at higher altitudes, but nap-of-the-earth fighting was Legion work.

Little Horus Aximand sat alongside Durso in the pilot's compartment at the head of fifty Sons of Horus. They were oathed to the moment and eager to fight.

Ten Stormbirds held station with Aximand's craft in a staggered echelon. The drop-ships of Seventh Company flew above, their weapons already in acquisition mode.

'They're eager,' said Aximand.

'Rightly so,' answered Durso.

'Too eager,' said Aximand. 'The Seventh Company were mauled at Avadon. They don't have the numbers to indulge in pointless heroics.'

The threat auspex trilled as it sniffed out the unmistakable emissions of weapons fire. Flickering icons appeared on the slate, too many to process accurately. The Imperial host became a red smear blocking the way onwards to Lupercalia.

'So many,' said Durso.

'We do our job there'll be a lot less soon,' said Aximand. 'Now look for gaps in the line.'

Aximand hooked into the various vox-nets, parsing the hundreds of streams in discreet synaptic pathways, sorting the relevant from the inconsequential. All they needed was for just one enemy commander to let hunger for glory overcome tactical sense.

Company level vox: tank commanders calling in targets, spotters yelling threat warnings and enemy attack vectors.

Command level vox: pained orders to abandon damaged tanks, pick up survivors or overtake laggardly vanguard units.

A screaming wall of encrypted scrapcode howled behind it all. Dark Mechanicum comms screeching between the towering battle-engines. He turned it down, but it kept coming back. The sound was grating on a level Aximand knew was simply *wrong*.

'No machine should sound like that,' he said.

Aximand listened to the streams of vox-traffic long enough to gather the information he needed: unit positionals, vox-strengths and priority enhancements. Taken together it painted a picture as vivid and complete as any sensory simulation. As the Stormbird broke through the clouds, Lupercal's voice broke through every Legion channel.

'*My captains, my sons,*' he said, '*Warriors' discretion. Engage targets of opportunity. Withdraw only on my command.*'

'Take us in, Yade,' ordered Aximand.

'Affirmative,' responded Durso, lifting the golden Eye of Horus he kept wrapped around his wrist and putting it to his lips and eyes. 'For Horus and the Eye.'

'Kill for the living and kill for the dead,' said Aximand.

Durso pushed the Stormbird down.

✠ ✠ ✠

THE PAIN OF his failed Becoming was nothing compared to the agony he suffered now. The neural interface cables implanted in Albard's scabbed spinal sockets were white-hot lances stabbing into the heart of his brain. They'd never properly healed from the day they'd been cut into him.

Banelash was fighting him. It knew he was an intruder and sought to throw him off like a wild colt. The spirits of its former masters knew that Albard was broken, knew that he had failed once already to bond with a Knight.

The dead riders did not welcome the unworthy into their ranks. Albard fought them down.

For all their loathing, he had decades of hate on his side. He felt the echo of Raeven's presence in *Banelash*'s machine heart, but that only made him more determined. His stepbrother had violated everything that Albard had once held dear.

Now he would return the favour.

The Knight's systems glitched and continually tried to restart and break his connection. The modifications his Sacristans had made kept them from shutting him out. The heart of the Knight was screaming at him, and Albard screamed right back.

Forty-three years ago, he had sat opposite Raeven and let fear get the better of him. Not this time. Blinded in one eye by a raging mallahgra in his youth, the simian beasts had always held a special terror in Albard's nightmares. When one had broken free on his day of Becoming, a day that should have been his proudest moment, that terror had consumed him.

His Knight had felt his fear and rejected him as unworthy. Condemned in the eyes of his father, he'd been doomed to a life of torture and mockery at the hands of his stepbrother and sister.

Raeven had killed his father? Good, he'd hated the miserable old bastard. Albard had taken his vengeance with a hunting knife and an intimate knowledge of human anatomy learned on the other side of the blade. His faithless step-siblings were now entwined in an irrigation ditch, bloating with nutrient-rich water and corpse gases. Food for worms.

He winced as a fragment of Raeven's lingering imprint on the Knight's core stabbed at him. He felt Raeven's disgust, but worse, he felt a shred of his pity.

'Even in death you mock me, brother,' hissed Albard, guiding the twenty-two Devine Knights through the rear ranks of the Imperial regiments. Hundreds of thousands of men and their armoured vehicles awaited the order to move out. Tyana Kourion wasn't going to make the same mistakes Edoraki Hakon had made at Avadon.

This would be no passive defence line, but a reactive battle of manoeuvre. Opportunities for advance were to be exploited, gaps plugged. This latter task was the role she had assigned to the Knights of Molech, a glorified reserve force. The indignity of it was galling, the insult a gross stain on the honour of Molech's knightly Houses.

Knights from House Tazkhar marched past, weapons dipped in respect. Many mocked the sand-dwelling savages, but they knew their place – not like the uppity bastards of House Mamaragon, whose strutting Paladins jostled for position in the vanguard. As if they could *ever* rise to be First House of Molech. House Indra's southern Knights bore banners of gold and green, and Albard suspected that they flew fractionally higher than his.

A blatant attempt to eclipse House Molech in glory.

Such temerity would not go unanswered, and Albard felt *Banelash's* weapon systems react to his belligerent thoughts. Anger, insecurity and paranoia blended within his psyche, goaded into a towering narcissism by a lingering presence, an infection newly acquired within the sensorium.

Something serpentine and voluptuous, hideous yet seductive,

lurked in *Banelash's* heart. Albard longed to know it and brushed his mind-touch over it.

The combined fury of the Knight's former pilots surged in response. A reaction of fear. Albard gasped as the sensorium swam with static, phantom images and violent echoes of past wars. A system purge, but it was too little too late. The infection within the sensorium bled into *Banelash's* memories, twisting them with unremembered indignities and delusions of grandeur.

Albard heard sibilant laughter as his damaged mind tried to parse the now from the remembered, but those regions of the brain required for a full interface had been irreparably damaged forty-three years ago. His own memories poured into the sensorium, mingling with long-ended wars and imagined kills. He drew the venomous infection into himself, drinking it down like fine wine.

The sensory rendition of the battlefield around him blurred and twisted like a slowly retuning pict-feed, one image fading and another swimming into focus.

What had once been an ordered Imperial camp of machine fabricated shelters, supply depots, ammunition stockpiles, fuel silos and rally points became something else entirely. Men in boiled leather jerkins and iron sallets marched to and fro. Some wore gleaming hauberks of iron scale. They carried long iron-bladed swords and axes across their shoulders. They marched in dreary lockstep. Hundreds of hunting hounds snapped at their heels, goaded forward by whip-bearing packmasters.

A crash of thunder belched from the vast, dragon-mouthed carronades fringing the hillsides in their thousands. Entrenched in wicker gabions and earthen ramparts, the gunnery academies of Roxcia and Kyrtro had brought their finest culverin and mortars to punish the enemy with shot and shell. Colourful flags snapped in the conflicting thermals above the powder-hungry weapons.

Gunners sweated and heaved, running their iron behemoths back into firing positions. The barrels were swabbed out and fresh powder charges rammed down. Heavy stone spheres were lifted by barrel-chested Tazkhar slaves.

As impressive as the guns were, they were nothing compared to the splendour of the knightly host.

Incredible warriors in all-enclosing plate rode powerful destriers with fantastical caparisons depicting rearing beasts such as had not been seen on Molech for generations.

Albard turned to see the knights riding alongside him.

Cousins, nephews and distant relations, all of the Devine Blood. They rode into battle on wide-chested warsteeds, but not one of their mounts could match the golden stallion upon which he rode, a beast with a mane of fire and wide, powerful shoulders. A king among horsekind.

'My brothers!' cried Albard, letting the blissful serpentine venom spread to each of them. 'See what I see, feel what I feel!'

Some struggled, some almost resisted, but every one of them surrendered in the end. Their secret desires and ambitions were fuel to the infection and it took their every scrap of lust, guilt and bitterness and twisted into something worse.

He turned in the saddle, looking over at the twin lightning bolt emblem streaming from his vexillary's banner pole. The ancient heraldry of the Stormlord himself blazed in the noonday sun, an icon of such brilliance that it illuminated the battlefield for hundreds of metres in all directions.

This was his *banner.*

He was the Stormlord, and these knights were the same vajras who had ridden the Fulgurine Path with him all those centuries ago. A towering sense of self-importance filled him, and he raked back his spurs. Banelash *ploughed through regiments of infantry as the Stormlord saw a vast and monstrous creature through the billowing clouds of cannon fire.*

A titanic beast, a giant of inhuman scale.

Scaled in black and white, it bellowed with the sound of thunder. A world devourer.

This *was* the foe he had been summoned to slay.

PART THREE
GHOSTS

TWENTY

The Battle of Lupercalia

THE THUNDERHAWK WAS wrecked, a gutted carcass that had survived just long enough to get them on the ground. It would never fly again, but who cared about that? Abaddon staggered from the flames and ruin of the crash site, throwing out hails to the Justaerin.

Two definitely dead, one not responding.

So, call it three dead. About what he'd expected in getting this close to the guns of Iron Fist Mountain. They'd lose more by the time they seized the trenches and blockhouses spread around its base and lower slopes like a steeldust fungus. Gunships flashed towards the mountain, barrages of typhoon missiles rippling from their launchers and shells sawing from their assault cannons and hurricane bolters.

Streaks of artillery and anti-aircraft fire slashed overhead. Explosions, flak and the continuous bray of gunnery dropped a constant rain of dust and ember flare. Storm Eagles made a more difficult target than Thunderhawks, but the sheer volume of fire coming off the mountain was swatting more of them from the sky with every passing second.

The wrecks of dozens of gunships were spread over the low foothills. Crashing hadn't been the intent of the plan, but it had been a more than probable outcome and an accepted risk. Five hundred Terminators formed up amid the flames and smoke of the crash sites.

The Imperial gunners thought they'd repulsed the airborne assault on their right. They were wrong. Just because an aircraft went down didn't mean the warriors within were dead.

Especially if those warriors were Sons of Horus.

A Storm Eagle slammed down on the rocks to Abaddon's left. Exploding ordnance mushroomed from the wreckage. Falkus Kibre appeared through the swirl of black smoke surrounding it.

'Did you even crash?' asked Abaddon, seeing the Widowmaker's armour was undamaged by fire or impact.

'No. Pilot brought us down in the lee of a scarp,' said Kibre, gesturing with his combi-bolter. 'Five hundred metres east.'

'I swear you are the luckiest bastard I ever met,' said Abaddon, his voice grating and without the powerful tones he had once possessed. The Emperor's angel of fire had stolen that aspect of him, burned it clean out of him and left him with this gargoyle's rasp. Barring a few bruises, the Widowmaker had come through that encounter unscathed.

'The more I fight, the luckier I get.'

Abaddon nodded. He checked the counter in the corner of his visor.

Four minutes.

The smoke and dust of the crashing gunships was still obscuring their presence, but that wouldn't last for long. The thunder of artillery on the plain swelled. Still the heavier guns in the rear, the main assault waves yet to crash home.

'Everything still on target?' asked Kibre.

'Seems to be.'

'Best find some cover then.'

'That cliff ahead?'

'It's not much.'

'Best I can see.'

Abaddon nodded and opened the vox to the Justaerin.

'New assault position,' he said. 'Advance to my marker and keep your damn heads down.'

'Inspiring,' said Kibre. 'I can see why Lupercal made you First Captain.'

'Now's not the time for inspiring,' said Abaddon. 'Now's the time to hope the damn Mechanicum don't miss.'

VAR ZERBA WAS one of the oldest defence platforms orbiting Molech, and had accrued a sizeable arsenal over the decades. Torpedo racks, missile tubes, mass drivers, collimated boser weapons and innumerable batteries of macro-cannons had been designed with the goal of smashing attacking fleets to ruin.

But such weapons were equally capable of wreaking havoc on planetary targets.

Ezekyle Abaddon had seized Var Zerba virtually intact, and the frigates, *Selenar's Spear* and *Infinity's Regret,* had almost burned out their reactors dragging it from its geostationary position over Molech's oceans to a point fixed just above the agri-belt north of Lupercalia.

Farther west of the battlefield to account for the planet's rotation, but otherwise in the perfect position to wreak havoc from above.

Orbital barrages were not subtle weapons, nor were they discriminate. Their use during battlefield operations was almost entirely unheard of. Their vast quantities of fire were too dangerous, too unpredictable and too destructive should something go wrong. A misfiring munition, a flare of atmospheric discharge or a simple miscalculation could be enough to send city-levelling ordnance wildly off-target.

But when the target was the largest mountain on Molech, perhaps the risk might be deemed acceptable.

THE BLOODSWORN KNELT with their swords drawn and buried in the earth before them. Each warrior had anointed the crimson plates of their armour with the Black, and waited as Warden Serkan moved among them, smearing ash across the winged blood drop on their shoulder guards. As the shells crashed down on the advancing horde he offered each warrior a measure of his wisdom and listened to their last words.

No one was under any illusion that this would be anything other than a last stand. Drazen Acorah knew he would not live to see another sunrise, but the thought did not trouble him overmuch. That they had killed Imperial soldiers in the jungle was not in any doubt, even if he still could not explain how it had happened.

Not only had they murdered innocents and hunted like beasts, but they failed in their duties as exemplars of all that was good and noble in the Legions. The Warmaster had already tarnished the honour of the Legions such that none would ever trust them again, and the Blood Angels had allowed themselves to be party to that.

The Bloodsworn had come to Molech to fight, but they had come to this battlefield to die.

Vitus Salicar stood, and ninety-six Blood Angels rose to their feet behind him, each man holding his blade up to the sky in salute. Not to the enemy; they were unworthy of any recognition. This was a final salute to the Emperor and Terra, to Sanguinius and Baal.

Salicar used an oiling cloth to clean his power sword of dirt, and Acorah saw the ident-tags swing from the blood drop pommel. Acorah needed no psyker powers to feel the weight of guilt attached to them. The rust and unmistakable tang of mortal blood told its own tale.

Salicar saw him looking and sheathed the blade. The ident-tags rattled against the iron and leather scabbard.

'You are still set on this course?' asked Acorah.

'I am,' confirmed Salicar. He made a fist and lifted his arm, bent at the elbow. Ten Rhino armoured carriers fired their engines, jetting oilsmoke and setting the ground atremble.

'You should not seek to dissuade me, Acorah. I would not sully this moment with having to discipline you.'

'I seek to do no such thing,' he said, though the rebellious thought had already crossed his mind. He'd dismissed it immediately. His powers were strong, but not so strong that he could alter a will so set in stone.

'Do you believe this is penance?' he asked.

'I do,' said Salicar.

'You're wrong,' said Acorah, placing his hand on the partly obscured Legion symbol at his commander's shoulder guard. A familiar gesture, almost too familiar. He and Salicar were battle-brothers, but they were far from friends.

Salicar looked down at Acorah's hand. 'Then what is it?'

'It's justice.'

'GO!' SHOUTED AXIMAND.

Third Squad broke from cover, moving and firing as Ungerran Dreadnought Talon opened fire with their cannons and missile launchers. Streaming salvoes of high-calibre shells and spiralling missiles hammered the line of mesh fortifications. Filled with rubble and stacked like children's blocks, they were ideal temporary fortifications.

Temporary or not, they were going to be bloody to overrun.

Behind him, the Stormbirds smoked in the flames of impact and hard burn landings. Nearly five hundred Sons of Horus poured onto the rugged landscape of the Untar Mesas, less than a hundred metres from the stepped defences.

No matter whether an assault came by land, sea or air, that last hundred metres would always need to be crossed by warriors willing to face the enemy head on.

This flank of the Imperial line rested on the mountain foothills, stretching away in a gentle crescent until it reached the towering peak of Iron Fist Mountain.

The twenty kilometres between here and there was an unbroken line of Imperial tanks and infantry. Well dug in, well positioned and, by the looks of things, well led. Jaundiced clouds of smoke drifted across the lines, the ejecta of Imperial guns mixed with the explosions of Lupercal's heavy artillery.

Titans duelled with city-levelling ordnance, the thunder of their steps felt even from here. The Imperator at the centre of the line wasn't marching. Its upper section turned only enough for it to bring its apocalyptic weaponry to bear. Its guns were tearing bloody wounds in the Warmaster's army with every shot. Hundreds were dying with every blast of its hellstorm cannon and hundreds more to the plasmic fury of the annihilator. Missiles, laser blasts and hurricanes of bolter fire wreathed its upper towers and bastions in smoke.

Single-handedly, the Imperator was gutting Lupercal's army.

Or at least the mortal portion of it.

Aximand's attention was drawn from the destroyer Titan to a flash of brightness at the Titan's base. Crimson-painted Rhinos surged forward in a wedge to split the attack in two. A glorious charge into the enemy ranks, the kind that only Legion warriors would dare.

'Bold, but foolish,' hissed Aximand. The enemy host was too vast for so few warriors to break apart, even warriors of the quality of the Blood Angels.

The hiss of a passing las-bolt brought him back to his own fight.

'There,' shouted Aximand, pointing at the base of a stepped salient where a flurry of Stormbird rockets had split the reinforced mesh. Rubble threatened to pour out. All it needed was a little encouragement. 'Squad Orius, bring that wall down! Baelar, take it when it's open.'

A burst of missile contrails arced from a patch of rocks to Aximand's left. A towering explosion of rubble detonated from the defences. Blasted rocks fell in a rain of shattered stone and debris. Even before the dust of the explosion blew out, Squad Baelar were moving. Jump packs flared from the cliff above, where Aximand's pure assault elements had landed.

Gunfire reached out to them. Six were blasted from the air before they reached the apex of their powered leap.

'Did you see that?' asked Yade Durso.

'I did,' said Aximand.

'No mortal shooters did that.'

'Agreed, that's Legion.'

Thudd guns punished the defences where the shots had come from, but Aximand knew they'd hit nothing. If he was right in who was there, they would have already displaced. Squad Baelar landed just before the emplaced blocks and braced their legs for another leap.

The ground erupted in a sheet of fire as a line of remote-activated melta mines detonated.

Aximand ducked back as his auto-senses shut down to protect him from the brightness. Squad Baelar were all but incinerated. A single warrior got airborne, but only his upper half. Stuttering jets carried his corpse over the wall.

'Just far enough away to need two jumps,' hissed Aximand. 'They knew assaulters would need to land there.'

'Definitely Legion,' said Durso.

'Not Blood Angels,' replied Aximand, which left only one possibility. 'The Ultramarines are here.'

'Third Squad is in position,' Durso voxed. 'Ungerran are ready.'

'Hit them with everything,' said Aximand. 'Maximum suppression. We're taking this wall ourselves.'

A PRESSURE WITHIN Abaddon's helmet was the first sign of the incoming barrage. His teeth ached and his visor dimmed in anticipation of impact.

'You're looking up?' asked Kibre. 'Do you *want* to be blinded?'

'How often do you get to be this close to such awesomely destructive firepower?'

'Even once is too often.'

Abaddon grinned, an unusual enough occurrence for him that he surprised himself. Since his injury he'd had precious little to laugh about. The angel's fire had done more than take his voice, it left him with a constant smoulder in his bones. Like an underground fire that never goes out, but burns and burns even when no fuel remains to sustain it.

'Think of it this way,' said Abaddon. 'When it hits, we'll either walk right through the ruins or we'll be dead. Anyway, if I die, Lupercal will need someone to be First Captain.'

'I don't want it earned this way.'

Anger touched Abaddon at Kibre's sentimentality. 'How else do you think you'll get it?'

Kibre didn't answer, and Abaddon turned his gaze to the heavens. Molech's skies had been ripped with electrical storms and raging atmospheric disturbances since the invasion began. Low-hanging clouds seethed like overloading generators. Finally they burst apart, unable to contain the rampant energies within them.

Forking traceries of blue light arced between them and the mountain's highest peaks, as though the holdfast were a vast lightning rod. Squalling clashes of expending void shields filled the sky with blooming oilspills of light. The lightning danced on the invisible barrier, stripping it back with every strike.

And with every screeching blast, the void shields grew closer to their extreme tolerances. Like a bubble stretched to its maximum expansion, they screamed as they blew out. A micro-storm blasted skyward as feedback detonated the generators and explosions geysered around the throat of the mountain.

But this was just the precursor.

Glassy rods of laser fire touched the mountain peak, coring deep into the rock. Superheated steam blasted skyward. Spurts of molten rock garlanded the high peak in a fiery golden crown.

Yet even this was a prelude.

Torpedo volleys and macro-cannon shells launched from Var Zerba at hyperfast velocities punched through the clouds on the coat-tails of the lasers. The mountain's defensive guns sought to bring them down, but the catastrophic detonations of the void shield array had blown out almost every targeting cogitator.

Orbital munitions designed to penetrate subterranean bunker complexes slammed into the mountain, punching into the shafts bored by the orbital lasers. Iron Fist Mountain was hardened to resist aerial bombardment and ground based artillery, but an orbital barrage was many orders of magnitude greater than anything the builders of Legio Crucius had envisioned.

The top five hundred metres of the mountain simply vanished.

Warheads just short of atomic power struck deep into its heart, tearing apart the internal structure of the hollowed out mountain in a hellish firestorm. Vast buttresses of adamantium buckled and melted in temperatures normally found in the cores of stars.

Bracing beams and load-bearing archways collapsed and a cascade of structural instability shook the entire mountain.

A flaming caldera formed as the weight of the mountain's exterior fell inwards. Iron Fist Mountain crumbled like a sand sculpture, every second of collapse adding to the speed of its dissolution. Kilometres-high plumes of explosive gases and dust clouds billowed in a fire-shot mushroom cloud.

The shock wave of impacts and the instantaneous destruction of an entire mountain raced outwards in a pulsing series of seismic pressure waves. Abaddon gripped tightly to the rock as though the earth sought to shake him loose. Explosions of rock and flame shot from the mouth of the newly formed volcano.

An avalanche of debris spilled downwards, millions of tonnes of shattered rock and steel. A tidal wave of destruction that buried the Imperial defences clustered around the mountain under hundreds of metres of rubble.

'First Company,' said Abaddon, as the shock waves began to dissipate.

Five hundred Terminators rose from cover and marched into the hellstorm surrounding the mountain's destruction.

VITUS SALICAR RODE at the head of the Blood Angels, his crimson Rhino's engines roaring like a mesoscorpion in heat. He'd ordered the Techmarines to overcharge the engines. They'd burn out within minutes, metal grinding on metal and erupting in flames as oil feeds burst under pressure. It wouldn't matter. These Rhinos would never need to move again once this task was done.

'An end for all of us,' he said.

They left burning trails behind them where fuel manifolds had already cracked. The flames spread quickly through the fields, and a wall of smoke and fire rose behind them.

There could be no retreat now, even if they desired one.

The traitor line was an unbroken wall of flesh and iron, tanks and marching soldiers as far as the eye could see. Smoke banks from booming artillery obscured the rear ranks. Gunfire snapped and explosions cratered the ground.

Shots punched the up-armoured glacis of his Rhino, but didn't penetrate. A las-round clipped his shoulder guard, vitrifying the ash and dirt smeared over his Legion symbol. A glassy scab formed over the blood drop.

He looked left and right. Like him, Drazen Acorah and Apothecary Vastern rode in the cupola of their Rhinos, while Warden Serkan squatted atop his vehicle like the savage tribal chiefs of Baal Secundus atop their chariots in ages past.

'For the Emperor and Sanguinius!' shouted Salicar as linked bolters on the roof of the Rhino opened fire. A few traitors in deliberately ripped Army fatigues and fetishised helms were punched from their feet.

He picked his target. Army Chimera with the Eye of Horus daubed in umber on the frontal glacis. A banner of ragged cloth streaming behind it with a bleeding eagle upon it. A vehicle for a commander or soldier of rank.

The engine behind Salicar blew out with a hard bang and a solid, concussive thud. He tasted burning promethium and lubricant. The vehicle gave one last spurt of power to the tracks before seizing with a dreadful clash of splintering metal and ripping gears.

The Rhino slammed head on into the painted Chimera. Metal buckled and deformed. The heavier Space Marine vehicle smashed the Chimera's frontal section like foil paper. Salicar vaulted from the Rhino's roof, using the collision to propel him deep into the enemy ranks.

His scaled cloak billowing behind him like golden pinions, the captain of the Bloodsworn sailed through the air and crashed down in the midst of the charging traitors. His sword swept out, its edges blazing with amber fire. Men died.

Behind him, the Rhino's spiked bull bar had disembowelled the enemy vehicle like a carcass on a butcher's slab. Black smoke billowed as the assault doors opened and the Blood Angels poured out. They slammed into the scattered traitors, bludgeoning them from their path with kite shields and short, stabbing thrusts of their swords.

Salicar moved and killed with grace and beauty, like a dancer whose every move was choreographed to match those of his foes. Mortals tried to cut him down, but his movements were too fast, too supple and too beautiful. His flame-lit edge opened their bodies, his gold-chased pistol spat headshots with every pull of the trigger.

Gun fire struck him on the chest and shoulders. Some of it even cut down the soldiers he was fighting. They knew they couldn't fight Salicar on an equal footing and were looking to kill him any way they could. He kept moving, putting as many of the enemy around him as he could. If they planned to shoot him down, they would kill their own men to do it.

The Blood Angels formed arrowheads of red-armoured killers around their war-leaders. Warden Serkan smashed through a knot of bare-chested warriors with their flesh scarified by knife blades. His eagle-winged symbol of office carved them new wounds, but none that would ever heal.

Alix Vastern, the Apothecary who knew every inch of human physiology and who had spent a lifetime repairing it, now bent his every effort to destroying it. Drazen Acorah fought with a monstrous twin-bladed axe, hewing a red path through to a squad of augmented soldiers adorned in blood-lined flesh cloaks and whose weapons were those of the techno-barbarians that once warred over the ruined hellscapes of Old Earth.

Salicar pushed through the masses of packed soldiery to link with him. No blade touched him, but las-rounds and solid slugs gouged and bit his plate. In any other fight, the goal was to make space. To move, to find the gaps between the foe and drink deep of the killing thirst. Here, the aim was to fill that space with their flesh, to make them his shields.

All around, the charge of the enemy continued unabated. Chimeras roared past towards Tyana Kourion's Grand Army of Molech. For all their trappings of savagery, the Warmaster's army was disciplined.

Salicar beheaded a pair of mortals bearing a heavy bolter and kicked another with a demolition charge in the chest. The man's ribs shattered and he flew back through the air. The charge he'd carried detonated and tore the sponson from a nearby battle tank. It slewed around and exploded a moment later.

Salicar knelt as the shock wave washed over him.

He rose to his feet and pushed on, his honour guard finally catching up with him. They had discarded their shields. Defence was now irrelevant, attack was all that mattered.

The bladed formations of the Blood Angels converged to form a single spear thrust right through the centre of the enemy. Perhaps a quarter of Salicar's warriors were dead. Sheer weight of fire had done what the enemy's individual prowess could not. They fled before his wetted blade. Gunshots smacked his arms and legs.

His visor display flickered with warnings, but he cared nothing for them. He was to die this day, and no warning would change that.

Drazen Acorah now fought at his side, his axe blades gleaming red and wet. His lieutenant saw him and gave a curt nod. All that could be spared in the fight's fury. Salicar returned the gesture as he saw a hellish fire silhouette the mortals before him.

Acorah cried out and dropped to his knees, the axe falling from

his grip. The press of bodies closed on him, knives and rifles
and swords stabbing for him. Salicar thrust and cut, keeping the
rabble back. A shot smacked into his back, a heavier round. He
staggered. Another clipped his helmet and he fell to one knee.

He reached out and gripped Acorah's shoulder guard.

'Stand, brother!' he ordered.

Acorah looked up.

Crackling lines of power hazed his helmet, and the lenses shone
with inner light. A blood-red radiance of arterial wonder.

'It's here!' cried Acorah. 'Throne save us, it's here!'

Salicar sprang to his feet as a towering fury surged through him,
a killing rage like nothing he had ever known.

No, that wasn't true.

He had known this once before.

Months before in the Kushite jungle. A red mist of unimaginable hatred and rage, the unbridled anger of a million souls. Every
hostile thought and primal impulse given free rein.

Salicar gasped, an exhalation of feral savagery.

A figure moved through the flames before him, a warrior of
transhuman scale. Its armour was blackened red and wreathed
in fire.

Worse, it was armoured as he was. Wreathed by flames that
seared the eye, the winged blood drop on its shoulder guard was
unmistakable.

Whatever this thing was, it had once been a Blood Angel.

Chains dragged behind it and it hovered a full metre above
the bloody ground. Its face was a scorched horror of eternally
burning meat, fire-blackened and pulled tight in a rictus grin
of horrified anger. In one hand it carried a severed head, that of
Warden Agana Serkan.

'Behold our kin,' it said, and Salicar felt his ears bleed within
his helm.

The mortals gathered around him fell to their knees. No longer seeking him dead, but supplicating themselves to the monstrous hellspawn. Salicar wanted to murder every one of them. Not fight them, not kill them, but slaughter them. He wanted to bathe in their blood, to strip himself of armour and slather his naked flesh with their entrails.

Their hearts he would devour. From their bones he would suck the marrow. Their eyes would be sweet, their blood ambrosia. Salicar's every civilised move was stripped away as he saw himself drowning in the blood of his kills, each skull taken paving the way for his immortality.

'This is what you all want, Vitus,' said the fallen angel, reaching out to him. *'Accept it. Your brothers have already drunk from the bloody chalice I offered them on Signus. They now slay in my name. They slake their thirst for blood without remorse. I know you felt the echoes of that moment in your own slaughters, Vitus. Feel no guilt for that,* embrace *the killer angel within. Join your brothers. Join* me.*'*

Salicar felt a presence beside him and reluctantly averted his gaze from the daemon-thing. Drazen Acorah stood at his side, one hand holding his axe before him like a talisman.

'I name you warp spawn!' cried Acorah, the witch-light within his helm spreading over his body to envelop the blades of his axe.

'I am the **Cruor Angelus,** *the Red Angel!'* cried the fire-wreathed abomination as a pair of flaming swords erupted from its gauntlets. *'Bow down before me!'*

Apothecary Vastern moved to stand between the Red Angel and his captain. 'I know you,' he said. 'You are Meros of the Blood Angels! My battle-brother of the *Helix Primus,* now and always. No power in the galaxy can break that bond!'

'I am the ragefire, I am the sinister urge, the red right hand and the ender of lives!' said the warp-thing. *'Meros is long gone. He*

and Tagas lit the soulfires within me, but the soul of your primarch and his corruption is the blood in my veins.'

Salicar fought to contain his rage and resist surrendering to its red temptation. Every fibre of his willpower was fraying, searing to ash within his mind. To give in would be easy, to submit and accept the bloodlust within him.

Acorah reached out and placed a hand on Salicar's shoulder guard. The fulgurite lightning bolt carved through the ash flickered and danced with golden light. Salicar drew a great draught of air into his lungs, like a drowning man finally reaching the surface.

He blinked away the bloody haze that had fallen across his vision. He ripped off his helmet and threw it aside. The fetor of the battlefield waxed strong in his sense. Blood and opened meat, urine and mud.

His Blood Angels knelt in the dirt around him, looking to him for guidance. Traitors surrounded them, looking to them as avatars of murder and slaughter, as newfound gods to worship. The thought sickened him, that they might be venerated by such dregs.

Firelight reflected on the ident-tags wrapped around the pommel of Salicar's sword. And what had once been guilt became the promise of salvation.

We are the Blood Angels.

We are killers, reapers of flesh.

But we are not murderers, we are not savages.

Vitus Salicar turned so that every one of his warriors could see him. He reversed his grip on his sword. They met his gaze. They knew. They understood. They aligned their blades as he did.

'Join me,' said the Red Angel. *'Be my blood-letters.'*

'Never,' said Salicar, driving his gladius up through the base of his jaw and out through the top of his skull.

✠ ✠ ✠

TWO WARHOUNDS OF Interfector, a snapping engine named *Lochon* and a limping beast dubbed *Bloodveil*, gave covering fire. Aximand and the Fifth Company charged under a blitzing hurricane of turbo fire and vulcan shells. Portions of the mesh-block wall had already given way. The new-birthed volcanic explosion on the far flank had toppled loose blocks from the top of the makeshift barricade, and the fire from the two Warhounds did the rest.

'Over it,' shouted Aximand. 'Take the fight to them.'

The Sons of Horus wove a path through the rubble, some firing from the hip, others pausing to aim. Aximand did neither. He kept his weapon pulled tight to his chest. Speed was his best hope of reaching the defences alive.

Ten Scimitar jetbikes flashed overhead, strafing the defenders with heavy bolter fire. Detonations rippled behind the blocks. The jetbikes turned hard, bleeding off speed for a quick turnaround.

A mistake, Aximand knew. As below, so above.

Speed was survival.

Shots from something rapid firing reached up and tore half the Scimitars from the sky, but a trio of larger attack speeders followed up with barking lascannon fire. An explosion clawed skyward, quickly followed by another. Gunfire chased the speeders, but by now the Scimitars were back on station and let rip over the defenders.

The crash of Titans made Aximand look up in time to see *Lochon* stamp down on a distant section of the walls. Debris spilled out and Sons of Horus swarmed over the breach. *Bloodveil* shadowed its impulsive cousin, firing controlled bursts of vulcan fire. Ejected shells spat from the rear of the weapon in a waterfall of scrap metal.

Behind the Warhounds came *Silence of Death*, a Reaver with deep gouges burned into its carapace. It had been wounded in the fight for Molech and one particular burn scar imparted a lopsided grimace to its pilot's canopy.

The Titan braced its legs, appearing to squat slightly, like an animal about to defecate.

'Down!' shouted Aximand, dropping to a crouch with his helmet tucked into his chest as far as it would go. The Reaver's blastgun and melta cannon fired with a shriek of rupturing air. The path of the weapons ignited, an instantaneous flashburn of light.

Aximand's armour warned of a cataclysmic spike in temperature that vanished almost as soon as it registered. Thunderclaps of superheated air washed over him in a thermal shock wave.

Paint blistered on his back and shoulders.

Aximand pushed himself upright. The middle of the wall was gone. Apocalyptic explosions had tossed what remained around, leaving the way open for the infantry.

Aximand ran towards the flaming ruin of the wall, threading a path through the blistering heat haze. The rock underfoot was molten and glassy. His auto-senses were lousy with thermals, just a bleeding mass of false target readings.

A series of ferocious explosions hurled Aximand into the air.

Massed battle cannon fire.

He came down hard on the fused remains of a block that had once been part of the defences. He rolled, his armour cracked open in a dozen places. His helmet was split down the middle. He tore it off, and struggled to find his feet. His innards felt like they'd been compressed in a Warlord Titan's assault fist. Concussive trauma. His lungs fought to take a breath. When they did it was searing hot, painful. He tasted burned meat, scorched metal and stone.

Sons of Horus lay dead all around him, split plates and boiled meat. Yade Durso picked himself up, holding his hand as though he was in danger of losing it. Aximand saw an Interfector War-hound lying across the remains of the wall. One side was ripped away, its mechanical innards spilled and its crew a burned smear on the inner faces of its carapace.

Bloodveil or *Lochon*, he couldn't tell.

Vapour ghosts made visibility a joke beyond forty metres. His eyes burned with the acrid fumes of melta residue. Shapes moved in the smoke. Tall, loping. Hunched low and racing through the geysers of superheated air.

Knights. At least a dozen. Aximand struggled to remember the force disposition documents he'd read.

Green and blue heraldry, a fire-topped mountain: *House Kaushik.* Arcology-dwelling House, low tech resources. Estimated six Knights maximum. Threat level: medium.

Coiled snake icon over a field of orange and yellow. *House Tazkhar,* southern, steppe-dwelling nobles of noted savagery and cunning. Estimated eight Knights in total. Threat level: high.

They came in pairs; one moving, one shooting. Heavy stubbers raked the walls and thermal cannons stabbed like bright lances through the smoke. Aximand experienced a moment of paralysis when he thought they were coming for him, but the Knights had bigger prey in mind.

Void shield flare blazed like sheet lightning behind him as the Knights went after the remaining Warhound and the Reaver. An unequal fight, but when had that ever mattered? The Knights swept past, over the ruin of the block wall, hunting horns blaring from their carapaces.

Then Aximand saw who was *really* coming for him.

Armoured in cobalt-blue and gold, a transverse crest of white on a legate's helmet. Bright silver blades unsheathed.

XIII Legion.

Ultramarines.

THE JUSTAERIN WERE wasted in this fight. Nothing remained of the Imperial right flank. Ashen statues that had once been men, buried wrecks of tanks that had become inescapable ovens. Artillery positions were buried in rock, and the twisted barrels of Basilisks and Minotaurs jutted from drifts of hot ash.

Mewling survivors begged to be pulled from avalanches of rock that were slowly cooking them to death. Abaddon didn't give them the mercy of a bullet.

He saw a Warlord on its knees, its lower legs fused and melted to the rock of the mountain. Its back was bent as it tried to right itself. All that was keeping it upright were its weapon arms, buried in ash to the elbows. Two Warhounds lay sprawled on their bellies, their canopies cracked open and wounded skitarii frantically digging to reach the crew.

The Terminators killed them without breaking pace.

The real fight was coming to them.

The Imperator Titan was on the move.

IN THE WAKE of the Ullanor campaign, Aximand had spoken at length to the warriors of the Ultramarines. It had been a tense time between the XVI and the XIII Legions. Together with the White Scars, the Ultramarines had acted as Lupercal's unwitting decoy in force while the Luna Wolves struck straight to the heart of the greenskin empire.

Neither Guilliman's nor the Khan's warriors took kindly to being used as bait while the glory went to others. Many fanciful stories grew out of that campaign; some aggrandising it, some belittling it, but all agreed on the spectacular nature of the victory, with Horus and the Emperor fighting back to back. Aximand wondered if that particular story would ever be retold in years to come.

Ezekyle had been merciless in his not-so-gentle mockery of the laggardly Ultramarines.

'Always late for the fight,' Ezekyle had roared, strutting like a peacock. The challenge had come from a sword-champion named

Lamiad, and Ezekyle had accepted. He had a head of height on the slender Ultramarine, but Lamiad had him on his back in under a minute.

'If you must fight an Ultramarine, you have to kill him quickly,' Lamiad warned Ezekyle. 'If he is still alive, then *you* are dead.'

Sound advice, though until now, Aximand had never realised just *how* sound. The Ultramarines had seen the threat of the *Silence of Death* and withdrawn to positions prepared for just such an eventuality. Practical, indeed.

Now three hundred warriors in the blue of open skies came at the scattered warriors of the XVI Legion with hatred in their hearts. Aximand had somewhere in the region of four hundred, but they were scattered and spread through the ruins. At best, he had a hundred, maybe a hundred and twenty immediately to hand.

The odds favoured the Ultramarines.

But since when had that ever mattered to the Sons of Horus?

'Lupercal!' shouted Aximand, swinging *Mourn-it-all* from its shoulder harness. The blade gleamed in the murder-light of battle. The runic script worked into the fuller shone with anticipation.

The Sons of Horus rallied to the Warmaster's name as Aximand swung his blade up to his shoulder and charged the Ultramarines. Bolter shells filled the rapidly diminishing space between them. Armour cracked open, bodies fell. Not enough to halt the tides.

Aximand picked his target, a sergeant with a notched sword that struck him as being the very antithesis of all the XIII Legion stood for. He would be doing Primarch Guilliman a favour by killing this legionary – what sort of example was he setting his warriors?

The ocean green and cobalt-blue slammed together in a shattering crack of plate and blades. Pistols blazed, swords crashed and armour sundered. Aximand split the Ultramarines sergeant from clavicle to pelvis with one stroke. No photonic edge was ever sharper. He backswung and hacked through a legionary's waist. The hosts became entangled, a heaving, grunting press of armoured bodies. Too close and cramped for sword work. Aximand slammed the hilt against a warrior's visor. It cracked and spat sparks. A pistol shot blew it out.

Yade Durso's sword had broken. He spun through the melee with two pistols. He took shots of opportunity, heads, spines and throats. Like a pistol master of the Scout Auxilia, he never stopped moving.

The fight was brutal. The blue had the better of it, fighting in ordered ranks, like a living threshing machine. Their blades and guns worked tirelessly, as though the Ultramarines fought to the unheard recitation of an unseen combat master.

It was war without heroics, without art.

But it was winning.

Already outnumbered, the Sons of Horus were fighting on their own, each warrior the hero in his own battle. But heroes could not win on their own, they needed battle-brothers. Aximand saw that ego had hamstrung them. They had come to Molech expecting an easy fight. It had made them forget themselves, and the XIII Legion were punishing them for that complacency.

Aximand roared and swung *Mourn-it-all* in a wide arc, clearing space. Ultramarines fell back from his unnaturally keen edge.

'Sons of Horus, close ranks!' shouted Aximand. 'Show these eastern dogs how the mongrel bastards of Cthonia fight!'

Warriors gathered around him. Not enough to keep them from being pushed from the field, step after backward step.

A warrior of the XIII Legion came at Aximand with a long-bladed polearm. The leaf-shaped blade shimmered with power. It gave him reach. Aximand jumped back as the golden blade stabbed for him. The warrior was a vexillary, Aximand now saw, the long-shafted weapon he bore having once borne a flag. Its burned remains hung limply from corded red fasteners.

'You lost the standard,' said Aximand. 'You ought to impale yourself on that spike of yours.'

'You will all die here,' said the Ultramarine.

Aximand turned the polearm aside with *Mourn-it-all*'s blade. He spun inside its reach. His elbow smashed the Ultramarine's face.

The warrior staggered, but didn't fall. 'If you must fight an Ultrama–'

Aximand plunged *Mourn-it-all* through the vexillary's breastplate until the quillons struck the glittering Ultima on his plastron.

'I know,' said Aximand. 'Make sure you kill him.'

FROM THE FIRE-WARMED heat of his war tent, Horus watched a holo-lithic representation of the battle unfolding. With each update fed into the cogitator by the kneeling ranks of calculus logi, Horus barked manoeuvre orders to Scout Auxilia runners who carried them to the vox-tents.

Beyond the war tent, hundreds of Rhinos, Land Raiders and Thunderhawks waited to carry thousands of Sons of Horus into battle. The remaining Titans of Vulcanum, Mortis and Vulpa were spread through the legionaries. A force capable of utter destruction, but they too waited.

Maloghurst stood at his side, but had said little since the battle's opening shots. Horus sensed his confusion at giving battle with a full third of the army yet to engage. Horus did not explain. His reasons would become clear soon enough.

'Ezekyle's Justaerin are pushing hard for the centre,' said Maloghurst. 'The destruction of Iron Fist Mountain has blown the left flank wide open.'

They'd felt the monstrous shock waves of the orbital barrage from Var Zerba like the rumblings of a distant earthquake. Fire-streaked smoke spread like embers on the horizon. It would rain ash for weeks, turning the entire agri-belt into a benighted wasteland.

'Ezekyle will need support if he's not going to be annihilated by *Paragon of Terra.*'

'He'll have it, Mal,' Horus assured him.

'From where, sir?' said Maloghurst. 'The Red Angel was supposed to drive the Blood Angels into madness, to break the centre for our Army forces to exploit. But the sons of Sanguinius are dead, and our centre has yet to make any significant impact. They're dying in droves out there.'

Horus gestured over the hololithic display, already knowing what he would see. The Imperial guns were decimating his Army units at the heart of the advance. The fields before the ridge line were a killing ground of burning wrecks and corpses. Thousands were dead, thousands more still would die.

It irked Horus that the *Cruor Angelus* had not made good on its promise to turn the Blood Angels. Given that he had upset the schemes of Erebus to prevent that very thing on Signus, the irony was not lost on him.

'And Aximand is bogged down on the right against forces from the Thirteenth Legion,' continued Maloghurst. 'It's going to take a Sons of Horus speartip to get through that line. You need to deploy the rest of the Legion and Titan forces.'

'Mal, are you telling me my business?'

'No, sir.'

'Good,' said Horus. 'Because I see the complexity of war differently to other men. Killing on this scale isn't only about numbers and movement on a battlefield. Just by observing them I shape them and bend them to my will. Can you imagine any of my brothers mastering so chaotic an endeavour as war as I do?'

'No, sir.'

Horus waved an admonishing finger. 'Come on, Mal, you're

better than that. Stop sounding like a sycophant. Answer honestly.'

Maloghurst bowed and said, 'Perhaps Guilliman.'

'Too obvious,' said Horus. 'Some think he has no heart for war, that all he cares about are grand plans and stratagems. They're wrong. He knows war as well as I do, he just wishes he didn't.'

'Then perhaps Dorn?'

'No, too hidebound,' said Horus. 'Nor the Lion or Vulkan. And not the Khan, though he and I are so very close in alignment.'

'Then who?'

'Ferrus,' answered Horus, tapping the lid of the ornately wrought box of lacquered wood and iron that sat next to him.

'If he was so capable, then why is he dead?'

'I didn't say he was perfect,' said Horus, leaning forward as the hololith hazed with static as it updated. 'But he knew war like no other. Terra would already be ours if he had joined us, if my Phoenician brother had handled the approach with a modicum of subtlety.'

'Subtlety was never Fulgrim's strong suit,' said Maloghurst.

'No, but that lack has played in our favour here.'

'It has?'

'The power Fulgrim so willingly embraced has whispered honey in the dreams of Molech's rulers for many years,' said Horus. 'Those dreams are about to become reality. And when they do, trust me, Mal, you'll be glad we kept so far away.'

A STONE LINTEL cracked and slammed down, blocking further progress along the trench. A firestorm raged overhead and Abaddon pressed himself flat against the vitrified stone wall as flames roared along its length. Fire was little threat to Terminator armour, but this was weaponised plasma from a Titan's weapon.

An Imperator Titan.

Paragon of Terra's guns were ripping the world apart.

Missiles, explosive shells, hurricanes of bolter fire, laser fire and killing beams from volcano cannon. What little was left of the trenches and strongpoints of this flank were being reduced to shot-blasted powder.

The Justaerin could survive a great deal, more than any other living thing on the battlefield, but the damned Imperator was going to kill them all. The walls of the trench blew inwards with the shock wave of another weapon system. Abaddon pushed away chunks of hot stone and metal.

A veteran hauled Abaddon clear with his one remaining arm. The other ended at the shoulder where the pressure wave of a passing gatling shell had ripped it away. Another weapon fired overhead, something with solid rounds, though Abaddon could no longer pick one weapon's fire from another. The overpressure of the cycling rounds battered his armour like an army of aggrieved forge-smiths.

Everything merged into one continuous thunder of explosions, percussive hammer blows on the ground and searing thunderstorms of impossibly bright light that burned everything they touched.

The trenches had provided some cover, but they were no match for the holocaust-level destruction an Imperator could unleash. He doubted half his warriors had survived this far. Another few minutes and they would all be dead.

'What was the Warmaster thinking sending us into this?' yelled Kibre, stumbling from a blockhouse of adamantium made soft as butter by the plasma fire. Abaddon saw the corpses of at least a dozen Justaerin within. More filled the trench system around him, but he couldn't see them. Too many red icons to know how many were dead, how many alive.

More dead than he'd ever thought to see among the Justaerin.

'How are we supposed to get past that Imperator?'

Abaddon had no answer for the Widowmaker, and set off down the trench. Movement was their only ally. To remain static was to die.

More explosions shook the trenches. The ground split and vomited earth and smoke. It felt like the very bedrock of Molech was breaking apart. Abaddon half expected to see lakes of magma ooze up from the cracks in the earth. Hundreds of las-blasts roared overhead, a horizontal rain of killing light. More explosions, more fire, more detonations, more death.

His one-armed rescuer died as three spinning pieces of rebar sliced through his chest, pinning him to the rock. Two plunged into the ground less than half a metre from Kibre. Abaddon grinned and shook his head.

A world-shaking impact burst the walls of the trench. Fire-fused glass cracked and fell to the ground. Burned earth poured in from above. Ruptured bodies came with it, threatening to bury them alive with the men they had killed.

'Now what?' demanded Kibre, pushing along the corpse-choked trench behind Abaddon. Explosions chased them. Debris rained and the sky turned to fire.

Abaddon paused.

'That wasn't a weapon,' he said.

'Then what in the nine hells was it?'

'A footstep,' said Abaddon. 'It's the Imperator. It's coming to crush us.'

The End Times had come to Molech. This was to be the last ride of the Stormlord, a final sally into the jaws of death. His noble vajra knights rode with him as they faced the daemon beast and the world's ending.

It towered over everything, a mountain-sized creature of darkness that was swallowing the world with its every breath. The black and white of its scales was only eclipsed by the fire surrounding it.

Fire from its daemonic breath and fire from its sorcerous fists.

It was unmaking the world, and though it would surely cost him his life, he knew he had to try and stop it. His steed bucked beneath him, its animal brain understandably reluctant to ride into the fire of its doom.

He quelled it with a sharp thought.

But on the back of that thought came another, a treacherous and unbecoming one. A mortal thought.

This is not real, *it said,* this is fantasy...

The voice grew louder until it was screaming in his skull. The Storm-lord tried to shut it out, but it only grew more intense. And for a moment the towering form of the dragon wavered. Its outline blurred and Albard saw just what he was charging towards.

Albard? Yes, Albard...

He was the Stormlord.

No, he was Albard Devine. Firstborn Scion of Cyprian Devine, Knight Seneschal of Molech, Imperial commander in the Imperium of Man. This was his world.

A poison veil fell from Albard's fevered eyes and he saw the interior of the *Banelash*'s canopy through the mist of his one remaining eye. He reclined in a fluid place of unnatural angles and billowing musks. Of silks and gold and gems. The interior was no longer machine-smoothed metal, but possessed the fleshy, furred texture of a pleasure palace.

Where before he had interfaced with the Knight's operation via the spinal implants, now his wasted body was a mass of writhing, serpentine ropes that oozed from the warped interior. Their ends were puckered with lamprey-like mouths. Tiny needle teeth buried in the meat of his limbs as they fed on him and filled his veins with their scented toxins.

'No!' screamed Albard, but laughter was his only answer.

One brother rejects me and tries to kill me – do you think I will let another do the same?

'I am Albard Devine!' he cried, holding onto his sense of self as blissful ecstasies filled his mind with pleasure. 'I am...'

His protests died as the fronds caressing his limbs withdrew and he saw what he had become. Beneath the mouths of the mass of snake-like feelers, he was naked, but he was not the ravaged specimen of wretchedness he'd expected.

Albard wept to see strong thighs with well-defined quadriceps. His belly was flat and cut with abdominal muscles. His pectorals were the very epitome of sculpted perfection. He was a god among men, as perfect as the gilded statues of the Emperor's sons that flanked the approach to the Sanctuary.

The years since his failed Becoming were wiped away and all that he could have been was revealed. This was what he should have been, this was what Raeven and Lyx had stolen from him.

This was what the Serpent Gods had offered Raeven and what he had selfishly thrown back in their faces. He would not make that mistake. Albard would live up to the promise of all he had been raised to expect. His would be a life of glory lived for the Serpent Gods.

What they offered was everything he had been denied.

The broken psyche that was Albard Devine had no chance against such blandishments and the force of his own ambitions.

'I am yours...' he whispered, and the lamprey-like mouths of the snake fronds fastened on his limbs once again. The pain of their teeth upon his perfect body was a welcome pain. He convulsed as the heady mix of daemonic elixirs coursed around his body. The sensation of bliss was unstoppable, matched only by his horror at the crippled thing he had once been.

Albard blinked and the interior of the pilot's canopy was wiped from his sight.

The Stormlord's warhorse rode towards the towering beast of black and white as it turned its killing fire on a host of brave foot knights

*making a last stand by a flame-belching crater where once had stood
a mighty fortress.*

'Vajras!' *he bellowed.* 'Ride with me to victory!'

IN THE END, it wasn't natural Cthonian ferocity or hot-as-hell-in-
the-heart resilience that saved Aximand's Sons of Horus. Nor was
it any small-unit tactics of uncommon brilliance or heroic leadership from a charismatic officer.

In the end it was Titans that saved them.

Mourn-it-all had reaped a fearsome tally, its edge as sharp as the
day the Warmaster had restored it. But a sharp sword and an arm to
swing it weren't enough. The Sons of Horus fought a desperate retreat
through the maze of shattered blocks that was all that remained of
the flanking wall, harried at every turn by vengeful Ultramarines.

Hundreds of warriors grappled and stabbed and shot one
another in the fog of explosions and burning propellant. Wrecked
vehicles lay strewn in the rubble. Random rounds cooked off
and crackled in the flames. Mortal soldiers unlucky enough to be
caught in the middle were killed within moments, crushed in the
fray, hacked open or shredded in withering crossfire.

This was Legion war. Mortals had no place in it.

Bolter shells caromed off Aximand's armour, swords gouged the
bonded ceramite and explosions battered him with debris. All
semblance of purpose and control among the combatants was
eroded in the smoking, flame-lit nightmare. Even in the chaos,
Aximand knew the Ultramarines held the upper hand. With every
hacking sweep, every snatched pistol shot, the Sons of Horus were
a step closer to defeat.

Aximand had killed seventeen Ultramarines.

An admirable ratio, but not without its cost.

Aximand's right shoulder guard was gone, torn away by the
heavy blast of an emplaced autocannon. The flesh beneath was

burned black and every movement of the arm brought a hiss of pain to his lips. His plastron was cracked and the coolant pipes crossing underneath spewed chemicals down his legs in oily sheets. Regrown vertebrae protested at his sudden movements, the grafted bone not yet fully bedded in.

But the fight wasn't lost.

For all their damned *practical*, for all that they held the upper hand, the Ultramarines couldn't put the Sons of Horus to rout. Almost any other foe would have broken in the face of such a relentless killing machine of war, but the Sons of Horus were weaned on blood. They gave ground only in blood.

And that had earned them a reprieve.

Unimaginably powerful weapons discharged behind Aximand. The kind that would kill you without you even knowing it, the kind that would atomise every molecule of your body before the brain even registered the muzzle flash.

Now that weaponry was turned on the warriors of the XIII Legion.

A column of incandescent light erupted in the heart of the blue-armoured warriors. Plasma washed up like a geyser as the white heat of a blastgun turned its heat on the enemy infantry.

A one-armed Warhound climbed to the top of the rubble, its hull pitted with stubber impacts. Void shield haze clung to its ripped carapace like corposant, and oily blood streamed from its underside.

Bloodveil.

Its remaining arm unleashed a withering fan of turbo fire. Ultramarines were hollowed out, sliced open and boiled within their armour. Killing light speared through the ruins. Five metre spurts of vapour and fragmented armour stitched through the rubble. Two dozen warriors were cut down in the blink of an eye.

The white-heat of the laser weapon's discharge burned the fog and Aximand punched the air like the old days when he saw the limping giant, *Silence of Death*, approaching. The Reaver had been taken apart, its armour in tatters and both its arms destroyed. The Knights had almost brought the Reaver down, but going head to head with a Battle Titan, any hope of victory had always been slender.

The Reaver's apocalypse launcher filled the sky with dozens of missiles. Then a dozen more. Streaking darts of light arced overhead and slashed down in a hammering series of explosions that merged into one continuous roar of detonation.

Atop the rubble, *Bloodveil* threw back its head and loosed an ululating blast of its warhorn. A bellow of victory or a paean of loss? Aximand couldn't tell.

Silence of Death crashed down onto its knees, its upper carapace swaying as flames erupted from the princeps canopy. The Interfector engine had turned the fight around, but it would take no further part in the battle.

The thunder of explosions shook the earth and Aximand gripped a bent iron girder jutting from the ruins to take a breath.

In the precious moment he had, Aximand reloaded his bolter.

Last magazine.

Then he saw he wouldn't need it.

Withdrawing in good order from battle was one of the most difficult manoeuvres a formation could make. Doing it under fire made it next to impossible.

Yet that was what the Ultramarines had done.

Yade Durso staggered through the smoke, looking as though he'd gone toe-to-toe with the Knights himself.

'You made it,' said Aximand.

'Lupercal helped me,' said Durso, holding up his hand.

The golden Eye of Horus that Durso had carried was melted into his palm, forever to be part of his gauntlet. Its outline was heat softened, but still clearly recognisable.

'I was bolter dry and sword broken,' said Durso. 'A Thirteenth

Legion bastard had me dead to rights.'

'So what happened?'

Durso clenched his fist. 'I had to punch his damn head off.'

THE HOLOLITH FILLED with multiple inloads coming from orbital survey tracks. A wealth of data filled the slate. New icons, new force vectors. Unknown contacts.

Unknown to the battle cogitators, corrected Horus. Not unknown to me.

'You are a wonder, my indomitable brother,' said Horus. He stood and his presence filled the pavilion with bellicose intent.

Maloghurst bent to the slate, his eyes darting between the multiple inloads.

'Send word to the Legion,' said Horus, lifting *Worldbreaker* from the nearest weapon rack. 'Full advance. It's time to end this.'

'Is that...?' began Maloghurst, his finger tracing a line of sigils advancing from the south.

'It is,' said Horus. 'Right where I need him to be and just when I need him.'

'How could you know he would arrive right at this moment?'

'I'm the Warmaster,' said Horus. 'It's not just a pretty title.'

TYANA KOURION FOUGHT the Battle of Lupercalia from the interior of her Stormhammer. Even protected by many centimetres of layered adamantium and steel plating, the *sturm und drang* of the apocalyptic conflict was still a symphony of thunder and hammer blows on the side of the superheavy.

The roar of its engine and the world-shaking crash of its multiple weapon systems made ear-defenders a necessity. It was cramped, deafening and stank of oil and sweat and fear. Each second this battle raged, hundreds of her soldiers were dying. It was her job to win this battle quickly.

Half a dozen data-slates parsed inloading information from vox-reports, pict-capture, auspex feeds and visual tagging.

No battle ever went according to plan, and today was no exception. The loss of the Blood Angels had horrified her, but their suicidal charge had bowed the enemy line, giving her guns more chance to savage the advance.

Was that worth the deaths of a hundred Legion warriors?

No, but better to make use of it than lament it.

The fighting had evolved naturally into a shifting tide of heady charges, strategic withdrawals, outright routs and flowing thrusts. Imperial and traitor tanks duelled in their own miniature battlefields, each one a tiny piece of a greater whole; hooking flanking manoeuvres, pincer traps and staggered echelons.

The Titans of Gryphonicus and Crucius waged war on a plane far removed from that of the mortals fighting in their colossal shadows. They fought with weapons whose venting could burn an entire company to death. It was war on a scale where ejected shells could crush a squadron of armoured transports and a misplaced step could destroy an entire battalion.

Sensible commanders avoided being anywhere near engines at war, but sometimes there was no escaping their monstrous presence. Like giants among ants, the Titans crashed and battered one another and their deaths took hundreds of warriors on both sides with them.

Gryphonicus's complement of Titans was primarily Warhounds, and they had harried the flanks. At least four were gone, either buried in the mountain's ruin or surrounded and gunned down by Legio Vulcanum's more numerous Reavers.

The enemy Titans had started the day with the numerical advantage, but *Paragon of Terra* had steadily eroded that advantage to the point where the engine forces were more or less at parity. At the current rate of attrition, the Imperial engines would soon outnumber those of the Warmaster.

'More Chimeras and mass-transit carriers coming through on the right,' observed Naylor. 'We can't ignore it any longer. Soon they'll have enough massed to pose a serious threat there.'

'Crucius and Gryphonicus aren't stopping them?' asked Kourion.

'They're wreaking bloody murder on the Mechanicum war machines and their superheavies, but they're ignoring a lot of the infantry carriers.'

'They're beneath them,' replied Kourion.

'They'll be right on bloody top of us unless we push them back before they've enough numbers to threaten that flank.'

'Agreed,' said Kourion, pulling the battle-inload from the right flank to her main slate. Her eyes scanned the dozens of icons there, quickly assessing their worth and combat effectiveness.

Nothing left alive there with the strength to mount an effective counterattack. She haptically swept up the centre and reserves.

One force icon stood out above all others.

'There,' she said, jabbing a finger. 'That's our best chance to throw them back. Get them in the damn fight.'

Naylor nodded. 'Good choice. No combat degradation and perfectly positioned to support the Titans.'

'Send the orders,' said Kourion, turning her attention to the confusing haze of gross-displacement weapon discharges on the left where Castor Alcade's Ultramarines were deployed. She didn't know what was happening there and that was unacceptable.

Naylor dialled into the local vox-net.

'Lord Devine,' said Naylor, exloading a series of engagement vectors. 'You and your Knights are ordered to immediately engage the enemy at the following grid-sectors.'

Vox-static hissed in reply.

✠ ✠ ✠

THE MULTI-TIERED COMMAND bridge of *Paragon of Terra* smelled of oil and incense, hot circuitry and anger. Two hundred calculus logi, servitors and deck crew were plugged into tactica-engines and command consoles, reviewing encrypted vox from every element of Tyana Kourion's battle-net. A constant drone of low-level binary and hushed voices blended with hot, grainy static and clicking prayers. Heat bled into every system, the anger of the Titan's machine-spirit rendering every system with a red haze.

Angled slates projected news from all over Molech, hanging in drifting entoptic veils of light. Each one only served to stoke the nuclear heart of the Titan's rage.

An Imperator Titan was a land-bound starship, as powerful and as demanding a mistress as any void craft. Crewed by thousands throughout its towering height, it was as complex a machine as had ever been built by the hands of man. Only the secret designs of the Ark Mechanicum dared approach the complexity of an Imperator.

To give life to so immense a machine and set it to motion was an entirely different thing to setting a ship in space. Zero gravity forgave a great many things that planetary environments did not.

Its Manifold was a proud, regal thing. An apex predator without rivals, a lord of battle with fangs no other could match and a fury equalled only by its commander.

Princeps Kalonice stood at the jutting prow of the strategium, hands braced on her hips as she drank in the data inloads feeding into the Manifold. She swiped a mechanical hand through the various projections, parting them like smoke and inloading them instantaneously.

Encased in the body-carapace of a Lorica Thallax, all that remained of Etana Kalonice was her skull and spine, fused within the mechanised body of meticulous construction. With reverse-jointed piston legs and wheezing, clicking mechanical joints, she was a robot in all but consciousness.

Contoured plates of porcelain-white armour encased her organic material, and hair-fine copper mind impulse unit cabling allowed her to interface with the fiendishly intricate mechanisms of *Paragon of Terra* without a gel-filled casket. To be so bound to a machine body was exquisite agony, but Kalonice would rather face a lifetime of pain than permanent entombment.

<Mister Sular,> she said. <Assessment?>

Algorithmic resonators translated synaptic activity into sounds and allowed Kalonice's voice to sound virtually human. It almost took away the edge of pain, but not quite.

A flurry of topographical images bloomed at her senior moderati's station. Maps, threat vectors, combat prognoses. *Paragon of Terra*'s preferred targets jostled for his attention, but Sular suppressed them in favour of answering his princeps.

'The Warmaster has fatally underestimated the resistance he would face, ma'am,' said Sular, a torso with mechanised arms fused with the battle-logister. 'The Imperial line has collapsed in a number of places, but not enough for a breakthrough. A good defence in depth and numerous flanking sallies have allowed General Kourion's reserve forces to meet each breakthrough and contain it.'

<Except this one,> said Kalonice.

'With respect to General Kourion, the destruction of Iron Fist Mountain was unthinkable.'

<The Warmaster thought it,> she said, feeling the spike of the Imperator's desire for revenge through her spine like a shank.

The Legio Crucius fortress was gone, reduced to a seething, volcanic ruin by orbital fury. All their history, all their connections to their sister Legios gone. In one fell swoop, the Warmaster had brought Legio Crucius to the edge of extinction.

'And we'll make them pay for that,' said Carthal Ashur, pacing the deck like a man on a crowded stage with no role to play.

<That we will, Mister Ashur, but please sit down. You are distracting me, and I do not need distractions now.>

'Apologies ma'am,' said Ashur, forcing himself onto a vacant supplicant's bench.

She'd met Carthal Ashur many years ago, had even once bedded him when there was still enough of her to make such a prospect tenable. He'd been a disappointment, but his talent with words and mortals had persuaded her to keep him around as Calator Martialis.

'Multiple targets inbound,' reported Moderati Sular. 'Two dozen main battle tanks. Six superheavies. Supporting infantry, battalion strength.'

'Any Titan killers?' asked Ashur.

Kalonice could taste his sweat over the scented oils of the bridge, a mix of eagerness and unfamiliarity. He'd been part of Legio Crucius for decades, but this was only his third time aboard a Battle Titan. His first in battle.

Moderati Sular looked to Kalonice, and she nodded her assent for him to answer Ashur's question.

'Shadowswords, aye,' said Sular, sweeping the data over to the strategium. 'Some traitor Mechanicum elements too. Highlighting.'

The local area around the Imperator was rendered in cascades of binary, illuminating forces both friendly and enemy. Tanks, infantry, Knights, artillery.

Each of the enemy icons already had a target solution plotted, the Mechanicum elements and superheavies assigned kill-priority.

Paragon of Terra was anticipating her, and Kalonice let it.

Ten Shadowswords with volcano cannons. Unidentified Mechanicum battle-engines – a mix of Ordinatus and Titan, each armed with weapons capable of wreaking great harm on her.

If they could be brought to bear.

<Ready the hellstorm,> she ordered. <Magos Surann? How long until the annihilator is ready?>

'Information – five seconds,' answered Magos Surann from the raised gallery behind her, where plugged Mechanicum adepts sat in rows like a binary choir.

<Perfect,> said Kalonice, bunching a fist at her side as readiness icons flashed up from the multiple weapon systems atop the battlements at the Titan's shoulders. Her Thallax body was limber and agile, but the sensory weight of the Imperator was immense. At times like this, she could accept there were some benefits to being held weightless within amniotic gels.

She felt stabbing prickles all across her body. Her void shields were taking hits, scrappy and uncoordinated, but hits nonetheless. The infantry she'd stepped over had heavy weapons. Nothing individually capable of harming her or taking out a void shield, but irritating nonetheless.

The Shadowswords were firing, the bright spears of their volcano cannons bursting shields and overloading the pylons.

'The voids are taking hits,' said Ashur, as though she wouldn't already know that.

<I said no distractions,> said Kalonice, issuing an engagement order to every weapon section. <Open fire.>

Kalonice let each of her weapon systems have its head, allowing the moderati and techs to wreak their own devastation. They all deserved a measure of the spoils of vengeance. The recoil from so many vast weapon systems was dampened by multiple suspensor webs and pneumatic compensators, but still shook the command bridge with the force of so many discharges.

Enemy icons vanished from the Manifold, dozens at a time.

But she kept the plasma annihilator for herself, zeroing in on a towering engine of bronze and brass worked with skulls and lurching towards her on spiked wheels. A corrupted engine of the Mechanicum, a hateful reminder of treachery within her own order.

Kalonice drew power from the boiling reactor core at her heart. The heat was immense, and she drew and drew from the well of plasma fire until the screaming agony in her right fist was almost too much to bear.

<You're mine,> she said, but even as the algorithmic resonator formed the words, Kalonice felt an icy cold knife slide into her lower back. Illusory, but no less painful for that.

The pain broke her hold on the plasma fury encased in her fist and the arm vanished in a furious supernova of white fire that rocked the Imperator back on its heels. Kalonice screamed, the resonators having no problem rendering the depths of her agony.

Her Thallax body fell to the deck, bio-feedback bathing her machine-wrapped spinal column in pain signals. The pain was overwhelming, all-consuming. Kalonice fought to shut herself off to the sensations, but *Paragon of Terra*'s pain was hers now. The reactor at her heart convulsed. Armour plating buckled, atomic bleed-off vented explosively from cycling louvres on the Titan's rear quarters.

Alarms blared. Binaric horns screamed their agonies into the command bridge. Damage controls blew out in overload and the red light of anger became a blood light of horrifying pain. Kalonice struggled to hold on, to not let the loss of her arm break her grip on the Manifold. She heard the machine-spirit of the Titan howling, an animal vocalisation of impossible pain.

'Etana!' cried a voice. A flesh voice. One she knew.

<Carthal?> she gasped.

'It's me,' he said, hauling her to her feet. She looked down at her right arm, expecting to see it as a mangled, molten mess. But, of course, it was undamaged. *Paragon of Terra* had borne the hurt, but she had felt it. Oh, how she had felt it!

<What happened?>

'They hit us,' said Ashur. 'The bastards hit us hard.'

<How?> she said, gradually inloading jagged shards of data. <We still have voids in place.>

'It came from inside the voids,' said Ashur, flinching as the Imperator rocked with the force of impacts.

Kalonice felt the impacts. Searing, stabbing blades plunging into her machine body.

'It's House Devine!' said Ashur.

<House Devine? Clarify.>

'The bastards have betrayed us,' hissed Ashur.

The dragon was screaming. It bled smoke and light from its wounds, and the Stormlord closed for the kill. He rammed his lance into the beast's flanks, hearing the splinter of bones and the hiss of slicing flesh. His other arm was a crackling whip, useless against such a towering beast, but lethal to the tiny, scurrying things that spilled from its legs.

He circled around again, bringing his lance to bear as a storm of spines blasted from the beast's carapace. A knight fell, pierced through by one such barb and he came apart in an explosion of blood and horsemeat.

The towering beast staggered. Their sudden attack had caught it off guard and almost brought it to its knees. But he had not thought to humble it with one strike. Already it was reacting to them, but the Stormlord had not earned himself that name without good reason.

He wheeled around the crashing footfall of the beast. The thunderous impact shook the ground for kilometres in all directions. His horse reared in panic, but he quelled it with the force of his will.

His knights circled back and forth, closing in time and again to deliver thrusts of their lances and stabbing cuts from their reapers. They were hurting it, but it was too big to be brought down by such wounds.

He looked up and saw the beast's wounded heart, a pulsing shimmer of light where the source of its power lay. Thick scales of draconic armour protected its heart from a frontal attack, but from behind...

From behind it was vulnerable. Even more so now. The Stormlord's first thrust had hurt the beast and exposed its greatest weakness.

'Warriors of Molech!' *shouted the Stormlord.* 'No one lance can pierce this beast's armour. We must be as one in our ardour, as one in our thrust into its heart.'

A breath of fire incinerated another of his vajras. If the killing blow was not struck soon, the beast would overwhelm them. It was already turning its wounded heart away.

'Your lances!' *screamed the Stormlord.* 'Unite them with mine!'

His knights formed up around him as they rode with all possible speed to chase the dragon's wounded heart. It bled light and steam, the exhalations of a monster the world needed slain.

The Stormlord laughed as he felt the strength of his knights fill him. Their lance arms were now his. What he stabbed, they stabbed. What he killed, they would kill.

The leavings of the beast still streamed from its gigantic legs. Ants and bacterium shed from a desperate creature that knew its ending was at hand, but still clung to life. Hundreds of them, thousands perhaps. The vajras fought and killed them with their battle blades alone, for their lance arms were now his to command.

His armour shuddered with impacts, his shield arm was just as strong as his lance arm. He felt the heat of the conjoined lances in his fingers, the potency of a weapon on the brink of release.

The dragon knew what he was doing.

It knew he had the power to kill it.

He was too fast for it, the fleetness of his steed more than a match for its cumbersome power. No matter how fast it tried to turn, he would be quicker. It spat a breath of fire to the ground, incinerating a host of its own defenders in its desperation. The Stormlord felt one of his vajras die, and cried out as he felt the righteous fury of the knight fill him.

The spirits of the dead flowed into him, filling his skull with their
death screams. Any other man would have been driven mad by now,
but he was the Stormlord. He was the hero, the saviour of Molech and
he would end this beast.
And then he saw it exposed, the beast's one weakness.
The Stormlord thrust his lance deep into the exposed heart of his prey.
And where he stabbed, so too did his warriors.

WHAT REMAINED OF the XIII Legion forces followed pre-prepared
evacuation routes down the Untar Mesas. Three Rhinos with little
of the cobalt-blue of Ultramar left on their structure after the
devastating barrages of plasma fire.

Barely a handful had survived the slaughter. The Sons of Horus
had the left flank, and were pouring in heavy armour. Army units
of artillery were racing to occupy the high ground and more
Interfector engines were pushing to complete the flank's collapse.

The slate before Arcadon Kyro completed its auspex sweep, but
came up empty. No Ultramarines armour locators that weren't
already aboard the withdrawing Rhinos.

'Are there any more?' asked Castor Alcade, and the desperate
hope Kyro heard was a whip to an already bloodied back.

'No, sir,' he replied, his voice strained and hoarse. A breath of
superheated air had scalded the inside of his lungs. If he survived
this battle, they'd need replacing. 'This is it.'

'Three damn squads!' hissed Alcade, slamming a fist against the
buckled interior of the Rhino. 'How can that be all that's left?'

'We were hit by Titans,' said Kyro. 'We're Thirteenth Legion, but
even we can't soak up that kind of firepower.'

'Keep looking,' insisted Alcade.

'If anyone else made it out, I'd know by now,' said Kyro.

'Keep looking, damn you. I want more of my men found.'

'Sir, there's no one left,' said Kyro. 'It's just us.'

Alcade sagged and Kyro hated that he had to be the bearer of yet another turn of fate that saw his legate further humiliated.

He'd lost his helmet in the fighting, and his armour was blackened all over where a backwash of plasma had caught him. He'd suffered burns to most of his exposed flesh, and could feel the puckering tightness of wounds that would never heal.

Hot winds rammed into the Rhino through a gaping wound in the glacis. Virtually the entire frontal section had been sheared off in an explosion, leaving the driver's compartment exposed. Instead of seeing the battlefield through external pict-feeds or a slender vision block, Kyro had a gaping hole large enough for two legionaries to climb through abreast of one another.

'Any word from Salicar?' asked Alcade. 'We should link with the Blood Angels, pool our resources.'

Kyro didn't answer, his attention snared by the hideous sight far across the battlefield. Even the intervening smoke of battle couldn't obscure the horror of what he was seeing.

'What in Guilliman's name is going on over there?' said Alcade.

Kyro shook his head. What it looked like was impossible.

The Knights of House Devine were attacking *Paragon of Terra*. Something had already wounded it. One arm was missing, and it staggered with shrieking feedback agonies. It bled corrosive fogs and fire. It had been hurt badly.

The Knights' battle cannon punched craters in its legs. Their reapers were cutting down the skitarii and Army troops stationed in its leg bastions by the hundred. They darted in to fire thermal lances into its upper sections, peeling back its rear armour like foil paper.

'What do they think they're doing?' demanded Alcade.

'They're traitors,' hissed Kyro, unwilling to believe it, despite the evidence of his own eyes. 'Raeven Devine has been with Horus this whole time!'

'Then his life is mine,' said Alcade.

Kyro ignored the legate's bombasts, and fixed his attention on the lead Knight. A red gold machine with a golden banner streaming from its carapace and a crackling energy lash whipping at its side. He knew it as *Banelash*.

It skidded to a halt behind the Imperator and braced its legs.

'They can't hurt it, can they?' said Alcade. 'They're too small, surely. An Imperator's far too big to–'

Raeven Devine's Knight unleashed a stream of white-hot fire from his thermal lance. And for a fleeting second, Arcadon Kyro believed his legate might be correct.

Then that hope was dashed as every Knight of House Devine combined their lance fire into one incandescent beam of killing light. Combined to hideous effect, the lance fire punched through the weakened armour of *Paragon of Terra*.

Kyro's senses were enhanced. He saw in spectra beyond those of unaugmented mortals, and knew immediately that the Imperator was doomed. He read the breaching of the vast reactor at the heart of *Paragon of Terra* as clear as the slate before him. Soaring temperature increases, coupled with spewing gouts of radioactive fire throughout the Titan's superstructure told a cascading tale of the Imperator's death.

The Knights knew it too and were already fleeing from their murder. *Banelash* led the Knights of House Devine towards the rear of the Imperial Army, sprinting for all they were worth.

Paragon of Terra stood unmoving, and Kyro wept to see so magnificent an icon of mankind's mastery of technology brought low.

'Come on, come on,' he hissed, willing the Mechanicum adepts and their servitors to vent the reactor, to eject what they could and save the rest, even though he already knew it was too late.

The thermal auspex blew out in a haze of sparks.

Kyro turned away and his auto-senses dimmed in response.

'Don't look at it,' he warned.

CASTOR ALCADE WAS more or less correct when he surmised that the Knights were far too insignificant to do more than inconvenience an Imperator. Their uncannily concentrated fire had caused a cascading series of reactor breaches within the engineering decks, but even that damage could have been contained.

As the adepts aboard *Paragon of Terra* initiated damage aversion protocols to avert a catastrophic reactor breach they were betrayed from within as well as without. Many of the Sacristans they had been forced to employ within the reactor spaces were those belonging to the Knight Households.

And by some considerable margin, the majority of these men had come from House Devine.

Quiet sabotage of venting systems, disabling of the coolant mechanisms and, in the end, the brutal murder of senior adepts, made an apocalyptic reactor breach inevitable.

The reactor empowering a Titan was a caged star.

Not a tamed one, never that.

And the reactor at the heart of an Imperator was orders of magnitude greater than all others.

The breach vaporised the entirety of *Paragon of Terra* in the blink of an eye and a seething eruption of plasma blew out in a cloud of expanding white heat.

The flash blinded all who looked upon it, burning the eyes from their skulls. Everything within a fifteen hundred metre radius of the Imperator simply vanished, incinerated to ash or reduced to molten metal in the blink of an eye.

Nightmarish temperatures and pressures at the point of detonation turned the earth to glass and blasted hot gaseous residue from the centre of the explosion at ferocious velocities. Contained within a dense hydrodynamic front, the explosion was a hammering piston compressing the surrounding air and smashing apart everything it struck. A hemispherically expanding blast wave raced after the roaring plasmic fireball, but quickly eclipsed its blazing fury.

The overpressure at ground zero was enormous, gouging a crater deep into the surface of Molech and hurling even the largest of war machines through the air like grains of wheat blown from a farmer's palm.

In the first instant of detonation, the death toll on both sides was in the tens of thousands. It rose exponentially in the following seconds. Mere mortals within four kilometres of the explosion were killed almost instantly, pulped by the overpressure as it rolled outwards.

Beyond that, those soldiers in cover or within reinforced blockhouses survived a few seconds longer until thunderous blast waves hammered down. Every strongpoint and trench system collapsed, and only the very fortunate or heavily armoured survived this stage of the explosion.

Towards the flanks, the seismic force swatted soldiers to the ground and halted the fighting as the enormity of what had just happened hit home.

A smoke-hazed mushroom cloud of plasma bled into the sky, reaching up to a height of thirteen kilometres and surrounded by ever-expanding coronas of blue-hot fire. Searing winds roared across the agri-plains north of Lupercalia, searing them of vegetation and life.

Those that survived would have plasma burns to rival any mark earned on other worlds torn apart by war. The centre of the Imperial line was gone, but thousands of soldiers and armoured vehicles remained to fight.

The destruction of *Paragon of Terra* was only the beginning of the end for Molech.

To the north and south, just beyond the farthest extent of the blast wave, dust clouds hazed the horizon as fresh forces were drawn to the vortex of battle.

Castor Alcade gripped tight to the battered flank of his Rhino, disbelief warring with horror at the sight of the Imperator's destruction. The field of battle was in disarray, men and women crawling from the wreckage and trying to make sense of what had just happened.

Virtually the entire muster of Imperial war engines had fought in the shadow of *Paragon of Terra*, and were little more than smouldering wrecks, barely enough of them remaining to identify which engine was which.

'It's over,' said Didacus Theron, stepping down from his Rhino.

'No,' said Alcade, pointing to where scattered command sections struggled to impose a semblance of order on what was left of their forces. 'We march for Molech.'

'But we don't have to *die* for it,' said Theron.

'Hold your damn tongue,' said Kyro.

'And remember your place,' snapped Theron, coming over to stand beside Alcade. 'Legate, we don't have to die here, not when Ultramar is at war and the Avenging Son needs us at his side.'

Alcade said nothing, for once in his life at a loss of what to do. Theoretical was everything, but what was the theoretical when every practical ended in death?

Amid the raging fire-swept wasteland below, Alcade saw the enemy had not been spared the horror of the explosion either. Their numbers were just as devastated. Only the enemy Titans had survived the blast intact, though even they had suffered heinous damage.

They stalked as shadows through the wall of dust and smoke thrown up by the explosion. Giant killers with nothing to oppose them. Even if the Imperial commanders below could rally their troops, what weapon did they have remaining that could fight traitor war engines?

'We need to go back to Lupercalia,' said Theron.

'And then what?' demanded Kyro.

'We leave Molech,' said Theron.

'How? We have no ship.'

'Then we take one from the enemy by force,' said Theron. 'We find an isolated vessel and storm it. Then we blast out-system and get back to the Five Hundred Worlds.'

'You already censured a dozen legionaries that dared to voice that sentiment, Theron,' said Kyro. 'I see a few red helmets among our pitiful survivors.'

'That was before the war was ended at a single stroke,' countered Theron, turning his attention back to Alcade. 'Sir, we can't stay here. Dying on Molech will achieve nothing. There's no practical to it. We need to go home and fight in a battle we can actually win.'

'We have a duty to Molech, Theron,' said Kyro. 'We're oathed to its defence, bound by the word of the Emperor.'

Castor Alcade let his subordinate's words wash over him, knowing both were right, and both dead wrong. He rubbed a hand over his face, wiping away the grit and blood of battle. He blinked at yet another black mark against his name, another failure to add to the tally of near-misses and also-rans.

'Sir, what are your orders?' asked Kyro.

Alcade turned and put one foot up on the running board of the scorched Rhino, sparing a last look at the hell unleashed below. On the horizon were the unmistakable dust clouds of advancing armour. Lots of armour.

'Get us to Lupercalia,' said Castor Alcade.

'Sir–' began Kyro, but Alcade held up his hand.

'That is my order,' said Alcade. 'It's to Lupercalia.'

TYANA KOURION CRAWLED from the wreckage of her Stormhammer, half blinded and burned. Her dress greens were black with oil and stiff with blood pulsing steadily from her stomach. Some ribs were broken, and she doubted her left leg would ever bear her weight again. Her right hand was a fused mess of blackened stumps. It didn't hurt yet. It would hurt later, assuming she lived long enough for there to be a later.

The superheavy lay on its side, one half black and folded in on itself like a plastek model left too close to the fire. The rubber of its joints and cupolas dribbled like wax and she saw the skeletal remains of her crew that had been flung from the explosion.

She didn't know where they were.

Her ears were ringing with detonation and concussion. Sticky fluid leaked from each one. She could hear, but everything was muted and subdued, as though filtered through water. Dust gritted her eyes, but she saw flashes of the nightmare through lifting clouds of smoke, as though the rogue thermals knew enough not to haunt her with too many scenes of horror in too short a time.

She heard howls of wounded soldiers. Ammunition cooking off. Fuel tanks ablaze and thudding footfalls that could only be enemy war engines on the hunt. Bloodstained soldiers sometimes wandered through her blurred field of vision. Men and women with missing limbs and shattered, glazed looks on their faces. Some turned at the sight of her, but if they recognised their commanding officer, they gave no sign.

Her army was gone. Destroyed in a heartbeat of Devine treachery.

She'd heard the last snatches of vox-intercept from *Paragon of Terra*, but hadn't understood them until she'd reversed the

Stormhammer to face the Imperator. She'd only just turned away from the pict-slate when the explosion came.

How long ago had that been? Not long surely.

Her tank was nowhere near where it had been dug in, swatted hundreds of metres by the force of the blast. She should be dead, and didn't like to think what horrendous forces had been exerted on the Stormhammer's hull. The impact of landing had crushed pretty much everyone in her tank but her.

Right about now, it felt like she'd gotten the raw deal.

Kourion propped herself up against the underside of the Stormhammer. Blood pooled in her lap. She knew a mortal wound when she saw one. She fumbled for her pistol with her left hand. She'd never bothered to procure a fancy sidearm, and had no family heirlooms like some of the more stuck up regimental commanders. This was just a standard, Mars-pattern laspistol. Full charge, textured grip and iron sights. Functional, but without embellishment.

Just like her.

It would have to do. It was the only weapon she had left, and she'd read somewhere that it was good for a soldier to die holding a weapon.

A shadow moved in front of her. Something with a living being's bulk and fluidity. Something that shouldn't be here. A huge monster covered in grey-furred scales lumbered past her, its arms and shoulders corded with inhuman musculature.

She struggled to remember the local name for the beast.

Mallahgra. Yes, that was it.

What the hell was a mallahgra doing this far north? Weren't they all confined to the mountains and jungles? Then she saw it wasn't alone. Dozens of identical beasts rampaged through the bloodied survivors of her army, mauling and feasting with abandon. Their speed was prodigious and they swept injured soldiers with clawed arms and tore them apart before feeding them into their meat-grinder mouths.

Giant feline predators the size of cavalry mounts bounded across the battlefield. Uniformed bodies hung limp in their jaws. Packs fought for spoils of flesh as though starved. Flocks of loping bird-like creatures with long necks stampeded over the battlefield. Their snapping jaws snatched up fleeing soldiers and bit them in half. Only a few hours ago, this had been Kourion's grand army. The noise of the beasts receded, replaced with the rumble of engines and the tramp of heavy, booted feet.

Shapes moved in the smoke and dust, humanoid, but bulkier and taller than even the abhuman *migou*. Armoured in filthy plates of ivory, they ploughed through the fog as though born to it, led by a giant in rags and plate who bore a towering reaper blade.

And marching towards him, with arms open, was a warrior of equal stature, shrouded in shadows, but upon whose breast burned an amber eye. He hadn't even deigned to draw the great maul slung across his shoulders.

Words passed between the giants, words of a battle fought and a world conquered. Blood poured out of Kourion, and she fought to hear what the giants said, knowing now who spoke. She should despise these traitors, these godlike beings who had slaughtered her army, but hated that she felt only awe.

Her vision began to fade.

Spots of grey grew in her peripheral vision.

The Warmaster took Mortarion's hand in the old way, wrist to wrist. A way that in an earlier epoch had been born of mistrust, but which now stood as the grip of honourable warriors.

'Let your plans be dark and impenetrable as night, brother,' said Mortarion, 'and when you move, fall like a thunderbolt.'

Horus looked around him at the devastation, the dead bodies, the ruined weapons of war and the bellowing monsters. He grinned.

'In war, they will kill some of us,' said Horus. 'But we shall destroy all of them.'

The last thing Tyana Kourion saw was the two primarchs coming together in a clatter of plate, embracing as dearest brothers.

Embracing in victory.

TWENTY-ONE

Hope to die
The man next to you
Legacy of Cortez

THE STREETS OF Lupercalia were crowded with people flocking towards the transit platforms. Alivia watched them through the vision blocks of the Galenus as it rumbled towards the upper reaches of the valley. Men, women and children were carrying everything they could on their backs or in overloaded groundcars.

Near the top of the valley she saw vapour trails of packed shuttles, lighters and supply barges struggling to get airborne.

'What do you see?' asked Jeph from farther back in the Galenus.

'I see a lot of frightened faces,' she answered.

Alivia knew they were right to be frightened.

None stood better than a one in hundred chance of getting off-world. Yet for all the fear she saw in the crowds pushing uphill, they still allowed the Galenus through. Some deep-rooted respect for the symbol of the Medicae made them get out of the way, and Alivia hated the fact that she considered her need greater than theirs.

After all, who was she to judge who should get off Molech and who should remain behind? And for the briefest moment she resented the one who had put her here and charged her with keeping watch over his secret.

She glanced down the length of the medicae vehicle, where Jeph, Vivyen and Miska sat with Noama Calver and Kjell. Five people she needed to get off-world. Five people whose escape would deny five others a chance of life. It was a trade off Alivia was more than willing to make.

But that didn't make it sit any easier in her heart.

The vox-caster crackled, repeating the same message it had been transmitting for the last two hours. The speaker was concise, direct and eloquent in the way only career military men could be.

She'd suspected a trap, of course. False hope dangled for the sake of spite or some other malicious reason, but as she listened to the message, she'd heard the gloss of unvarnished truth.

There was a way off Molech.

An Imperial ship had survived the void war and found refuge in the asteroid belt. Repaired and rearmed, its captain had brought his ship back in an act of supreme courage.

Molech's Enlightenment stood ready to evacuate refugees and survivors of the Warmaster's invasion. The window of opportunity was narrow and shortening by the minute. Enemy ships would even now be lighting their reactors to break orbit and intercept it.

If *Molech's Enlightenment* didn't get away soon, it never would.

'Coming up on the Windward Platforms,' said Anson from the driver's compartment. Alivia heard the anxiety in his voice. He wanted nothing more than to halt the Galenus and go get his girl, but Alivia didn't have time to indulge him.

The Warmaster's army would be here soon and she was already risking far too much by coming here first. But mission be damned, she wasn't going to let her children die on Molech.

She smiled. *Her children.*

'Don't worry, Anson,' said Alivia, clouding his anxieties and imparting a sense of wellbeing to him. 'I'm sure Fiaa's waiting for you here. She wouldn't leave without you.'

'No, she wouldn't,' said Anson, sounding relieved.

She justified the lie by telling herself it would keep him alive.

The Galenus rumbled to a halt and Alivia hauled open the side door of the vehicle. The smell of the city hit her first, warm spices and metallic smoke coming down from the fires burning beneath Mount Torger.

That and the smell of the thousands of shouting people mobbed before the gates to the landing platforms. The mood was ugly and ranked units of Dawn Guard were doing their best to keep a riot at bay. The mix of emotions was potent. Alivia did her best to shut them out, but there was only so much she could do.

She stifled a sob and leaned back into the Galenus.

'Jeph, bring the girls,' she said. 'Noama, Kjell, time for you to get out too.'

She banged the driver's door with her palm.

'Anson, get out,' she said. 'I need you too.'

Jeph clambered out of the Galenus, his mouth dropping open in wonder at the scale of the city around him. Noama Calver and Kjell helped the girls down and kept them close as the press of nearby bodies closed in.

'What about us?' asked one of the wounded soldiers who'd hitched a ride with them back to Lupercalia.

'You all stay put,' she said, adding an emphatic push to her words. 'I'm going to need you all. You, what's your name?'

'Valance. Corporal Arcadii Volunteers.'

'Ever driven a Galenus before?'

'No, ma'am, but I put some time in on a Trojan,' said Valance. 'Won't be that much different.'

'Good, get up front and keep the engine running. When I'm

done here, we're going to have to move fast to get to the Sanctuary. Are we clear?'

The man nodded and went forward into the driver's compartment.

Alivia turned to the others and said, 'Hold hands, and don't let go for anything. Not for *anything*, you understand?'

They nodded, and she felt their fear. They linked hands and Alivia held hers out. Vivyen took one hand, Miska the other, and with the adults trailing behind her in a narrow V, she pushed into the crowd.

The gates to the landing fields were perhaps a hundred metres away, and with every roar of struggling engines lifting off the mood of the crowd was souring further. She didn't know what criteria the Dawn Guard were using for deciding who got through and who didn't, but she guessed that most of the people here wouldn't meet them.

Hostile stares and curses met her as she pushed forward, but she turned them all aside. The effort was draining. She'd never found this sort of thing as easy as John seemed to. Her talents lay towards empathic, less overt, means of manipulation. It took real effort and each calming touch took more out of her than the last.

But it was working, the crowds were moving aside for her.

She had her Ferlach serpenta loaded and tucked in the inside pocket of her coat should things get *really* ugly. She didn't want to think what might happen to the girls if things got that bad.

Angry voices came from the gates. Querulous demands, pleading entreaties and desperate attempts at persuasion. Most were falling on deaf ears, but the occasional clang and clatter of a postern told her that at least some were getting through.

Alivia pushed her way to the front. A man in a richly embroidered frock coat turned to berate her, but stepped aside with a puzzled expression.

'No, after you, miss,' he said.

Alivia nodded and turned her attention to the gate guards. She'd have to work fast. The man beside her might be accommodating enough to let her past, but the people behind him wouldn't be so understanding.

The guard through the gate had a slung rifle and held out a data-slate and stylus. A list of approved personnel, quotas? It didn't matter, it was her passport into the landing fields.

'We need to get through,' said Alivia, using a blunter form of persuasion than she would normally employ. 'We're on the list.'

'Name?'

'Alivia Sureka,' she said, turning to push the others to the front and giving the guard their names. His face furrowed as his eyes scanned the slate. Alivia struggled to alter the perceptual centres of his brain. He was Munitorum. Unimaginative. A man born to live his life by lists.

'Look, there,' she said, reaching through the gate to put her hand on his wrist. 'We're on that list.'

The man shook his head, but Alivia conjured the image of her family's names and those of Kjell and Noama into his mind.

'I'm not seeing your... ah, wait, here they are,' he said, nodding to the squad of soldiers at the gate controls. 'Five coming in.'

The gate was a turnstile affair, unlocked to allow the requisite number of people through. The kind of gate that couldn't easily be stormed once it was open.

Kjell and Anson went first, only too happy at this unexpected chance to get off-world. Noama went to follow them, but Alivia pulled her into a tight embrace before she went through.

'Look after them for me,' whispered Alivia.

Noama nodded and said, 'I would have done anyway. You don't need to do whatever it is you've done to the guard to me.'

'Sorry,' said Alivia with a flush of guilt. 'I know you will.'

'Take care,' said Noama. 'And whatever it is you're going to do, be quick about it. These girls need you.'

Alivia nodded as Jeph steered the girls towards the gate. She put her arms around him and said, 'Be safe, and take care of our beautiful girls.'

He smiled. Then the import of her words hit him.

'Wait, what? You're staying?'

'Yeah,' she said. 'I have to.'

'You're not coming with us?' said Vivyen, her eyes brimming with tears. Alivia knelt beside the girl and took her in her arms.

'There's something I still need to do here,' she said.

Miska put her arms around her. 'Come with us, Liv. Please.'

Alivia hugged them tightly and just for a moment she considered just going through the gate. Getting on a shuttle and heading up to *Molech's Enlightenment*. Who would blame her? What could she do against the might of an entire army?

The moment passed, but the thought of never seeing the girls again was a cold knife in her heart. Tears ran down her face as she held Vivyen and Miska tight.

'I'm sorry, but I can't come with you.'

'Why not?' sobbed Vivyen. 'Please, don't leave us.'

'You've got your father,' said Alivia. 'And Noama and Kjell will look after you. I've got something I need to do here, so I can't leave. Not yet. I made a promise a long time ago, and I can't break it. As much as I want to.'

'Come with us,' said Miska. 'Please, I love you and I don't want you to die.'

'I'm not going to die,' said Alivia. 'And once I get done I'll come and join you.'

'You promise?' said Vivyen.

'Hope to die,' said Alivia, knowing she'd never make good on that promise. She'd broken a lot of promises over the years, but this one hurt worst of all.

She eased the girls' fears with a gentle push.

'Listen, you've got to go now. There's a shuttle that's going to take you to a starship, and that's going to be the biggest adventure you've ever had. And once I get done here, I'll see you on board. We'll share the adventure together, yeah?'

They nodded, and the belief she saw in their faces almost broke her heart. Alivia wanted nothing more than to get on that shuttle with them, to turn her back on Molech forever, but that earlier promise had a stronger hold on her.

She reached into her coat and pulled out the battered storybook. It had been with her for longer than she could remember, but it wouldn't do any good where she was going. She didn't like the thought of the book ending its days lost forever beneath the surface of Molech and pressed it into Vivyen's hands.

She closed the girl's fingers around the book's spine.

'I want you to look after this for me, Viv,' said Alivia. 'It's a very special book, and the stories in it will keep you from getting scared.'

Vivyen nodded and clutched the book to her chest.

'Is everything going to be okay?' asked Miska.

'Yeah,' said Alivia through her tears. 'It's going to be okay.'

OLD BREATH SIGHED across his neck, chill and sharp despite the insulation of his armour. Loken moved slowly, trying to fix on the backplate of Ares Voitek's armour. Three of the servo-arms were drawn in tight, a fourth with a passive auspex monitoring the surrounding spaces.

This high in the *Vengeful Spirit*, there were internal security surveyors, and each time Voitek raised a palm, they would stop and Tubal Cayne would develop a workaround. Often these would take them to places worthy of marking, and Bror's futharc symbols became ever more elaborate in their directions.

'What if one of the Sons of Horus sees these?' asked Varren.

'They won't,' said Bror. 'And if they do, so what?'

'Well, won't they just erase them?'

Loken had wondered the same thing, but Bror just shrugged. 'They will or they won't. No use worrying about it.'

Loken heard a sound, like a palm slapping on pipework. He halted and dropped to one knee with a fist in the air.

'What is it?' hissed Nohai.

'Thought I heard something.'

'Severian? Anything ahead?'

The vox chirruped with burbling static. There'd been a lot of that the closer they'd moved to the vessel's prow. Voitek said it was the increased density of machine-spirits, but Loken wasn't so sure, though he couldn't have named what he thought it might be.

'Don't you think I'd have said so?' answered Severian.

'Is that a no?'

'Yes, it's a no. Now shut up and let me work.'

THEY PASSED INTO the forward galleries, taking one of the service tunnels that ran the length of the ship. Following Cayne's plotter towards the prow, Loken realised that this portion of the ship was one he *had* seen before.

Or, more accurately, it *felt* like somewhere he'd visited.

He paused to make sure he wasn't mistaken.

No, this was one of the places, a lonely forgotten pocket within the ship's layered superstructure. Dark now as it had been then, brackish water drizzled from conduits bolted to the roof. The remains of burned down tapers floated in oily puddles.

'Something wrong?' asked Varren.

'I can't say,' replied Loken.

Varren grunted and moved ahead. Loken let Nohai and Tyrfingr pass him. Rubio paused at his side.

'You'll tell me if you start hearing things, yes?'

'Of course,' said Loken.

They moved on, entering, as Loken had known they would, a stagnant, vaulted space of old echoes and drifting flakes of ash. Iron bars framed the interior and numerous empty oil drums lay scattered throughout, spilling grey mulch over the deck.

The pathfinders circled around Severian and Cayne, who knelt in the centre of the space, conferring softly over a map hastily scrawled in the ash.

'Where are we?' asked Nohai. 'This doesn't look like anything worth marking. I thought the plan was to seek out places of importance.'

'This place *is* important,' said Loken. 'More than you know.'

'It's just a hold,' said Rubio, wrinkling his nose. 'It stinks.'

'This is where they first met, isn't it?' asked Qruze.

Loken nodded.

'Where who met?' asked Voitek.

'The Quiet Order,' said Loken.

'The what?'

'A warrior lodge,' said Rubio, circling the chamber. Scaffolding still clung to the walls, ribbing them like steel bones. Discarded dust sheets hung like unpainted banners, as though a host of craftsmen might return at any moment. 'This is where it began, the corruption.'

'No,' said Loken. 'It began long before this place, but here's where it took root.'

'Were you a member?' asked Severian.

'No. You?'

Severian shook his head. 'After my time. What about you, old man?'

Qruze pulled his shoulders back, as though offended by the

notion. 'I most certainly was not. When Erebus brought it to the Legion I didn't know why we needed such a thing. Said so then, and I say so now.'

Loken moved through the space, thinking back to the time he'd attended a meeting with Torgaddon at his side.

'I came here once,' said Loken. 'Not this space exactly, but one just like it.'

'I thought you said you weren't a member,' said Bror.

'I wasn't. Torgaddon brought me here, thinking I might want to become part of the order.'

'So why didn't you?' asked Varren.

'I went along to see what sort of things the order did,' said Loken. 'A warrior of my company had... died. He'd been a member and I wanted to see if the order had anything to do with his death.'

'Did it?'

'Not directly, no, but even after I'd seen that it looked like nothing more than a harmless gathering of warriors, I felt there was something *off* about it. They'd gotten too good at keeping secrets, and I couldn't bring myself to entirely trust any group that shrouded itself in that much secrecy.'

'Good instincts,' said Rubio.

Loken nodded, but before he could answer, Rama Karayan dropped from the scaffolding lining the walls. A Space Marine in full armour was a considerable weight, but he managed to land almost soundlessly.

'Get into cover,' said Karayan. 'Someone approaches.'

THEY CAME IN groups of three or four, mortal men in masks and heavy, hooded robes. Loken watched them assemble around what he'd at first assumed to be a defunct conduit hub. Roped down tarpaulin covered it, but when the first intruders to the chamber cut the ropes and pulled the covering away, Loken saw how wrong he'd been.

This wasn't a lodge space, at least, not any more.

He groped for the word.

Temple. Fane.

An altar lay beneath the tarpaulin, a blocky plinth of dusty, baked ochre clay that looked oddly familiar. It took him a moment to recall where he'd seen stone just like it.

'Davin,' he whispered. 'That altar stone, it came from Davin.'

Severian looked up as he spoke, shaking his head and placing a finger to his lips. The devotees continued to arrive, silently and reverently, until the space was filled with over a hundred bodies.

No words were spoken, as though they were about some solemn business. Some knelt before the altar, while others righted the toppled oil drums and relit the fires with rags, sheafs of paper and vials of viscous oils.

The fuel took hold swiftly and the heat of the flames soon warmed the chamber. Shadows swayed on the walls, cut and sliced by the bodies moving in time to some unheard music.

At last a group of eight appeared, marching a partially naked figure towards the altar. His physique was clearly transhuman, bulked out with muscle and sub-dermal bone sheaths. A long chasuble of purple cloth draped his shoulders and hung to just below his waist.

Severian tapped two fingers against his eyes and then pointed them towards the naked figure with his eyebrows raised.

Loken shook his head. No, he didn't recognise him.

The figure was led to the altar, where he was bound with chains to the deck. The chasuble fell from his shoulders, and only then did Loken see the Ultima tattoo on the legionary's scapula.

The warrior was of the XIII Legion.

Loken looked across the space to where Rubio was hidden. He

couldn't see him, but a barely perceptible movement in the darkness showed that he too had seen the warrior's tattoo.

'Why doesn't he fight?' whispered Loken, and this time Severian answered.

'Drugged maybe? Look at his movements.'

Loken did and saw Severian was most likely correct. The warrior had the slack features of a sleepwalker. His arms were loose at his sides and his head sagged over his chest.

With the Ultramarine bound to the deck, the robed figures began a droning chant of garbled syllables, a collision of unsounds that Loken's auto-senses registered as piercing static like insect bites.

At the height of the chant, another figure entered the chamber, this one just as genhanced as the bound warrior. He too was robed and hooded, but Loken instantly recognised him by his purposeful stride and swaying shoulders.

'Serghar Targost,' he said. 'The lodge master.'

LOKEN'S FINGERS CURLED around the hilt of his chainsword, but Severian reached down and clamped his hand around its pommel. He shook his head.

'He has to die,' said Loken, as Targost scooped a handful of ash from a blazing drum and pressed it against the bound warrior's chest.

'Not now,' said Severian.

'Then when?'

Targost lifted a short bladed sword from beneath his robes, a gladius with a hemispherical pommel. The Sons of Horus did not favour the gladius. Too short and too mechanical. More suited to warriors who fought as one entity.

Its blade glittered dully as though sheened with coal dust, and Targost used it to cut radial grooves in the captive's flesh. The Ultramarine did not cry out, whether due to his own fortitude or an induced fugue state, Loken couldn't tell.

'When?' demanded Loken. Too loud. Heads turned upwards, searching the darkness. They were invisible, but Loken held his breath as the lodge master continued his ritual mutilations.

Severian's eyes blazed with anger, then flicked over to the highest point of the scaffolding across the chamber. Loken could see nothing, just a confluence of girder and roof. A place the flames cast no shadow where they ought to.

'Karayan?'

Severian nodded. 'Let him take the shot.'

It irked Loken that someone not from the XVI Legion would get to kill Targost, but Severian's logic was sound. He released the sword hilt and opened his fingers to show assent.

'Be ready with that blade,' said Severian. 'No one gets out.'

Severian looked up to the shadows and tapped a finger against the centre of his helmet, right between the eye lenses.

He held up three fingers. Two. One.

A muted muzzle flash lit the shadows and Rama Karayan's outline flickered against the roof. Loken paused just long enough to see Targost fall before pushing himself out from hiding.

He dropped seven metres and landed with a booming thud that buckled the deck plate. His sword roared from its sheath as he waded into the cultists. The blade's teeth ripped them up, chewing meat and bone and robes with every slash and downward cut.

Loken raced to the arched entrance through which they'd entered and stood like a mythical sentinel barring a hero's passage onwards. But these were no heroes, these were the scum of humanity, flotsam and jetsam swept up by the promise of easy gain offered by the corrupt powers at work within the Legion.

Unfit for war, all they could do was chant and pray and spill more worthy blood to corrupting alien powers. They came at him in a rush, with curved blades or clubs sourced from debris around the ship's degenerating interior.

He let them come and cut them down without mercy.

The other pathfinders dropped into the midst of the cultists. Varren's chainaxe hacked a bloody path. Voitek's servo-arms lifted men from the deck and pulled them apart like a cruel child with a captive insect. Tyrfingr fought with his bare fists, roaring as though raucously brawling with trusted comrades.

Loken lost count of how many he killed.

Not enough, but eventually there were no more to slay.

He was blooded from head to foot. Through the entirety of his killing fury, he felt the presence of another at his shoulder, like a fencing master guiding his every strike. The sound in his helmet was hoarse, echoing, though he was not out of breath.

He blinked away the seconds the slaughter had taken.

Rubio stood amid a pile of corpses, his fists wreathed in killing fire. Cayne's axe was dripping with gore, and Severian cleaned his combat blade on the robes of a headless corpse. Bror Tyrfingr spat blood not his own and wiped an elbow over his smeared chin.

Qruze and Cayne warily approached Serghar Targost, but Loken ignored the fallen lodge master. Instead, he went to help Ares Voitek and Nohai with the captive Ultramarine. While Voitek's servo-arms cut through the chains binding him to the deck, Nohai knelt beside him, lifting his head and pressing a hand to the side of his neck.

'What have they done to you, my friend?' asked Rubio, tearing off his helmet. The light no longer danced in the crystalline matrix around his head, but the fire in his eyes was banked high.

'You know him?' said Loken, seeing recognition in Rubio's eyes.

'Proximo Tarchon,' said Rubio. 'An officer of the Twenty-Fifth Company. We marched with them on Arrigata, when Erikon Gaius led us.'

Loken recalled that blood-soaked world all too well. He glanced up at Varren and saw he too remembered it. But now was not the time for past regrets.

'How in the Throne's name did he end up here?' asked Loken.

Rubio knelt beside the swaying captive and said, 'How do any of us end up where we are? Chance, bad luck? The Sons of Horus must have taken him in battle.'

'So Ultramarines are letting themselves get captured now, are they?' said Varren, picking the blood from his axe-teeth.

Rubio shot him an angry glare, but didn't waste words with the former World Eater. Instead, he turned to Altan Nohai.

'What have they done to him?'

'I don't know yet,' said Nohai, sliding a data-slug into the threaded sockets cored into Proximo Tarchon's body. 'Powerful drugs most likely, but I'll know more soon. Don't worry, we'll get him back.'

Rubio's fingertip followed the cuts made in Tarchon's flesh, and Loken felt distinctly queasy at their precise nature.

'You recognise these?' asked Loken.

'I have seen similar markings in primitive tribal cultures the Thirteenth Legion were forced to eradicate during the early years of the Crusade,' said Rubio, his fists clenched and his voice betraying the depths of his fury. Cold fire shimmered at his hood, and Loken's breath misted.

'What are they?' he asked.

'Precursors to evocation.'

'What does that mean?'

'It means maleficarum,' said Bror Tyrfingr, jerking a red thumb back towards Targost. 'The dead one was trying to raise a wight of the Underverse and clothe it in this one's flesh.'

'A simplistic way of putting it,' said Rubio, holding up a hand to forestall Bror's rising choler, 'but essentially correct.'

'And this isn't his first time,' growled Bror. 'Look at the cut lines. No hesitation, no mistakes. He's cut them before. On too many other bodies, many other times. Lucky for this one we were here.'

Loken left them to it and returned to where Qruze and Cayne knelt beside the body of Serghar Targost.

The lodge master lay on his back, his hood ripped away by the passage of Karayan's custom shell. What was left of his head was a splintered mass of leaking brain matter and bent metal fasteners. Bone hooks dangled from flaps of skin and skull fragments. One eye was a pulped scrap of exploded tissue, the other a blood-filled orb that wept red tears.

'Too easy an end for you,' said Loken.

'*Samus is here,*' said Targost and sat up.

Qruze fell back on his haunches as the lodge master's fist punched into Cayne's throat, tearing through the gorget seals with his bare hands. The former Iron Warrior didn't have breath to cry out as the ruined, dead thing ripped out the ropy, meat-pipes of his throat.

The blood spray was catastrophic. Life ending.

Cayne fell back, vainly trying to stem the flood as Targost got to his feet. A black flame in the vague outline of a skull filled the ruined space where Targost's head once sat.

'*Samus is the man next to you,*' he said.

SABAEN QUEEN BURNED fiercely, pillars of thick black smoke boiling from the Stormbird's gutted interior and drawn up to the cavern hangar's roof. The other gunships were just as useless. Melta bombs had turned their engine cores to slag and handfuls of kraks and frags smashed every control mechanism in their cockpits to scrap metal.

The thirty Ultramarines who'd survived the slaughter watched their escape from Molech's surface burn to ruin. Their Rhinos idled behind them, engines coughing and retching as they too died.

Arcadon Kyro stood defiantly before the inferno of his own making and planted an Ultima vexil of the XIII Legion next to him, the one thing he had saved from *Sabaen Queen*'s interior after emptying it of weapons and ammunition.

His helmet was mag-locked at his waist and the ribbed arms of his experimental servo-harness were folded at his shoulders.

Tears streaked his ash-smeared features.

'What did you do?' said Castor Alcade in disbelief.

'What I had to,' replied Kyro. 'I did it because you wouldn't.'

Didacus Theron marched towards the unrepentant Techmarine, but Alcade held him back. Bad enough that legionary was fighting legionary, but for Ultramarine to fight Ultramarine? Unthinkable, even in a time when such thoughts were the norm.

'You've killed us all,' said Theron. 'You've dug our graves on this miserable rock.'

'A miserable rock entrusted to us by the Emperor,' Kyro reminded him. 'Or have you forgotten the oath we swore?'

'I have forgotten nothing,' said Theron.

'You've forgotten where the power of your oath comes from.'

'Then remind me.'

'That by making it you ask the Emperor to bear witness to the promises you make with an expectation of being held account-able for how you honour them.'

Theron wrapped his hand around the hilt of his sword. Alcade knew that with but a moment's provocation, he would draw it and strike Kyro down. Theron was Calth born and bred. Rough and ready, but with a nobility of heart that was all that kept him from killing Kyro where he stood.

'My home world is burning,' said Theron. 'But Ultramar can still be saved. This world is lost. What will it achieve if we all die here? How does that serve the Emperor, Kyro? We are His Angels of Death, and this war against Horus has upset the board.'

Theron reached up to the scorched oath paper fluttering at his shoulder guard where a melted seal of wax affixed it to the curved plate. He tore it off and threw it aside.

'An oath to die in vain is no oath at all,' he said. 'Calth needs us and you have kept me from her.'

'Trying times don't negate our duty to keep an oath,' said Kyro. 'They demand it, even more than when it's easy to keep.'

Theron drew his sword, knuckles white.

Alcade took a breath. This had gone on long enough.

'Centurion!'

Theron turned, his face ruddy with anger.

Alcade knew that anger. He felt it too, but with the horror of the massacre in the north behind them, cold practicality reasserted itself.

'Leave him be, Didacus, he's right,' said Alcade, letting out a long, resigned breath. 'An oath is not an oath if it can be set aside when it suits our desires. We swore to defend Molech, and that's what we're going to do.'

'We can still get off-world, legate,' said Theron, his anger undiminished, but bleeding out of him with every word. 'We can seize another orbital craft. Capture a warp-capable ship and fight on. We can still make a difference. Thirty Ultramarines is not a force to be easily dismissed.'

'I have made my decision,' said Alcade. 'The matter is closed. We march for Molech.'

Theron mustered his arguments, but Alcade cut him off before he could argue any more.

'I said the matter is closed.'

For a moment he wondered if Theron might attack him, but decades of devotion to duty crushed any thought of disobedience.

'As you say, legate,' said Theron. 'We march for Molech.'

Alcade waved his warriors towards the piled crates of ammunition and weaponry Kyro had removed from the gunships.

'Gather up all the guns and blades you need,' he said.

He marched to stand before Kyro and said, 'On any other day I'd have you bear the red of censure, but I need every bolter I can muster. Rejoin the ranks, and bring that vexil with you. If we're going to die here, we're going to do it under the Ultima.'

Movement at the mouth of the hangar drew Alcade's attention.

A wide-base Army vehicle lurched into the cavern, and thirty bolters snapped to face it. Automated weapon systems tracked it, but Kyro swiftly issued an override command at the sight of the red caduceus emblazoned on its glacis.

A heavy door rolled back on its side and a slender woman in a bloodstained coat and hard-wearing fatigues several sizes too big for her jumped down. Five men emerged behind her. Army by their bearing. Each was armed, but they were no threat.

'Who the hell are you?' he demanded.

The woman smiled in relief.

'Legate Alcade,' she said. 'My name is Alivia Sureka and I very much need your help.'

TWENTY-TWO

Not Ullanor
This is fear
Hellgate

IN CONTRAST TO Alivia Sureka's arrival, Lupercalia felt deserted when the Warmaster entered the city. Columns of Legiones Astartes came first, marching beneath wolf-headed vexils and tribal runes of Barbarus as the sun dipped towards dusk.

Aximand's company bore bloody trophies taken from the vanquished XIII Legion, while Ezekyle's Justaerin dragged scorched Legio Crucius banners behind them for others to trample.

Tyana Kourion's body was nailed to a Contemptor's sarcophagus.

Smoke-blackened tanks and the striding engines of Vulpa, Interfector, Vulcanum and Mortis came after the infantry, their warhorns braying in triumph.

Those citizens who had not already fled to the surrounding countryside or risked travelling to the upper transit platforms in the hope of securing passage off-world huddled fearfully in their homes. Farther ahead, a last few shuttles blasted skyward.

Suspicious eyes watched the arrival of his army from the cover of parapets and shutters. Behind the curiosity, behind the masochistic need to see their conquerors, Horus recognised bone-deep fear.

'The last time I entered this city, I was parading in glorious triumph with Jaghatai and the Lion,' said Horus. 'I marched at father's right hand, and the people cheered my name.'

Mortarion grunted with grim amusement. 'Aye, not exactly Ullanor, is it?'

Horus turned to address the three members of the Mournival who marched behind him. They were a sorry looking group, scarred and burned by war, but victorious nonetheless. Ezekyle in particular was looking the worse for wear, his eyes downcast and his mien truculent.

'What do you think, my sons?' he asked as they passed beneath the towering arch of the second wall.

'About what?' asked Aximand.

'Why do these people not welcome our arrival?'

'Aside from the fact that we killed their army?' said Kibre.

Horus waved that trifling objection aside.

'They're afraid,' said Aximand.

'Of what, that I'll have them all put to death?'

'Perhaps, but more likely they fear change. Right now, most of these people are wondering what our arrival will mean for them. Will they be enslaved or freed? Richer or poorer? Like all tiny cogs in a great machine, they know that it matters little whose hand is at the crank, only that it turns.'

'Give it time,' said Horus. 'They'll be cheering my name again when I bring them the crown of Terra.'

'A crown is it now?' said Mortarion. 'Being made Warmaster wasn't enough, so now you're going to be king?'

'Have you forgotten already?' said Horus as the citadel's rearing towers and gilded domes came into view.

'Forgotten what?'

'I'm not going to be king, nor even Emperor,' said Horus. 'I'm going to be a god.'

TARGOST, OR THE thing within Targost, reached for Iacton Qruze. The flesh of its face was bubbling like the surface of a muddy swamp. The stench was appalling. Qruze scrambled away on his backside, fumbling for his pistol.

Bror Tyrfingr charged the Samus-thing, but it was like trying to tackle the leg of a Warlord Titan. Samus slapped the Fenrisian away, like a man swatting an irritating fly. Bror landed on a flaming drum and rolled, spilling its contents in a shower of embers.

The creature's jaw cracked wide open and oozing black ichor boiled up from the interior of its skull. Serrated triangular teeth pushed out from the stump of its neck and a host of lashing, vertical tongues emerged, rough and forked. A multitude of glowing eyes formed in the roiling, glutinous mass of its phantom skull.

Its form stretched upwards, diseased roots sprouting from its lower limbs and infesting the deck like oily ropes.

'*I'm Samus...*' it gurgled with mucus-thick breath, and the name struck a dreadful chord in Loken's heart. The air tasted of static and biting on metal. Shadows moved on the wall, independent of the firelight.

Samus, he knew that name. He knew it from a world made compliant a long time ago in another life. He'd heard it over the vox and in the air of Sixty-Three Nineteen. He'd heard it spoken by Xaver Jubal just before he'd opened fire on his brothers.

The Whisperheads.

Loken was there again, in that glistening cave, fighting his fellow legionary as the foundations of his world came apart.

He had a sword in his hand, but he couldn't raise it.

This is fear.

This was what mortals dealt with every day of their lives. Fear of the alien, fear of war, fear of pain, of disease. Fear of failing those who trusted them.

How could anyone live like this?

Loken was paralysed, his limbs leaden at his sides.

Varren charged, burying the smile of his axe in the Samus-thing's belly. Sawing teeth bit deep. It bent over and plucked Varren from the ground, its circular mouth fastening on his shoulder. Blood sprayed and Varren's arm spasmed, releasing the axe grip.

Voitek's arms hacked at its flanks, as Severian sliced through gristle-like fronds whipping from Targost's transforming flesh. A shot from above punched through its wraith skull.

Karayan.

Qruze finally had his pistol out and was pumping shot after shot into the creature's chest. The mass-reactives were swallowed whole without effect.

The Samus-thing laughed and tossed Varren aside. He landed forty metres away beside the altar of Davinite stone. Bror Tyrfingr picked himself up, shouted something to Qruze and Severian. Loken heard Altan Nohai shout something in return, sounding surprised.

Loken's armour registered a sudden drop in temperature.

Then Rubio was there.

The former Codicier threw himself at the Samus-thing, his sword a sliver of flame-wreathed bluesteel. Varren's axe had achieved little, but Rubio's blade sliced deep into the meat of the thing. The fire leapt from his weapon onto Samus, and the remains of Targost's robes went up in flames with a roaring whoosh of ignition.

It screamed, finally hurting.

Loken felt something grip his leg and looked down to see Tubal Cayne's hand scrabbling at his armour.

The other hand was clamped around his own neck. Blood welled between his fingers, pumping enthusiastically from the awful chasm in his throat. He'd ripped his helmet off and his eyes took Loken's in an iron grip. Anger, vindication and something Loken couldn't identify poured out of Tubal Cayne. Flickering reflections of Rubio's white fire shimmered in his widening pupils. The dying warrior tried to speak, but only wet, liquid gurgles emerged.

Loken watched his eyes turn to glass and knew that he was dead.

And the fear that held him rigid vanished.

He'd fought Samus before.

He and Vipus had killed it.

Loken brought his sword up and charged.

RAMA KARAYAN TRACKED the battle below through his bolter's scope. Something was affecting it. The thing his brothers faced wasn't registering. He could see Bror, Macer and the others, but not the thing they fought.

But prey could be hunted by its absences as much as by its leavings.

His hunter's eye had been honed as a youngster in the darkened mine workings of Lycaeus. The lords of the Ravenspire had recognised his gift and developed it. Not invisible enough for the Shadowmasters, but perfect for the silent killers of the Seeker squads.

His auto-senses were linked directly with the scope of his modified bolter, and he took a breath, innately interpolating the locus of his brother's attacks. Peripheral sight picked out the pellucid white flames of Rubio's sword.

He found his centre and drew in a breath.

Held it.

He fired. A spent casing dropped to the scaffold boards.

It bounced, slower than should be possible. A web of frosted lines crazed its surface in a pale web.

Strange shadows moved on the walls. Impossible shadows. They were all around him, like stalking wolves in a twilit winter forest or the dust devils of Deliverance's ash wastes.

Karayan felt grave-cold air and the hard, sharp edge of a blade at his throat.

'Nice rifle,' said a rasping voice. 'I think I'll take it.'

Karayan moved. Not fast enough.

The blade sliced deep, cutting back to bone.

LOKEN'S SWORD TORE through the Samus-thing's scorched belly. Bubbling laughter spilled from its smoking skull. Ash and greasy meat cinders billowed around it. Furnace-red light shone through wounds torn in its charred flesh.

Targost's arms reached for him, stretching and cracking like timbers splitting in a fire. Loken put a bolt-round into its chest and hacked the hand from the arm. Another writhing append-age squirmed into existence at the stump, but it was a twisted, malformed thing.

'It's vulnerable!' cried Rubio. 'Its link to the warp is fraying.'

The pathfinders surrounded the daemon-thing, hacking and shooting it. Even in such desperate straits, each shot was carefully aimed, each strike precisely placed.

'*I know you, Garviel Loken,*' it hissed, looming over Loken. '*I claimed your brother's soul in that mountain cave. He screams in torment still.*'

'Don't listen to it,' shouted Rubio, blocking a whipping append-age of glistening dark flesh. The Librarian's hood blazed with blue white fire.

'*Silence, witcher!*' bellowed the Samus-thing. The force of its words drove Rubio to his knees. It spat a torrent of black fire from its writhing, toothed gullet. Rubio threw up a shimmering wall of witchfire and the flames guttered and died.

Severian closed and slashed his blade into the daemon's back, tearing upwards. Loken hadn't even seen him move. Looping coils of what might once have been guts, but were now mouldering loops of dead meat spilled out.

The beast spun around and clubbed Severian to the deck with unnatural speed. It hurled Voitek and Qruze away with a scream of pure force and slammed Loken to the deck with slithering arms like blistered snakes.

Loken saw the gladius Targost had used to mutilate the Ultramarine prisoner. The ivory Ultima on its pommel glittered in the firelight. Its blade was dark, yet sheened with starlight. He reached for it, but a hand of scabbed knuckles and bruised fingers picked it up first.

'This is mine,' said Proximo Tarchon.

Loken sprang to his feet as the carved warrior of Ultramar threw himself forward. He rolled beneath the Samus-thing's writhing arms and thrust his gladius up into its belly.

The effect was instantaneous and devastating.

Targost's body fell apart, as though every single molecular bond within its flesh was instantly sundered. Its form turned to liquid and collapsed in a stinking pool of rancid matter.

The pathfinders scattered. Severian dragged Cayne's body away from the spreading lake of smoking fluid. Loken lowered his sword and let out a shuddering breath that felt like it had been held within him for decades.

Altan Nohai rushed to Cayne and knelt beside him.

'There's nothing you can do for him,' said Loken.

'He that is dead, take from him the Legion's due,' said Nohai as the reductor portion of his gauntlet slid into place.

Loken registered the muted crack of the gunshot a fraction of a second before the faceplate of Nohai's helmet exploded outwards.

The Apothecary slumped over Cayne's body, a smoking entry wound drilled through the back of his helmet.

Armoured warriors dropped to the deck from the upper reaches of the chamber. Sons of Horus. Two dozen at least, armoured in blackened plate the colour of night. Their helm lenses flickered with dead light, as though cold flames seethed behind them.

Most were armed with bolters. He saw a plasma gun. A melta too.

Loken fought the urge to reach for his own weapons.

'Raise a single weapon and you all die,' said a warrior without a helmet. Loken didn't recognise him, but saw the planed features of what they'd once called a *true son*.

'Noctua? Grael Noctua of the Warlocked?' said Severian.

Loken's head snapped around.

Severian shrugged. 'He was Twenty-Fifth Company, same as me.'

'Severian?' said Noctua, his shock evident. 'When the Warmaster said two faithless cowards had returned with the prodigal son, I had no idea he meant you. And Iacton Qruze? Your name has been a curse ever since you deserted the Legion at the moment of its greatest triumph.'

Qruze flinched at Noctua's words, but he squared his shoulders and said, 'You mean the moment my Legion died.'

Loken had never respected Iacton Qruze more.

The pathfinders reluctantly divested themselves of their weapons as the black-armoured Sons of Horus closed the noose on them. Now that he looked closely, Loken saw their proportions were subtly wrong, asymmetric and out of true, as though the warriors within were not legionaries at all, but things ill-formed and unnatural.

Or that was what they were *becoming*.

'And you, Thirteenth Legion' said Noctua. '*Especially* you.'

Proximo Tarchon slowly laid down his gladius, and Loken saw a depth of calculating hatred in his clear eyes like nothing he'd ever seen before. The blood had hardened to scabs on the ritual cuts, and the smeared ash would mark the scars forever.

'When I hold this again, it will be to put it through your heart,' said the Ultramarines warrior.

Noctua smiled at that, but didn't reply.

'Grael Noctua, you little bastard,' said Severian, setting his blade down. 'Did you know I advised against your advancement three times when your name came up? I always said you were too sly, too eager to please. Not good qualities in a leader.'

'Looks like you were wrong,' said Noctua.

'No,' said Severian. 'I wasn't.'

'I think you were, I'm Mournival now.'

Loken's heart skipped a beat at the mention of the Mournival, that confraternity to which he and Torgaddon had once belonged. A brotherhood as close to the Warmaster as it was possible to be.

'Did someone say Mournival?'

The speaker dropped from the roof spaces, and Loken groaned as he saw the modified bolter he carried. Rama Karayan's weapon. Blood dripped from the breech and muzzle.

'I remember the Mournival,' the warrior said.

Like the others surrounding them, his armour was black and non-reflective. Like Noctua, he went without a helm, and something in his saturnine, cocksure swagger struck him as hideously familiar.

He retrieved Tarchon's gladius from the deck and turned the darkly sheened blade over as though curious at what had been done to it. He shook his head and slid the weapon into an empty shoulder sheath.

'Poor bloody Samus,' he said to Loken with a grin. 'He'd only just earned his return after a warrior as straight up and down as you killed his host flesh on Calth. It's getting to be a thing.'

'Who are you?' said Loken.

'No one remembers me,' said the warrior. He grinned, exposing perfect white teeth. 'I'd be hurt if I wasn't already dead.'

'You're Ger Gerradon,' said Qruze. 'One of Little Horus Aximand's scrappers.'

'The body is his, admittedly,' said Gerradon. 'But he's long gone, Iacton. I'm Tarik reborn, he-who-is-now-Tormaggedon.'

ALIVIA LED THE Ultramarines and her five soldiers ever downwards along a twisting series of switchback stairs beneath the Sanctuary. The walls were glassy and smooth, cut down through the geomantic roots of Mount Torger by the colossal power of the galaxy's most singular mind.

No light shone this deep, and only the Ultramarines suit lights pierced the darkness. It felt like nobody came here precisely because nobody *ever* came here.

'How much deeper is this gate, mamzel?' asked Castor Alcade. The smell of plasmic fire still clung to his armour, and his breath had the hot flavour of burned stone to it.

'It's not far,' she said, though distance would become a somewhat subjective quantity the deeper they went.

'And how is it that you know of it?'

Alivia struggled to think of a way to answer that without sounding like a lunatic.

'I came here a very long time ago,' she said.

'You're being evasive,' said Alcade.

'Yes.'

'So why should I put my trust in you?'

'You already have, legate,' said Alivia, turning and giving him her most winning smile. 'You wouldn't be here if you hadn't.'

She'd told them of what lay beneath the Sanctuary, a gate closed in ages past by the Emperor and which Horus planned to open. She told them that beyond the gate lay a source of monstrously dangerous power, and thankfully that was enough for them.

She'd not relished the prospect of trying to exert her empathic influences over the legionaries of the XIII Legion, but as things turned out there hadn't been any need to apply pressure to the legate's psyche.

It wasn't hard to see why.

She'd offered him a last lifeline to achieve something worthwhile, and he'd seized it with both hands.

'Thirty men facing the might of two Legions sounds grand in the honour rolls,' he'd said after she'd told him what she wanted of him and his men. 'But last stands are just the sorts of theoreticals we've trained our entire lives to avoid.'

'This isn't a fight we'll walk away from either,' she'd warned.

'Better to fight for something than die for nothing.'

He'd said it with such a straight face too. She hadn't the heart to tell him that sentiments like that were what had kept men fighting one another for millennia.

They'd found the citadel filled with refugees. Most had ignored them, but some begged for protection until Didacus Theron fired a warning shot over their heads.

The Sanctuary and its secret levels, the really *interesting* levels that not even the Sacristans or Mechanicum knew about, were beneath the deserted Vault Transcendent. Alivia took every confounding turn through the catacombs and located every hidden door as though she'd walked here only yesterday.

The last time Alivia had climbed these particular steps, her legs were like rubber and fear sweat coated her back like a layer of frost. She'd helped *him* come back to the world; her arm around his waist, his across her shoulder. She'd tried to keep his thoughts – normally so impenetrable – from reaching into her, but he was too powerful, too raw and too damaged from what lay beyond the gate to keep everything inside.

She'd seen things she wished she hadn't. Futures she'd seen in her nightmares ever since or inked in the pages of a forgotten storybook. Abominable things that were now intruding on the waking world, invited in by those who hadn't the faintest clue of what a terrible mistake they were making.

'Do these steps ever bloody end?' asked Theron.

'They do, but it'll seem like they won't,' answered Alivia. 'It's kind of a side effect of being so close to a scar in the space-time fabric of the world. Or part of the gate's defence mechanisms, I forget which. It's amazing how many people just give up, thinking they're getting nowhere.'

'I've been mapping our route,' said a Techmarine called Kyro with a superior tone that suggested he was equal to anything this place could throw at him.

'You haven't,' said Alivia, tapping a finger to the side of her head. 'Trust me.'

Kyro flipped up a portion of his gauntlet and a rotating holographic appeared. A three-dimensional mapping tool. Right away, Kyro frowned in consternation as multiple routes and divergent pathways that didn't exist filled the grainy image.

'Told you,' said Alivia.

'But *do* they ever end?' asked Alcade.

Alivia didn't answer, but stepped out onto a wide hallway that she knew every one of the Ultramarines would swear hadn't been there moments ago. Like everything else here it had a smooth, volcanic quality, but light shone here, glittering within the rock like moonlight on the surface of an ocean.

Wide enough for six legionaries to walk comfortably abreast, the hallway was long and opened into a rough-hewn chamber of chiselled umber brick. The Emperor never told her how this chamber had come to be or how He'd known of it, save that it had been here before geological forces of an earlier epoch raised the mountain above.

Ancient hands had cut the stone bricks here, but Alivia never liked looking too closely at the proportions of the blocks or their subtly *wrong* arrangement. It always left her strangely unsettled and feeling that those hands had not belonged to any species known by the galaxy's current inhabitants.

The Ultramarines spread out, muscle memory and ingrained practical pushing them into a workable defensive pattern. Alivia's human allies, Valance especially, kept close to her like a bodyguard.

'Is that it?' asked Alcade, unable to keep the disappointment from his voice. 'This is the Hellgate you spoke of?'

'That's it,' agreed Alivia with a smirk. 'What did you expect? The Eternity Gate?'

She'd told them something of what lay beyond the gate, but Alivia had to agree it didn't exactly look like the most secure means of keeping something so hideously dangerous out. Irregular chunks of dark stone veined with white formed a tall archway in the darker red of the mountain's foundations.

The space between the arch was mirror-smooth black stone, like a slab of obsidian cut from a perfectly flat lava bed. Nothing within the chamber was reflected in its surface.

'We expected something that looked like it would take more than a rock drill or a demo charge to breach,' said Kyro.

'Trust me,' said Alivia. 'There's nothing you or the Mechanicum could bring that would get that open.'

'So how does Horus plan to open it?'

'He's blood of the Emperor's blood,' she said. 'That'll be enough unless I can seal it.'

'You said the Emperor sealed it,' said Theron.

'No, I said He *closed* it,' said Alivia. 'That's not same thing.'

Alcade looked at her strangely, as though now seeing something of the truth of what she was.

'And how is it you know how to seal it?' he asked.

'He showed me how.'

Kyro tapped the black wall with one of his servo-arms. It made no sound whatsoever. At least in *this* world. 'If what's beyond here is so terrible, why didn't the Emperor seal it Himself?'

'Because He couldn't, not then, maybe not ever,' said Alivia, remembering the gaunt, aged face she'd seen beyond the glamours. He'd been gone no more than a heartbeat to her, but she saw centuries carved into the face she'd watched go into the gate.

'The Emperor couldn't seal it, but you can?' said Kyro. 'You'll forgive me, Mamzel Sureka, if I find that hard to believe.'

'I don't give a damn what you find hard to believe,' snapped Alivia. 'There are things a god can do and things He can't. That's why sometimes they need mortals to do their dirty work. The Emperor left armies to guard against obvious intruders, but He needed someone to keep out the lone madmen, the seekers of dark knowledge or anyone who accidentally stumbled on the truth. Since I've been on Molech, I've killed one hundred and thirteen people who've been drawn here by the whispered poisons that seep from beyond this gate. So don't you dare doubt what I can do!'

She took a calming breath and shrugged off her coat, tucking the loaded Ferlach serpenta into the waistband of her fatigues. She felt foolish for losing her temper, but every emotion was heightened in this place.

'How old are you, Mamzel Sureka?' asked Alcade.

'What's that got to do with anything?' said Alivia, though she knew exactly where he was going with this.

'The Emperor was last on Molech over a century ago,' said Alcade. 'And even with juvenat treatments, you're nowhere near old enough to have been at His side.'

Alivia laughed, a bitter, desperate sound. 'You don't know how old I am, Castor Alcade. And, right now, I wish I didn't either.'

LOKEN FELT AS though every cubic centimetre of air had been crushed from his lungs. He wanted to deny what the thing wearing Gerradon's face had said, but the voice, the posture... *everything*, told him it was true.

When you see me, kill me.

The words he'd heard whispered in the shadows of his quarters on the *Tarnhelm* returned to him. No, that wasn't right. They weren't a memory, it was like he'd heard them again. As if some fragment of what had once been his friend was still speaking to him.

Loken's sword and bolter lay on the ground before him. It would be easy to sweep them up, but could he put a bolt through Gerradon before the others gunned him down? Did that even matter?

He forced down the killing urge.

'Tarik?' he said, the name forced through gritted teeth.

'No,' said Gerradon with an exasperated sigh. 'Weren't you listening? I'm Tormaggedon. I was waiting in the warp when Little Horus cut off Tarik's head and plucked the bright bauble of his soul before any of the warp whelps could feast on it. He screams and begs like a whipped dog, you know. Fulgrim did the same, and he was a primarch. Just imagine how bad it is for Tarik.'

'Don't listen to it, Loken,' warned Rubio. 'Warp spawn feast on the pain their lies cause.'

Grael Noctua kicked the back of Rubio's knee, driving the psyker to the deck. The butt of a boltgun sent him sprawling. Bror Tyrfingr snarled at Noctua, but Severian shook his head.

Loken knew sorrow. He'd grieved at the death of Nero Vipus and had mourned battle-brothers he'd lost along the way. Tarik's death on Isstvan had all but broken him and driven him into an abyss of madness he wasn't sure he'd ever really escaped.

Until now.

He lifted his head and the fists he'd made unclenched.

'No,' he said. 'Tarik would never beg. Even in death he'd be stronger than that. You say he's screaming? I believe you. But he's not screaming in pain, he's screaming at me to kill you.'

'I am the first of the *Luperci*,' said Gerradon. 'The Brothers of the Wolf. And you can't kill me.'

Loken rubbed a hand across his chin and tipped his head back. When he next looked at Ger Gerradon, he was smiling.

'You know, if you'd just let him die, I wouldn't be here,' said Loken, now able to admit out loud to the sights and sounds that had plagued him since the visitation on the edge of the Mare Tranquillitatis.

'I've seen and heard Tarik Torgaddon at every step of this journey,' said Loken. 'He's long dead, but he brought me back to the *Vengeful Spirit*. He brought me back to kill you and set him free.'

Gerradon tossed Karayan's rifle to one of the dead-eyed legionaries and took a step towards Loken with his arms open.

'Then take your best shot,' said Gerradon.

'Stand down,' said Grael Noctua. 'He can't kill you? Well, you can't kill him, either. The Warmaster wants him alive.'

Gerradon grinned and gestured to the transformed warriors in black, those he had called the Luperci.

'Take a good look, Garvi,' said Gerradon. 'You're going to be just like them. I'm going to put a daemon in you.'

TWENTY-THREE

Blood price
Obsidian Way
A god amongst men

'So THIS IS the best defence our father could muster?' said Mortarion as bolter shells punched the walls of glassy rock beside him. The Death Lord snapped off a pair of eye-wateringly bright shots from the *Lantern*.

Aximand didn't see if they hit, but it was safe to assume the XIII Legion were two warriors fewer.

'A few petty cantrips and a handful of legionaries?'

Aximand heard the Death Lord's disdain, decades in the making, but even in the heat of battle, he couldn't let the comment go unremarked.

Not after the blood he had shed.

Not after so many warriors under his command had died.

'That's not all he left,' snapped Aximand as a grenade thrown back along the passageway detonated with a compressed bang. 'He left millions of men and tanks. He left armies the Sons of Horus fought and crushed. What did the Death Guard do? Razed a jungle and massacred a defeated enemy.'

Mortarion regarded Aximand with the scrutiny a man might give an upstart child. His fingers tightened on *Silence*. Those Death-shroud who weren't shooting along the passageway took a step towards Aximand until Mortarion waved them back.

'You might once have been a *true son*, Little Horus,' said Mortarion, his voice a low, rasping growl, 'but look in a mirror. You're no Sejanus any more.'

Aximand leaned out to shoot. A blue helm vanished in a fan of ceramite and blood. 'What has that to do with anything?'

The Death Lord leaned in close, his words for Aximand alone. 'It means that you think you're special? You're nothing. It means that, Mournival or not, I'll end you if you speak that way again.'

'Lupercal would kill you.'

'My brother would be displeased at your death, but he would forgive me. You'd still be dead though.'

Horus appeared at Aximand's side with a feral grin of anticipation making him seem younger and more vital than ever. He leaned out into the passageway and unleashed a roaring blaze of fire from his gauntlet-mounted bolters.

'There will be others,' said Horus ducking back into cover as an interlocking pair of bipod-mounted heavy bolters raked the passageway. 'Father wouldn't rely on mortals to keep his secret. He'll have a failsafe of some kind.'

'All the more reason for you to let me send Grulgor up there,' said Mortarion over the hammering impacts and detonations of explosive munitions. 'He'll end this quickly.'

Horus shook his head. 'No, we do this my way. So close to the gate, Grulgor could kill us all.'

Grulgor?

Aximand knew the name, he'd read it in casualty lists. He looked back to where the Justaerin were locking their boarding shields into position. Aximand was not surprised to see Abaddon and

Kibre holding flanking positions. Their shields were splashed with blood in bladed radial patterns that were not accidental.

'Ready, Ezekyle?' asked Horus of his First Captain.

Abaddon slammed his shield on the floor and slotted his combi-bolter into the firing notch by way of answer.

'All yours, brother,' said Horus, moving back and taking up position at the head of the Justaerin's formation. One of the Terminators locked a shield onto Lupercal's armoured forearm. Against his mighty frame it looked woefully inadequate protection.

Mortarion waved forward two warriors armed with rotary missile launchers.

Horus nodded and a hammering salvo of bolter shells filled the passageway. The two Death Guard stepped forward and ripped out a volley of missiles. Warheads streaked down the passageway. Aximand heard the metallic cough detonations. Shroud bombs and frags.

One warrior dropped to his knees with the back of his helmet blown out. The other staggered with most of his ribcage detonated from the inside by penetrating mass-reactives.

'Lupercal!' shouted Abaddon as Horus led the Justaerin forward.

Shields braced, marching in relentless lockstep. Boots like mechanised pistons as they pushed into the passage. Heads down, shields out, they filled its width. Gunfire pummelled them.

Not enough to stop them.

Nowhere near enough to stop them.

ALIVIA TRACED THE patterns she'd memorised all those years ago over the surface of the gate. Each movement sent a rippling shiver of painful disgust through her.

She knew what lay beyond the gate better than most.

She knew how it hungered for what lay on this side.

A closed gate was better than no gate, and the howling, mad, devouring *things* on the other side weren't about to give up even this tenuous hold without a fight.

Alivia's empathic gift was now a curse. This close to the gate, every hateful thought she'd ever had was magnified. She relived the pain of every lover who'd betrayed her, every attacker who'd wounded her and every person she'd abandoned.

And not just hers. Valance and his four men knelt beside her with their rifles shouldered. They were soldiers, and had a lot of bad memories. All of them crowded her thoughts. Tears streamed down her face and wracking sobs spasmed in her chest.

Not for the first time, she cursed in a dead language that she had been left to do this. She knew that *he* couldn't do it. After what he had taken from the realm beyond, it would be suicide for him to draw so near to those whose power he'd stolen.

Every mantra she whispered was faltering, every line she drew in lunar caustic was fading before she could empower it. She couldn't focus. All the years she'd spent waiting in readiness for this moment and she couldn't bloody concentrate.

Hardly surprising, really.

The sound of battle was incredible. Bolters and other, heavier weapons were filling the passageway with explosive rounds, but she knew it wouldn't be enough to stop the Warmaster.

She had known that Horus would find this place eventually, but he had found it quicker than she'd hoped. She'd never agreed with the decision to obscure the existence and nature of the warp, but if Alivia's long life had taught her anything, it was that finger-pointing after the fact was beyond futile.

Four Ultramarines stood with her and her bodyguards, a living shieldwall of flesh and ceramite. This was the only place mortals could survive – being without armour in the midst of a Legion firefight was a sure-fire way to end up dead.

Castor Alcade oathed the warriors protecting her little band to fight as though the Emperor Himself stood behind them.

These men would die for her.

They weren't the first to do so, but she dearly hoped they'd be the last.

An explosion shook the chamber and she coughed on the acrid propellant fumes. She could taste aerosolised blood misting the air. Not good. Especially with the aggression flaring from every man in the chamber. Ultramarines were all about their *practical*, but they had sacrificed too much to fight clinically with the cause of their hurt so close.

Alivia breathed deeply, picturing Vivyen and Miska. Even Jeph, with his sad, hangdog eyes and absurd belief that he had to protect her. She missed them, and hoped *Molech's Enlightenment* was already accelerating towards the system's Mandeville point.

No, that wasn't helping. She needed something more, something cherished. She remembered when the auspex of a trans-loader from Ophir had failed and it ran into a submerged mine in Larsa's harbour. She hadn't been on the ship, but had seen it go down with all hands. Only when she returned home did she find out that Vivyen and Miska thought she'd been aboard, and they'd wept for hours believing that she was dead.

She remembered her arms wrapped around them both when they finally succumbed to sleep. Their warm breath and the smell of their hair reminded Alivia of a time long gone, of a life now ended, when she'd been blissfully ignorant of her true nature and the doom approaching Arcadia.

She had been happy then, and she used that to push down the violent thoughts intruding on her psyche. Alivia pictured the symbols she'd been shown: precise arrangements of intersecting lines that couldn't possibly intersect; curves that broke every established rule of calculus; the geometry of the insane.

She spoke the words that weren't words, pouring every inch of her desire to see this gate sealed into what she was doing. Her hands described the motions she pictured, moving across the surface of the smooth black barrier.

It looked and felt like a solid barrier, but it wasn't.

It was a scab over a hole that should never have been torn open, an impossible object that existed in an infinite number of possible existences. It was neither real nor unreal.

A doorway to hell Alivia now attempted to unmake.

Her surroundings faded to grey, a monochrome facsimile of the world where she was the only splash of colour. She heard gunfire, screams of pain and explosions. All were muted and dulled, as though coming from a distant battlefield.

Her hands were radiant, leaving echoes of warp light in their wake. A pattern began to emerge, disjointed knowledge seeded throughout her psyche coming together in a multi-dimensional lattice that was part unbreakable seal, part demo charge.

She smiled, seeing the cunning that had gone into its design, the care it had taken to hide within her. So intricate was its construction, she almost didn't mind being used like this.

She certainly didn't mind that its completion would kill her.

A spray of blood drenched Alivia and she cried out as one of her protectors dropped with a hole blown through the cobalt-blue of his breastplate. A concussive pressure wave hit her and slammed her to the ground. A spinning fragment of hot metal sliced across her shoulder. Pain blazed as blood ran down her back.

Her surroundings bled back into her awareness. The noise, the fear and the choking clouds of smoke. She heard heavy footfalls, all thudding in unison. Short, tramping steps and the scrape of iron on stone. Alivia rolled onto her side, blinking away tears of pain from her shoulder.

Her left arm felt useless and the stink of burned meat filled her senses. Valance lay on his back next to her. He'd taken the brunt of the blast that had knocked her to the ground. What was left of him was only recognisable by the half of his head that remained.

She looked up in time to see a ridged line of interlocking shields barge its way into the chamber. Sons of Horus with breacher's shields. The Ultramarines couldn't hope to hold their position, scattered by the missile explosions and overwhelmed by suppressive volleys.

Concentrated bursts of fire took them down in twos and threes.

The shield line widened as the chamber opened up. Sons of Horus warriors following behind pushed the line out and brought yet more guns to bear.

Arcadon Kyro put a hole in the shield line with coordinated blasts from the plasma one-shots on his mechanised arms. Each bolt impacted at precisely the same time, and blew apart one of the shields and the warrior behind it.

Massed bolter fire brought him down, a ridiculous amount of overkill that shredded his flesh unrecognisable and thoroughly dismantled his mechanical augmentations. Didacus Theron and Castor Alcade pushed into the gap Kyro had opened, looking to tear it wider.

Theron's power sword cleaved through a shield and the arm holding it. His bolt pistol fired point-blank into the face of a Terminator. Such hulking war-monstrosities all but eliminated the need for mortal flesh entirely. The bolts detonated on impact, but left the warrior beneath unharmed.

The Terminator's crackling energy-fist pistoned out and rammed through the centurion's body. He came apart in an explosion of disembodied limbs and shattered plate.

Alivia tried to drag herself back to the gate, pushing along the floor on her backside with her heels.

Her work was almost done. Just a little more and her obligation would be over. No more long, wearying years, no more lies and isolation. No more anything.

A towering figure broke free of the shield line.

A giant, a demigod, a beautiful avatar of all that humanity could achieve in greatness. She'd heard all these epithets and more used to describe the Warmaster, but they'd been coined by those viewing him at peace.

Seeing him in battle was something entirely different.

Horus Lupercal was a monster. A daemon of war and ruin made flesh. He was a destroyer, an unmaker and the face all humanity ought to have turned its back on millennia ago.

His was the face of uttermost evil...

And he didn't even know it.

It was the worst thing Alivia had ever seen.

Castor Alcade vaulted away from the Terminator bearing down on him and ran to put himself between her and the Warmaster. There was no way Alcade could defeat the Warmaster, no hope of even a fair contest.

Alcade was dead the moment he moved, but he did it anyway.

It was the best thing Alivia had ever seen.

The legate of the XIII Legion thrust with his gladius.

It snapped on the amber eye at Horus's breast.

The Warmaster's titanic maul swept out and Castor Alcade was obliterated as though he had never existed.

Alivia pushed onto her feet and threw herself at the gate, her hands slippery with blood. She traced the final lines and opened her mouth to speak the last of the apotropaic words.

All that came out was a scream of pain.

Alivia looked down and saw four parallel blades jutting from her chest. They pinned her to the black wall and her blood ran down the blades and into the gate.

'I don't know who you are, but I need that open,' said the Warmaster.

'*Please,*' said Alivia as the pain finally caught up to her.

Horus snapped the talons of his gauntlet from Alivia's body. She fell, and it felt like she fell for a very long time before she hit the floor.

She looked up into the Warmaster's face.

She saw no pity, no mercy. But, curiously, she saw regret.

Alivia struggled to speak, and the Warmaster knelt to hear her valediction as the life bled out of her.

'Even... souls ensnared by evil... maintain a small... bridgehead of good,' she said. 'I want... you... to remember that. At the end.'

Horus looked puzzled for a moment, then smiled. And for a moment, Alivia forgot that he was the enemy of humanity.

'You shouldn't put your faith in saints, mamzel,' said Horus.

Alivia didn't reply, looking over the Warmaster's shoulder.

The gateway of black obsidian was bleeding.

HORUS STOOD FROM the body of the dead woman.

He wished she hadn't died so he could ask her how she had come to be here. But she had stood against him and tried to stop him from achieving his destiny. And that was a death sentence.

'Who was she?' asked Mortarion.

'I don't know, but I felt the touch of father upon her.'

'She met Him?'

'Yes,' said Horus, 'but a long time ago I think.'

Mortarion looked up at the gate, clearly unimpressed. Horus saw his brother's expression and put a hand on his shoulder.

'Don't underestimate what our father did here,' said Horus. 'He broke through into another realm, a realm no other being has breached and lived. Such a journey would make the climb to your first father's hall seem like a pleasant stroll.'

Mortarion shrugged. 'I don't much care what He did,' he said. He tapped the butt of *Silence* against the body of the woman. 'She was here to seal the gate. Do you think she succeeded?'

Horus reached out and laid his palm flat against the black wall. He felt micro-tremors in its surface, too faint to be perceived by anyone save a primarch.

'Only one way to find out,' said Horus, unsnapping the seals across his breastplate. 'Take that reaper of yours and cut me.'

'Cut you?'

Horus shed his armour, letting each plate fall to the ground until he stood clad only in a grey bodysuit.

'I was told this gate can only open in blood,' said Horus. 'So cut me and don't spare the edge.'

'Sir,' said Kibre coming forward. 'Don't. Let one of us do it. Spill *my* blood, use as much as it takes, even if it kills me.'

Little Horus and Ezekyle joined their voices in opposition to his desire for Mortarion to cut him deep.

Horus folded his arms and said, 'Thank you, my sons, but if I've learned anything from Lorgar, it's that somebody else's blood won't do for something like this. It has to be mine.'

'Then let's get this done,' said Mortarion, hefting *Silence* and readying its blade. Where some of Horus's brothers might baulk at the thought of wounding him, Mortarion had no such qualms. If his brother sought to usurp him, this was his chance.

Horus locked his gaze with his brother.

'Do it.'

Mortarion spun *Silence* around his body.

The blade flashed.

Horus howled as the Death Lord's reaper cut him from clavicle to pelvis. The pain was ferocious. Its savagery took him all the way back to Davin's moon, and Eugan Temba's stolen blade.

Blood jetted from the wound and sprayed the black wall.

Through eyes wet with pain, Horus saw unfinished sigils and arrangements of arcane significance. Their brightness was dying, washed away by the tide of his blood.

The gouges his talons had torn were bleeding.

His blood and the woman's mingled, and Horus saw hair-fine cracks spreading from where he'd marked the wall.

He grinned through the pain. *Worldbreaker* swung to his shoulder.

'Time to earn your name,' he said.

The Emperor's gift swung round in a sledgehammer arc.

And smashed the wall to shards.

ABSOLUTE DARKNESS SPILLED into the chamber like a physical thing, as though an ocean of dark matter filled the mountain above and was now pouring out.

Horus felt hurricane winds tear at him, yet was unmoved.

He felt the cold of space, a soul-deep chill that enveloped him in ice. He was alone, floating in an empty void.

No stars illuminated him.

He had no memory of passing through the gate, then berated himself for so literal an interpretation. The gate beneath the mountain was not a literal portal separating one space from another, but an allegorical one. Just by spilling his blood upon stone that was not stone he had passed through. By enacting his desire with *Worldbreaker*, he had hurled himself heedless into the domain of gods and monsters.

A realm he knew of only in myth and the ravings of lunatics put down in proscribed texts and lurid works passed off as fiction. This was a place unconstrained by the limits of the physical world. The laws governing existence in the material world held no sway here and were endlessly flouted.

Even as he came to that understanding, the void surrounding

him conspired to refute that notion. A world faded up, a terrible place of bone white sands and blood-red mountains and orange skies lit by global fires.

The air tasted of ash and regret, of sorrow and fecundity.

Horus heard the clash of swords, but no battle. The plaintive cries of lovers, but no flesh. Whispers surrounded him, plotting and scheming as he felt the cyclic entropy of his flesh. Old cells dying, new ones born to replace them.

He blinked away the heat of the sky, now seeing it wasn't the orange of a reflected blaze, but the blaze itself.

The heavens were on fire from horizon to horizon.

A firestorm blazed over distant mountains, swollen by forks of ruby red lightning rippling upwards from their summits.

Horus felt the ground beneath him become more solid, and looked down to see that he stood within a circle of flagstones fashioned from obsidian. Eight radiating arms vanished into the far distance, and the landscape twisted in hideous ways along each of the pathways.

Acres of wire grew with the moaning bodies of his closest sons hung upon barbed spikes. Flickering lights skimmed desolate bogs that burped and hissed with the decay of rotting corpses. Silken deserts of serpentine fogbanks of perfumed musks. Labyrinthine forests of claw-branched trees clung to a series of rounded hills, each with eight doors set around their circumferences.

'I've travelled realms like this before,' said Horus, though there was no one to hear. No one obvious, at least.

Each of the four cardinal paths ended at a mountaintop fortress to rival that of the Emperor's palace. Their walls were brass and gold, bone and earth. They glimmered in the ruddy light of the firestorm. Screams issued from each of them and booming laughter of mad gods rolled down from the peaks.

'They are mocking you,' said a voice behind him.

Horus turned, knowing what he would see.

The *Cruor Angelus* was the red of a battlefield sunset, its armour no longer splintered and broken, its face no longer a charred nightmare of agony. The chains encircling its body were gone, but the light of extinguished suns still burned in its dead eyes.

'Why are you here?' said Horus.

'I am home,' said the Red Angel. *'I am unbound. The cold iron Erebus hung on me has no power here, nor do the warding oaths cut into my skin. Here I am the sum of all horror, the thirster after blood and the devourer of souls.'*

Horus ignored its grandstanding. 'So why are they mocking me?'

'You are a mortal in a realm of gods. You are an insect to the Pantheon. Insignificant and unworthy of notice, a fragment of dust in the cosmic wind.'

Horus sighed. 'Noctua was right, all you warp-things are ridiculously overwrought.'

Razored bone talons ripped from its gauntlets. Curling horns tore from its brow. *'You are in my realm, where you will see only what we wish you to see. I can snuff you out like a candle flame, Warmaster.'*

'If you're trying to intimidate me, you're doing a poor job of it,' said Horus, taking a step towards the daemon. 'Let me tell you what I know. You exist in both realms, but if I destroy your body, your time in *my* world is over.'

The Angel laughed and stepped to meet his advance.

'Daemons never die,' it said.

'No, but they do get incredibly tiresome,' said Horus, reaching up to wrap his hand around the Red Angel's throat. He lifted it from the ground and squeezed. It spat black ichor and the fire in its eyes blazed.

'Release me!' it roared, clawing at his arms. Blood welled from

the cuts and splashed the mirror-black flagstones. Black veins of disintegrating blood vessels spread down Horus's arm at the daemon's touch. He felt the internal mechanisms of his body decaying, but only crushed the daemon's neck harder.

'*You will die for this!*' spat the daemon.

'One day perhaps,' said Horus. 'But not today. You weren't sent here to kill me.'

Horus nodded to the vast citadels in the mountains. 'You're here to guide me. Your masters *need* me, so take me to their fortresses, speak my name and tell them the galaxy's new master would treat with them.'

Horus dropped the Red Angel and for a moment he thought it might fly at him in a rage. Booming thunder rolled down from the mountains, bellows of anger, squeals of delight and more sibilant whispers. A million voices swept the nightmarish landscape, and the Red Angel's claws retreated into its gauntlet.

'*Very well, I will take you to the Ruinous Powers,*' it said with a hiss of venom that curdled the air. '*The Obsidian Way is the eternal road. It is perilous for flesh and soul. It is not for mortals to walk, for its dangers are–*'

'Shut up,' said Horus. 'Just shut the hell up.'

AXIMAND CRIED OUT at the awful sensation of blindness. His helmet's auto-senses had failed the instant the Warmaster's hammer struck the black wall. He tore his helmet off, but was still in the dark. Not just a darkened space, but a place of utter absence, as though the very idea of light had yet to become real.

'Ezekyle!' he yelled. 'Falkus! Sound off!'

No response.

What had happened? Had they failed? Had Lupercal inadvertently unleashed some hideous apocalypse on them? Aximand felt as though his entire body was enveloped in viscous glue. Every breath was laden with toxins, with bile and with sweet, cloying tastes that sickened him to the core.

'Ezekyle!' he yelled again. 'Falkus! Sound off! Anyone!'

And almost as soon as it had begun it was over.

Aximand blinked as the world came back again. He spun around, seeing the same confusion in the faces of his brothers. Even Mortarion appeared discomfited. The Deathshroud gathered close to their master as the Justaerin looked around for someone to protect.

'Where is he?' demanded Abaddon, though Aximand wasn't sure who he was addressing. 'Where is he?'

'Exactly where he intended,' said Mortarion, looking at the black gate. It had previously appeared to be a slab of polished obsidian, but now it was a vertical pool of black oil. Rippling concentric rings spread over its surface, as though raindrops were falling on it from the other side.

'Do we go in after him?' asked Kibre.

'Do you want to die?' said Mortarion, rounding on the Widow-maker. 'Only one other being has passed into the warp and lived. Are you the equal of the Emperor, little man?'

'How long has it been since he went in?' said Abaddon.

'Not long,' said Aximand. 'Moments at most.'

'How do you know that?'

Aximand pointed to the ruby droplets running down the Death Lord's reaper. 'His blood is still wet on the blade.'

Abaddon appeared to accept his logic and nodded. He stood before the portal, as though trying to drag Lupercal back with the sheer power of his will.

Kibre stood with him, Abaddon's man to the last.

Aximand took a breath of deep-earth air. Not even the horror of Davin could have prepared him for this moment. The Warmaster was gone and Aximand didn't know if he would ever see him again.

A cold shard of ice entered his heart and all the light and colour bled from the world. Was this what the Iron Tenth had felt when Ferrus Manus died?

Aximand felt utterly alone. No matter that his closest brothers stood with him. No matter that they had just won a great victory and fulfilled the Warmaster's ambitions for this world.

What would they do without the Warmaster?

No use denying that such a thing could ever happen. Fulgrim's slaying of Manus proved a primarch *could* die.

Who else but the Warmaster had the strength of will to lead the Sons of Horus? Who among the *true sons* could achieve what Horus had failed to achieve?

Horus is weak. Horus is a fool.

The words struck him like a blow. They were without source, yet Aximand knew they had issued from beyond the black gate. Delivered straight to the heart of his skull like an executioner's dagger.

He blinked and saw a time a long time ago or yet to pass, an echoing empty wasteland of a world. He imagined a death. Alone, far away from everything he had once held dear, dying with a former brother at his feet whose cruel wounds bled out onto the dust of a nameless rock.

Breath sounded in his ear. Cold and measured, the breath of nightmares he'd thought banished with the ghost of Garviel Loken.

A fist of iron took Aximand's heart and crushed it within his chest. He couldn't breathe. *Transhuman dread.* He'd felt it briefly on Dwell, and now it all but overpowered him.

The feeling passed as a bitter wind blew from the gateway.

'Stand to!' yelled Abaddon. 'Something's happening.'

Every weapon in the chamber snapped to aim at the portal. Its surface no longer rippled with the gentle fall of raindrops, but the violence of an ocean tempest.

Horus Lupercal fell through the oil-black surface of the gate and crashed to his knees before Abaddon and Kibre. Behind him, the darkness of the gate vanished with a bang of displaced air. Only a solid wall of mountain rock remained, as though the gate had never existed.

Aximand rushed forward to help them as the Warmaster held himself upright on all fours. His back heaved with breath, like a man trapped in a vacuum suddenly returned to atmosphere.

'Sir,' said Abaddon. 'Sir, are you all right?'

Even through his gauntlets, Aximand felt the glacial ice of the Warmaster's flesh.

'You're still here?' said Horus without looking up, his voice little better than a parched whisper. 'You waited for me... after all this time...'

'Of course we waited,' said Aximand. 'You've only been gone moments.'

'Moments...?' said Horus, with a fragile, almost frantic edge to his words. 'Then everything... everything's still to be done.'

Aximand looked over at Abaddon, seeing the same lingering doubt in the face of the First Captain. None of them had the faintest clue as to what might happen beyond the gate or what the consequences of venturing into such an alien environment might be.

They had let their lord and master walk into the unknown and not one of them had known what to expect.

That lack of forethought now horrified Aximand.

'Brother,' said Mortarion, cutting through Aximand's self-recrimination. 'Did you find what you were looking for?'

Horus stood to his full height and Aximand's eyes widened at the sight of him.

The Warmaster had aged.

Cthonia had shaped him, moulded him into a warrior of

flint-hard lines and cruel beauty. Two centuries of war had left no mark upon him, but moments beyond the gate had done what the passage of time could not.

Silver streaked the stubble upon his scalp, and the grooves at the corners of his eyes were deeper and more pronounced.

The face Aximand had devoted his life to serving was now that of an ancient warrior who had fought for longer than he could ever have imagined, who had seen too much horror and whose campaigning days had bled him dry.

Yet the fire and purpose in his eyes was brighter than ever.

Nor was that fire simply confined to his eyes.

What Aximand had taken to be cold flesh was the power of the empyrean distilled and honed within the body of an immortal being. Horus stood taller, fuller and more powerfully than before. Lupercal had always found *Warmaster* to be an awkward fit, a term never fully bedded in or taken as read.

Now he owned the title, as though it had been his long before there was any such office to take. He was now, naturally, and without equivocation, the Warmaster.

Aximand, Abaddon and Kibre backed away from Horus, each of them dropping to their knees in wonder as the power filling the primarch bloomed in the material world.

Even Mortarion, that most truculent of primarchs, bent the knee to Horus in a way he had never done for the Emperor.

Horus grinned and all trace of the war-weary ancient was banished in the blink of an eye. In his place was a mortal god, brighter and more dangerous than ever. Filled with a power that only one other being in all existence had wielded before.

'Yes,' said Horus. 'I found *exactly* what I was looking for.'

TWENTY-FOUR

Leaving Lupercalia
Ill met by moonlight
Hunter's eye

LUPERCALIA WAS BURNING.

The Sons of Horus had not lit the fires, but Aximand watched them spread through the knotted streets of the lower valley as the Warmaster's Stormbird cleared the citadel's walls. The Knights of House Devine stalked the streets of their city like vengeful predators, burning and killing with wanton abandon.

One machine, a burn-scarred thing with a lashing whip weapon, danced in the light of the revel fires, its warhorn hooting as though its pilot were drunk.

Aximand forgot the Knights as the angle of the gunship's ascent became steeper and a number of Thunderhawks took up station on either wing.

'It's strange to be leaving a world so soon after arriving,' said Falkus Kibre, scrolling through a data-slate bearing a force disposition assay. 'Especially when there's still armies to fight.'

'No one *worth* fighting,' grunted Abaddon from farther along the compartment. He'd said little since they'd emerged from the catacombs beneath the citadel. 'The fight before Lupercalia destroyed the best of them.'

Kibre shook his head. 'Orbital surveys say tens of thousands of soldiers and dozens of armoured regiments have fled across the mountains on the edges of the southern steppe.'

Abaddon said nothing. Aximand knew Ezekyle better than most and knew when to leave well alone.

This was one such moment.

'The Kushite Eastings and Northern Oceanic were largely wiped out at Lupercalia and Avadon,' continued Kibre who, as Abaddon's second, should have known not to press the issue. 'But van Valkenberg and Malbek are still unaccounted for.'

'Then you go down and bloody finish them!' snapped Abaddon.

Kibre took Abaddon's outburst stoically and replaced the slate in its niche.

'Ezekyle,' said Kibre. 'We fought the hardest down there, you and I.'

Aximand scowled at that. The Fifth Company had fought their way through the XIII Legion to break the line, and they'd done it without the support of an orbital weapons platform.

'We faced a bloody Imperator and lived,' continued the Widow-maker, 'so don't make me come up there and slap you for being unmindful of what we did.'

Aximand revised his assumption that he knew Ezekyle better than most when, instead of killing Kibre, Abaddon grunted in laughter.

'You're right, Falkus,' said Abaddon. 'It does feel somehow... *unfinished*.'

That at least, Aximand understood. Like all true fighting men down through the ages, he hated to abandon a mission before it was finished. But Ezekyle had things wrong.

'It *is* finished,' he said.

Abaddon and Kibre looked back down the fuselage at him.

'We came here for Lupercal,' he said. 'This was his mission, not ours. And it's done.'

'We're just going to have to fight those men again on the walls of Terra,' said Kibre.

'You're wrong,' said the Warmaster, emerging from the pilot's compartment and sitting on the dropmaster's seat. 'Those men will be dead soon. Mortarion and Grulgor will see to that.'

Horus had always been a demi-god among men, but looking into the Warmaster's eyes now was like looking into the heart of a star on the verge of becoming a self-immolating supernova.

'We're leaving the Fourteenth Legion to finish the job?' said Kibre.

Horus nodded, shifting his bulk on the seat. It was patently too small for him, more so now that his natural presence was enhanced by his journey across the dimensions.

'Molech now belongs to Mortarion and Fulgrim.'

'Fulgrim?' said Aximand. 'Why does the Phoenician get a share of the spoils?'

'He played his part,' said Horus. 'Though I doubt he'll remember his time here fondly. Plasmic fire to the face tends to be an unpleasant experience. Or so Lorgar told me from Armatura.'

'What was Fulgrim doing?' asked Aximand.

Horus didn't answer immediately and Aximand took a moment to study the chiselled lines of the Warmaster's face. The extended age Aximand saw in his gene-father still unnerved him. He dearly wanted to ask Lupercal what he'd found, what wonders he'd seen and how far along the road he'd travelled.

One day, perhaps, but not today.

'Fulgrim reaped a crop sown here many years ago,' said Horus. 'But enough of my brother, let's savour the moment ahead.'

'What moment?' said Kibre.

'A reunion of sorts,' said Horus. 'The confraternity of the old Mournival is about to be remade.'

LUPERCAL'S COURT. THE dark jewel in the crown of Peeter Egon Momus.

If Loken's return to the *Vengeful Spirit* had been hard before, moving stealthily through its hidden corridors and secret niches, being within Lupercal's Court was an exquisite torture. Loken had stood at the Warmaster's side when they had planned the Isstvan campaign.

He'd been proud then, prouder even than the day he'd been chosen to be one of the XVI Legion. All he felt now was confusion.

Gerradon and Noctua had dragged them through the ship, marching them onto a pneu-train bound for the prow. At first, he'd thought they were heading to the strategium, but after debarking at the Museum of Conquest, he'd realised exactly where they were going.

The high ceiling was still hung with uncommon banners, some fresh, some mouldering and dusty. Shadows clung to the thick pillars, making it impossible to tell if they were alone. The twenty-three Luperci – he'd counted them as they passed through the Museum of Conquest – spread out and marched them towards the towering basalt throne at the far end of the chamber.

'Kneel,' said Gerradon, and there was little to do but obey.

Iacton, Bror and Severian were to Loken's left, Varren, Tarchon, Rubio and Voitek to his right. The Luperci surrounded them like executioners. They knelt facing the throne, looking out into the vastness of space through the one addition to the chamber, a cathedral-like window of stained glass.

Pinpricks of light from distant stars glittered at unimaginable distances, and Molech's moons painted the floor in lozenges of milky radiance.

'Nice throne,' said Varren. 'The traitor still thinks he's a king, then. Should have seen this coming long before.'

Ger Gerradon kicked the former World Eater in the back. Varren sprawled, and bared his teeth, reaching for an axe that wasn't there. Four Luperci kept their bolters trained on him as others hauled him back to his knees.

'A king?' said Gerradon with a grin Loken wanted to split wide open. 'You World Eaters always did think small. Horus Lupercal doesn't think he's a *king*. Haven't you felt it? He's a god now.'

Severian laughed and Grael Noctua backhanded a bolter across his face. Still laughing, Severian rolled onto his side and picked himself up. Loken wanted to mock Gerradon's theatrics, but he could barely take a breath. That he would soon be face to face with the Warmaster was sending his sense memory into overdrive.

The corners of Lupercal's Court were shadowed ruins where the dead of Isstvan gathered, hungry for flesh. The moonlight painting the floor was the flash of atomic firestorms, and the breath at his ear was that of his killer.

'Loken,' said Qruze.

He didn't answer, keeping his gaze fixed on the black throne.

'Garviel!'

Loken blinked and lifted his head.

The great iron doors to Lupercal's Court were opening.

And there he was, looking right at Loken with paternal pride.

His gene-father, his Warmaster.

Horus Lupercal.

THE WARMASTER HAD always been the mightiest of the primarchs, a fact acknowledged by all Sons of Horus, though hotly debated by legionaries from most other Legions.

To see him now would surely end that debate.

Horus was possessed of a powerful dynamism, a charge that

passed from him to those he beheld. To be in his presence was to know that gods walked among men. A hyperbolic sentiment, but one borne out by those fortunate enough to have met him. That power, that *essence* was magnified now.

It was magnified a hundredfold, and it all but emptied Loken's reservoir of hate to keep from throwing himself at the Warmaster's feet and begging for forgiveness.

His feet, look at his feet.

A piece of advice he'd been given when Lupercal still served the Emperor. As true now as it was then. Loken kept his eyes down. He took a breath and held it. His heart thundered, a hammer beating on the fused bone shield of his ribcage.

His mouth was dry, like the eve of his first battle.

'Look at me, Garviel,' said Horus, and every pain Loken had suffered since the first bombs had fallen on Isstvan was washed away in that moment of recognition.

He couldn't help but obey.

The Warmaster was an all-conquering hero, clad in armour as black as wilderness space. The volcanic eye on his chest was slitted and veined with black, his claws unsheathed like a jungle predator closing on a kill.

His face was as heroically self-aware as Loken remembered.

Loken knew other warriors accompanied Horus, but they were as ghosts in the obscuring corona of the Warmaster's presence. He heard their shocked voices and understood that he knew them, and they him, but he could not tear his gaze from his former commander-in-chief.

The urge to remain kneeling through fealty rather than captivity was overwhelming.

Horus said, 'Stand. All of you.'

Loken did so, and told himself it was because he chose to.

None of the other pathfinders followed his example. He faced the Warmaster alone. Just as he'd always known he would. However this ended, now or in years to come, it would come down to just two warriors locked in a fight to the death.

The figures surrounding the Warmaster emerged from his shadow, and Loken felt his choler flare at the sight of his former Mournival brothers.

Ezekyle, scarred and bellicose, hatred etched on his eyes.

Horus Aximand, pale and wide-eyed, his face pressed onto his skull like badly set clay. He looked at Loken, not with hatred, but with... *fear?*

Was it possible for Little Horus to fear anything?

Falkus Kibre, hulking and unsubtle. Following Abaddon's lead. Nothing new there.

Grael Noctua took his place with them, and Loken immediately understood the skewed dynamic between them. A reborn Mournival, but one with its humours grotesquely out of balance.

'I never thought to see you again, Garviel,' said Horus.

'Why would you?' said Loken, mustering his reserves of defiance to speak with clarity and strength. 'I died when you betrayed everything the Luna Wolves ever stood for. When you murdered Isstvan Three and the loyal sons of four Legions.'

Horus nodded slowly. 'And despite all that, you come back to the *Vengeful Spirit*. Why is that?'

'To stop you.'

'Is that what you told Malcador?' said Horus, before turning to regard the rest of the pathfinders. 'Is it what he told *you?*'

'It's the truth,' said Loken. 'You have to be stopped.'

'With what, a squad?' said Horus, cocking an eyebrow. 'I don't think so. The galaxy isn't a sterile place without a love of melodrama, Garviel. You know as well as I that this doesn't end with kill teams or assassins or a pre-emptive strike thousands of light years from Terra. It ends with me looking into my father's eyes, my hands around His neck, and showing Him everything He loves burned to ash by His lies.'

'You're insane,' said Bror Tyrfingr. 'The Wolf King will stop you, he'll carve his name on your heart and give your bones to the wyrd to tell the future for eternity.'

Horus snapped his fingers and said, 'Russ? Ah, so that's what this is.'

Loken willed Bror to shut up, but the damage was already done.

'Leman didn't slake his thirst for blood on Prospero?' continued Horus with a rueful shake of his head. 'I wonder, does the Emperor even know you're here or did the Wolf King set this up himself? He always was eager to spill his brothers' blood. Did he convince Malcador that sending you here was the only way to end the war before it got to Terra?'

'Russ stands on Terra's walls a loyal son,' said Qruze. 'Walls the Master of Stone has strengthened beyond your power to breach.'

'Perturabo assures me differently,' said Horus. He bent to take Qruze's chin in his hand. 'Ah, Iacton. Of all my sons, you were the one I never expected to turn from me. You were old guard, a warrior with roots on both Terra and Cthonia. You were the best of us, but your time is over. Tell me, how did you even get aboard?'

Loken kept his face neutral and hoped Qruze could do the same.

He doesn't know about Rassuah or the Tarnhelm.

'We came here to mark the *Vengeful Spirit* for Russ,' said Loken, hoping a measure of truth might divert the Warmaster from Rassuah.

'Yes, Grael told me he saw some futharc scraped on the walls.'

'Bloody Svessl,' hissed Bror. 'Is there anyone he *didn't* tell?'

Horus moved on and walked a slow circuit of the remnants of the pathfinders towards his throne.

'Marking a route for Russ,' he said. 'That sounds plausible, but come on, Garviel, you and I both know that's not the only reason you're here. There's more to your return than you're telling.'

'You're right,' answered Loken, turning to face Ger Gerradon. 'I came to kill him. To free Tarik's soul.'

'Maybe that's part of it,' conceded Horus, taking his place upon his throne, 'but why don't you tell your comrades why you really came here? And don't be coy, Garviel. I'll know if you're lying.'

Loken tried to speak, but the Warmaster's gaze pinned him in place, dredging the very worst of his treacherous fears out through his eyes. He tried to repeat what he'd just said, but the words wouldn't come.

Enthroned in the glow of the moon shining through the stained glass windows, Horus was regal and magnificent, a lord for whom it would be worth laying down a life.

A hundred lives, a thousand. As many as he asked for.

'I...'

'It's all right, Loken, I understand,' said Horus. 'You came back because you want to rejoin the Sons of Horus.'

THIS WAS THE moment Bror Tyrfingr had feared since they'd left Terra. Not death, that moment held no fear for him. He'd considered himself dead the moment he foreswore the frost blue of the Rout and taken Yasu Nagasena's outstretched hand.

No, death was not his fear.

Loken took a step towards the Warmaster's throne.

Bror had watched Garviel Loken's mental dissolution the way an aesthete might lament the slow degradation of a great work of art.

If Loken bent the knee to Horus, Bror was under orders to kill him. He understood why the duty had fallen to him. He was VI Legion, the Executioner's son, and could be counted on to do the unthinkable, no matter what bonds of brotherhood might be forged in adversity.

He let his breath come slowly.

The warriors gathered around him could be counted on to rally to him, but they were grossly outnumbered. Bror had the positions of the Luperci embedded in his mind. They wouldn't stop him. They might once have been Legion warriors, but now they were maleficarum.

Bror was unarmed, but a warrior of the Rout needed no weapons.

He could break Loken's neck without blinking.

And if he died a heartbeat later, so be it.

Bror closed his eyes, feeling the hackles rise on the back of his neck. He'd first felt it in the forests of Fenris, stalked by the great silver wolf the Gothi said would one day kill him.

He'd proven them wrong and taken its pelt for a cloak.

Bror looked up and saw Tylos Rubio staring at him. His eyes were wide and pleading. They flicked over towards Ger Gerradon. No words passed between them, but the meaning was clear.

Be ready.

LOKEN FELT HIMSELF moving forward. Step by step towards the Warmaster's throne. What Horus was saying was ludicrous. He couldn't go back to the Legion, not after all the blood and betrayal that had passed between them.

And yet...

He wanted it. Deep down, he wanted it.

'Loken, don't do this,' said Qruze, rising to his feet. 'Don't listen to him. He's betrayed us all, made us monsters in the eyes of the very people we were wrought to protect.'

Abaddon's fist sent Iacton to the deck, streaks of red in his hair like blood on snow.

'Shut your mouth, Half-heard,' said Abaddon.

'Loken!' cried Qruze, coming forward on his hands and knees.

...he is the Half-heard no longer... his voice will be heard louder than any other in his Legion.

Loken blinked as he heard Mersadie Oliton's words in his head.

No, they weren't Mersadie's words, they were Euphrati Keeler's.

If you saw the rot, a hint of corruption, would you step out of your regimented life and stand against it? For the greater good of mankind.

He'd heard those words aboard this very ship, on the residential decks once occupied by the remembrancers. Euphrati had reached out to him, scared and alone. She'd tried to warn him of what was coming, but he'd dismissed her fears as groundless.

'Garviel,' said Horus, and he turned to see the Warmaster holding out his gauntlet. 'Don't hate me for what's happened.'

'Why shouldn't I hate you?' said Loken. 'You did the worst thing that anyone can do to another person. You let us believe we were loved and valued, then showed us it was all a lie.'

Horus shook his head, but his hand remained outstretched. Behind him, a crenellated warship passed over the face of the moon. The Eye of Horus adorned its prow, but it was a crude thing, painted on like graffiti.

'Come back to me, my son. We can rebuild what was lost between us, renew our bonds of fellowship. I want you at my side as I reforge the Imperium anew.'

Loken looked back at the warriors on their knees behind him. Men he'd fought and bled with. Men he'd called brother in the darkest of times. He looked into their eyes, seeing their defiance and more. Rubio's fists were clenched and the tension in Voitek's neck was like a straining machine about to throw a gear.

He saw the cold eyes of Bror Tyrfingr upon him and remembered the words he had spoken at their first meeting.

If I think your roots are weak, I'll kill you myself.

He gave an almost imperceptible nod to his fellows and took a step away from the Warmaster, feeling the threads of loyalty and brotherhood that bound him to this moment pull tight.

Horus rose to his feet as the passing warship completed its transit of the cathedral window.

Dazzling moonlight poured into Lupercal's Court once more.

It haloed Lupercal, limned him in silver to cast the darkest shadow across the deck. The flared back of the Warmaster's throne gave that shadow wings, like the faceless daemons from the lurid books Kyril Sindermann had loaned him.

'Part of me wishes I could, sir,' said Loken. 'Believe me, I want the warmth that being part of something greater brings. I want to *belong*. I had that with the Legion, but you took that away from me when you stabbed us all in the back.'

'No,' said Horus. 'Garviel, no. That's not–'

But Loken wasn't about to stop now. 'Turning my back on everything I knew, being cut off from the Legion that made me who I am? That was the worst moment of my life. It drove me insane. More than Tarik's death or being buried alive on Isstvan, it was the heartbreak and yawning emptiness that finally broke me.'

'Then come back to me, Garviel,' said Horus. 'Feel that warmth again. Don't you want to be part of the greatest endeavour the galaxy has ever seen?'

'I already was,' said Loken, turning his back on Horus. 'It was called the Great Crusade.'

RUBIO NODDED AND Bror Tyrfingr vaulted across the deck, his hand a hard axe blade. He rammed into Ger Gerradon and barrelled him from his feet. Voitek moved with him. The leader of the Luperci went over backwards, sprawling on the deck in surprise.

Gunfire exploded and the harsh blurt of binaric pain told Bror that Ares Voitek was hit. He smelled lubricant and hot oils.

Qruze and Severian were moving, turning on the Mournival.

Bror hadn't time to spare for them.

More gunfire. Shouts. He'd taken in the positions of the Luperci, but that was seconds ago, and his situational awareness was now hopelessly outdated.

'Kill him, Bror!' shouted Rubio. 'He's blocking my powers!'

'Trying,' grunted Bror. 'He's stronger than he looks.'

Gerradon's face twisted in rage. For a moment Bror saw the dark flame twisting within him. He slammed his forehead against Gerradon's face. His cheekbone caved in and foul-smelling blood burst across his split skin.

Even as they struggled, the blood flow stopped and the cut in Gerradon's cheek sealed itself.

He laughed. 'You think you can hurt me? You Wolves really are stupid.'

Voitek's servo-arms pinned one of Gerradon's, and Bror scrambled to drag the man's blade from its sheath. Gerradon's fist thundered into Bror's belly, cracking the plate and driving the air from him.

Gerradon kicked him away and he lost his grip on the handle.

He staggered as a bolter shell punched him in the back. Another blew out the meat of his thigh. Pain swamped him, but he hurled himself at his enemy again.

Gerradon caught him around the throat with his free hand and slammed him against Ares Voitek. The impact was ferocious. Plate cracked.

Bror saw something glitter at Gerradon's back. A gleam of moonlight on an ivory Ultima. A stolen weapon jutting from a shoulder scabbard. He reached for it. Too far away. Gerradon's grip tightened, crushing the life from him. He tensed every muscle in his shoulders and neck, his face purpling with the effort.

Then he saw it.

Proximo Tarchon's gladius held aloft like a gift from the ancient gods of Asaheim.

Grasped in the manipulator claw of Ares Voitek.

The servo-arm stabbed the blade into Gerradon's back.

The daemon within Gerradon howled as its hold on the dead man's mortal flesh slipped. The iron grip on Bror loosened.

Not much, but just enough.

Bror pulled Gerradon's arm from his neck. He pounced and fastened his sharpened fangs on the Luperci's flesh.

Their eyes met and Bror relished the sudden fear he saw.

He wrenched his jaw back and ripped out Ger Gerradon's throat.

LUPERCAL'S COURT WAS in uproar. The Luperci filled the space with sporadic bolter fire, their outlines wavering as though something bestial sought to escape their flesh. Muzzle flare split the cold glow of moonlight. An arcing sheet of blue lightning from Rubio's gauntlets hurled six of them back in a coruscating blast.

Their armour clattered to the deck, the monsters within burned to ash. Loken ran towards Aximand, scooping up a fallen chainsword that still smoked with Rubio's witchfire.

He knew he couldn't hope to kill Aximand, but was past caring.

He'd faced the Warmaster and rejected him.

None of them were going to leave the *Vengeful Spirit* alive.

Severian was right. Getting in had been the easy part.

IACTON QRUZE HAD come back to the flagship with one aim in mind and one alone. As gunfire filled the chamber, he dived towards where Ger Gerradon fought to stem the tide of blood from his mauled throat.

The sinews and skin were trying to knit, but the wound was too awful, the blood loss too catastrophic for the daemon's host to survive. He dragged Gerradon's sword from its sheath as bolt shells cratered the deck beside him.

A ricochet sliced the skin of his cheek. If he lived he would have a neat scar from jawline to temple.

Loken and Bror were struggling with Little Horus Aximand and Falkus Kibre, a brutal, gouging, bloody brawl they were losing. Kibre was all strength and ferocity, but Bror Tyrfingr was giving as good as he got.

Loken had a chainsword, Aximand a blade with a powered edge. That wasn't going to end well. Rubio fought Abaddon with a sword wrought from blue lightning and bolts of witchfire. The First Captain was a monster now, a giant with cadaverous features and black, gem-like eyes.

Rubio bled from where Abaddon's tearing fists had ripped open his armour, its steeldust plates sheeted with red.

The Librarian had ploughed all his powers into attack, sparing nothing for defence. Varren lent what aid he could, but the wounds bound by Altan Nohai were bleeding freely again.

Qruze couldn't see Severian. Armed once again with his altered gladius, Proximo Tarchon stood sentinel over Ares Voitek, who spilled litres of sticky red-black fluid from half a dozen sword cuts and bolter craters.

An impact smashed into Qruze's hip, a searing bloom of pain that almost drove him to his knees. He turned as four of the Luperci raced towards him. They carried axes, swords and weapons that looked like they'd been looted from the Museum of Conquest.

'Come on!' roared Qruze, mashing the sword's activation trigger. 'Let this old dog show you he still has some bite.'

The first swung his axe for Qruze's neck.

'Too risky for a first attack,' he said, ducking low and hacking his chainblade through his opponent's gut. 'The beheading cut leaves you far too exposed against a low blow.'

He swayed aside from a sword thrust, bending to snatch the bolt pistol from the downed warrior's holster. Fully loaded, safety off. Sloppy.

'Too much weight on your forward foot,' he grunted. 'No control to evade a counterstrike.'

He drove the tip of his sword through the Luperci's spine. He spun and wrenched the sword blade out through its chest.

The last of the Luperci had at least learned from the deaths of their fellows. They split up and circled Qruze warily, swords in the guard position, their footwork cautious.

Qruze shot them both in the face, a classic double-tap. Their helmets exploded as the mass-reactives registered threshold densities for detonation.

'And if your opponent has a gun when all you have is a sword,' he said, turning towards the Warmaster upon his basalt throne, 'you're going to die.'

WITH EVERY MEETING of their swords, Loken lost teeth – whickering triangular shards flew from his chainsword as Aximand's shimmer-edged blade bit the unshielded metal.

'*Mourn-it-all* is going to kill you,' said Aximand.

Loken didn't reply. He'd come to slay Aximand, not waste unnecessary words on him.

'No words of hate for the life I took on Isstvan?' said Aximand.

'Just deeds,' said Loken, fighting to keep his temper.

An angry swordsman was a dead swordsman.

He cursed as Aximand used his momentary inattention to launch a lightning fast thrust to the groin. Loken swept the blade aside with the flat of his sword, trying to keep the disruptive edge from further damaging his weapon.

'Tarik always said you were so straight up and down,' said Aximand, using small wrist movements to move the tip of his sword in tight circles. 'I never really knew what he meant until now. It's only when you try to kill a man that you see through to his true character.'

Loken was too experienced a swordsman to fall for so obvious a gambit and kept his eyes fixed on Aximand's. Alone of his once-proud features, his eyes remained unchanged from how Loken remembered them.

Pale blue, like ice chips under a winter sun.

'Who gave you the new face?'

Aximand's reattached dead skin mask twitched.

'Who was it that beat you?' asked Loken, ducking a waist-high sweep of *Mourn-it-all*. He aimed a low cut at Aximand's knees.

'A Chogorian named Hibou Khan,' said Aximand, driving the blade into the deck. It screeched with red sparks. 'Why do you care?'

'So I can tell him I finished the job.'

Aximand roared and attacked with relentless fury. Loken blocked as fast as he could, but every killing blow he warded off cut portions from his weapon until it was next to useless.

He tossed the broken blade, looking over Aximand's shoulder.

'Now, Macer!' he shouted.

The former World Eater's fist crashed into the back of Aximand's helmet. And had Macer Varren not been horrifically wounded, his strength might have split Aximand's skull wide open. As it was, he crashed into Loken and the three of them fell to the deck in a thrashing tangle of limbs.

Mourn-it-all skittered away, its edge dimming without its bearer's grip.

Aximand smashed his elbow into Varren's face.

Loken kicked Aximand in the gut. They grappled. Fists bludgeoned, elbows cracked and knees slammed. It was an inelegant fight, not one the sagas would speak of in glowing heroic terms.

Even outnumbered two to one, Aximand was having the better of the fight. Loken reeled from a hammering series of body-blows. Varren stumbled as Aximand thundered his foot against the wounds Altan Nohai had bound.

'I dreamed of you,' said Aximand between breaths and sounding more regretful than angry. 'I dreamed you were alive. Why did you have to be alive?'

Loken rolled upright as Aximand curled his fingers around *Mourn-it-all*'s leather-wrapped grip.

He brought the sword around. Its blade bit plate and flesh.

Blood rained.

'No more dreams,' said Aximand.

PROXIMO TARCHON WAS down, sprawled over the body of Ares Voitek with three mass-reactive craters blasted through his body. Ger Gerradon's legs still kicked weakly, but whether he was still alive or was just twitching in death was open to interpretation.

Severian had a combat blade in one hand, a bolt pistol in the other.

He'd killed a dozen Luperci in as many shots or cuts, moving through the fighting like a ghost. People saw him, but they didn't *see* him, didn't recognise the significance of what they were seeing until it was too late.

Severian never needed more than one cut.

Usually that was enough, but Abaddon had merely staggered at his thrust and kept fighting. At least it had allowed Varren to break from the fight to go to Loken's aid.

The battle had devolved into individual skirmishes, but it couldn't go on like that for long. His pistol was empty. He tossed it as dead weight.

Severian saw his target and moved like a displaced shadow towards Grael Noctua.

The sergeant of the Warlocked saw him coming, which was unusual enough in itself. He grinned and took out his own blade.

'Twenty-Fifth to Twenty-Fifth,' said Noctua. 'A battle with a pleasing symmetry to it, yes?'

'So long as you're dead at the end, symmetry can go to hell.'

The two of them faced one another as though in the training cages. Crouched low, blade to blade, hands extended, eyes locked.

Noctua made the first move, feinting right. Severian read it easily. He countered the real blow, spun low and stabbed into Noctua's groin. Forearm block, return elbow smash that hit thin air. Severian trapped Noctua's arm, slammed his forehead forward.

Noctua threw himself backwards, dragging Severian with him.

They rolled, fighting to free their knife hands.

Severian got his free first. He stabbed into Noctua's side. The blade scraped free as Noctua rolled with the blow. Severian pushed clear. Noctua's weapon sliced the side of his neck, a hair's breadth from opening his throat.

'I always hated you, Severian,' said Noctua. 'Even before ascension.'

'I never cared enough about you to feel hate.'

They came together again. Thrust, cut, block, spin. Their blades like striking snakes. Both warriors had drawn blood. Both were evenly matched. Much longer and it wouldn't make any difference.

'You're good,' said Severian.

'The Twenty-Fifth teaches its warriors well.'

Severian flicked his blade at Noctua's face. Blood spatter hit his eyes, and Severian slipped into that fraction of a second's distraction.

He rammed his dagger through the centre of Noctua's chest, twisting the blade into his heart space.

Noctua's face contorted in pain.

'Not as well as Cthonia,' said Severian.

The pain was incredible, the worst Loken had known.

It filled him and crushed him. It bypassed every bio-engineered suppression mechanism. It kept the pain gate in his spinal column wedged open.

Where *Mourn-it-all* had cloven his ribs, he felt the toxic afterburn of something vile enter his bloodstream. Had the blade been poisoned?

He fell onto his side, struggling not to curl up and weep.

Aximand stood over him and the script worked along the length of the fuller drew threads of crimson from the edge. Loken turned onto his front, keeping one hand clamped to the rift gouged in his armour. He crawled away, knowing it was useless.

Varren lay moaning in a pool of his own blood. Aximand's return stroke had taken his right arm at the elbow and split open his chest. Old wounds bled afresh, and his helmet was cracked across the centre.

Loken lifted his head. The air in Lupercal's Court grew thick, and he saw their last stab at a measure of victory horribly snatched away.

Abaddon had finally put Rubio down and had Bror Tyrfingr pinned to the deck. The Fenrisian was still fighting the First Captain, but even his strength was not the equal of Terminator armour. Voitek's servo-arms wheezed and clicked, trying and failing to lift him upright. Proximo Tarchon lay unmoving next to him. The Ultramarine still clutched his bloody gladius, but his head hung low over his cratered chest.

Only Severian still stood, but he was surrounded by the Luperci with nowhere to go. The bodies of Ger Gerradon and Grael Noctua lay at his feet, their blood mingling in a spreading lake.

Severian's eyes darted from side to side, seeking a way out, but finding nothing.

Loken heard his name being shouted and blinked.

The gelid quality of the air receded and he took a great sucking draught into his lungs. It burned and the pain stabbed through him from the grievous wound in his side.

He turned to the source of the shout.

But what he saw made no sense.

Iacton Qruze knelt before Lupercal's throne with his back to Loken. The Warmaster held him clasped to his breast, whispering something in the Half-heard's ear.

Then Loken saw the Warmaster's talons jutting from Qruze's back.

Horus wrenched his arm back and pushed Qruze away.

Iacton crashed to the deck and Loken saw the gaping wound in his chest. Held aloft in the Warmaster's dripping gauntlet were the twin hearts of Iacton Qruze. Both organs were bright with oxygenated blood and beat one last time.

'No!' cried Loken. 'Throne, no!'

HE FOUGHT THROUGH the screaming fire saturating his body and scrambled over to where Iacton Qruze lay. The Half-heard's eyes were wide and filled with pain. His jaw worked up and down, trying to speak, trying to make his last words meaningful.

But nothing was coming. The pain was too intense, the shock of his imminent death too much.

Loken held him, helpless to do anything more.

Even had Altan Nohai lived, there would be no saving Qruze.

Lupercal's Court held its breath. None of the gathered enemies moved. A hero was dying and such a moment was worthy of pause, even in the midst of bitter fratricide.

Loken's pain was inconsequential in the face of what Qruze

was enduring. Loken met Qruze's gaze and saw an urgent need to communicate in them, a desperate imperative that superseded all other concerns.

Qruze took Loken's wrist in an iron grip.

His gaze was unflinching. His ruined body spasmed as pain signals overwhelmed his brain. Yet even in the throes of the most agonising death, Qruze still put his duty first.

'Iacton, I'm sorry...' said Loken. 'I'm so very sorry.'

Qruze shook his head. Anger lit his face.

He held his free hand out to Loken. He pressed something into his palm and closed his fingers over it. Loken went to lift it, but Qruze shook his head again, eyes wide. A pleading imperative.

Not now, not here.

Loken nodded and felt Qruze's grip slacken on his wrist.

The light in the Half-heard's eyes went out, and he was dead.

Loken laid Qruze down on the blood-soaked deck plate and reached down to a pouch at his waist. He pulled out the two Cthonian mirror-coins Severian had given him in the shadow of the Seven Neverborn and placed them on Iacton Qruze's eyes.

Loken's grief was gone, burned away by anger.

He pulled himself to his full height and looked up at Horus.

The Warmaster stood before his throne, Iacton Qruze's blood still weeping from the long talons of his gauntlet.

'I didn't want it to come to this, Garviel,' said Horus.

Loken ignored the ridiculous platitude and stood taller than he had ever stood before. Prouder than he had ever stood before.

All the uncertainty, all the confusion and every shred of the madness that had kept him wrapped in delusions vanished. All compunction to revere the Warmaster was purged in an instant of loathing.

Iacton Qruze was dead, and the last link with what the Legion had once been was broken.

And with it, any last shred of belief that the Warmaster possessed any nobility or trace of the great man he had once been.

Loken felt the words well up from a depthless reservoir of certainty within him. A valediction and threat all in one.

'I guarantee that before the sun sets on this war, even if you win, even if I die here, you'll rue the day you ever turned your back on the Emperor. For every planet you take, the Imperium will exact a fearful tally of Cthonian blood. I guarantee that even if you conquer Terra the fruits of victory will taste like dust in your mouth. I guarantee that if you don't kill me today, you'll meet me again. I will stand against you at every outpost, every wall and every gate. I will fight you with every sword at my command, with every bolter and every fist. I will fight you with bare hands. I will fight you with the very rocks of the world you seek to conquer. I will never give up until the Sons of Horus are dead and no more than a bad memory.'

Loken took a breath and saw the Warmaster's acceptance of his threat. Horus understood that Loken meant every word of what he had just said, that nothing could ever sway him from his course.

'I wanted you back,' said Horus. 'Tormaggedon wanted to make you like him, but I told him you would always be a Son of Horus.'

'I was *never* a Son of Horus,' said Loken. 'I was and remain a Luna Wolf. A proud son of Cthonia, a loyal servant of the Emperor, beloved by all. I am your enemy.'

Loken heard a chirrup of crackling vox.

He heard it again, coming from the helmet mag-locked to Qruze's belt. He recognised the voice and despite the body at his feet and all they had lost to get this far, Loken smiled.

He bent and lifted the helmet to his lips as a ghost-shadow moved across the silver orb of the moon through the glass of the great cathedral window.

'How's that hunter's eye, Rassuah?'

'*I have him,*' replied the *Tarnhelm*'s pilot. '*Say the word.*'

'Just take the damn shot,' said Loken.

THE WINDOW BLEW out in a blizzard of shards. Sheeting lasers blasted into Lupercal's Court as the *Tarnhelm*'s guns filled it with killing fire. The loss of atmosphere was sudden and absolute, over in an instant of ruthless annihilation.

Air blasted into space, along with weapons, bodies and anything not mag-locked to the deck. Spent bolter rounds, stone fragments blasted from the walls and chips of broken ceramite. Glass and debris went too.

Loken let the explosive decompression take him, hurling him from the *Vengeful Spirit* and into the void of space. Qruze's body spun away from him.

A crushing sensation of awful solidity seized his chest. His internal organs were shock freezing. Life-support systems in his armour registered the sudden change. It fought to equalise the pressure differential and forced his lungs empty to avoid lethal hyperdistension, but without a helmet it was a losing battle.

Silver light bathed Loken.

Fitting that a Luna Wolf should die by the light of a moon.

Loken's vision fogged. He felt sudden, shocking cold in his throat, as though his windpipe was filling with liquid helium.

He tried to howl a last curse, but hard vacuum kept him silent.

Loken closed his eyes. He let the moon's light take him.

And the *Vengeful Spirit* spun away in the darkness.

TWENTY-FIVE

The road to Terra
Half-heard no more
Okay

GREAT SKEINS AND shawls and clusters of bright stars winked through the great viewing bay. The light of a galaxy that would soon belong to him.

Horus stood at the farthest prow of the strategium, his hands laced behind his back. He was no longer clad in armour, but a simple training robe of pale cream, belted at the waist with a thick leather belt.

The Sons of Horus fleet was breaking anchor, mustering for the next stage of the march to Terra. Scores of transports still ferried men and machines from Molech's surface, but Boas Comnenus expected to be ready for system-transit within four hours.

Ezekyle and Kibre wanted to send fast cruisers after the Imperial Cobra-class destroyer, but Horus denied them. His First Captain had railed against that decision, as he had when Horus refused to remove the futharc sigils.

Horus was adamant – *Molech's Enlightenment* was to be unharmed.

Let word of this world's fate fly ahead of the *Vengeful Spirit* on wings of terror. Despair would be as potent a weapon as tanks and Titans, warriors and warships in the coming years.

Horus turned from the vista of stars and made his way back to the ouslite disc at the heart of the strategium. The Mournival awaited his orders, standing patiently as though the natural order of things would continue as it had before.

He saw them all differently now.

Horus knew them better than they knew themselves, but now he saw the things they kept hidden; the secret doubts, the cancerous thoughts and, deep down, the fear that they had taken a path that could only end badly.

The war on Molech had stoked the fires of Ezekyle's ambitions. Not for much longer would he be satisfied with a captaincy, even a First Captaincy of the Sons of Horus. Soon he would need something grander to lead. A Legion of his own perhaps? With the power Horus now commanded and the ancient sciences of Terra, the means to create new Legiones Astartes was within his grasp.

Why shouldn't his greatest warriors become their own masters?

Falkus Kibre... a simple man, one unfettered to grander ambitions. He knew his place and any thoughts of bettering his station were purely in service of the Warmaster. Falkus would be loyal unto death.

After his moment of doubt in the wake of Isstvan V, Aximand had painstakingly rebuilt himself. Even Dwell, with all its painful associations, had served to invigorate Little Horus with the desire to see the war won. The revelation of Garviel Loken's survival had shaken them all, but it had hit Aximand particularly hard. The melancholy he had so long denied was his ruling characteristic now shrouded him with the fear that Loken had been right to reject the Warmaster.

Yet it was Grael Noctua who had experienced the most profound change. Horus saw the twin flames burning within him, one darkly gleaming and malevolent, the other bruised and subjugate. The Fenrisian had ruined Gerradon's flesh, and the daemon that Targost had summoned needed a new body to host its essence.

'Sire, what are your orders?' asked Kibre.

Horus smiled at the extra vowel at the end of the honorific. A natural development, given the power that now filled him.

Power that had almost cost him his life to obtain.

Not that to look at him anyone would know that.

The many hurts he had suffered to win Molech had healed years ago it seemed. It was hard to be sure. His sons told him he'd only been gone moments, how could he tell them different?

Molech was a far distant memory to Horus now.

He'd fought wars, slain monsters and defied gods in those moments. He'd wrested the power of those same gods at the heads of vast armies of daemons. He'd fought in battles that would rage unchecked for all eternity.

He'd won a thousand kingdoms within the empyrean, billions of vassals to do with as he pleased, but he'd refused it. Every pleasure and prize was his for the taking, but he'd denied them all. He'd taken the power his father had taken, but he'd done so without deception.

He'd taken it by force of arms and by virtue of his self-belief.

There was no bargain made, no promise to honour.

The power was his and his alone.

Finally, after everything, Horus was a god.

'Sire, what are your orders?' said Ezekyle.

Horus stared at the veil of stars, as though he could see all the way from Molech to Terra. He extended a clawed hand, as though already cupping the precious bauble of humanity's cradle.

'I am coming for you, father,' said Horus.

✠ ✠ ✠

THE TARNHELM HAD always been a cramped ship, but hidden in the shadow of *Molech's Enlightenment*, it now felt obscenely spacious.

Loken sat on his bunk, stripped out of his armour and wearing nothing but a bodyglove, a chest-hugging synth-skin bandage and dermal-regenerative.

Varren was in an induced coma, as were Proximo Tarchon and Ares Voitek. The former Iron Hand's servo-harness had exercised a hitherto unsuspected level of autonomy to take hold of Proximo Tarchon as Lupercal's Court vented into space.

Rubio sat alone at the table where they had shared a drink in the company of Rogal Dorn. The empty spaces where their brother pathfinders used to sit weighed heavily on the former Ultramarine.

That any of them were here at all was nothing short of a miracle. Or rather, it was thanks to Rassuah's preternaturally dextrous hands at *Tarnhelm*'s electromagnetic tether controls and their armour translocator beacons. She had followed their progress through the *Vengeful Spirit* and got them back aboard the *Tarnhelm* within a minute of shooting out the shielded window to Lupercal's Court.

She'd blasted clear of the *Vengeful Spirit*, weaving a path back through the gaps in the defensive net she and Tubal Cayne's device had torn. There'd been no pursuit, which she'd attributed to *Tarnhelm*'s superior capabilities, but Loken wasn't so sure.

They'd caught up to the Imperial destroyer as it powered past the system's fifth planet. Its engines were burning hot, its captain clearly expecting pursuit.

But nothing was coming.

The Warmaster's fleet was still anchored around Molech.

Loken looked up at a knock on the hatchway.

Severian and Bror Tyrfingr stood at his door, clad in bodygloves and simple knee-length chitons. Loken hadn't spoken to any of the pathfinders beyond operational or medical necessity since the *Vengeful Spirit.*

Severian looked as fresh as he had the day they'd set out on their mission, but Bror's face was bruised and raw from the beating Ezekyle Abaddon had given him.

'It's not as bad as it looks,' said Bror.

'He's lying,' said Severian. 'It's far worse.'

'He's lucky to have walked away from a fight with Ezekyle at all,' said Loken. 'Not many people can say that.'

'I'll get him next time,' said Bror. 'When the Wolf King leads the Rout back to the *Vengeful Spirit.*'

'What is it you want?' asked Loken.

Bror held out a plastic bottle filled with clear liquid. Loken could taste its caustic flavour from the other side of the room.

'What's that?'

'Dzira,' said Severian, pulling over a stool and producing three cups into which Bror poured them all a measure.

'I thought we drank it all,' said Loken. 'And Voitek can't possibly be well enough to distil more.'

'He might be mostly metal, but we'll be back on Terra before his sedation wears off,' said Bror, limping over to take a seat. 'No, I made this. There's not a lot one of the *Vlka Fenryka* can't rustle up after we've tasted it.'

Loken took a cup and swallowed a fiery mouthful.

He sucked in a breath as it went down. 'Tastes just like it. Maybe even stronger.'

'Aye, well, can't have folk thinking the Wolves make something weaker than the Tenth Legion,' said Bror. 'We'd never hear the end of it.'

'So what is it you really want?' said Loken. 'I'm not much in the mood for company.'

'Don't be foolish, man,' scoffed Bror. 'Any time you walk away from a fight is just the time to be with your brothers.'

'Even when I failed?'

Bror leaned forward and aimed his cup at Loken. 'We didn't fail,' he said. 'We did what we set out to do, we marked the *Vengeful Spirit*. When the Wolf King comes to fight Horus, he'll have an easier time of it because of what we did.'

'That's not what I meant,' said Loken not wishing to dwell on broken promises. 'But Lupercal knows about the futharc sigils.'

Bror sighed. 'He won't find them all, and do you think I'd make them all work by being *seen*. Ah, Loken, you've a lot to learn about how clever the Rout really are.'

'I lost half the men under my command.'

Bror refilled his cup and said, 'Listen, *you* didn't lose them. They died. It happens. But you don't make sense of deaths in solitude. Mortals might, but we're not mortals. We're a brotherhood. A brotherhood of warriors, and that's what makes us strong. I thought you knew that?'

'I think maybe I'd forgotten,' said Loken.

'Aye, you and this one both,' said Bror, nodding towards Severian.

'Alone is where I do my best work,' said Severian.

'That's as maybe, but the rest of us fight best when we fight with our brothers,' said Bror, knocking back his drink and continuing without pause. 'It's fighting for the man next to you. It's fighting for the man next to him and the one next to him. I heard what you said to Horus, so I know I'm not telling you anything you don't already know. But what you're after? You already have it. Right here, right now. With us.'

Loken nodded and held his cup out for a refill.

'Right, enough with the sermonising,' said Severian. 'We want to know what Iacton Qruze gave you. Do you still have it?'

'I do, but I don't know what to make of it.'

'Let's see it then,' said Bror.

Loken reached up to a small alcove above his bunk and lifted down a metal box. A box very like the one he'd left aboard the *Vengeful Spirit*, filled with his few keepsakes of war.

He opened it and lifted out the object Qruze had pressed into his palm. A disc of hardened red wax affixed to a long strip of yellowed seal paper.

'His Oath of Moment?' said Severian.

'The one Mersadie Oliton had me give to Iacton.'

Loken turned it around, so that Bror and Severian could see what was written on the oath paper.

They read the word and looked at Loken.

'What does it mean?' asked Bror.

'I don't know,' said Loken, staring down at the word.

Its letters were inked in red that had faded to rust brown.

Scratched by something needle-sharp and precise.

Murder.

THE CORRIDORS OF *Molech's Enlightenment* were cold and cramped. Vivyen didn't like it here, there were too many people, and no one seemed to know anything about what was happening. She'd seen lots of soldiers, and daddy told her that meant they were safe.

Vivyen certainly didn't feel safe.

She huddled in a widened transit corridor, below a ventilation duct that sometimes blew warm air and sometimes blew cold. Her daddy talked in low voices with Noama and Kjell, and they gave her funny looks when she asked if they'd ever see Alivia again.

Miska had her head on Vivyen's shoulders.

She was sleeping.

Vivyen needed to pee, but didn't want to wake her sister.

To take her mind off her filling bladder, she pulled out the dog-eared storybook Alivia had given her in the press of bodies at the starport. She couldn't read the words, they were in some old language Alivia had called *Dansk*, but she liked looking at the pictures.

She didn't need to know the words. She'd heard the stories often enough that she could recite them off by heart. And sometimes when she looked at the words, it was like she *did* understand them, like the story *wanted* to be read and was unfolding itself in her mind.

The strangeness of that thought didn't register at all.

It made sense to her and it just… *was*.

She flipped through the yellowed pages, looking for a picture to conjure the right words into her head.

A page with a young girl sitting at the edge of the ocean caught her eye and she nodded to herself. The girl was very beautiful, but her legs were fused together and ended in the wide tail of a fish. She liked this story; the tale of a young girl who, for the sake of true love, gives up her existence in one realm to earn a place in another.

Someone moved along the corridor. Vivyen waited for them to pass, but they stopped in front of her, blocking the light.

'I can't see the words,' she said.

'That's a good story,' said the person in front of her. 'Can I read it to you?'

Vivyen looked up in surprise and nodded happily.

'Didn't I tell you it was going to be okay?' said Alivia Sureka.

ABOUT THE AUTHOR

Graham McNeill is the author of seven Horus Heresy novels, most recently *Vengeful Spirit* and *Angel Exterminatus*, along with the *New York Times* bestseller *A Thousand Sons*. He has written a host of other novels for Black Library, including Warhammer 40,000 series based on the Ultramarines, the Iron Warriors and the Adeptus Mechanicus. His work in the Warhammer World includes The Legend of Sigmar for the Time of Legends, the second book of which, *Empire*, won the *David Gemmell Legend Award*. Originally hailing from Scotland, Graham now lives and works in Nottingham.

THE HORUS HERESY

John French

THE CRIMSON FIST

Stone and iron

The Iron Warriors launch their attack on the
Imperial Fists fleet at Phall

WHEN I REACHED the bridge the *Hammer of Terra* was already a spreading globe of gas and glowing debris. The warship's death filled the pict-screens, burning in silence above the hundreds of servitors and crew that filled the cavernous space. The sight of it made me freeze for a second, my eyes locked on the image. I thought of Pertinax, captain of the *Hammer of Terra*, a warrior who had already fought in a hundred campaigns by the time I became part of the Legion. I remembered his green augmetic eyes watching me steadily, and the soft accent of Europa that had never left his voice.

I shook my head, and the noise of the bridge washed over me. Officers were shouting at each other as servitors and machines spat out reams of data. Raln was at my side, already calling orders to the serfs. I needed to get hold of the battle before it spun further beyond my grasp, but there was one fact missing I needed to know.

'Who is the enemy?' I asked. Raln half turned to me, the red lenses of his helmet briefly meeting my gaze as he spoke.

'The Iron Warriors,' he said and turned back to issue a stream of rapid orders to the bridge officers. For a second I stood still, like a man with a bullet hole through him yet to fall. Then I nodded and snapped my helmet over my head.

The holo-projection above spun, showing me battlegroup and enemy positions, auspex readings and tactical data in growing clusters of glowing runes. Screeds of data from my helmet display overlaid the projection: inter-ship communication, links to the battlegroup commanders, the Legion-contingent details from each ship. To a Space Marine not conditioned to process such levels of information it would have been bewildering. To a normal human it would have been overwhelming. I took a deep breath, felt the focused calm enforce itself through my body and mind. Training and conditioning blanked out every other instinct. I was the centre of a storm, a clear point of will and strength.

'Bring us above the plane of attack,' I called to Raln. I felt the ship judder. The holographic projection blurred and flickered for a second. I glanced back to the raw data of the battle that floated in front of me. Four minutes had passed since the *Hammer of Terra* had died. We had lost ten ships; thirty were crippled, forty-six had suffered severe damage. Ordnance had degraded to sixty-two per cent across the fleet. We were close to disaster.

The *Tribune* was taking fire. I could read it in the flow of activity on the bridge as if it were the movements of my own body. Shields were down across the forward batteries. Power had been diverted to bring them back up. Plasma reactors were straining to maintain output.

Inbound enemy bombers.

Batteries firing.

Dorsal line accelerators approaching optimal fire angle.

Turn at thirty per cent.

Course correction…

I let out a slow breath, and blanked out the details of the *Tribune*'s situation. I was the fleet master. The *Tribune* was under Raln's hand, and was only one part of the battle. I focused on the information in front of me; the hololithic projection was a tangle of trajectories and amber engagement makers.

The position was clear and chilling. The enemy fleet had penetrated a third of the way into our lines. Their formation resembled a jagged cone, the largest vessels set back from screens of escorts and heavy-hulled strike cruisers. It had punched into our fleet and was moving towards the centre of our spherical formation. To my eyes it looked like a fanged worm eating to the core of a ripe fruit. It was methodically brutal in its ugly efficiency. So typical of the Iron Warriors.

The Iron Warriors. Our enemies are the Iron Warriors.

The thought was like a sliver of ice thrust into my guts, as if that fact had only just registered in my mind. They had scrambled their communications but I recognised their ships. These were vessels we had fought beside, crewed by warriors I had bled with and called brothers. *If the Iron Warriors were with Horus, then how many others might be as well?* Could more have turned on the Imperium? Terra might have already fallen. The Imperium might already be no more. Our fleet might be the last fragment of loyalty surviving. The possibilities made my head swim, as if my mind was screaming after the dead Imperium as it vanished into an abyss. For a moment I felt the old crack in my strength, the weakness that had nearly made me curl up and accept death on the ice of Inwit.

I cannot fail now, I will not fail. My eyes flicked across the projected sphere showing the battle, green and blue smeared with red like leaking blood. The contingency plans I had made over the long months surfaced in my mind, aligned with the possibilities of the present. I could see it, a way not only of recovering but fighting back. *If we bleed*, I thought, *so will they.*

Order the novel or download the eBook
from *blacklibrary.com*
Also available from